DEATH, T... ...AM

"[A] sure-shot success!" —*Fresh Fiction*

"*Death, Taxes and Green Tea Ice Cream* is pure Diane Kelly—witty, remarkable, and ever so entertaining."
—*Affaire de Coeur*

DEATH, TAXES, AND HOT PINK LEG WARMERS

"Be prepared for periodic unpredictable, uncontrollable laughing fits. Wonderful scenarios abound when it comes to Tara going undercover in this novel about tax evasion, drugs and (of course) guns. Good depth of characters and well-developed chapters are essential when casting a humorous series, and Ms. Kelly excels in both departments." —*Night Owl Reviews*

"Tara's sharp mind, sharp wit, *and* sharp skills are brought to life under the topnotch writing of Diane Kelly."
—*Romance Reviews Today* (Perfect 10)

DEATH, TAXES, AND PEACH SANGRIA

"Great action, screwball comedy similar to the misfortunes of Stephanie Plum, and relationship dynamics entertain the reader from start to finish."
—...*ews*

"In anoth... ...series, D... ...ead-liest case... ...*tles*

"Diane Kelly knows how to rock the romance, and roll the story right into a delightful mix of high drama with great characters." —*The Reading Reviewer*

DEATH, TAXES, AND A SKINNY NO-WHIP LATTE

"Readers will find Kelly's protagonist a kindred spirit to Stephanie Plum: feisty and tenacious, with a self-depre-cating sense of humor. Tara is flung into some unnerving situations, including encounters with hired thugs, would-be muggers, and head lice. The laughs lighten up the scary bits, and the nonstop action and snappy dialogue keep the standard plot moving along at a good pace."
—*RT Book Reviews*

"Readers should be prepared for a laugh fest. The writer is first-class and there is a lot of humor contained in this series. It is a definite keeper." —*Night Owl Romance*

"A quirky, fun tale that pulls you in with its witty hero-ine and outlandish situations . . . You'll laugh at Tara's predicaments, and cheer her on as she nearly single-handedly tackles the case." —*Romance Reviews Today*

"It is hard not to notice a sexy CPA with a proclivity for weapons. Kelly's sophomore series title . . . has huge romance crossover appeal." —*Library Journal*

"An exciting, fun new mystery series with quirky charac-ters and a twist . . . Who would have ever guessed IRS investigators could be so cool!"
—*Guilty Pleasures Book Reviews*

Death, Taxes,

and Cheap Sunglasses

DIANE KELLY

St. Martin's Paperbacks

This is a work of fiction. All of the characters, organizations, and events portrayed in this novel are either products of the author's imagination or are used fictitiously.

DEATH, TAXES, AND CHEAP SUNGLASSES

Copyright © 2015 by by Diane Kelly.

All rights reserved.

For information address St. Martin's Press, 175 Fifth Avenue, New York, NY 10010.

ISBN: 978-1-250-04832-5

Printed in the United States of America

St. Martin's Paperbacks edition / March 2015

St. Martin's Paperbacks are published by St. Martin's Press, 175 Fifth Avenue, New York, NY 10010.

10 9 8 7 6 5 4 3 2 1

To my friend Cindy Barron-Taylor, who is always a sparkling ray of sunshine

$\mathscr{A}$cknowledgments

First, a shout-out to my repeat offenders.

At the top of the list is my fantastic editor, Holly Ingraham. You always know which way to steer me when I veer off course. I appreciate all you do to make my books better!

Thanks to Sarah Melnyk, Paul Hochman, and everyone else at St. Martin's who has helped to publicize my novels and get this book to readers. You're a top-notch team!

Thanks to Danielle Fiorella, Monika Roe, and Iskra Design for another perfect cover. You guys sure do know your stuff!

Thanks to my agent, Helen Breitwieser. I'm grateful for all you do!

Thanks to the awesome Liz Bemis-Hittinger of Bemis Promotions for my wonderful Web site, newsletters, and bookmarks. I don't ever want to find out what I'd do without you!

Thanks to the many members of Romance Writers of America for your support and camaraderie, as well as the hardworking national office staff. Joining RWA was the smartest decision I ever made!

Thanks to Aimee Mata for answering my questions about banking, and for Sandra Castro for putting me in touch with Aimee. Sandra, I owe you a margarita.

Thanks to my son, Ross, for schooling me in World of Warcraft. Figures you'd know the hot animated babes. ;)

And, lastly but not leastly, thank you to my readers. It makes my day when I hear from you, and I hope this book will bring you lots of laughs!

chapter one

$\mathcal{N}$ick's New Assignment

I slid my gun into my purse, grabbed my briefcase, and headed out to my car. Yep, tax season was in full swing once again, honest people scrambling to round up their records and receipts, hoping for a refund or at least to break even. As a taxpayer myself, I felt for them. But as far as tax cheats were concerned, I had no sympathy. The most recent annual report indicated that American individuals and corporations had underpaid their taxes by $450 billion. Not exactly chump change. That's where I came in.

You've probably heard of my earlier exploits, but just in case you haven't, let me introduce myself. I'm IRS Special Agent Tara Holloway. My hair is chestnut brown, my eyes are grayish blue, and I comport myself with the style, manners, and grace expected of all graduates of Miss Cecily's Charm School—except when I don't. I might stand just five foot two, but I stand my ground. When men say I've got a nice rack, they're not lying. My gun rack holds five rifles. My bra, on the other hand, holds a couple of 32As.

After earning my accounting degree from the University of Texas—*hook 'em, Horns!*—I spent four years preparing tax returns at a CPA firm here in Dallas. I learned a lot about taxation, business, and business people, which was great. But I sat at a desk for eight to twelve butt-numbing hours a day, which was *not* great. When my butt refused to stay in that chair a second longer, I applied for a job with IRS Criminal Investigations.

The agency accepted me as a candidate for the program, then did its best to kick my ass in training. Fortunately, I'd learned how to study hard at UT, developed a good work ethic at the accounting firm, and been taught by my father how to shoot an empty can of root beer off a fence post at a hundred yards. I aced both my written exams and my physical and weapons tests, so now here I was, fighting for truth and justice on behalf of honest taxpayers like you.

You're welcome.

And can I get a raise, please?

It was a gorgeous spring morning in late March as I drove through downtown Dallas with the top down on my red convertible BMW. Despite being mere knockoffs of the more expensive Brighton brand, my tortoiseshell sunglasses blocked the early sun's rays with reasonable effectiveness. My stereo speakers blared Miranda Lambert's feminist revenge anthem, "Gunpowder & Lead." Yep, Miranda got it right. Those two things were what little girls were made of, at least where I was concerned. Nobody had ever accused me of being made of sugar and spice. Not unless that spice was cayenne pepper.

As I turned into the parking lot of the IRS building, my eyes noted a sporty Volvo C70 in the rear of the lot. Given the rolled-up purple yoga mat standing in the backseat, the pink hoodie hanging from the driver's headrest, and the

"Above the Influence" bumper sticker gracing the back bumper, I knew the car belonged to DEA Agent Christina Marquez. She and I had worked several cases together in the past and become fast friends. You pair two badass female federal agents together and sic them on a drug-dealing ice cream man and they're bound to bond.

I pulled into the spot next to Christina's car, punched the button to raise the top on mine, and removed my sunglasses, sliding them into the breast pocket of my blazer. Before climbing out I performed one last visual check in my vanity mirror, fished my tube of Plum Perfect gloss out of my purse, and applied a fresh coat. Probably not necessary since I'd been dating my coworker, Senior Special Agent Nick Pratt, for months now and he'd seen me many times without any makeup on. Still, it never hurt to put some effort into it, right? Our relationship was solid, but we had yet to officially seal the deal with rings and a license. Of course we'd only been dating a few months and it was too soon to think about marriage. It wasn't too soon to think about thinking about it, though. I was already in my late twenties and Nick had hit thirty. We weren't exactly kids anymore. That fact didn't prevent us from acting like children on occasion, though.

I rode up in the elevator, sipping my skinny latte as I thumbed through e-mails on my cell phone. Mom had sent me a recipe for pecan-encrusted fried okra. *As if I ever cook. Give up on it, Mom!* My favorite clerk at Neiman Marcus had e-mailed to let me know the petite department had a new line of suits in stock. I'd stop by on my lunch hour to take a look. My best friend and roommate, Alicia, who worked at the same downtown accounting firm I'd escaped from nearly a year ago, had sent me a message from her office at 6:08 this morning that simply read *Ughhhhhh . . .* Poor girl. Looked like tax season was getting her down. I'd have to make up a pitcher of peach sangria later and have it waiting for her when she got home.

As I stepped off the elevator, my eye caught a flash of lima-bean green over which towered a pinkish-orange bee-hive. My boss, Lu "the Lobo" Lobozinski, was heading down the hall that led to my office. Christina, dressed in black slacks and a gray blouse, walked beside her. The two slowed in the hallway as they approached my office, but rather than turning right into my digs they turned left into Nick's office, which sat across the hall from mine. After they slipped inside, Christina pulled the door closed behind them.

Hmm . . .

What was Christina doing meeting with Lu and Nick? Did the DEA have another case that called for an agent with financial skills? If so, why hadn't she recommended *me* for the gig? Christina and I always had fun working together. Performing stakeouts, plotting tactics and strategies, taking down criminals. Heck, I think some of the criminals got off on being manhandled by a couple of young women.

It was totally nosy and unprofessional of me to stop in front of Nick's door and put my left ear to the frame to listen. But, yeah, sometimes I'm nosy and unprofessional.

Lu's voice was the first I heard. "Got a new drug case for you, Nick."

"Oh, yeah?" Nick replied.

Drug cases were standard fare at IRS Criminal Investigations. Drug dealers rarely reported their earnings and paid their taxes to Uncle Sam. The few that did usually laundered the money in an attempt to make it appear as if the funds were legit.

Christina spoke next. "We've been working with Mexican drug authorities for years trying to bring down an extensive drug network. We recently got a break that could help us nail these guys."

Nick spoke now. "A break? What kind of break?"

"A guy on the inside who wants out," Christina replied. "An informant. Alejandro was forced into the family business, so to speak. He never wanted to be involved."

And apparently he was now willing to spill the *frijoles* to help law enforcement. *Bueno.*

Despite my best efforts to eavesdrop, my ears couldn't quite make out what she said next. Was she asking Nick to help track a money trail? To review financial records to prove money laundering? While Nick had the financial skills to perform a financial analysis, any agent in the office was equipped to handle that type of work. So, why Nick? What did he have to offer that the rest of us didn't? Only one way to find out. I pressed my left ear closer to the frame and stuck a finger in my right to block out the soft *whir-whir-whir* of the copier down the hall.

"I'm going to pose as Alejandro's girlfriend," Christina continued. "We'll bring you in as a friend who can help move the money."

"So we'll be going undercover?" Nick asked.

"*Deep* undercover," she replied.

"Meaning what, exactly?"

I had the same question myself.

"No contact with the outside world until the case is resolved."

The outside world? Wait a cotton-pickin' minute here. Would I be considered part of that "outside world"? Or, as a fellow member of law enforcement, would I be exempt from the no-contact rule?

Nick hesitated for a moment before responding. "How long do you expect the investigation to take?"

"Weeks," Christina said, "maybe months. But we've got

to put some people on the inside if we're ever going to break up the ring. This could be our chance to finally nail El Cuchillo."

"El Cuchillo?" Nick repeated. "The Knife?"

Uh-oh.

That doesn't sound good at all.

I swallowed hard and kept listening.

"He's a key member of the network," Christina said, "one of its most trusted drug runners and a suspect in dozens of kidnappings and murders in Mexico. His weapon of choice is a butcher knife. Evidently, he thinks using a gun to kill someone is too impersonal. If we can get him, we could take down an arm of the Sinaloa cartel."

Ohmigod.

My hand, still clutching my cell phone, flew involuntarily to my chest. A soft crunch told me the sunglasses in my breast pocket were DOA. Nick, too, could end up DOA if he worked on this case.

From previous conversations with Christina, I knew the DEA had been after the Sinaloa cartel for years. Known previously as *La Alianza de Sangre,* or Blood Alliance, the cartel worked with other drug-trafficking organizations in a loose federation that extended upward all the way from Argentina to the northernmost parts of the United States. Not only did the cartel supply drugs to distributors in Latin and North America, it also supplied parts of Asia and Europe.

Though the cartel often bought its way into power via bribes and threats, its members were not above kidnapping, torture, and murder to achieve their aims. In recent years, the cartel clashed violently with the Juárez cartel in Ciudad Juárez, a Mexican city just across the border from El Paso, Texas. The battle for power left thousands of innocent residents dead, along with untold numbers of rival cartels members. The cartel had kidnapped numerous people and held them for ransom, including at least one high school student. The cartel had also kidnapped reporters in Mexico in an attempt to force them to spread criminal communications, and gone so far as to invade a wedding being held by purported members of another drug ring. They'd kidnapped the groom, his brother, and uncle, and left their tortured, lifeless bodies in the back of a pickup truck that was found days later. A fourth person was killed at the wedding. Men with ties to the cartel were responsible for the execution-style murders of seventeen people at a drug rehabilitation center in Mexico. When one of their own lost hundreds of pounds of marijuana in a drug seizure by law enforcement, the cartel beat the man to death and severed his hands above the wrists, placing them on his chest and dumping his body on a Juárez street as a reminder to others within the cartel to carefully tend to their business.

Things had become so bad the U.S. State Department had issued travel warnings for people considering visits to Mexico. Texans who had previously flocked to Mexican border towns and beaches for vacation were now thinking twice before heading south.

Of course the violence didn't stop at the border. Not only did it spill over into Texas border towns like El Paso and Laredo, but it headed farther north as well. The cartel had hired thugs from MS-13, a gang founded by former members of the El Salvador military who fled to Los Angeles in the 1980s following the civil war in their country. In St. Paul, Minnesota, the gang members kidnapped and tortured two teenagers whom they'd suspected— *wrongfully*—of stealing drugs and money from the cartel.

Forbes magazine had estimated the fortune of the cartel's leader, Joaquín Guzmán Loera, known as El Chapo, or "Shorty," at $1 billion, making him the wealthiest drug lord of all time. He'd escaped from a Mexican prison in 2001 and later evaded apprehension at his home in Culiacán by escaping into a secret tunnel system through a hidden hatch under a bathtub. Finally, in early 2014, he was captured by Mexican marines in a pre-dawn raid in Mazatlán.

The arrest of El Chapo had left a power void within the cartel. As those who remained vied for control, the violence had escalated even further. The instability posed not only further threats to security in Mexico, but also provided a unique opportunity for law enforcement to go after the cartel while it was vulnerable.

My stomach flooded with acid and my mind went fuzzy from fear. When it cleared, I knew one thing for certain. *The only way Nick would be going undercover inside a violent drug cartel would be over my dead body.*

I grabbed the handle and threw the door open. It banged against the wall with a resounding *BAM* that rattled the window behind Nick's desk.

Nick, dressed in his customary white business shirt, navy Dockers, and cowboy boots, stood from his desk, his tall, broad-shouldered form blocking some of the light streaming in the window. He cocked a dark brow in question.

"No!" I shrieked. I turned rage-filled eyes on Christina and Lu before returning my focus to Nick. "You are not going to work on this case. You'll get killed!"

Lu leaped from her seat and closed the door behind me. "Tara! Keep your voice down!"

"No!" I cried again, shaking my head so violently it's a wonder my brains didn't rattle. "No. NO. NO!"

Nick sent me a pointed look, his amber-colored eyes on fire. "Get a grip, Tara."

Oh, I'd like to get a grip all right. I'd like to grip him by the ears and shake some sense into him!

"Were you listening in the hall?" Lu demanded.

"Yes," I spat, "and if you're expecting an apology you're sorely mistaken."

"Well, now." Lu pursed her lips. "If you're expecting me not to note this unprofessional outburst in your performance report, you, too, are mistaken."

My boss had probably hoped her threat would bring me to my senses, but frankly it only added fuel to the fire, making me more upset.

"This is a big case, Tara," Nick said, a defensive tone in his voice. "This type of opportunity doesn't come along every day."

"Opportunity?" I was flabbergasted. "This isn't an opportunity. This is a suicide mission!"

Nick crossed his muscular arms over his muscular chest. "Call it what you want but I've been waiting my entire career for a case like this."

Looked like I'd get nowhere with him. After all, he could be just as stubborn as me. Fueled by terror and rage, I turned to, *and on,* Christina. "You've told me how dangerous the Sinaloa cartel is. How could you drag Nick into this?"

She knew how I felt about Nick. *I loved the guy, dammit!* What kind of friend was she to involve him in this case?

Christina gave me a look that was both pointed and apologetic. "You know why, Tara." She gestured at Nick. "He's got the perfect set of skills for this case."

I could understand why the DEA would want Nick on the case. He'd lived in Mexico for three years and was virtually fluent in the language. Of course the time he'd spent there was in forced exile after his cover had been blown in an earlier undercover investigation. Nevertheless, he knew more about the language and culture than any other special agent in the Dallas office.

Nick was also especially equipped to handle cases calling for physical intimidation and defensive skills. Not only had he been a linebacker on his high school football team, he'd been raised on a farm and engaged in physical labor that had further developed his muscles and stamina. Thanks to time at the shooting range with me, his aim had improved vastly. He'd never match my sharpshooting skills, of course, but he was nonetheless one of the best shots in the office.

Despite Christina's undeniable logic, I wasn't about to surrender. "How can you call yourself my friend?"

Lu intervened. "This is *business,* Tara. It's not personal. Besides, putting Nick on the case was *my* call, not Christina's."

I turned on Lu now. It took every bit of my restraint not to rip off her false eyelashes and beat her with them. "There's gotta be someone else," I said. "Another special agent who could handle this. What about . . ."

I racked my brain. There was my usual partner, Eddie Bardin, of course, but he had two young girls and a wife to think about. No way could I suggest him as a replacement for Nick. The new guy, William Dorsey, was smart and capable but he, too, was a family man. Josh Schmidt would also be a poor choice. Though his cybersleuthing skills were top-notch, he was a total wimp when it came to the physical aspects of our job. Hell, he'd probably wet himself if he just heard the name El Cuchillo.

"Me," I said finally. "Put *me* on the case instead."

"Tara," Nick said in a tone probably meant to be soothing but which instead struck me as patronizing. "Come on."

"I mean it." My gunmetal-gray eyes locked on his whiskey-colored ones. "You're an only child and your mother is already a widow. If something happened to me my parents still have each other and my brothers." I turned back to Lu. "Please, Lu," I pleaded. "*Please*. Assign me instead."

Lu offered no acquiescence, only a feeble smile rimmed in bright orange lipstick. "Nick's a big boy, Tara. He can take care of himself."

"Not always," I spat. "He was getting the shit beat out of him at Guys and Dolls until I showed up and saved his ass."

Nick, Christina, and I had worked undercover together on a previous prostitution and drug case at the strip club. Three of the club's bouncers had attacked Nick and, despite his impressive efforts to fight the trio off, he'd been seriously injured. If I hadn't shown up and shot each of the bouncers in the foot, who knows if he would have survived the ordeal.

Nick scowled, his eyes aflame now. "Hell, Tara, why don't you just kick me in the balls? What went down at Guys and Dolls wasn't a fair fight and you know it."

I slammed my fists down on his desk and leaned over it to stare him directly in the eye. "And you expect drug lords to fight fair?"

Without taking his eyes off mine, Nick addressed Lu and Christina. "Could you two excuse me and Tara for a moment?"

Lu nodded. "We'll be in my office."

With that, she and Christina stood from their seats and headed to the door.

Christina turned in the doorway and looked back at me. "For what it's worth, Tara. I'm sorry to have to involve *anyone* in this."

The sincerity in her words and expression cut right through me, taking my emotions down several notches.

"For what it's worth," I replied, my voice quavering. "I hate that *you* have to be involved in this, too."

She offered me a feeble smile and left.

Once we were alone, Nick and I stared at each other for a long moment. The flame in his eyes flickered out and cooled. He walked around his desk and enveloped me in his strong arms, wrapping a warm hand around my head to tuck my face against his chest. He gave me a soft kiss on the top of my head. "I've got to do this, Tara."

I let out a long sigh, grabbed fistfuls of his white dress shirt, and turned to bury my face between his rock-hard pecs. "I know."

Fighting bad guys was our job, after all. We'd willingly signed up for this. Still, the fact that we'd volunteered to put our safety at risk didn't mean it didn't suck sometimes. Besides, this separation was coming at a bad time. Nick and I had just gone through a rough patch in our relationship when I became all starry-eyed over a country-western singer I'd been assigned to pursue. We'd only just patched things up, and were still enjoying make-up sex. I'd hoped to parlay the make-up sex into a make-up changing of the air filters in my town house. I tended to neglect the darn things and the dust always made me sneeze when I replaced them. Looked like I'd just have to tough it out.

Nick reached down and put a finger under my chin, lifting my face to his. "I love you, Tara."

Tears pooled in my eyes. "I know that, too."

I was glad he loved me, but a fat lot of good that love would do me if he was killed. I clung to him for a moment longer, then finally mustered the courage to extricate myself from his embrace. Time to man up. Or, in my case, *woman* up.

He chuckled. "You made a mess of my shirt."

I glanced back to note a smear of Plum Perfect gloss on his chest, along with a smudge of beige foundation. "That's nothing compared to what a knife could do."

chapter two

Art . . . Or Not?

After the incident in Nick's office, I went to my office, fished my broken sunglasses out of the breast pocket of my blazer, and tossed them into my trash can.

Thunk.

Plunking myself into my chair, I logged on to my computer and Googled the words "El Cuchillo" and "Sinaloa." Many of the Web sites that came up were in Spanish, which I could not *comprender.* Stupid me. I'd taken French in high school. Growing up so close to the Louisiana border, I'd thought it was a *bon* idea at the time. Besides, several of *mes amies* had signed up for French, too. We'd planned to one day take a trip together and go to the top of the Eiffel Tower. The closest we'd come was the time we'd climbed the windmill in Junior Huffnagle's parents' cow pasture.

The sites that were in English offered gruesome details. Until recently, El Cuchillo often worked with a man known as Motosierra, or "Chain saw." The two were suspects in dozens of brutal murders in Colombia, Guatemala, Mexico, and the United States. They had split ways due to disruptions caused by the arrest of El Chapo. Police

suspected that each had taken control of an arm of the
Sinaloa cartel, thus moving up in the ranks.

There was only one photo of El Cuchillo online and it
caused my sphincter to clench so tight I'd need a triple
dose of Ex-Lax to compensate. The man's dark hair was
shorn to the scalp in an extreme, military-style cut. His
face was a roadmap of scars earned in knife fights. He
looked directly into the camera with eyes as hard and
cold as a glacier as he licked a victim's blood from his
blade.

"Oh, God," I whispered. "Oh, dear God!"

I slammed my laptop closed and shut my eyes. I willed
my mind to erase the image, but it was seared into my brain
as if branded there.

There was only one thing that could take my mind off
what I'd just seen.

Kittens.

Cute, cuddly ones.

And lots of them.

I opened my laptop and hurriedly went to YouTube,
pulling up video after video of adorable, playful kittens
romping in a yard, batting a ball of yarn, licking the camera
lens. My sphincter relaxed a little. Maybe a mere double
dose of Ex-Lax would do me now.

Once I'd gotten my kitten fix, I did my best to force
my attention back to my work. It wasn't easy.

At two in the afternoon, Eddie came down to my office
to round me up. "Ready to go to the art museum?"

"Ready as I'll ever be."

I'd spent all morning sick with worry, trying not to cry
or throw up or kick my filing cabinet. Okay, so I'd actually kicked my filing cabinet, putting a big dent in the side
that I'd then had to try to push back out. But I was damn
upset. It was dangerous enough working for a cartel.
After all, they killed their own members regularly if

they screwed up. But if anyone found out that Nick and Christina were undercover law enforcement they'd be in for some unique and special type of torture. El Cuchillo might decide to try out his entire Ginsu collection on them, starting with a paring knife and finishing up with a meat cleaver.

What would I do if Nick were julienned to death?

Thanks to these lovely thoughts, I'd managed to force down only a single piece of sushi at lunch. The new pantsuit I'd bought at Neiman's afterward hadn't helped much, either, though the glittery Michael Kors cap-toe pumps I'd scored for a mere $97 on sale improved my spirits slightly. I vowed to wear them on my first date with Nick when he returned from working the cartel case . . . *if* he returned from working the cartel case.

Damn.

Should've bought myself a new purse, too. Maybe some earrings.

I'd looked over the selection of sunglasses, but none had looked as good on me as my Brighton knockoffs. I wasn't willing to spend a hundred dollars on a pair of shades that didn't totally knock my socks off.

Eddie eyed me as I grabbed my blazer and briefcase. "You okay?"

Eddie and I had been partners since I began at the IRS a year ago. He'd been the only special agent who'd agreed to train the newbie. We'd come to know a lot about each other over the months we'd worked together. While familiarity might breed contempt in some cases, our familiarity had somehow led to respect and understanding and the occasional good-natured ribbing. Each knew how the other worked, and we could sense each other's moods.

"Okay?" I let out a long, loud breath. "Not really. Nick's going deep undercover. He won't be allowed any contact with anyone until the case is resolved."

Eddie's brows lifted. He knew without my saying that

a deep cover investigation would be particularly risky. "So he'll be completely out of touch?"

I nodded. "God only knows for how long."

"That sucks. When does he leave?"

"Tomorrow. He's over at the DEA right now being debriefed." Of course Nick and I had planned our own type of debriefing for later tonight, one last good-bye boink before he disappeared into the underworld like Hades descending into his realm.

"You'll just have to keep yourself busy," Eddie suggested. "That'll keep your mind off things."

"Busy? No problem there." I gestured to the towering stack of files on my desk. "Lu's given me enough work to choke an elephant."

Ironically enough, one of my cases actually involved an elephant. An auditor who'd been assigned to perform a routine records check on a tax-exempt animal welfare organization had referred the matter to criminal investigations when those operating the place hadn't been able to produce any documentation. Eddie and I planned to drive out to the sanctuary tomorrow to see if we could get to the bottom of things.

Eddie and I made our way to the elevator, rode down in silence, and headed to his G-ride, our name for the plain sedans assigned to us by Uncle Sam. I understood that we had to use the taxpayer's money wisely, but did the cars have to be so darn boring? Why couldn't we have souped-up cars like the Dodge Chargers driven by Dallas PD? After all, I might get into a high-speed chase attempting to catch a tax evader. It could happen.

We climbed inside, snapped our belts into place, and settled into our usual routine in which the driver picks the radio station and the passenger plays navigator. Eddie, who had a penchant for easy-listening music, slid a Harry Connick, Jr., CD into the player while I used the GPS app on my phone to pull up directions to the Unic Art Space. The name was probably intended to be a creative way to spell "unique," but my mind read it as "eunuch." I supposed if you were a male who'd been castrated, you wouldn't be distracted by sexual yearnings and your hands would have plenty of free time to finger paint.

"It's in Deep Ellum," I told Eddie, referring to the nearby entertainment district that featured numerous art galleries, restaurants, and nightclubs.

"Gotcha." He backed out of the spot and headed out of the parking lot, taking a right onto Commerce Street, then easing over onto Main. In less than six minutes we circled back onto Elm and pulled up to the curb in front of the Unic Art Space.

Eddie and I glanced up at the two-story red-brick building. While the commercial art galleries that flanked the museum on both sides featured colorful signs and displays to lure shoppers into their stores, the Unic's front window bore only inch-high black lettering that read THE UNIC— OPEN MONDAY THRU FRIDAY 1 TO 4.

Sheesh. That schedule made banker's hours seem demanding.

Eddie's brow contorted in skepticism. "Doesn't look like much."

"Didn't expect it to," I replied.

The museum was run by Sharla Fowler, the mother of former NFL player Rodney Fowler. A Heisman nominee, Rodney had played for various teams back in the 80s and early 90s, earning one of the league's highest salaries, before retiring from the Dallas Cowboys. Rodney, now in his mid-fifties, was divorced with three grown daughters. Two years ago, he'd decided to follow in the footsteps of philanthropic professional athletes Troy Aikman, Tim Tebow, and Serena Williams, and formed a charitable foundation called the Fifty-Yard Line

Foundation. The Fifty-Yard Line Foundation funded the Unic Art Space.

Although the organization's mission statement claimed the foundation existed "to educate the public about the arts by funding a space where creative works will be displayed and contemplated," I suspected the space truly existed for the purpose of enabling the former football player to shelter his income from high taxes by shifting it to family members and others to whom he or his family had close personal ties. It wouldn't be the first time someone had established a sham nonprofit organization to evade taxes.

Eddie and I climbed out of the car and stepped inside. The interior was equally unimpressive, comprising primarily empty space with a piece of art hanging here and there on the vast walls or displayed on widely spaced pedestals. A wide staircase with white steps and chrome banisters led up to the second floor. A young woman with shocking red hair and contrasting black brows sat at a glass table in the foyer, a small cash register and credit card swiping machine within reach.

"'Ello," she said with a French accent. "Welcome to the Unic. You would like to see the exhibits today?"

Eddie began to pull his badge from his pocket, but I stopped him with a nudge of my elbow. Perhaps we'd learn more from this woman if she didn't yet know we had come to interrogate her boss.

"Yes," I told the girl. "Two tickets, please."

She held out a delicate palm. "Sixty dollars, *s'il vous plaît*."

Eddie and I exchanged glances. As sparse as the offerings appeared to be, thirty bucks per person seemed a hefty price. Besides, the ticket income would only further pad the pockets of those involved in this sham. On the other hand, there appeared to be no one else here and I knew from my review of the museum's financial records that it would be operating at a significant loss if not for the constant influx of contributions from the Fifty-Yard Line Foundation.

"Let me get this," I told Eddie. This was my case, after all. My partner was along only as a sounding board and backup. I performed the same role when I assisted on his cases.

I pulled out my Visa card and handed it to the clerk. She slid it through the machine, and, in a feminine and genteel gesture, used her pinky to depress the print button. She ripped the paper tape from the machine and handed it to me along with a pen. "Your signature?"

After signing the slip, I returned it to the woman, who exchanged it for a couple of brochures. "This guide will tell you about the pieces on exhibit." She offered a smile and extended the palm once again, this time to indicate the few pieces of art in the room. "If you have any questions, please to let me know. My name is Josette. Enjoy."

After thanking Josette, Eddie and I walked into the room, our footsteps and voices echoing off the stained concrete floor and brick walls. Instinctively, we both began to tiptoe and whisper. We made our way to the first work of art, an enormous painting that hung on the left wall. Other than the artist's signature in the lower right corner, the canvas appeared to be blank.

Eddie consulted his brochure. "This piece is called *There's No Such Thing as a Good Cry*."

"It should be called *Wasted Canvas*."

Seriously, what was up with this? Wouldn't an artist want to show off his or her talents by actually doing more than hanging what appeared to be an empty canvas? Then again, I didn't have an artistic bone in my body. Not a single cell, even. Art to me was a velvet painting of dogs playing poker. Was it possible I just didn't get it? That I was too unsophisticated?

Eddie held up the pamphlet. "Says here the entire canvas was painted with the artist's tears."

"Huh?" I read the entry on my copy. Sure enough, the huge canvas had purportedly been swabbed end to end with tears. The statement provided by the artist, Aly Pelham, said she sought to unify art and spirit by using bodily fluids as a linking medium. I supposed it was creative, but I *knew* it was bizarre.

The pamphlet went on to describe Aly Pelham as "an emerging avant-garde artist" with "a brave, bold style sure to earn her a spot in the annals of modern art history." As for me, I was just glad she hadn't painted with anything that came out of an *annal*.

My partner took another gander at the exhibit. "What do you think she was crying about?"

"A man," I said. "Only one of your kind could upset a woman enough that she'd cry the two gallons of tears it would take to fill this canvas." Hell, as worried as I was about Nick I could probably paint ten of these canvases with the tears I was sure to shed over the next few weeks until he returned home.

Eddie and I shuffled along to the next painting. This one was a tiny canvas approximately the same dimensions as a wallet-sized photo. This canvas bore a small, cock-eyed reddish-brown smear along the right edge.

"This is by the same artist," Eddie said. "It's called *Picking at Scabs*."

"Ew!" I cringed and backed away lest I catch hepatitis.

"What's next?" Eddie said. "Saliva? Earwax?"

I was almost afraid to find out. If the next piece was called *Wigglers, Conception on Canvas,* I was out of here. Fortunately the next piece contained neither saliva, earwax, or sperm, though it was nonetheless disturbing. *Bad Hair Day* was painted by the artist using brushes made from her own hair to apply the acrylic paint in an abstract pattern of tangled brushstrokes. Some of the artist's hair had stuck in the paint and was clearly visible on the canvas.

Eddie leaned in for a closer look. "Aly Pelham's a blonde."

"A *bleached* blonde," I said, pointing out a piece of hair with a dark end.

"Nah. That's just brown paint," Eddie replied. "Or is it?" He took another step closer to verify.

"This isn't art," I whispered. "This is a freak show."

Wasn't art supposed to make you think? I mean, at least to think something other than *what the hell?* The only thought I had about Aly Pelham's art was that she seemed to be trying awfully hard to shock her audience, to grab attention with odd, disturbing images. Her art didn't seem to me as much a personal expression as a cry for attention. But perhaps I was being too harsh. After all, who didn't like a little attention now and then?

We turned and approached the three pedestals. Sitting on the first was a rusty oscillating fan, its cord plugged into the wall behind it. The fan chugged along on low speed, creaking as its jerking movements turned it first left, then right, then left again. The air blew across our chests as we stood watching.

Creeeeak . . . creeeeeak . . . creeeeeak.

"This fan could use some WD-40," I said. "It's creakier than the Tin Man from Oz."

I read the entry in the brochure. According to the pamphlet, the artist was someone named Jackson T. Reavis. "This one is called *Winds of Change*," I told Eddie. "Apparently the artist uses air as his medium."

Interesting, perhaps, but shouldn't it take more than finding a junky old fan at a garage sale and plugging it into a wall to prove your worth as an artist? If not, then I was making art every time I used the ancient harvest-gold hand mixer my grandmother had passed down to me.

As we walked to the next pedestal, Josette scurried up. "Let me turn on this piece for you. It is very loud so we do not leave it running."

Josette plugged the cord into the wall and turned the dial on the stand to activate the 1950's-era dome-style hair dryer. As the device forced warm air down toward our shoes, Josette shouted over the noise, telling us about the piece. "This exhibit is *The Portal to Hell*. Such creativity, no?"

"Such a load of crap," Eddie muttered next to me.

Josette spun the dial to turn off the machine, putting an end to the warm air and racket. "What do you say, sir? I could not hear over the noise of the art."

"I . . . um . . ." Eddie cleared his throat. "I said 'such good craft.' "

"Oui." Josette offered another smile and led us to the next pedestal, where a vintage salmon-pink canister vacuum sat in repose. She retrieved the frayed cord, holding it aloft between her fingers as if it were a fancy cigarette. "The title of this piece is *Sometimes Life Sucks*. Such a true sentiment, would you not agree?"

Hmm. I never knew how to answer a question posed in that manner. If I said "yes," would that mean I agreed or disagreed? Instead, I chose to answer with an unambiguous, unequivocal declaration. "Life does indeed suck on occasion." *Like when your boyfriend has to go on a dangerous undercover mission involving a man known as the Knife.*

Josette crouched down to plug in the cord, activating the device. The vacuum emitted a sound like a mechanical burp—*BRUPP*—and belched a plume of grayish-brown dust into Josette's face. She shrieked, inadvertently sucking in the dust the vacuum had expelled. As she launched into a coughing fit, I bent down and yanked the plug out of the wall before the thing could burp again and suffocate her completely.

"Excusez-moi!" Josette cried, blinking dust out of her eyes and waving her hands as if performing a jazz dance routine. "I must go clean myself!" With that, she scurried off to a frosted-glass door on the far wall, opened it, and disappeared into the administrative wing of the building.

Having viewed and contemplated the meager offerings on the first floor, Eddie and I ascended the staircase to the second story. This floor, which contained no administrative wing, was wider than the downstairs room had been. The works here were of no less questionable quality, however. We took in *Vacation in Venice,* a colorfully painted and somewhat abstract macaroni mosaic depicting what appeared to be a boat on a Venetian canal. The gondolier sported the typical black pants and striped shirt formed from linguini, while the girl riding in the boat wore a piece of bowtie pasta on her head. The pasta appeared to be mounted on cheap poster board, though the gilded gold frame around it provided an illusion of grandeur.

"Is this art?" Eddie asked, his tone and expression incredulous. "Or dinner?"

According to my brochure, the masterpiece—or should I say the *pasta*piece?—had been the brainchild of artist Hunter Gabbert. "The artist really used his noodle to come up with this idea."

Eddie groaned. "Do you have to be so silly?"

"Don't you mean *fusilli*?"

Eddie groaned again. "If I thought I could get away with it, I'd shoot you right now."

"No you wouldn't," I said. "That's a bunch of *bolognese*."

"You're right," he said. "Guess I'll have to shoot myself then."

Having run out of pasta puns, I moved on. Next was a large sculpture by an artist named Emily Raggio. The sculpture, called *Rx: Death,* comprised a full-sized coffin completely covered in assorted colorful prescription pills. The same artist had created *Shooting Up,* a rocket-shaped sculpture made from plastic syringes, a needle on top pointing skyward.

I gestured to the coffin and rocket. "What do you think about those?" Seemed to me it took some creativity and sculpting ability to put the rocket together, and the coffin, no matter how weird, sent a clear message about the pill culture in America and the dangers of overmedicating. "Is that real art?"

Eddie shrugged. "Heck if I know."

My favorite by far was artist Mallory Sisko's piece entitled *Life's Compost,* in which a wooden composting bin was filled with the detritus of a young woman's life. A junior high yearbook. A pair of pink ballet slippers with a hole in the toe. An empty tube of acne cream. A letter the artist had received from her boyfriend while she was at summer band camp and in which he broke up with her offering the usual platitudes of *it's not you, it's me* and *I can't love someone else until I learn to love myself.* The guy had the nerve to ask *Do you know if Nicole Green is still seeing Colt Reynolds? If not, can you tell her hi for me?*

Sheesh. What a dumbass.

chapter three

*O*ne Tough Mother

Eddie and I made our way back downstairs and over to Josette, who had cleaned herself up the best she could and was back at her desk, taking a last dab at her eyes and nose with a tissue.

She glanced up as we approached. "I trust you enjoyed the exhibits, no?"

I exchanged a glance with Eddie. "They were very . . . intriguing."

"Oui," she agreed. "The Unic features only the most creative contemporary artists. None of those tired haystacks or landscapes." She waved a hand dismissively.

"I do have a question, though," I continued. "How can you tell if the art is good? Whether the artist has any talent?"

Josette sat up straighter and pulled her head back as if offended. "Well, whether art is good is up to the observer to decide, is it not?"

"Is it . . . not?" I asked, again confused on how to respond to her question. "I mean, the art here is certainly interesting, I'll give you that. But the museum paid good money for these pieces, right? So there must be some consensus whether they are real art or just some gimmick that a person threw together when they decided to clean out their pantry or attic."

Josette's lips formed a tight line. "I assure you that each of our featured artists is a professional."

"Do you know anything about them?" I asked. "What art schools they attended? Or whether they even attended an art school?"

She no longer appeared merely taken aback, she appeared thoroughly appalled by my questions. She managed to maintain her composure, however. "I see that on the subject of art you are quite ignorant."

"Totally." She'd obviously meant to insult me, but I rolled with it. What did this snit's opinion matter to me? "I'm curious what specific artistic techniques were used in these pieces. You know, learned skills. Can you tell me?"

She waved her hand again, though this time it seemed as if she were trying to shoo me away. "One does not *learn* art. One *feels* it, gives birth to it."

Next to me, Eddie snorted, then covered it with a fake sneeze. I was tempted to snort, too. Sure, creative instincts originated from within, but if a person could not learn artistic techniques, then what were the art schools and college art departments teaching? This woman's explanations were as transparent as the air blowing its way across the gallery from the oscillating fan.

Besides, I'd done some research before coming here today. Even the most original and imaginative modern artists generally had some formal art training and employed both personal creativity and learned techniques in their works.

Herb Williams, dubbed the "King of Crayola," fashioned interesting sculptures using crayons as his medium. He'd created a life-sized Johnny Cash and a three-dimensional sculpture of Marilyn Monroe. Prior to launching his colorful career in Crayolas, Williams had earned a BFA and worked casting sculptures at a bronze foundry. Heck, the White House had commissioned Americana works from the artist and made them part of its permanent collection.

Billy Tripp, a metalworking artist, created an evolving, abstract outdoor piece of monolithic proportions as a tribute to his parents. In response to the FAQs on Tripp's Web site, the artist noted that he'd taken college-level art courses at two institutions.

Although Banksy, the secretive and subversive British graffiti artist, denied having any formal art education beyond that provided in public schools, I noticed he'd made a reference in an interview to Rodin. Obviously he knew something about the masters. Self-taught, perhaps? If nothing else, the fact that Banksy refined his graffiti technique over time to include the use of stencils and that he was so prolific showed a true dedication to his art form.

I doubted that some of the artists featured here were so devoted to their work. Then again, that macaroni piece must have taken a long time. Of course that could simply evidence an addiction to carbs.

"Are you a trained artist, Josette?" I asked.

"But of course." She offered a smile, but no details.

"Where did you study?"

"What is it you Americans say?" She looked up as if the answer might be written on the ceiling. "Here and there?"

An evasive answer if ever I'd heard one and, trust me, I'd heard a lot of evasive answers. Though I was curious, there was no point in pushing her further. Her artistic education wasn't the issue here. The issue was whether this museum was a sham or whether the place was "for reals." Frankly, I still couldn't say for sure.

At this point, I retrieved one of my business cards from my purse and held it out to Josette. Eddie did the same. Josette's brows angled in as she tried to decipher why two agents from IRS Criminal Investigations would be at the Unic.

"We have an appointment with Mrs. Fowler," I said. "We're a little early." We'd expected our tour of the museum to take more than fifteen minutes, after all. "If she's available we'd be glad to get started."

Josette stood. "I will see if she is ready for you. Wait here." She carried our business cards with her as she made her way again through the glass door that led to the museum offices.

Eddie and I stood in front of the oscillating fan while we waited. When Josette hadn't returned in twenty seconds I grew bored. I put my face directly in line with the airstream and called "oooooh" into the fan. The spinning blades gave my voice a warbling, eerie sound. I turned my face up to Eddie. "Do I sound like a ghost?"

"A little," he said.

"What about now?" I said, stepping back, throwing out a hip, and tossing my head to let the breeze blow my hair back. "Do I look like a fashion model on a photo shoot?"

"No," he said. "You look like a dimwit who needs to grow up."

Yeah, Eddie and I had that kind of brutally honest relationship.

As the glass door opened again, I stood up straight. No sense in me also giving the museum's director the impression I was an idiot.

As Josette continued out and took a seat again at her desk, Sharla Fowler stepped into the doorway.

"Holy mother of God," Eddie whispered on a breath. "I wish I had shoulders like that."

Sharla stood six feet tall in her flat business loafers and, like the defensive tackle she'd borne, had a big-boned frame and the strong, broad shoulders of a water buffalo. Though she had to be in her late seventies, you'd never know it from looking at her. Her skin was a latte brown, her hair a shiny honey gold. She wore a tasteful ivory blazer over beige slacks, along with chunky gold jewelry and an expression so intimidating I was tempted to cross my legs lest I wet myself. If she'd passed that look on to her son along with those shoulders, it was no wonder he'd had such a successful career on the football field.

"Come on back," she called without introduction, though I suppose it was clear who each of us was. Her voice, like her expression, was also intimidating, deep and throaty and commanding.

Eddie and I followed her to her office, one of two doors positioned off the small inner hall. The other was a unisex restroom.

Sharla motioned to two contemporary barrel chairs upholstered in a trendy lemon yellow. "Take a seat."

As Eddie and I sat down, she continued around her modern desk, which, with its outwardly angled legs and flat top, resembled an oversized breakfast tray. As she settled in her high-backed desk chair, I took a chance to glance around. Notably, the room was devoid of art, though a number of books on the subject filled a narrow bookcase. The like-new condition of the books told me they'd probably never been opened and had probably been recently purchased and put there for show.

I noted several printouts on her desk. The first detailed several Hawaiian vacation options. The second provided information on resorts in Bermuda. A third featured tours of the California wine country.

Sharla noticed me noticing them and gathered the papers up. "It's been a busy day for me."

Yeah, right. Busy planning her next vacation. Given

that she pulled down a cool quarter-million-dollar annual salary, you'd think she could manage to keep her focus on her work.

Sharla slid the printouts into a desk drawer. "Josette says you toured the museum. Impressive, isn't it?"

"It's quite a collection," I said, not quite agreeing with her but not directly refuting her, either. "In fact, I'd love to hear more about the pieces and the artists. I know zilch about art. Can you tell me what types of techniques the artists used? What about their other pieces? Do they have art on exhibit elsewhere?"

Sharla only chuckled. "Now, now, Ms. Holloway. If you want an art lesson, take a class. I know you're not here to learn about art. You're here to snoop."

So she was direct. That meant I could be, too.

"Snooping is our job," I said unapologetically. "We have to make sure that organizations claiming an exemption from tax are truly qualified for the exemption."

"Oh, I know that's true." She clucked her tongue and smirked. "I heard all about the IRS taking its sweet time making sure those Tea Party organizations were qualified for their tax exemption. Those shenanigans made you folks look like a bunch of fools, wouldn't you say?"

Although Criminal Investigations had had nothing to do with the recent scandal that rocked the IRS, I'd only appear defensive if I said so to Sharla Fowler. Instead, I went on the offensive. "Lots of things take time. Like completing a valid art appraisal, for instance."

The appraiser hired by the Unic's board had completed his analysis of the museum's entire collection in a single day. The Unic didn't have many pieces but, still, it seemed it should have taken him longer to come up with accurate figures, especially since, according to the appraiser's own documentation, only one of the artists had a previous sale to use as a reference point. That piece, a three-by-four-foot sculpture entitled *Aaah* in the shape of a human head with mouth gaping open, had been constructed entirely of tongue depressors. The sculptor was the same person who'd made *Rx: Death* and *Shooting Up,* the pieces Eddie and I had seen in the museum only a few minutes earlier. *Aaah* had sold for $125 to a pediatrician, who probably had the thing on display in his waiting room next to an aquarium full of goldfish and a rack full of *Highlights* magazines.

Despite the modest sales price for *Aaah,* the appraiser had valued *Rx: Death* at $18,000. Per the records the audit department had forwarded on to Criminal Investigations, the Unic had paid the artist the full appraised value for the piece. *Shooting Up* had fetched another $9,500. Mallory Sisko had been paid three grand for *Life's Compost.*

But the real question regarding valuation surrounded the other artists. Aly Pelham's pieces had garnered her a grand total of $60,000. Jackson Reavis, the "air artist," had been paid $75,000 for his pieces, even though one sucked and the others blew. Hunter Gabbert, the crown prince of pasta, earned forty big ones for his noodle doodle. Heck, maybe I should dig my old grade-school art projects out of the attic and see if the Unic would buy them. I could become an overnight millionaire.

"Let's not beat around the bush here," Sharla said. "We're all busy people. What do I need to tell you people to make you stop wasting my time?"

"Fair enough," I said. *Hey, my time is valuable, too.* Worth as much, if not more, than *Vacation in Venice.* "Tell me how you found your appraiser."

"He was personally recommended to me," Sharla said.

"By whom?" Eddie asked.

"If I could remember"—she glanced his way—"I'd tell you. I interact with so many people in the art community

I lose track. I just know his name came up on several occasions."

I pulled the appraisal from my briefcase. "Weren't you curious how he came up with such high valuations for all the pieces given that only one of the artists had a previous sale?"

Sharla lifted a noncommittal shoulder. "I trusted him to do his job. Besides, people go nuts for these types of unusual pieces."

True, in some cases. Brad Pitt and Angelina Jolie had paid $1 million for a Banksy. But I doubted the Unic's pieces carried such artistic weight.

"Have any of your artists sold pieces since?" I asked.

Sharla lifted two noncommittal shoulders this time. "You'd have to ask them."

I was tempted to say *maybe I will*. But I knew I would definitely sound petty then. Besides, there was no maybe about it. I planned to contact the artists for more information.

"Do you, or anyone associated with the Unic, have a personal relationship with any of the artists?" I asked.

She chuckled condescendingly. "What a ridiculous question. Of course we know these artists. We've held galas here at the museum to feature them and their work. I'm sure you've seen the photographs on our Web site?"

I had, of course. I'm nothing if not thorough. "I meant *before* the Unic bought their work," I clarified. "Did anyone associated with the Unic have a personal relationship with any of the artists before their work was purchased?"

She hesitated an instant before snapping, "You think I know everyone that every board member and employee knows?"

More evasiveness, answering my question with a question of her own was not an answer.

"There are only three board members for the Unic," I

pointed out. "And only two employees. You and Josette. That's not a big number."

Her eyes flashed. If she'd thought Tara Holloway would back down, she'd thought wrong. More than likely her aggressive tactics had worked on others. I knew they'd worked on the auditor. His personal notes in the file referred to Sharla Fowler's personality as sharklike.

When Sharla said nothing in response, I picked up the conversation. "Do I need to personally interview every board member and every employee?"

"I don't know," she snapped. "Do you?"

Clearly we'd get nowhere with this woman. I'd have to take a different tack. I motioned to Eddie that it was time to call it a day here.

"We'll be back," I told her as Eddie and I stood to go.

Sharla Fowler didn't bother getting up from her chair. "You do what you have to do," she said, giving us the evil eye. "And so will I."

chapter four

Sweet Sorrow, My Sweet Ass!

Shakespeare's a dumbass. Parting isn't sweet sorrow, it's agony. Especially when you know that the next time you might see the man you love he could be zipped up in a body bag . . . assuming his body could even be found.

Nick and I stopped at a strip mall with a Kohl's store, where I scored a cute pair of bright blue sunglasses for just ten bucks. They weren't nearly as nice as my Brighton knockoffs, but they'd do for now. Afterward, we went to dinner at his favorite barbecue joint. He downed approximately two thirds of a cow, while I merely pushed some beans around on my plate, poked at my potato salad, and contemplated the fact that cole slaw was essentially the edible equivalent of confetti. Plus mayonnaise.

"It's going to be okay, Tara," Nick said, jabbing his fork into an enormous slab of pecan pie. Who could blame him for his gluttony? This could be his last supper.

"I'll believe that when you come back home." I pushed my plate away and crossed my arms over my chest. I hated to act like a petulant child, but that's exactly how I felt.

I wasn't getting my way. If I were, Nick wouldn't be working the cartel case and he and I would be on vacation in Maui, sitting on a sunny, sandy beach, sipping piña coladas.

"Don't worry," Nick said. "I'll squash La Cucaracha like the filthy, nasty bug he is."

"It's El Cuchillo." I picked up my steak knife and brandished it at him in illustration. "*The knife.* And you damn well know it."

Ignoring my demonstration, Nick held his bite of pie aloft. "I'm counting on you to be strong for my mother, Tara. She's going to need reassurance."

"Don't worry. I can fake a happy face. See?" I forced my lips into a grin so broad it hurt my cheeks.

"Your eyes still look upset."

"I'll wear my new sunglasses." I reached into my purse, retrieved my bright blue sunglasses, and slid them onto my face. "How's this?"

"Better," he said.

I took the sunglasses back off and set them on the table in front of me. I continued poking at my potato salad and rearranging my beans while Nick ate his dessert in silence.

Just as Nick finished his pie, a busboy walked up with an empty plastic bin. He eyed Nick's empty plate and my messy one. "All done here?"

I nodded.

Holding the bin in one arm, the kid used the other to quickly sweep the plates, cups, and utensils from the table. The items clunk-clunked into the tub, followed by a suspicious crunch.

"Crap." I looked down into the tub to see my new sunglasses crushed under my still-full plate. The nosepiece had snapped in two and the right lens had popped out. I grabbed the earpiece and pulled them from the wreckage to see if they were salvageable. The bean juice dripping from them said no.

The boy's eyes went wide. "Sorry! I didn't see your glasses on the table."

I tossed the sunglasses back into his bin and raised a palm. "Not your fault. I should've put them back in my purse."

His face relaxed in relief as he headed off to bus another table.

Nick and I walked out to his truck and drove to his town house, which sat just down the street from mine. Close enough to make overnight stays convenient, but far enough to give each of us the illusion of independence.

His dog, Daffodil, greeted us at the door, her tail wind-milling behind her so fast it threatened to take her airborne. Daffy was an Australian shepherd mix with gorgeous blue eyes much prettier than mine. Her multicolored fur, which had been missing in spots when Nick recently adopted her from the animal shelter, was filling in nicely. The dog was filling out, too, her ribs no longer easily palpable. Though it had been my idea for Nick to take a look at the dogs available for adoption, I had to admit I was a bit jealous of the attention Nick lavished on Daffodil. I wouldn't mind him rubbing my tummy or brushing my hair now and then. And I bet Nick would never wipe sleep crud from *my* eyes or clip *my* toenails.

Nick knelt down and gave Daffy's ears the same ruffle he used to give his sweet old dog Nutty, who had recently gone to the big dog park in the sky. While Nutty had merely wagged his tail in manly appreciation, Daffodil shame-lessly licked Nick's face from chin to forehead and ear to ear. What a suck-up. Then again, maybe he just smelled like barbecue and she was hoping to get a taste.

Nick chuckled and turned his face aside lest she put her

tongue in his mouth for a French kiss. "How's my best girl?" he asked. "Huh? How is she?"

"I'm fine," I said, though I knew perfectly well he was talking to his dog. "Thanks for asking."

Nick glanced up at me. "You're just jealous."

"I am. You never greet me with that kind of enthusiasm."

"Neither do you."

"All right. Next time I see you I'll lick your face."

"You can do it right now if you want."

"After Daffy got her dog germs all over you? Ew. No, thanks."

Of course I was all bark and no bite. Despite my envy, I knew there were some things only *I* could do for Nick. Besides, it wasn't the dog's fault she was an irresistible cutie pie. And even though I might be jealous of her relationship with Nick, I still adored the dog.

I knelt down next to Nick and Daffy's tongue attacked my face next. "Hi, girl," I managed between licks. "How ya' doin'?"

Once Nick and I had been fully cleaned by his dog's saliva—or sullied, depending on your view—we let her out back for some yard time and headed upstairs to his bedroom.

Nick flopped backward onto his bed. "I'm not sure I can perform after all that food."

"I told you to skip the pie."

His mouth spread in a naughty grin. "I *never* skip pie." He reached out, grabbed my wrist, and pulled me onto the bed, flipping me over until he had me pinned to the spread.

I could give you the details of what happened next, but no sense sharing Nick's trade secrets and voiding his patent. Suffice it to say that clothing hit the floor, sheets became sweaty, orgasms were exchanged, and a good time was had by all. Nick had even spoken to me in Spanish during the deed. Whether he'd been whispering sweet nothings or talking dirty I wasn't sure, but either way it had worked its magic.

Though the sex was mind-blowing, as always, it was the tender moments afterward that I treasured even more, those moments of serene intimacy shared in each other's arms. Tonight, especially, I didn't want to let him go, wishing I could freeze time and hold on to Nick forever. But, alas, time marched on, stomping all over my heart.

After a few moments in which Nick stroked my hair and nuzzled into my neck, we both knew we had to get moving. We reluctantly dressed, me in the work clothes I'd still had on prior to said rendezvous and Nick in a pair of shorts and a T-shirt. He reached down and retrieved the duffel bag he kept his workout clothes in. Unzipping it, he pulled out a small plastic bag from which he then pulled out two tiny, prepaid phones.

I knew exactly what they were.

A way for the two of us to stay in touch while he was undercover.

He handed one to me. "This could get me in deep shit, you know."

"I know." My eyes filled with tears. "Thanks, Nick. I'll feel better having this."

No one, not even Lu or the other higher-ups at the IRS, would know the two of us had these untraceable, secret phones. It was a somewhat risky move.

"One rule, though," he said. "I only contact you, okay? To let you know I'm all right. I can't risk your call or text coming in at an inopportune time and someone discovering that I've got the extra phone."

"What if it's an emergency?" I asked.

"Then you call Lu," he said. "She'll know how to reach

me through the secure network the DEA has arranged for us."

"How are you going to hide the phone?"

Nick grabbed his left boot, angled it so I could see inside, and pulled out the bottom liner to reveal a jagged-edged compartment he'd cut into the heel, probably with his pocketknife.

"Wow," I said. "That's clever. Like *Get Smart*."

"Let's only hope I don't *get caught*."

chapter five

Going Under

Tuesday morning, as I drove down to Nick's place, my
stomach and head seemed to be rotating in opposite directions as if they were playing a game of rubber baby
buggy bumpers. The problem was caused in part over my
worry about Nick and in part because, last night after I'd
returned home, I'd downed two thirds of the pitcher of
peach sangria I'd made for Alicia. Talk about trying to
drown your sorrows.

Nick stepped out of his house into the gray, drizzly
morning with Daffodil dancing on his heels. Poor girl. She
probably thought he was taking her for a walk when, in
reality, he was taking her for an indefinite stay with
grandma.

Nick situated Daffy in the backseat of my car, then slid
into the front. He leaned over and gave me a peck on the
cheek. "Good morning."

I didn't want to be a downer, but I couldn't minimize
my feelings, either. I was nothing if not an emotionally
honest person. "I've had better."

"Me, too." Nick stared out the rain-spotted windshield

with a faraway look on his face before turning back to me. "But we'll have more good ones. Soon. You'll see."

I reached over and ran the back of my fingers over the dark stubble on Nick's cheek. "This is sexy."

He cut his eyes and a soft smile my way. "Does it make me look tougher?"

"Hell, yeah," I said.

"Maybe my stubble will stop a bullet if someone tries to shoot me in the face."

I knew Nick was only trying to lighten the mood, but I didn't find his attempts at humor to be funny at all. "Stop it. You're only making me worry more. Besides, it's not bullets I'm worried about. It's that knife."

"There's just no pleasing some people." He reached out and gave my knee an affectionate squeeze.

I slid the car into gear and we drove to his mother's house. As we climbed out of the car, Bonnie opened her front door with a worried frown on her face. Bonnie's hair was dark like Nick's, though longer and streaked with hints of silver. Her blue eyes were clouded with worry. Before we could even reach her door, she began to throw a hissy fit like the one I'd thrown the day before.

"You've done enough for that agency!" she told Nick. "You haven't even been home from Mexico a full year yet. There's got to be someone else in that office who can handle this case instead of you!"

"They assigned me to the case because I know Spanish," he said, giving her a peck on the forehead. "Besides, I'm the baddest badass on the force."

"Oh, ho!" I called, stepping up behind him to give Bonnie a hug. "I beg to differ."

Bonnie looked from one of us to the other. "You might both be badasses," she said, "but you're both crazy, too. Why don't you two hang out a shingle and start a tax firm together? Pratt and Holloway, CPAs. It would be much safer than working for the IRS and I bet you'd rake in the dough."

I'd asked myself the same question time and time again. *Why do we do this?* The IRS paid reasonably well, but the private sector would likely reward us better, with partnerships, perks, and client dinners at Dallas's most exclusive restaurants. But it wasn't about the money. Never had been. Never would be. Serving as a special agent wasn't so much a job as it was a calling. And the call, once received, couldn't be ignored. Sort of like a persistent bill collector.

Nick retrieved Daffy's bed, toys, hairbrush, treats, and food from my car and brought them into his mother's house. The dog sat in the front hallway watching him, a confused and frightened look on her face, like a child beginning to realize her parent was leaving her. Nick bent down, cupped her furry chin in his hands, and looked into her eyes. "It's going to be okay, girl. Daddy will be back in a few weeks." He gave her a kiss on the snout.

He stood and repeated the same basic process with his mother. Though it was clear Bonnie was trying her damnedest to fight back the tears, several spilled down her cheeks nonetheless.

"Look, Mom," Nick said softly, putting a hand on her back. "I gave Tara a secret phone. I'll check in with her when I can, let her know I'm okay. She'll pass that information on to you."

Bonnie turned to me. "You call me immediately when you hear from Nick, okay? No matter what time of day or night it is."

"I will."

She gave her son one last hug, clutching him so tight it was a wonder he could take in oxygen. "I love you, son."

"Right back at ya', Mom."

I drove Nick over to the DEA office, pulling up to the curb near the front doors. "Get out."

"That's a fine good-bye."

I said it again, this time through a fresh stream of mascara-tinted tears. Two days in a row the guy had ruined my makeup. "Get out." My chest heaved with barely contained sobs. "And . . . come back."

Nick tilted his head and cupped my face, rubbing his thumb back and forth across my cheekbone like a windshield wiper to remove the moisture. "I'm going to remember you just like this."

I shook my head. "Don't remember me like this. Remember how I looked on New Year's." I'd worn a fabulous, shimmery gold gown. Of course Nick had been so jet-lagged from working two international cases that he'd slept right through the midnight countdown.

"That's a better idea," he replied. "You're kinda gooey right now."

I narrowed my eyes at Nick, grabbed a napkin from my console, and wiped my eyes and nose.

"That's okay." He leaned in and pulled me toward him. "I'm not afraid of a little goo."

We held each other for a long moment and I thought my heart would explode in my chest.

"I love you," he said into my hair.

"I love you, too," I mumbled into his warm neck. *Maybe too much.* Love was a double-edged sword. It could make a person happier than they'd ever been, but it could fill them with pure, raw misery, too.

He finally released me. "I'll be in touch."

Despite my best efforts to hold it in, a fresh sob escaped me. "You better."

chapter six

$\mathcal{W}$elcome to Paradise

Later that morning, Eddie and I loaded into my G-ride and headed southeast out of Dallas.

I glanced over at Eddie. "Remember the last time we came out this way?"

He gave a mirthless snort. "I remember coming out here," he said. "But I don't remember coming back."

He'd been unconscious and riding in a medical helicopter on his return. We'd tracked our target, a con artist running an investment scam, down to a lake house. Unfortunately, the creep had turned his gun on me and Eddie and put a bullet in my partner's skull, taking part of his earlobe with it. I'd suffered a broken arm when I'd leaped out a window to avoid being shot.

Good times.

Our targets today were Quent and Kevin Kuykendahl, a couple of cousins operating an alleged animal sanctuary known as Paradise Park. Whether the two were running a legitimate wildlife sanctuary or something else remained to be seen. I only hoped Eddie and I would have better luck extracting information from the Kuykendahl cousins than we'd had with Sharla Fowler the day before.

I had to admit I was curious, not only about the place, but about the two men running it. The auditor had described them in her notes as Charles Manson look-alikes.

The clouds broke on the drive, the sun shining through and reflecting off the moisture on the roads, creating a blinding glare that fried my retinas.

"I need to make a quick stop." I whipped into a gas station and, while Eddie waited in the car, ran inside to buy a cheap pair of shades to replace the pair I'd lost at the barbecue joint the night before. The pickings were slim. I tried on several pairs, eyeing myself in the tiny mirror at the top of the revolving display, before settling for a mirrored aviator-style pair that, even at $4.99, seemed over-priced given how flimsy they were.

"I'll take these," I told the clerk, gingerly placing them on the counter next to the cash register along with a bag of Skittles. "And a scratch-off."

When I returned to the car, Eddie smirked. "You trying to look like a motorcycle cop? Or a fighter pilot?"

"I'm just trying not to go blind." I handed him the scratch-off. "Here. A little something to thank you for driving all the way out here with me."

Eddie took the lottery ticket from me and fished a penny out of my cup holder to rub off the adhesive. "Winner, winner, chicken dinner!" He waved the ticket in the air. "I won fifty bucks."

"Damn. Should've kept that ticket for myself."

"Too late now." Eddie slid the ticket into his wallet and glanced over at me. "You gonna share those Skittles?"

"You've got fifty bucks. Go buy your own."

He snatched the bag out of my hand, poured a dozen or so of the colorful candies into his palm, then held the package out to me.

I snatched it back from him. "You stink."

"I'll split my winnings with you. How's that?"

"Better." I could use the $25 to upgrade to a nicer pair of shades once we returned to Dallas.

We made our way through the small town of Kemp, then turned south on State Highway 274. As we ventured down the country road on which the sanctuary was located, I noticed the fence erected on the left side of the road was made of thicker wires than most and stood at least a dozen feet tall. No doubt the fence contained something that was either unusually big or could jump awfully high. With the trees impeding our view onto the property there was no way to tell.

I gestured to the fence. "What do you think is in there?"

Eddie cocked his head. "King Kong? Bigfoot? Dinosaurs replicated from mosquitoes stuck in tree amber?"

I had my doubts whether anything like Jurassic Park would fly in Texas, where playing God with DNA was considered a sin as treacherous as rooting for a team other than the Cowboys.

The GPS app on my phone interrupted our conversation. "In one-half mile the destination will be on your right."

Eddie and I turned our attention away from oversized fictional creatures and back to the road in front of us. Other than trees, barbed-wire fencing, and an occasional gate, there wasn't much to see. A couple minutes later, the disembodied voice announced, "You have arrived at your destination."

I stopped the car and Eddie and I looked around. There was no mailbox. No numbers indicating an address. No sign marking the sanctuary property.

"You see anything?" I asked.

He pointed. "Just that rusty old gate up there."

Thirty feet ahead a wide gate with a loose top hinge hung cockeyed from a rotted wooden post. A dirt road led back from the gate onto the property, turning left behind a copse of scraggly trees and disappearing from sight. No animals could be seen, nor was there any structure visible.

I turned back to Eddie. "Could that be the sanctuary?"

"Only one way to find out."

We drove up to gate. I honked my horn three long times to get the attention of anyone who might be on the property. Venturing onto a rural property unexpected and unannounced was a good way to end up with buckshot in your ass, especially in Texas. Our residents loved their guns. After all, it was two guys from the Lone Star State who'd gone into a Chipotle restaurant waving their semiautomatics in a flagrant display of their rights under the state's open-carry law. What a couple of shit-for-brains dumbasses. They were lucky someone with the sense to keep their weapon concealed hadn't assumed they were there to rob the place and plugged them full of lead. If I'd been working the counter, those two would've taken a ladle of scalding refried beans to the face and a knee to their nards.

Hooonk. Hooonk. Hoooooonk.

Eddie and I waited a full minute with no response. I tried again.

Hooonk. Hooonk. Hooooooooooonk.

Still nothing.

"Do we risk it?" I asked. If it were solely up to me my answer would be yes. But after what Eddie had gone through on the earlier case, it was only right for me to give him a vote in the matter, even if I was the lead investigator on this gig.

"We've come all this way," Eddie said. "Might as well go in."

I slid my gearshift into park, hopped out of my car, and opened the gate. After I drove through, Eddie slid out of the passenger door to close the gate behind us.

We proceeded slowly along the dirt road, bouncing in our seats as we hit the ruts caused by recent rains. As we rounded the bend, a small trailer came into view. It was a basic beige model with metal stairs and no ornamentation, the type often used as a temporary office on construction sites. Its windows were covered in a thick layer of dust. One of them was cracked. An enormous black barrel grill stood off to the side, the top gaping open like a mouth ready to take a big bite. The grill was dirty, chunks of burnt meat stuck to the surface, flies swarming about. Bones of various shapes littered the ground around the grill, some of them surprisingly large. What the heck had these Kuykendahls been cooking out here? Antelope? Feral hogs? Tyrannosaurs?

Eddie snorted. "This is *paradise*?"

"Definitely not what I envisioned, either."

A muddy army-green ragtop Hummer was parked in front of the trailer. Behind the building sat a dilapidated wooden shed probably used to store animal feed and supplies. Next to the shed was a rusty horse trailer that had been modified to include metal bars over the windows. The trailer must be used for more than horses.

I gave my horn one more quick push to announce our arrival. *Honk!*

Seconds later a hairy face appeared in the dusty, cracked window.

"I was wrong," Eddie said. "Bigfoot doesn't live back at that other ranch. He lives here."

chapter seven

What Kind of Game Are They Playing?

The front door opened, giving us a better look at the man. While it was clear now that he wasn't an ape, the amount of coarse, dark facial hair he sported put him on par with those furry-faced dudes from *Duck Dynasty*. He had crazy eyes, too, the wide, wandering kind that seem to be taking in something surprising no one else could see. It was clear now why the auditor had compared him to Charles Manson. There was definitely a likeness, though he was too far away for me to tell whether he sported Charlie's forehead swastika tattoo.

Long-limbed and lanky, this man wore a khaki canvas hat with a chin tie that disappeared under his beard, a black T-shirt with the sleeves cut off, camouflage pants, and black rubber boots. A hunting knife that looked big enough to fillet a rhino was strapped to his belt next to a walkie-talkie. Looked like El Cuchillo wasn't the only one with a blade fetish. Two orange and white hunting dogs stepped up on either side of him and began barking in stereo. *Woof! Woof-woof!*

"Hello!" I called, raising a hand in a friendly wave. "Is this Paradise Park?"

The guy eyed me, then ran his gaze over my car, his eyes narrowing as he apparently realized it was a government vehicle. "Who wants to know?"

"We're from the IRS. Just need to talk to you a bit."

"Is that so." It was a challenge rather than a question. The man cocked a wild and woolly brow. "'Bout what?"

"About your financial records," I said, easing myself from the car. More precisely, I was here to talk about their *lack* of financial records. Every business should keep good documentation regarding their income and expenses, but recordkeeping was even more important for nonprofits, the records of which were required by law to be open for public inspection. What's more, these guys had filed only the electronic postcard return, intended for small nonprofits. Without records, it wasn't clear whether their organization qualified for the simplified form or whether they should have filed a full-fledged report detailing their board members, programs, and activities.

"We already done talked to the IRS." His crazy eyes narrowed so that they virtually disappeared between his brows and beard. "I thought we was all done with you folks."

I closed my car door behind me. "We have a few follow-up questions."

Eddie followed me and we stepped up to the trailer with our briefcases in our hands. At this range, I noted the man had worked up quite a stench. I also noticed that the man's lips were dry and cracked, as were his knuckles. The guy must spend a lot of time outside and neglect to properly hydrate. I was tempted to offer him a swipe of my Plum Perfect gloss and a squirt of the vanilla-scented hand lotion I always kept in my purse, but figured he'd turn me down. Or worse, that he *wouldn't*. No way would I use the products again if he touched them. I wasn't about to risk getting his stinky cooties.

I pulled a business card from my breast pocket and held it out to the man. "I'm IRS Special Agent Tara Holloway." I tilted my head to indicate Eddie. "This is my partner, Eddie Bardin. Are you Quentin or Kevin Kuykendahl?"

"I'm Quent." He took my card and looked it over, even going so far as to turn it over to see if there was anything written on the back. "This says you're from Criminal Investigations." He looked back up at us, and he didn't look happy. "What the hell, man?"

"Just a routine check," I lied. Our investigation was anything but. Still, no sense getting the guy all riled up, not when he had that knife on his belt and appeared more than capable of gutting us on the spot. "May we come in?"

He hesitated a moment, as if mulling over his options. Finally, he stepped back a foot or two to allow us inside. We headed up the rickety stairs and into the trailer, which smelled like sweat, dogs, and pork rinds thanks to an extra-large bag sitting open on a table inside next to a two-liter bottle of Mountain Dew with the cap off. The air inside the building was still and stifling. Why didn't the guy open a window? Was he trying to save electricity? Or was he just used to living like this?

The only chairs in the place were cheap folding canvas lawn chairs. Quent flopped down into one behind the table, while Eddie and I grabbed a couple situated haphazardly in the room and pulled them over to face Quent.

Seated now, I took a quick glance around the place. An ancient fridge stood along the left wall next to a short countertop housing a small stainless steel sink. A toaster oven sat on the counter. An uncovered trash can overflowed with paper plates, plastic utensils, and empty Mountain Dew bottles. Along the right wall stood a flat-screen television, what looked to be a forty-inch size. It was tuned to *Let's Make a Deal*. On screen, Wayne Brady negotiated with a woman in a Little Bo Peep costume while her husband or boyfriend, dressed as a sheep, stood by her side, offering advice. "Take the box, honey! Take the *baaa*x!"

The woman took the box. The pretty assistant lifted the lid with a smile, revealing a plate of spaghetti and meatballs. *Some prize.* Bo Peep turned to her sheep partner and brandished her staff as if ready to beat the woolly thing to death. That would be the last time she'd listen to him.

While I opened my briefcase and pulled out my notes, Quent tugged the walkie-talkie from his belt and pushed the talk button with a dirty, jagged-nailed thumb. "Kev. Come to the office. Folks is here from the IRS criminal department wanting information."

The radio's speaker crackled and a man's voice came back. "What the fu—" He stopped himself, apparently realizing we might be able to hear him. "I'm down at the crick but I'm headin' your way."

Quent set the radio down on the table and turned his crazy eyes back on me and Eddie.

"I'm sure you've got a lot to do," I told Quent. *Like bathe or get a manicure.* "We might as well get started." I pulled out a pen and clicked it open. "The auditor noted that your records were incomplete." "Incomplete" was an understatement. The records were *nonexistent*.

He rocked back in his chair until he was leaning against the wall and put one mud-caked boot up on the table. In one smooth movement he pulled the knife from the sheath on his belt. *Swiff.* My hand instinctively went for my Glock, relaxing only when he began using the knife to dig dirt from under his nails.

He wiped the dirty blade on his pants before moving on to the next fingernail. "Incomplete how?"

"You didn't have any."

Though the Kuykendahls had offered not so much as

a single receipt to the auditor, she had been able to scrape together some information by contacting their bank for account statements. The information contained therein had shed some light on their expenses, but provided virtually no information about their income, which consisted of sporadic cash deposits ranging from a low of $800 to a high of $9,600. The deposits were made shortly before the expenses were paid and were in commensurate amounts, as if they'd purposely deposited just enough to cover their impending debit card transactions. The average balance maintained in the operating account was a mere $63. The pattern was suspicious. Wherever the cash was coming from, it was unlikely that all of it had been deposited into the bank account.

The only indication Quent had heard me was a flexing of his foot on the table. Looked like he was expecting me to carry this conversation by myself. That or he was waiting for his cousin to show up and answer my questions instead.

"Do you take care of the financial matters, or does Kevin do it?" I asked.

"Depends," he said.

"On what?" I asked.

"On who's around to take care of things."

"So you two take turns? Share duties?"

The ankle flexed again. "I s'pose you could say that."

"We'd rather not suppose anything," I said with as much goodwill as I could muster. "We'd rather you gave us the facts straight."

Quent's only response was to use his knife to fish a pork rind out of the bag on his desk. He put the knife to his mouth, used his tongue to maneuver the pork rind off the blade, and proceeded to eat the fried skin. *Crunch-crunch-crunch.* He washed it down with a slug of Mountain Dew straight from the bottle. *Glug-glug.*

Eddie chimed in now. "We noticed that you two aren't paid a salary to run the organization."

"We both got other jobs," Quent said. "We're fishing guides out on the lake."

Each of them had reported net income from their guide business of only $17,000. Barely enough for a person to live on. Whether they had accurately reported their personal income was another matter, but for now I planned to focus solely on the nonprofit organization. One step at a time.

"Besides," Quent continued. "Kevin and I don't run this place for the money. We do it out of the goodness of our hearts." His dry, cracked lips curled up in what was equal parts smile and snarl.

"Of course," I said, though I had my doubts. I might have believed him had his woolly beard and hat been paired with a tie-dye shirt and his pork rinds replaced with trail mix. But he didn't give off that kumbayah vibe indicative of do-gooders.

"Can you tell me about the organization's income?" I asked. "The sources and amounts?"

Quent gnawed on his chapped lower lip now. "We'll have to hold off on this inquisition until Kevin gets here."

"Why's that?" I asked.

Another flex of his ankle. "He can answer your questions better."

"You seem to be doing just fine yourself."

He pulled his boot off the table now and set it firmly on the ground. "He might think of something I missed."

I suspected Quent wanted us to wait for Kevin more to ensure that the two of them got their story straight than to be forthcoming with additional information. But I also knew that the more I pushed, the more the guy would push back. Sometimes it was better to let the targets think they were the one in control. You can catch more flies with honey, after all. And once these flies were stuck in the honey, they'd be all mine.

We sat without speaking, the only noise coming from the game show. As we waited, a young man dressed as a frog won a Ford Fiesta, while another in a spaceman getup sacrificed five hundred dollars in exchange for a plastic toy harmonica. That was a deal he should never have made.

A few minutes later, Kevin pulled up outside in a long-bed Chevy pickup. Through the dirty window I saw him hop down from the truck. He wore the same type of rubber boots as Quent. Having been raised in the country with a small herd of goats and half a dozen barn dogs, I knew rubber boots were the best thing to wear when you'd be stomping through poop. They might not be fashionable, but they hosed off easily. Like Quent, Kevin wore camo pants and a belt with a knife strapped to it. Kevin's belt also contained a holstered handgun. I was glad I'd had the foresight to wear my hip holster for easy access to my Glock should the need arise. Instead of a black T-shirt like Quent, Kevin sported a white undershirt à la Bruce Springsteen, though Kevin's was adorned with assorted holes and yellowed pits. *Bruce Sweatstain.* Like Quent, Kevin was tall, thin, and bearded beyond belief. The tangled mass of hair on his head appeared as if it hadn't been washed or combed since the Bush administration. The *first* Bush administration.

The stairs clanged as Kevin stomped up them. He stepped through the door, his eyes first finding his cousin and holding a moment, then shifting to me and Eddie. At least his eyes weren't crazy like Quent's. Nonetheless, they didn't quite meet mine. Instead, they seemed to focus on a spot about an inch to the left, along my temple.

A broad smile appeared in the beard as he stuck out his hand. "Hello, there." Eddie and I introduced ourselves

and shook his hand. I made a mental note to stick my hand
in boiling water later to kill any germs I'd contracted.

Apparently the brains of the outfit, Kevin took over the
conversation. "Quent says you're hunting for information?"

"Routine stuff," I said. "Gotta make sure our auditors
have done their jobs right."

"So this is like, what?" he asked. "Some kind of performance review for the auditor?"

"Exactly." *Not at all.*

Kevin sat on the table, one long leg stretched to the floor,
the other crooked up beside him. He looked now at the
center of my forehead, which was unnerving. "What would
you like to know?"

"The audit file contained little information on the organization's income," I said. "The auditor failed to collect data on the sources and amounts. Can you show me
what she missed?"

Kevin stroked his beard as he appeared to be mulling
over my request. "That information may be hard to come
by. Quent and I know how to deal with animals, but we're
not so good when it comes to keeping track of our
finances."

"Where does most of the organization's income come
from?"

"Donations," he said, after a short hesitation. "You
know, charitable contributions."

I nodded in acknowledgment. "Makes sense. And most
of these contributions come from third parties, correct?"

His furry brows formed a V. "Third parties?"

"What I mean is, you and Quent aren't putting your own
money into the organization. You're getting the contributions from other people."

Kevin stroked his beard again. "Right," he said tenta-
tively, as if hoping he'd given the right answer.

"Show me your list of donors," I said, "along with copies of the receipts you've issued to them."

"Receipts?" Kevin repeated, this time twirling the end of his beard around his finger.

"Nonprofit organizations are required to issue a receipt to any donor who makes a contribution of two hundred and fifty dollars or more in any given year," I said. "You know that, right?"

He glanced over at Quent. "Nobody ever gave us that much," he said. "Least not all in one year."

It was my turn to glance at my partner now.

Eddie picked up the questioning. "Your records show that you spend around thirty grand a year running this place."

The figure should have been much higher given that the bank statements showed checks written or wire transfers to various parties for the purchase of forty-three animals, including three panthers, four black bears, a cheetah, and a lion, in the last five years. From what I could glean, most of the animals had been acquired from private parties, either people running roadside zoos or those who'd thought, wrongly, that a big cat would make a fun pet or protect their meth stash. Yep, in many parts of Texas it was still legal to own a large cat, even if you had no idea how to properly take care of the thing. To paraphrase Keanu Reeves from the classic movie *Parenthood,* any butt-reaming asshole could own a tiger in Texas.

Such concerns aside, how the Kuykendahls could provide food, water, and vet care for such a large number of animals on such a relatively small budget was beyond me. Things definitely didn't add up. It was up to me to figure out the math.

Eddie continued his questioning. "You've got to cover your expenses somehow."

The cousins said nothing and just stared at us. More accurately, Quent stared at us with his crazy eyes and Kevin simply stared through the space between me and my partner, failing to directly meet our gazes.

As if realizing a direct question was needed in order to get a response from the two, Eddie asked, "If you don't have any major supporters, do you receive a lot of smaller donations?"

"Small donations." Kevin pointed a finger at Eddie's face though his focus was on Eddie's shoulder. "You got it, bro."

Eddie cast me another glance that said *Did this lying piece of white trash just dare to "bro" me?*

Why yes, my return glance replied. *In fact, he did verily "bro" you, bro.*

I jotted a note on my pad that read "small donations=BS" and looked back up again. "Who did these small donations come from?"

"People." Kevin waved his arms around. "From all over the place."

I held my pen poised over my pad. "Can you give me some of their names?"

"Oh, I can't do that," Kevin said.

"Why not?"

"'Cause I don't know who they were."

"Not a single one? None of them were local? Friends? Family?" *Fellow members of the East Texas Dipshit Society?*

He shook his head. "Nope."

I played along. "How did your contributors get their money to you? Did they write you checks? Give you their credit card information? Send the money through PayPal?"

He stroked his beard again. "They was all in cash."

"All in cash?" I repeated. "Every single one of the donations?"

"Uh-huh."

How stupid was this guy that he'd thought Eddie and I would believe this crap? Little did he know that he was actually making things easy on us. It was much more difficult and time-consuming for us when we were given partial records than when we were given none at all. This matter would be a slam dunk. No records. No tax exemption. We'd seize their assets and shut them down. Case closed.

"How'd your donors get the cash to you?" I asked.

More beard twirling. The thing looked like an F-5 hair tornado now. "Some of them mailed it to us. Others stopped by and dropped it off."

More bullshit. Nobody in their right mind put cash in the mail. "You didn't get their names and contact information so you could hit them up later for more money?"

"Nope." He shook his head and stared at my chin. "That's a good idea, though. Wished we'd of thought of it."

"You two should hire a professional bookkeeper," I suggested.

"You're tellin' me!"

chapter eight

*L*et's Call It a Day

Kevin barked with laughter, raising the hackles on the dogs, who had settled on the floor at our feet. "Look," he said, leaning toward us. "Quent and me ain't the most s'phisticated guys you'll ever meet."

Eddie snorted next to me, doing his best to disguise it as a sneeze. "Excuse me."

"Bless you," I said, cutting him a look.

Kevin continued. "We may not be doing things 'xactly the right way when it comes to all that record-keeping and making Uncle Sam happy. But cut us some slack, here. We're saving animals. We're good guys!" He threw his hands in the air for emphasis before leaning back toward us and shifting his focus to my nose. "That's got to count for something, doesn't it?"

If I'd had a beard, I would've stroked it at that point as I pondered my next move. *Hmm . . .*

"You know, you're right," I said, once I'd come up with a fresh tactic. "We really don't mean to hassle you. I'm an animal lover, too, and I think you're doing a great service here. I don't want to cause any problems for the auditor, either. She's got five kids and she really needs to keep her job." I leaned toward him, as if he and I were in cahoots. "How about this. You two promise to start keeping better records from here on out, take me and Eddie on a tour of the place and show us your critters, and we'll call it a day." *As if.* "Deal?" I stuck out my hand.

Kevin reached out and took it. "Deal." He then turned to Eddie and shook his hand, too. He stood from the table and motioned for us to follow him. "Come on. We'll take my truck."

Eddie and I followed the two men and the dogs outside. While Eddie and I climbed into the cab with Kevin, Quent stepped up onto the back bumper and swung himself over the tailgate to take a seat in the bed. The dogs settled down in the shade of a nearby tree to take a nap.

The truck smelled like a blend of beer and urine, and had stained seat covers, no floor mats, and a cracked, dusty dashboard. The small black turds on the floorboard told me a raccoon or two had probably lived in the cab at some point. I could only hope one wasn't hiding under the seat, waiting to take a bite out of my ankle.

Kevin started the truck and headed farther down the dirt road, which rapidly devolved into nothing more than a couple of tire tracks separated by a strip of grass and weeds. Eddie slid a nervous glance at Kevin, then shared it with me. I patted my hip to let him know my Glock was within easy reach should a *Deliverance*-type situation arise.

Since playing along with their farce seemed to be working, I decided to build on our newfound camaraderie by asking about his fishing-guide business. "What do most of your clients like to catch?"

"Largemouth bass," he said, "or catfish."

"Channel cats? Blue? Flatheads?"

He cut me a surprised look, his eyes meeting mine for the first time. "You know fish?"

"Heck, yeah," I said. "I worked at a bait shop all through high school."

Thanks to three summers at Big Bob's Bait Bucket, I knew more about worms than Donatella Versace knew about fabrics. Nightcrawlers. Wax worms. Mealworms. Which ones worked best for catching which fish. The only thing I didn't know about worms was how they tasted. Despite my idiot male coworkers offering me a hundred dollars to eat one, I'd never taken them up on their offer. That was definitely one deal I was not willing to make.

Kicking up a trail of dust, the truck approached a chain-link enclosure no bigger than a dog run. A large make-shift shelter formed from scrap plywood sat at one end. Inside the cage, a lion paced back and forth on a well-worn strip of dirt. What else could he do in the tiny space? It took him only five steps in each direction to reach the limits of his cage. Some sanctuary. Keeping a big cat in such a confined space should be illegal. This king of the jungle had definitely been dethroned.

"'Fess up," I said to Eddie. "That song from *The Lion King* is running through your head."

"Actually," he said, "I was thinking of 'The Lion Sleeps Tonight.'"

"Even better," I said. "I actually know the lyrics to that one." Much to his chagrin, I began to sing the nonsensical part of the chorus. "Wee-ee-EE-ee, ee-ee-ee-EE-ee, wee-ah-bomba-way!"

At the sound of the truck pulling up, the lion stopped and looked our way, probably hoping we were bringing him something for lunch. He began to pant, his mouth falling slightly open, revealing what appeared to be a full set of secondary teeth but only three large fangs. His lower left fang was missing.

As Kevin stopped the truck, I gestured at the lion. "What happened to his tooth?"

"Got no idea," Kevin said. "Simba's like that when we got him."

With the information gleaned from the bank records, I'd been able to do some snooping on the Internet and determined that Kevin and Quent had acquired the lion from a roadside zoo outside Tupelo, Mississippi. The zoo had closed down after its black bear had taken a swipe at a child through the bars of its cage and come away with enough flesh that it took doctors thirty-eight stitches to piece the kid's face back together. The kid's parents sued, of course. According to an online news report, the zoo operator carried no insurance and was forced to sell off the animals to pay the $300,000 damage award. Too bad Simba hadn't ended up in a better place.

I nudged Eddie and motioned for him to let me out of the truck. When he did, I eased slowly toward the cage.

"Careful now," Quent called from his place in the bed of the pickup. "That ol' cat can be a little moody."

I would be, too, if I were stuck in a shoe box. I snapped a quick photo of the lion with my cell phone and turned to return to the truck, when—"Aaaaah! Rattlesnake!"

I leaped backward instinctively as a long, thick, brown snake slithered by in front of me. My new aviator sunglasses flew off my face and landed somewhere in the thick grass. I wasn't about to search for the damn things and risk my hand being bitten by a rattler. I bolted back to the truck and hopped in.

Kevin sniggered. "Forgot to mention there's quite a few diamondbacks and other snakes out here. Gotta be careful."

Now he tells me.

Ass.

Kevin started off again, driving to a similar set of enclosures where the bears were kept. The bears, too, appeared frustrated, bored, and miserable, their eyes dull and hopeless as they lay curled up on their sides on the bare dirt of their pens. It was sad and cruel. These bears should be running free in the Canadian wilderness or stealing pic-a-nic baskets in Jellystone Park.

Our final stop was at a pair of four to five-acre pastures enclosed on the sides with twelve-foot chain-link fencing. Chicken wire spanned the top. Wild vines had grown up the sides of the fence and across the chicken wire, providing shade across much of the space. Water troughs and feeders filled with deer corn were spaced throughout the pastures.

Inside the first corral milled two dozen or so hoofed beasts with expansive antlers, some kind of antelope or deer, though their legs and bodies seemed much longer than the typical white-tailed deer common in Texas. The animals ranged in size from small babies no bigger than the average dog to enormous stags nearly six feet in length and topping the scales at over five hundred pounds by my best estimate.

"What are those?" I asked, gesturing to the beasts.

"Barasingha deer," Kevin replied.

I pointed into the second corral, which contained another long-legged, hoofed species, though these were primarily white instead of brown. Rather than antlers, however, these animals bore two long, relatively thin, backward-angled horns on their heads. Like the deer in the first corral, these animals ranged greatly in size. "What about those?"

"Scimitar-horned oryx," he said. "Beauties, ain't they?"

"You can say that again." *You can also go jump off a cliff for all I care.*

"Oryx are extinct in the wild," he said. "If it warn't for Quent and me rescuing a small herd and letting them reproduce, the species woulda gone the way of the dinosaurs."

Eddie and I exchanged looks again. Perhaps his Jurassic Park comment earlier hadn't been too far off. Though this place was more like Jur*asshole* Park.

Kevin turned the truck around and headed back in the direction of the trailer. But we couldn't be done yet, could we?

"Is that all of the animals?" I asked.

"Yuh-huh," Kevin said. "That's all of 'em."

The small number of animals he'd shown us was far less than the number that should be here. That explained how they could spend such a paltry sum on food and supplies.

"Where are the panthers?" I asked. "And the cheetah? And the elephant?"

"Oh, you know," he said, lifting one shoulder. "They got old and died and whatnot."

"*Whatnot?* What do you mean by 'whatnot'?"

"You know," he repeated, though obviously I did not know or I would not have asked. "Diseases and stuff."

"So they all passed away? You didn't sell any of them or give them to another sanctuary?"

He hesitated again before answering, as if once more he was trying to decide what answer would pose the least chance of me catching him in a lie. "No. They all died. Some of 'em was old or in pretty bad shape when we got 'em."

I didn't doubt that. An inordinate number of wild animals were in the hands of people who had no business keeping them. Heck, there'd been multiple instances of wild animals escaping and mauling or even killing innocent victims, including children. Unfortunately, the more extreme members of the hunting lobby, which often sided with and supported the keeping of undomesticated animals, had a strong presence in Texas and many other states, and legislators often bowed to their will, relying on their contributions for reelection.

"What did you do with their bodies after the animals passed?" I asked. "Did you bury them here on the property somewhere?"

"We . . . uh . . ." His left hand tightened on the steering wheel while his right hand resumed stroking his beard. "We had them . . . what do you call it? *Cremated*, right?" He didn't wait for an answer. "That's it. That's what we do. We cremate them."

I nodded as if in understanding, when in reality I wanted nothing more than to pistol-whip some truthful answers out of the guy. I didn't think he'd given me a single honest answer yet. Well, maybe about the largemouth bass, but that was it.

"Must be hard to cremate such large animals," I said. "Who handled that for you?"

Kevin shifted in his seat, leaning slightly farther away from me. He was twisting the beard again now, as if it were a crank that ran his brain. "Quent and I do it ourselves. No sense spending money to have someone else do it when all it takes is a little gasoline and a match to get the job done."

Sheesh. No true animal lover would have ever phrased things like that. Still, I had to keep my disgust and dismay in check. If the Kuykendahls realized how upset I was, they might figure out that I planned to do whatever it took to shut down this sham rescue operation.

When we returned to the trailer, Eddie, Quent, and I climbed out of the truck, but Kevin remained in the cab, probably to head back down to the "crick." I thanked the two men for their time.

"So you'll be closing our file?" Kevin asked. "Like we agreed?"

"We'll call it a day," I said with a smile, repeating the same intentionally vague phrase I'd used earlier.

"We 'preciate that." With a nod, Kevin motored back down the path.

I turned to Quent, who had called his dogs and was heading back up the steps to the trailer.

"Kevin showed us where you buried the animals that died," I said, knowing he hadn't been able to hear the conversation taking place in the cab of the truck from his seat in the bed. "It was nice of you two to lay them to rest in peace. It must've taken y'all hours to dig a hole big enough to bury the elephant."

Quent's crazy eyes looked up and down a few times, rolling like a slot machine. I half expected lemons or cherries to appear in them and quarters to pour out of his mouth. "Yeah," he agreed. "Hours and hours."

Hours and hours, my ass.

"Bye, now." I lifted a hand as my partner and I returned to my car.

Once inside, Eddie let out a derisive snort, not bothering to mask it as a sneeze this time. "Lying sacks of shit."

"I'm going to get to the bottom of this," I vowed. Not only because it was my job, but because Simba and those other animals deserved so much better.

As Eddie and I headed back down the highway, we again passed the property with the high fence. I braked abruptly, nearly giving us both whiplash, and turned onto the smaller country road that ran alongside it.

Eddie rubbed the back of his neck and cut me an irate look. "Give a guy some warning next time. You nearly snapped my spine."

"Sorry, partner," I said. "I just had an aha moment. I think I know where the missing animals might have gone."

I'd learned to follow my hunches. Sometimes our subconscious mind is a step ahead of our conscious one. Then again, other times it is only punking our brain.

We continued on for three quarters of a mile until I spotted a sign. I pulled over to the side of the road and pointed at it. The sign featured a cartoonish picture of a stalking tiger with his sharp teeth exposed and a roaring bear standing on his hind legs, claws extended. The sign read:

SOUTHERN SAFARI GAME RESERVE
GUARANTEED KILL OR YOUR $ BACK
BIG CATS, BEARS, AND OTHER EXOTIC GAME

The outfit's Web address and phone number were printed across the bottom.

Eddie squinted as he read the sign. "Is this one of those canned hunting places?"

"Yep." I snapped a photo of the sign with my phone. "I didn't put it together until after Kevin showed us those deer and oryx and I noticed the high fences around their enclosures, too."

Though my father and brothers enjoyed hunting, they, like many outdoorsmen, frowned upon these places. Many of the animals at these canned hunting facilities were accustomed to humans and didn't fear them. A so-called hunter could virtually walk right up and shoot the poor beast in the head without the animal batting an eye. Where's the sport in that? What's more, with the fences confining them, the animals had no chance of escape, essentially trapped in a cage. It was shooting fish in a barrel, and it wasn't right or fair. Fair would be taking down the fences, dressing the animals in camouflage, and dousing them in Budweiser to mask their scent from the hunters.

Eddie shook his head. "I'll never understand why men

hunt. You want some fresh meat, just drive to Kroger. No fuss, no muss. They've already chopped off the head, pulled out the yucky innards, and peeled the skin off for you."

My stomach squirmed inside me. "That's it," I said. "I'm having a salad for dinner."

chapter nine

The Art of Lying

The first thing I did at work Wednesday morning was pull
the secret phone Nick had given me from the inside pocket
of my blazer to make sure I hadn't missed a call or text
from him. My hopes plunged as I looked at the screen.

Nope.

Nothing.

Ughhhhh.

I had no idea where Nick was right now. Was he still
in the Dallas area? Maybe in one of the border towns?
Could he be in Mexico? As I stared at the screen, I noticed my reflection. Worry lines crossed my forehead and
dark semicircles underscored my eyes. Another *ughh*. I
closed my lids so I wouldn't have to see myself.

As long as my eyes were closed, I figured I'd say a quick
prayer, not only for Nick, but for Christina, as well. As a
woman, she would be particularly vulnerable going inside
the dangerous cartel. Then again, I supposed she had more
places in which to hide a weapon. She could probably tuck
a small can of pepper spray between her boobs and no one
would be the wiser.

My prayers floating on the airwaves to heaven, I turned

my attention to my work. Sharla Fowler had been evasive when I'd asked whether anyone operating the Unic had a personal relationship with any of the five artists whose work was on display in the museum, but I had my own ways of finding these things out.

I logged on to my computer and accessed the 1099s filed by the museum for payments made to the artists. Armed with this information, I was able to determine the artists' current addresses and find driver's license data for all but Hunter Gabbert. The license detail provided me with their birthdates. Next, I pulled up their birth certificates.

Certificates for the two male artists were relatively easy to find. Both had unusual names—Jackson T. Reavis and Hunter Gabbert. Jackson had been born right here in Dallas in 1983, while Hunter, the artist who'd made the macaroni mosaic, had been born in Kissimmee, Florida in 2007. He was just a kid. *Sheesh.* That explained a lot, including why I'd found no driver's license in his name.

I backtracked two generations, tracing their family trees back to their parents and grandparents.

Bingo.

Jackson's mother, Taysha Young, was Sharla's daughter from her first marriage, which made Taysha the half sister of Rodney Fowler and made Jackson Sharla's grandson and Rodney's nephew. Hunter was Rodney's grandson, Sharla's great-grandson. Yep, the Unic's payments to these two young men appeared to be a classic case of income shifting, a way for the football player to claim a fraudulent tax benefit by disguising nondeductible gifts to family members as deductible charitable contributions.

I moved on to the female artists. Luckily for me, two of the three female artists were not married and thus retained their maiden names, making their records a cinch to locate. The name of the third female artist, Emily Raggio, was her married name. I was able to pull her husband's name from their joint tax return. Interestingly, I noted that in the "occupation" space in the signature block of the return he had listed his occupation as otolaryngologist. I wondered if Emily obtained her pills and syringes and other art supplies by pilfering the cabinets in her husband's medical office.

I used Dr. Raggio's name to find their marriage license, which had been issued by the state of Louisiana. The marriage license told me that Emily Raggio's maiden name had been Emily Heather Nix. Her birth certificate surfaced in the Illinois records, and I worked my way backward from there.

A half hour later, my cyber genealogy search was completed. Of the female artists, only Aly Pelham, the artist who'd painted with her tears and blood, had a clear connection to the families that ran the foundation and museum. Though Aly was half Rodney Fowler's age, an engagement announcement in the online version of the *Dallas Morning News* informed me that the two had been betrothed for a couple of years now. The paper's society pages, as well as the Unic's Web site, featured photographs of Aly and Sharla standing together with their arms encircling each other's waists. Sharla seemed to be quite fond of her future daughter-in-law, and from the smile on Aly's face the feeling was mutual.

Interestingly, Rodney and Aly's engagement had occurred just weeks before Rodney had formed his foundation and opened the Unic. Looked like she may have been the impetus behind the creation of the museum. My guess was that once Aly had planted the seed, an unscrupulous tax adviser had informed Rodney of the shady ways in which he could use the Unic to reduce his taxes, support his fiancée's hobby, and support his family via sham donations to the museum, which were then redistributed to his desired recipients.

Neither Emily Raggio nor Mallory Sisko appeared to bear any relation to anyone associated with the museum.

A listing on LinkedIn indicated that Aly had studied fashion design and worked as a buyer for an exclusive boutique in the Galleria. Aly's tax schedule for her art business showed only the payment from the Unic. She'd sold no other pieces. She had, however, deducted the costs of traveling to various museums and galleries all over the world. The deductions were specious at best. I found nothing else to indicate she was a professional artist, though she was clearly an art groupie. Her Facebook page, which she'd made public as those seeking attention are wont to do, featured numerous photos of her at gallery openings and museum fund-raisers, a champagne flute in hand and a smile on her face as she posed next to one artist or another. In fact, a post on her page noted that this coming Saturday she would be attending the opening-night event at the First Church of Art, a gallery housed in a converted church in the Bishop Arts District.

With Nick and Christina gone and Alicia tied up with tax season, I had nothing better to do this Saturday evening. I decided that I, too, would make an appearance at the gallery's opening.

Next, I Googled Emily's name, then Mallory's.

Although Aly hadn't sprung for a professional Web site to promote her art pieces, Emily Raggio had. Her site featured her headshot—*dark blond, blue eyes, thin nose and lips*—along with photographs of her work and a bio indicating she had studied art at the Kansas City Art Institute. After dabbling in pottery and ceramics, she'd discovered her love for sculpture. She'd settled on medical waste as her medium after meeting her husband when she'd gone to his office seeking treatment for strep throat. Instead of love at first sight, looked like it was love at first throat culture. Her Web site further noted that she maintained a studio in a converted, detached garage behind their house which, according to the address on her 1099, was in Bedford, a city lying twenty miles west of Dallas. Her tax returns for the past several years showed varying amounts of income from her art business, ranging from a low of $23,000 one year to a high of $87,000 the next.

Hmm . . . From what I saw here, Emily appeared to be a legitimate artist. What about Mallory?

My search for information on Mallory turned up three awards in regional art contests, as well as an entry in the archives of an art museum in Houston noting that one of her pieces had been on display in a student exhibit there. Her Facebook page indicated she'd earned a BFA from the University of Houston last May. The page also featured several posts in which she'd discussed her current projects. A quick look into her tax file told me that she currently worked for Pretty on the Inside, an interior design firm. She, too, appeared to be a legitimate artist, even if art wasn't her sole vocation.

Grabbing my purse and briefcase, I headed out of the office.

On the drive to Mallory's workplace, I pulled into a dollar store and bought a pair of sunglasses with bright red rims. They were a little on the casual side, but they were the right price. *Cheap.* I only needed them to last me until I could get to the Brighton store for an authentic pair of designer shades.

A half hour later, I pulled into a parking space in front of Pretty on the Inside, which was located in a one-story white brick strip center in the north Dallas suburb of Lewisville. Inside, a vacant reception desk greeted me. I looked around the space. A shaggy, oblong rug in a pale green sprawled in front of a peacock-blue couch. Pillows in assorted shades of blue and green accented the sofa. A large, aluminum flower with a green-hued stem and turquoise petals graced the wall space above the seating area. Though my tastes tended to be more traditional, I could appreciate the colors and style in this contemporary décor.

Through a glass wall on the left, I saw an older woman sitting at a conference table with Mallory, whom I recognized from her Facebook photos. The two pored over large books of fabric swatches, comparing and contrasting them with a striped wallpaper sample the woman held in her hand.

Mallory glanced up, apparently catching my movements out of the corner of her eye. She said something to the woman, stood, and headed my way. Once she'd stepped into the foyer and the glass door had closed behind her, she offered me a polite, businesslike smile. "May I help you?"

"I'm Special Agent Tara Holloway with the IRS," I said. "I need to speak with you about the Unic Art Space."

Mallory's smile quavered. "I'm with a client right now. I don't know how long we'll be."

She glanced back at the woman in the conference room, who was flipping back and forth between two pages of the book, having apparently whittled down the selection to two favorite choices.

"Looks to me like she's nearly made up her mind," I said, taking a seat on one end of the sofa. "I'll wait."

Mallory's expression was uncertain, but who could blame her? She was less than a year out of college, only in her early twenties. What did she know about dealing with federal law enforcement?

As I sat waiting, I flipped through some of the decorating magazines on the rack next to the sofa.

It took only five more minutes for Mallory to finish helping the woman make her selections and place her order for fabric. She walked the woman to the door.

"Thank you so much. I'll give you a call as soon as the material arrives."

The woman thanked her in return and walked outside to her car.

Mallory turned her attention to me now. "I don't have an office," she said. "I'm just an assistant. But the conference room is free for another hour. Let's talk there."

I followed Mallory into the room, slid into a seat, and got right down to business. "You probably know why I'm here."

She somehow managed to look simultaneously sheepish and insulted and hurt. "Mrs. Fowler called me yesterday and said you might contact me. She said that you don't think I'm a real artist."

"That's not exactly the case," I said. "In fact, I loved the piece you had there. *Life's Compost* was so . . ." I tried to think of the right word and came up with, "Relatable."

Mallory smiled. "Thanks. That was exactly what I was going for. I mean, who hasn't been dumped, right?"

I could tell I'd earned her appreciation if not her trust. I hoped she would give me some honest answers. "Look, I'll be straight with you. I suspect that the man who set up the foundation that funds the Unic did so primarily to impress his fiancée and to shift money to his relatives in lower tax brackets. Two of the five artists whose work is featured at the museum are relatives, and the third is the fiancée I mentioned. You and Emily Raggio are the only ones with an art background. I'm trying to figure out whether the place is a legitimate art museum. If it is, then they are entitled to a tax exemption. If it's just a phony tax shelter, then they don't qualify for an exemption."

Mallory tilted her head, her face clouding in confusion. "I don't know anything about tax exemptions."

"I don't expect you to," I said. "But you do know about art. That's what I came here to talk to you about. Can you tell me how you got involved with the people who run the Unic?"

She turned her head upright again. "When I first moved to Dallas after college last year, I toured all of the art museums and galleries. I was trying to get a start in the business and find a place where I could display my work, build a name for myself, you know? When I went into the Unic, it had only a few things on display. I asked the woman who was in charge—that was Sharla—if they might be interested in one of my pieces. She agreed to take a look, so a few days later I brought several pieces by and she offered to buy one of them. I was really excited. It was my first sale."

"So you didn't know anyone at the Unic or the Fifty-Yard Line Foundation before you sold your piece to them?"

"No," she said. "I've met some of them since. They have social events at the museum pretty often and they always invite the artists."

"So you've met the other people whose work is on exhibit?"

Her expression became sheepish once again. "Yes."

"And?"

"And what?"

I watched her closely. "What did you think of them?"

"Emily Raggio and I had a lot in common." Her gaze moved to a spot on the wall behind me for a moment before moving back. "The others . . ."

I filled in the blank for her. "Not so much?"

"Right."

"What do you think of their work? The oscillating fan and the hair dryer and the vacuum? The macaroni mosaic? The canvas painted with tears?"

Mallory paused a long moment before offering a small shrug. "Modern art encompasses a broad spectrum."

I could understand that she didn't want to be critical,

but I wanted her opinion. "Do you think those pieces show talent?" I asked. "Or acquired skills?"

She paused another long moment. "I think they show . . . *imagination*."

She'd given me the answer I'd been seeking, even if she'd done it in a very understated way.

"Have you sold any more pieces since selling the one to the Unic?" I asked.

She beamed. "I have. Three more. Two were three-dimensional pieces similar to *Life's Compost*. The other was a collage."

"How wonderful." I offered her a congratulatory smile. "Sounds like you're on your way."

"I hope so," she said, then, apparently feeling a little guilty, added, "I mean, interior decorating can be fun, and I'm happy working here, but if I could work on my art full-time that would be my dream job."

I already had my dream job. Playing financial detective, carrying a gun, making sure the bad guys paid their fair share to Uncle Sam like everyone else. *What's not to like?*

I thanked Mallory for her time and wished her luck with her art projects.

Once I was back in my car, I aimed it for Bedford. I found Emily Raggio in her studio behind her house. She was dressed in a pair of stretchy black spandex capris and a paint-stained promotional T-shirt for an allergy medication, probably a freebie given to her husband by a pharmaceutical salesman. Her garage door stood wide open, the strains of South American pan flute music pouring out into the yard. She worked inside, sculpting what appeared to be an abstract take on a weeping willow tree. An IV stand with fluid-filled bags and tubing hanging from it formed the trunk and limbs, while latex surgical gloves hung like leaves from the metal posts and hoses.

She was surrounded by shelves laden with spools of wire and string, tubes of assorted glues, and medical supplies including prescription pads, pill bottles, gauze bandages, and scalpels. Better keep an eye on those in case she decided to slit my throat. Then again, my worries about the cartel case were probably just making me paranoid.

"Mrs. Raggio?" I called, stopping at the three-foot wooden fence, removing my cheap red plastic sunglasses, and introducing myself. "I'm IRS Special Agent Tara Holloway. May I come in?"

"Please do. I could use the company."

I unlatched the gate and entered the yard. A few steps later I was in the garage, winding my way around a gray tabby who sat on her haunches, casually batting a water bug around with a front paw. I might've felt sorry for the bug if the darn things didn't creep me out so much.

Emily stepped back and eyed her piece, then reached out and moved the dangling fingers of a glove into a different position. "There. That's better."

I gestured to the sculpture. "Interesting piece."

"Thanks," she said. "I think I'm going to call it *Lifelines*."

"Seems fitting."

She moved to her right, to something nearly as tall as her that was covered with a hospital bedsheet. "Give me your thoughts on this."

She grabbed the bottom edge of the sheet and tossed it up and over the piece, revealing a plastic skeleton like those used in an anatomy class. The skeleton wore a ruffled, floor-length dress made from a number of light blue hospital gowns stitched together. Emily stared at me, her face expectant. "How does it make you feel?"

"Honestly?" I said. "Uncomfortable. A little scared, even."

"Good," she said. "It should. It's called *Death's Beauty*

Pageant. It's a statement about the dangers of anorexia."
She swung the sheet back over the skeleton, wheeled it
back against the wall, and turned to me again. "I'm fas-
cinated by life and death, and all we humans do to de-
stroy ourselves or keep death at bay. I like to explore those
themes in my art."

It also explained her fascination with medicine.

Emily began to sway with the pan flute music and
executed some type of hands-up pirouette before jabbing
the button to turn off the stereo. "Okay, let's talk." She offered me a short, square stool that looked as if it could serve
as either a seat or a platform for working on taller pieces.

"Did Sharla Fowler call you?" I asked as I sat. "Did
she tell you I might be coming to see you?"

"Yes," Emily said. "She said something about you not
believing that the Unic is a real art museum? Accusing
her and her son of trying to pull something over on the
IRS?"

Unlike Mallory, Emily didn't seem at all upset or concerned.

I pulled a pad and pen out of my briefcase to take notes.
"Would it bother you if someone questioned the value of
your art? Or whether it even was true art?"

"Oh, honey." She tittered. "I wouldn't last a second in
this business if I cared one iota what other people think.
There's always some critic or other telling an artist she's
a no-talent hack, then the next minute there's another critic
calling her the next Georgia O'Keeffe or Mary Cassatt or
Polly Morgan."

I'd heard of the first two artists, but not the latter. "Polly
Morgan?"

"British taxidermist and sculptor," Emily replied. "She
uses dead birds, rats, and squirrels in her pieces."

Art imitating life, I supposed. Or was it art imitating
death?

I shifted on the hard stool, trying, unsuccessfully, to find a more comfortable position. "Do you have any thoughts about the other pieces on display at the Unic? About the other artists?"

She offered a patronizing smile. "I have all sorts of thoughts, Miss Holloway. But what do my opinions matter? As long as an artist believes he or she has created something worth making, and as long as someone else decides a piece is worth buying or at least thinking about, hasn't the purpose of art been fulfilled?"

Hell if I know.

"But you were trained as an artist," I said. "You wouldn't have spent the time and money on an art education if you didn't think it would have value, right?"

"Of course not," she agreed.

"Then doesn't it bother you that someone with no training can just throw something together and call themselves an artist?"

"Not at all. I studied art because I wanted to hone my talents and learn more skills and techniques. But even untrained amateurs can have moments of brilliance. It's like cooking. Restaurants hire professional chefs to make gourmet meals, but people whip up all kinds of yummy stuff from scratch in their kitchens every night, too. It's just different approaches to the same end."

I supposed what she said was true. My mother had ordered that dump cakes cookbook after seeing the commercial on TV, and damn if some of those cakes weren't delicious.

Seeing I'd get nowhere questioning the art itself, I asked Emily how her work had ended up on exhibit at the Unic. She told me that Rodney Fowler had come to her husband's office to be treated for swimmer's ear.

"I was installing a piece I'd made specifically for my husband," she said, pulling out a portfolio of photographs and showing one to me. "See? I painted a half-dozen plastic ear models, posted them on flexible wires, and put them in a vase to resemble a bouquet. I call that one *Listen to Your Doctor.*"

She went on to say that Rodney had commented on the piece, mentioned that he was involved in an arts charity, and asked if she had any pieces available for sale.

"One thing led to another," she said, closing the book, "and the next thing I knew I had a nice, fat check in my hand."

"About that check," I said. "Did it surprise you how much the Unic paid for your work given that you had sold only one piece beforehand? And that you'd sold the earlier piece for much less?"

"On the contrary." She offered me a grin. "I thought I deserved much, much more."

A theory was beginning to develop in my mind. Maybe those running the Unic realized they had to spend significant sums on at least a few pieces from unrelated artists in order to give the place the air of legitimacy and to justify the amounts they'd paid for the pieces made by Sharla's grandson and great-grandson, as well as Rodney's fiancée.

Although I found Emily interesting on a personal level, it was clear that spending any more time with her would in no way further my case. If anything, I was more confused than ever.

What constitutes art?

What is the purpose of art?

Who has the right to call themselves an artist?

I thanked her and returned to my car, pondering art, life, death, and taxes.

chapter ten

$\mathcal{G}$one Phishing

Early Thursday morning, I sat at my desk and stared across the hall at Nick's empty office, missing the hell out of him even though he'd been gone only a short time. His chair sat at attention behind his desk, as if waiting for the return of the firm ass that had graced its seat for the last few months. An aluminum baseball bat leaned against his credenza and a gym bag sat on top of it. I wasn't the only one who missed Nick. The others on the IRS softball team had pitched a fit when they heard Nick would be gone indefinitely. He was not only the team captain but also their star player. Will Dorsey had stepped up to coach but, without Nick, the chances of the Tax Maniacs winning a game were slim to none.

The situation sucked. All around. Big-time.

Ly's secretary, Viola, stepped into my doorway with a huge bouquet of red roses interspersed with greenery and baby's breath. "Special delivery!" she sang as she set them on my desk.

"Wow!" I exclaimed, rising from my seat. "Thanks, Vi."

As she left my office, I grabbed the card from the plastic

holder. Tearing the envelope open, I pulled out the card. It read "I miss my gooey girl. Nick."

Tears of relief welled up in my eyes as I clutched the card to my chest. These flowers were beautiful, sure, and they smelled great, too. But it was more what they symbolized that had me getting so emotional. These flowers meant El Cuchillo's knife bore none of Nick's or Christina's blood. The two of them were alive and okay.

Or were they?

Just as quickly as the relief had hit me, so did the realization that Nick might not have ordered these flowers today. He might have placed the order on Monday or Tuesday before he'd gone undercover, and simply requested they be delivered today. There was only one way to know for sure.

I picked up the envelope from my desk, sat back down in my chair, and dialed the phone number of the florist listed on the envelope. When the clerk answered, I said, "Hi. I had a question about a floral arrangement from your store. It was ordered by Nick Pratt. Can you tell me when he placed the order?"

The woman hesitated a moment. "Can't you just ask him?"

Hmm . . . What can I say that will make her give up the goods?

"He's actually the one who asked me to call you. He couldn't remember what day it was. His credit card company said there'd been some fraud on his account. If you can't verify the date for me he'll be forced to have the charge reversed."

I felt absolutely evil, but I knew the best way to get information from someone was to make them believe that the cost of withholding it would be higher. Either this woman would tell me what I wanted to know, or she'd be out $75 or more.

"Just a moment," she said.

Good.

There was a clicking of keys. "It says here in the computer that he ordered them on Monday. Wait a minute. It also says he paid cash. Why would the credit—"

Click. I hung up on her.

Though I felt bad both about misleading the florist and hanging up on her, I was dealing with issues of much greater importance. The flowers were still undeniably gorgeous, yet their red blooms no longer bore the message of hope I'd thought they had. In fact, the red blooms seemed suddenly reminiscent of blood, the thorns like tiny little knives along the stems.

I closed my eyes. *Don't go there, Tara,* I told myself. *Chances are Nick and Christina are fine. Nick wanted you to enjoy these flowers. So do it already!*

I could be damned bossy with myself, huh?

I tweaked the arrangement, separating the blooms slightly to let them breathe and spread, and took a deep breath of the nearest blossom. *Heavenly.*

Forcing my thoughts back to my work, I pulled my regular cell phone out of my purse. Pulling up my contacts list, I stopped on *Mom and Dad* and hit the button to call home.

My mother didn't answer until the seventh ring. "Hi, sweetie!"

Ah, mothers. Even if we pack a gun and kick ass for a living, we'll always be their "sweeties."

"Hi, Mom. Did I catch you at a bad time?"

"Not at all." Of course she could've just cut her finger off in the garbage disposal and be standing there bleeding to death and she'd still make time to talk to me. That's the kind of mother she was. "I was just out in the garden, planting tomatoes."

"Wish I could be there to help you."

"Me, too, hon. Those bags of garden soil seem to get heavier every year."

Gardening together had been one of our favorite mother-daughter activities, second only to making road trips from our home in east Texas to the Neiman Marcus flagship store in Dallas. Gardening had always relaxed me. Digging in the ground made me feel, well, *grounded*. Between my long hours on the job and my romantic pursuits, I'd had little time to garden recently. With Nick gone now, maybe I'd find time to work on my flower beds. Brett, a landscape architect I'd dated before Nick, had hired a crew to install and maintain a nice bed in front of my town house. Unfortunately, when the relationship ended, so did my free lawn service. Weeds had snuck in among the plants, many of which had died off over the winter. Time for me to get things spruced up. Besides, the labor would help take my mind off my worries.

"Is Dad around?" I asked.

My mother's tone instantly changed from happy to concerned. "What's wrong?"

"Can't a girl ask to speak to her father without something being wrong?"

"She *can*," my mother snapped. "But you *don't*. Every time you want to speak to your father it means something's up."

True. I generally counted on my mother to share any of my news with my father. Not that my dad and I weren't close. We were. It's just that my mother's role in the family was serving as the central information center and my father's role was to pay for things, fix things, and teach us kids how to handle guns. It was thanks to his superb guidance that I'd learned to shoot as well as an army sniper.

"Last time you asked to speak to your father," my mother continued, "you wanted to borrow his long-range rifle."

"That's not why I need to speak to him," I replied. I had my own long-range rifle now. Dad had given it to me for Christmas, just like he'd given me my first Daisy BB gun when I was a little girl. Yep, some girls, including *moi,* are made of *gunpowder and lead.* "I need him to help me on a case. I'm pretty sure an animal rescue group I'm investigating is supplying animals to a canned hunting ranch."

"That's despicable."

"Yep. It's also illegal if they're claiming to be a tax-exempt sanctuary."

"Hold on a minute. I'll have to go find him." My mother set the phone down and a minute or so later returned to the line. "Here he is."

"Thanks."

Dad's voice boomed over the airwaves. "Hello, there, Tara. Your mother says you want to speak with me?"

"I've got a favor to ask you."

"Anything for daddy's girl. Ask away."

"I need you to come with me to a hunting ranch and shoot a lion."

There was a moment of silence followed by a, "Say what, now?"

"You won't actually shoot the lion," I clarified. "But I need you to pretend you're a trophy hunter wanting to bag a big cat."

I explained about the Kuykendahls and the canned hunting outfit. "My gut tells me those cousins may be supplying animals for hunts."

If I could prove it, I could charge Quent and Kevin with criminal tax evasion and put them out of business for good. As things stood right now, all I could do was revoke their organization's tax-exempt status for failure to maintain adequate records and issue them a tax bill. I wanted to do more than that. I wanted to put those losers in jail. And I wanted to rescue Simba and his furry, four-legged bear buddies and as many of those deer and oryx as possible.

"I'd be glad to help any way I can," my father said.

"Great," I told him. "I'll call Southern Safari and see if I can get it arranged."

As soon as we ended our call, I pulled up the photograph I'd taken of Southern Safari's sign on my phone and jotted down the phone number. I then placed a call to Southern Safari.

A man with a deep Texas accent answered. "Southern Safari, where your trophy is guaranteed. How can I he'p ya?"

I told him I wanted to arrange a hunt for my father as a gift for his birthday. "Any chance you've got a lion? He's always wanted to bag a big cat."

I knew they didn't currently have one on site. I'd had Eddie call them yesterday afternoon. He'd claimed to be a personal assistant for an unnamed Hollywood celebrity and asked for a full list of their available game. The manager of Southern Safari had e-mailed Eddie a complete list. Though it contained a variety of deer, scimitar-horned oryx, Nubian ibex, Dama gazelle, Mouflon sheep, and wildebeest, there was no lion on the list.

"I don't have a lion at the moment," the man said, "but if you can give me a few days I believe I can make arrangements to get one."

"What's the fee?"

"It'll depend on our cost, but my best guesstimate is that a lion'll run you at least five grand."

Holy crap! Being a bloodthirsty jackass was expensive. I supposed I shouldn't have been surprised. Canned hunting was a multimillion-dollar industry in Texas. Hence the state legislature turned a blind eye and failed to regulate it.

I arranged the hunt for a week from Saturday. Looked like Simba would be getting a stay of execution at least until then and, if I had anything to say about it, for the rest of his life afterward.

I turned my attention to the stack of files on my desk. Each of them was equally pressing and they had been assigned to me en masse, so there was no clear file to start on next. Beginning at the top, I pointed my index finger at each file in turn. "Eeny, meeny, miny, mo." I pulled "mo" from the stack and opened the file.

This particular case was something new and different. Someone, or perhaps multiple someones, had been impersonating an IRS employee online and phishing for personal banking information via e-mails purporting to be from the agency. The e-mails were designed to resemble official IRS letters, and included the Treasury Department insignia at the top. While the letters contained a valid mailing address for the IRS service center in Austin, they failed to include a telephone number.

The con artist had clearly had some fun when drafting the e-mails. The names of the fictional IRS employees who'd allegedly written the e-mail correspondence included such clever monikers as B. Andit, T. Hief, and U. R. Aschmuck. The scammer had included falsified employee identification numbers, as well.

The someone or someones used a clever and conniving method. Had the culprit told potential victims that they owed money to the IRS, the taxpayers would have likely questioned why and perhaps enlisted the assistance of a tax professional. After all, people didn't want to give a penny more to Uncle Sam than they had to. Instead, the perpetrator informed victims that a programming glitch in their tax software had caused a computation error and overstated their tax liability. As a result, they were due a

$427.95 refund that the IRS would be happy to send by check in the mail in the next six weeks or, if the taxpayer wanted their funds quicker, via direct deposit to their bank account within three business days.

Again, while the amount was nothing to sneeze at, it wasn't such a significant number as to set off warning bells. The thief seemed to realize that subtlety worked in his favor. Suspicions were also allayed by the fact that the letter purported to give the recipient the option of receiving a paper check. Of course anyone choosing that option would never receive the refund check.

The victims were asked to fill out a short form at the bottom of the letter. The form included spaces for their bank's routing number, bank account number, and signature. The letter stated that the recipient's social security number had not been included on the letter for security purposes, but requested that the taxpayer provide his or her social security number as verification that the person receiving the e-mail was the intended recipient. The letter said the number provided would be compared to the social security number on record with the IRS to authenticate the recipient's identity. The letter then requested that the taxpayer either scan the completed document or take a photo of it, and that the file or image be sent to the IRS via a reply e-mail to an address intended to look like an official Treasury Department address.

Because the e-mails requested no money from them, many people failed to perceive the threat. The general public was much more susceptible to scams that merely asked for information rather than money. Unfortunately, a con artist armed with a name, address, bank account number, and signature could cause substantial damage. This particular con artist had made withdrawals at the victims' banks, relieving the duped parties of more than $85,000.

The IRS had first become aware of the problem when a man named Roy Larabee barged into his local office in Farmer's Branch and demanded a return of the $1,800 withdrawn from his checking account shortly after he'd provided his banking information via e-mail to an IRS staff member named S. Teal. After being informed that no such employee existed, that the IRS does not send such letters by e-mail, and that he'd been duped, the enraged man had removed his size-ten loafer and lobbed it at the counter clerk. Fortunately, IRS counter clerks are used to dealing with all manner of crazies and the clerk ducked in time to avoid injury. The loafer did knock over a full coffee cup, however, spilling its contents onto a printer, which spewed sparks and smoke and activated the building's automatic sprinkler system before expiring.

Larabee was charged with assault on a government employee and destruction of government property. Since he had no prior record, his attorney had been able to plead the charges down to criminal mischief and an agreed punishment of twenty hours of community service. I phoned Larabee's attorney to get permission to speak directly with his client.

After identifying myself, I said, "I need to speak with Mr. Larabee about the fraudulent e-mail he received. Could you tell me where I might reach him?"

"He's completing his community service as we speak," his attorney said. "He's working with a cleanup crew from the city parks department at White Rock Lake."

"Thanks," I said.

"When you see him," the lawyer replied, "tell him my bill is past due."

"Will do."

I rounded up my purse and briefcase and headed out to my G-ride, sliding my cheap red sunglasses onto my face. Twenty minutes later, I turned into the park and took a spot in the lot near the playground. It was a bright but unusually chilly day. Given that no children were scampering about, it looked like the area moms had decided to keep their tykes inside today, where they could keep warm.

The cleanup crew, in their bright orange safety vests, were concentrated along the bank of a narrow, boggy creek that emptied into the lake. Some of the men worked with pincer-type devices while others, presumably non-violent offenders, used pointed metal sticks to spear the trash.

I made my way over and checked in with a man who, judging from the fact that he was reclining on the yellow plastic playground slide with his eyes closed, appeared to be in charge. His mouth hung open, emitting an odd gagging, snoring sound. Sleep apnea, I supposed.

I stepped up to him. "Hello, there."

Startled, the man jerked awake, throwing out his arms in an instinctive defensive gesture. My instincts kicked in, too, causing me to turn my head reflexively to avoid his flailing arms. The momentum caused my cheap, lightweight sunglasses to fly off my face. They hit the metal support pole of the nearby swings with a *plink* and fell to the ground, the left lens popping out of the frames. *Great*.

As the man sat up, I wiped dirt from the lens and tried to finagle it back into the frame. No luck. I tossed the lens in a trash can, slipped the damaged sunglasses into the breast pocket of my blazer, and handed the man my business card. "I'm with the IRS. I need to speak with Roy Larabee."

The man used my business card to gesture at a short, portly man with a bowl haircut using his pincers to fish a used condom out of the brush. "That's Roy right there."

"Thanks." I walked over, keeping an eye on the man lest he remove a shoe and lob it at me for an encore of his previous performance. "Mr. Larabee?"

The man looked up. When he spoke, his voice was equal parts anger and sad resignation. "That's me. Who are you and what do you want?"

"I'm Special Agent Tara Holloway from the IRS." I didn't bother extending my hand for a shake since both of Larabee's were occupied, one with the pincers, the other with a clear garbage bag. Also, since condom cooties were in the vicinity, I didn't want to risk catching them.

Larabee glowered at me for a moment before dropping the condom in the bag and turning back to poke around in the debris. "You've established who you are. Still waiting to hear what you want."

Jeez. What a crankypants. Besides, he should know better than to ask a compound question. This was America, where the average attention span is 2.3 seconds. *Now where was I again?* Oh, yeah. "What do I want? I want to catch the guy that stole from you."

He stopped poking around and looked up at me. "You for real?"

"Absolutely. You weren't the only victim. There are dozens of others like you in the area." The con artist had scammed over seventy-five innocent taxpayers.

Larabee issued a grunt. "Good to know I wasn't the only one dumb enough to fall for that stupid e-mail trick."

"You weren't dumb," I said, trying to assuage his self-loathing. This guy was a sad sack if ever I'd seen one. "You were just . . . naïve." Naïve and short-tempered, which was why he was out here today rounding up trash.

He snagged a beer can with the pincers and turned to

call to one of the other men. "Hey! You with the bin. Come over here."

The man scurried over with a special bin for recyclables. Larabee dropped the can inside with a tinny thunk and the man scurried off again.

Though my case file had contained copies of the e-mails he and some of the other victims had received, it hadn't given me a complete picture or a clear place to start my investigation. I hoped that by speaking with some of the victims and the bank tellers who'd handled the withdrawals, I'd have a well-defined plan of attack by the end of the day.

"I have a few questions for you," I said.

He waved his pincers in the air. "Ask away." He looked around the park and issued a sigh. "It's not like I'm going anywhere."

I pulled my notes and a pen from my briefcase, then set my briefcase on a bench nearby.

"Any idea where the thief might have obtained your e-mail and home addresses?" I asked.

"None," he spat.

"Had you received any suspicious e-mails before you got the one purporting to be from the IRS?"

"Sure," he said. "Same ones everybody else gets. The one where a friend supposedly had their wallet and passport stolen in a foreign country and needs me to wire them five grand. The ones that look like they're from a delivery service, telling me they attempted a delivery but I wasn't home and now they need me to click a link or open an attachment. Those ones about Asian women who want to do nasty things to my private parts or asking whether I want to meet a black woman with a big booty."

I'd received those same bogus e-mails myself. "Did you maybe enter a contest recently? Fill out one of those paper cards to win a boat or a free month at the gym?"

"No way," he said. "They just use that information to spam you. Besides, I've never won anything in my life. I'm not exactly what you'd call lucky. I was born with two undescended testicles and it's been downhill ever since. In the past year alone my house burned down, my wife left me, and the doctors had to do emergency surgery to remove my gall bladder."

Despite his having thrown a shoe at the IRS staff member, I was beginning to feel sorry for the guy. "I see from the documents in my file that you bank with Chase. Which branch do you normally use?"

"The one on Valley View," he said. "It's on my way home from work. Occasionally I go to the one on Josey, near my office." He extracted the pincers from the brush. A stiff, flattened pair of men's underwear was grasped between the pincers, the tighty whiteys having turned gray. With a look of disgust, Larabee dropped the undies into his bag.

I'd made some calls earlier and knew that the thief had made the withdrawal at the branch on Wycliff. Of course, banks required those making withdrawals to have some type of official identification. The thief must have presented the teller with a driver's license or state ID card in Roy Larabee's name.

"Did you lose your wallet recently?" I asked. "Or was it stolen?"

He shook his head. "That's about the only bad thing that *hasn't* happened to me."

"What about a change of address?" I asked. "Did you get a new license after your house burned down?" Maybe an employee at the DMV had kept the old license he'd surrendered. The employee could have used the license or perhaps even sold it on the black market.

Roy shook his head. "I lived at one of those rent-by-the-month hotels until my house was rebuilt."

So much for my DMV theory.

Out of ideas, I gave Larabee my card. "Call me if you think of anything new."

He took my card, though he didn't look hopeful.

"By the way," I said. "Your attorney said your payment is late."

Larabee's only response was a long, sad sigh.

chapter eleven

Skin Deep

After meeting with Roy Larrabee, I climbed back in my car, put on my defective sunglasses, and drove, squinting my one uncovered eye against the bright sun, to the office of Dr. Valentina DeMarco, a dermatologist. One of her aestheticians, a woman named Jessica Weiss, had lost $900 to the phishing scam. The missing lens wreaked havoc on my depth perception. It was a miracle I didn't have an accident on the way over.

The clinic was in a small, freestanding building two blocks down from one of the metroplex's many hospitals. I parked and went inside to check in with the receptionist.

"Just a moment," the woman said. She picked up her phone and held the receiver to her ear while punching a button. "There's a Tara Holloway here to see you." She paused a moment. "Okay. I'll send her on back." She hung up the phone and gestured to a door adjacent to the waiting area. "Right through there. Third door on the right."

"Thanks."

I went through the door and down the hall, stopping to rap on the designated door.

"Come in," called a female voice from within.

I stepped inside to find a thirtyish woman in pink scrubs. She had hair the color of ginger snaps and the smoothest, most flawless skin I'd ever seen this side of a baby's butt.

"Wow," I said, momentarily forgetting why I was there. "Your skin looks fantastic."

"Glycolics," Jessica said. "Great stuff. Have you ever tried it?"

I said, "No," though judging from the disgusted expression on her face as she ran her gaze over my cheeks she seemed to have already surmised the answer.

"My eleven o'clock canceled. I could give you a treatment while we talk if you'd like. It would do wonders for those bags under your eyes and those worry lines on your forehead."

Gee. Thanks a lot. "What does it run?"

"Seventy-five dollars."

I engaged in a quick mental debate. Seventy-five dollars seemed like a lot to spend on a skin treatment. Then again, maybe I'd earned a little pampering. I'd hardly slept last night, fighting off nightmares in which Nick and Christina disappeared forever. No ransom note. No bodies. No trace of them anywhere.

Dammit, I've earned this.

I hopped up onto the paper-covered examination table. "Let's do it."

I questioned Jessica as she pulled my hair back into a stretchy paper cap and used a moist wipe to remove my makeup. "Any guesses as to where the thief might have gotten your e-mail and home address?"

She retrieved a purple tube from a cabinet and sat on a rolling stool, using her heels to slide the seat closer to me. "I have no idea." She squirted a generous blob of creamy lotion into her gloved hand and began to dab it onto my forehead and cheeks. "I've given it out so many places. Where I went to school. Friends. Family. Different places that I've worked. And of course my landlord has it, as well as the electric company, gas company, and water company. Cable company, too." She lifted her palms. "Even my doctors' offices."

Her comment about the cable company got me wondering. The guys who came out to install the equipment were obviously very technologically savvy. What's more, they'd have access to the victim's e-mail address. "Who's your cable and Internet provider?" I asked.

"Charter," she said.

I made a mental note to contact Ray Larabee to see who his provider was. If it was also Charter, I might have just found my link.

While Jessica rubbed the cream into my skin, I continued to ask her the same questions I'd asked Roy Larabee. "Any chance you've lost your driver's license? Or maybe turned an old one in when you moved and gotten a new one?"

Like Larabee's, her response was negative. She'd had the same driver's license for three years. Also, like Larabee, she banked at branches near her home and work, with Bank of America in her case. The thief, on the other hand, had made the withdrawal from Jessica's account at a BOA only a mile from the Chase location where he'd withdrawn funds from Larabee's account.

My interrogation complete, I closed my eyes while the glycolics worked their magic, causing my skin to tingle. Twenty minutes later, a timer went off with a *beep-beep-beep,* letting us know the treatment was complete.

"Time to clean you up." She used a fresh wipe to remove the cream from my face, plucked the paper cap from my head, and tossed both into the trash. She picked up a hand mirror from the cabinet and handed it to me. "Take a look. What do you think?"

Gazing into the mirror, I turned my face from side to side, incredulous. There wasn't a single wrinkle, bag, or rough patch in sight. "My skin has never looked this good!"

"For best results you should get treatments at least once a month," she suggested, taking the mirror from me. "If you decide you want another, just give me a call. You've got my number."

After leaving the dermatologist's office, I ran into a nearby drugstore for a new pair of sunglasses. I found a cute pair with black-and-white-striped frames for $6.49. This was my fourth new pair in as many days. I hoped these would last me longer than the others had.

I slid into my car. *Bzzt-bzzt.* The secret cell phone hidden in the inside pocket of my blazer buzzed and jiggled. Letting out an involuntary squeal, I fished the phone from my pocket. No sense checking the phone's screen. Only one person would be calling this number.

I flipped the phone open. "Hello?"

The only response was silence.

"Hello?" I said a little louder. "Can you hear me?"

Still only silence.

I pulled the phone away from my ear and looked at it, realizing Nick hadn't called but merely sent me a text. All it said was *Miss you. Love to you and Mom.*

He'd told me earlier that he wouldn't be able to send me any details by text, just in case someone in the cartel got a hold of the phone. He couldn't risk them thinking he'd been feeding information to law enforcement or even a civilian inside or outside the cartel. Drug lords tended to like their privacy and encouraged the members of their networks to keep their mouths shut, both literally and technologically.

While I was thrilled to know Nick was okay, the uninformative text left me with renewed anxiety. Where was

he? How was the case going? Had he and Christina managed to collect any good evidence yet? Were they in danger? How much longer would this go on?

I closed the phone, clutching it tightly in my hand and
holding it to my chest as if it were a lifeline. In a sense it
was, my only link to Nick. A few seconds later, I'd com-
posed myself enough to return the phone to my pocket. I
grabbed my regular cell and called Bonnie.

"Tara, hi." She sounded breathless, as if she'd run for
her phone. "You've heard from Nick?"

"Just a few seconds ago," I told her.

"And?"

"He sends his love."

"That's it?"

The disappointment in her voice caused my heart to
writhe inside me. I wished I had more to offer her. But I
didn't. "That's it."

She was quiet a moment. "I suppose it's better than
nothing. But I'd hoped for more."

"Me, too. But I'm sure he did the best he could."

"That's right. We'll have to be grateful that at least we
know he's alive. How are you holding up?"

"Not too good," I replied. "I'm trying to stay busy to
keep my mind off things."

"Me, too. I've taken Daffodil for about a thousand
walks. She doesn't even get excited anymore when she sees
me pick up the leash. Maybe I'll do some work on my garden. It could use some weeding."

"How about I come over this weekend and help you
out?"

"That would be wonderful, Tara. I'll make a pitcher of
my famous peach sangria."

"Great! See you then."

After speaking with Bonnie, I made a quick detour to
the minor emergency clinic where Christina's fiancé, Ajay,

worked. The guy was a good doctor, but his bedside manner could best be described as smart-ass, at least where I was concerned.

Not sure if Ajay was on duty, I circled around the back of the building. Yep, Ajay's blue Viper sat in the back of the lot. Good. I continued on around to the other side and took a spot up front.

Kelsey, the redheaded, freckle-faced receptionist, looked up as I came in. "Good afternoon, Miss Holloway. We haven't seen you in a while."

For a while last year, it seemed like every time I turned around I was coming into the clinic for some type of injury or ailment. Burns on my head caused by a cigarette that had caught my hair on fire. A bloody stab wound in my thigh inflicted by a cockfighting rooster. A severe rash on my girly parts caused by a sexual enhancement product. Fortunately, I'd managed to avoid injury recently and had only seen Ajay socially.

"Good afternoon to you, too." I stepped up to the counter. "Is Dr. Maju available?"

"I'll check." Kelsey picked up her phone, punched a button, and spoke into the receiver. "Tara Holloway is here. Do you have time to speak with her?" She listened for a moment. "Great. I'll send her back." She returned the phone to the cradle and looked back up at me. "Room three."

"Thanks."

I stepped through the door that led back to the examination rooms. The door to room 3 stood open. Ajay sat on a rolling stool inside, entering patient data into a computer. He wore his usual Converse high-tops and jeans. When I stepped into the doorway, he looked up and stood, the gap in his white lab coat revealing a T-shirt with a Wonder Woman graphic.

"Hey, Tara." Though Ajay smiled in greeting, his eyes

remained hard and distant. He looked as tired and upset as I felt. No doubt he'd had trouble sleeping, too.

"Hey, yourself."

I closed the door behind me and hopped up onto the crinkly paper of the exam table. "I'm assuming Christina told you about the case she and Nick are working?"

"The cartel?" Ajay said. "Yes, she did. It's eating me alive. I've been popping Tums nonstop. I've got so much chalk in me I could poop drywall."

I could definitely relate. "I flavored my coffee with Pepto-Bismol this morning." It was true. And surprisingly, not nearly as disgusting as it sounds. "Can I trust you with a secret?"

He rolled his weary eyes. "Of course. I'm a doctor, remember? HIPAA requires me to keep my mouth shut so I've had lots of practice keeping secrets."

"Point taken." I leaned toward him and kept my voice low. "Nick took a secret phone with him. He contacted me this morning."

Ajay's face brightened. "So they're all right?"

I nodded, pulled my covert phone out of my purse, and held it out so Ajay could read the screen.

His shoulders relaxed. He looked up and put his palms together as if in prayer. "Thanks be to Vishnu."

Not to be outdone or to create jealousy between the gods, I looked up and issued a silent prayer of thanks to Jesus. While I had His attention, I asked for His continued protection. I'd already interrupted the Big Guy's morning. Might as well go for broke, right?

Ajay looked me over. "You look like you haven't slept in days."

"So do you."

"Touché. I can prescribe a sleeping aid if you'd like."

Though I appreciated the offer, I declined, thinking about that pill-covered coffin at the Unic. Rather than pop a pill, I'd self-medicate with the help of *el doctor* José Cuervo and a magical lime-flavored elixir.

As I stood to go, Ajay stepped toward me and gave me a long, warm hug.

"Thanks for coming by," he said. "You made me feel a lot better."

We chuckled at the irony.

When he released me, I gave him a smile. "I'll send you a bill for my services."

He opened the door for me. "You'll let me know if you hear anything else?"

"Of course."

He handed me a green lollipop from a plastic bowl on the counter. "Good girl."

After leaving the emergency clinic, I visited one more victim, an eighty-seven-year-old man named Freddie Babcock who lived alone in an older but well-maintained condominium northeast of downtown. His face was lined with age, but contained more laugh lines than worry lines, a sign of a life well lived. His hair, though stark white, remained thick and curly. He walked with one of those four-pronged canes, but managed to get around pretty well.

As I entered his place, my eyes spotted a sandwich sitting on a plate on his kitchen table. It had one bite taken out of the top left corner. Looked like he'd been just sitting down to lunch when I arrived. "I can come back in a half hour if you'd like."

"No, no," Freddie said, waving a hand dismissively. "It's not a problem at all. You know, I make a mean pimento cheese sandwich. Why don't I make one for you and you can join me?"

"Thanks," I said. "But we're not permitted to accept anything of value from a taxpayer."

"The sandwich would cost only forty-seven cents to

make," he said, disappointment registering on his face. "That's hardly anything."

I realized the man might be less interested in feeding me and more interested in simply having some companionship. "How about I run to that Chinese place across the street and get something for myself to bring back here?"

His mouth spread in a smile. "Now you're talkin'."

I returned in less than five minutes with a container of sautéed snow peas, an egg roll, a bottled water, and three fortune cookies. The counter clerk had thrown in a couple extra when I'd slid a tip into his jar.

Freddie had set me a place at his table.

"This is nice," he said, raising his glass of tea as if in toast. "Usually the only company I have is my TV set."

While we ate our lunch, I asked him the same questions I'd asked Roy Larabee and Jessica Weiss.

Though Freddie had once misplaced his license for a couple of weeks, he'd eventually found it in his toolbox. He gestured to his windows, which bore a silvery lining. "I'd been using it to get the bubbles out of the thermal window tint. I guess I'd accidentally tossed it into the box along with my cutter when I was finished."

"Understandable," I said. "Who's your television and Internet provider?"

"AT&T," he said.

Darn. There went my theory about the Internet installers. No sense calling Roy Larabee about it now.

I sighed inwardly. Again, my questions had proved fruitless. Maybe I was asking the wrong questions. Problem was, I didn't know what other questions to ask.

When we finished our lunch, I handed Freddie one of the fortune cookies and opened one of the others for myself. "What's your fortune say?" I asked.

"A fool and his money are soon parted." He shook his

head. "They got that right. I feel so stupid for giving out my bank information. My son wants to put me in a home!"

"Don't feel bad," I told him. "A lot of people were taken in by this scam. Many of them much younger than you."

His gaze moved to the slip of white paper in my hand. "How about yours?"

"Conquer your fears or they will conquer you." This fortune hit home. My fears about Nick and Christina were costing me sleep and making it difficult for me to concentrate at work. I wished I could be put into a medically induced coma until they returned. I wasn't sure how much more worrying I could take before I'd develop an ulcer.

I cracked open the third cookie, handing half of it to Freddie to eat. The fortune inside said *He who lives by the sword dies by the sword.*

Great. Just when I'd been trying to set aside those niggling fears about El Cuchillo, this darn fortune dredged up the horrifying thoughts all over again.

"You play cards?" Freddie asked me, pushing his plate aside and retrieving a deck from a basket on the table.

The last time I could remember playing cards was with Christina when we'd been working an undercover gig in a crack house a year ago. *Good times.* "I don't play often," I admitted. Still, I didn't want to leave Freddie disappointed. "But a game or two could be fun. Just promise you won't embarrass me too much."

We played fifteen hands of blackjack. Freddie beat me each time.

I gave him a smile. "What part of 'don't embarrass me too much' did you not understand?"

Freddie chuckled. "You need to get back to work?"

"Yes, unfortunately. If word got out that I was spending my afternoons playing cards with an attractive older man my boss would can me."

He walked me to the door, one hand on his cane and the other on the doorjamb as I turned around on his porch.

"I'll let you know if we find anything out."

He nodded. "I'd appreciate that. You take care now, Miss Holloway."

What a nice guy. He reminded me of my granddad. I hoped I'd get to the bottom of things, not only because it was my job and would be another successfully closed case for my upcoming performance review, but for Freddie's sake, as well. Nobody should take advantage of such a nice guy.

I headed next to visit some of the banks where the withdrawal had been made.

The manager of the first bank was a tall, narrow woman with dark hair cut in a short, layered style. She waved for me to follow her. "This way."

As we walked past her assistant, she asked the young man to summon the teller who had handled the bogus withdrawal. He nodded and picked up his phone as we continued on into the manager's office. After I stepped inside, she closed the door behind me.

As the woman took a seat behind her desk, I sat down in one of the sturdy chairs in front of it. She turned her computer monitor sideways on her desk so that we could both view it. "Our security team was able to pinpoint the car on the security video."

"Great!" If I could get a license plate number, this case could be solved in short order and I could move on to the next case in my stack.

The woman clicked a button on her keyboard to start the video. The clip playing on the screen showed a pickup truck with tinted windows pulling into the farthest drive-thru lane. No doubt the thief had picked that particular lane because it would be the easiest to escape from should the teller become suspicious. The truck was either black or dark blue. It was hard to tell for certain given the poor quality of the video. It was also difficult to tell the age of the truck given that models for pickups tended to vary much less than cars. The pickups being built today looked pretty much the same as those built even eight to ten years prior.

My eyes moved to the truck's bumper. Though Texas law required all vehicles registered in the state to bear license plates on both the front and back bumpers, this truck had no plate on the front. *Damn.* With any luck, there'd be one on the back. But given that it appeared the front one had been removed, I had my doubts.

As the driver's window rolled down, a man's face appeared. He was clearly not Roy Larabee, though, truth be told, it was hard to say what he looked like with much certainty. He sported one of those hats with the hanging flaps on the sides and back to keep the sun off his neck. The flaps covered part of his cheeks, making it difficult to determine exactly how wide his face was or its shape. He'd pulled the brim of the hat down low enough to meet the top of the dark sunglasses he wore. He wore an aloha shirt and a plastic Hawaiian lei around his neck. That was odd. Then again, maybe the guy was Jimmy Buffet.

On the screen, he slid a withdrawal slip and what appeared to be a driver's license into the heavy cylinder. He closed the end of the cylinder, inserted it into the bottom of the tube, and punched the button to activate the vacuum. The cylinder could be seen being sucked up into the channel.

As the thief waited for the cash, his fingers drummed the steering wheel, a sign he was anxious or excited or both. Or maybe there was just a good song playing on the radio. A moment later, the container reappeared, plummeting down the tube with its stolen contents. A smile broke on the man's face as he reached out, retrieved the envelope of cash and the counterfeit driver's license at record speed, and took off, wasting no time.

The camera angle showed the back of the truck now and, sure enough, there was no plate on the rear bumper, either. There were also no identifying bumper stickers. *Double damn.* Given that half of the vehicles on the road in Texas were pickups, it would be virtually impossible to narrow down who the truck belonged to.

A rap sounded on the door and the manager called, "Come in."

The teller, a fortyish woman with rail-straight brown hair, eased inside, closing the door behind her. She wore the bank's standard blue button-down with their logo embroidered on the chest pocket.

"Take a seat, Tammy," the manager said.

Tammy glanced from the manager to me and back again, her eyes bright with anxiety. She was smart enough to realize that being called into the boss's office unexpectedly was rarely a good thing, and when there was a strange woman in a suit there, too, the stakes had to be high. She slid into the chair next to mine, perching primly on the edge rather than settling back.

I introduced myself. "I have a few questions about a fraudulent withdrawal that was made here a couple months ago."

"What?" Tammy's eyes widened. Apparently this was the first she'd heard about the situation.

"You handled the transaction," I said. "We'd like you to watch this video and see if any of it seems familiar."

The bank manager played the video again.

I watched Tammy closely. There was always the possibility, however slim, that she might be in cahoots with the thief. I noted nothing unusual as she watched, though, no increase in respiration, no jitters. When the video finished, I asked, "Do you happen to remember that customer?"

Tammy shook her head. "I don't remember anyone coming through wearing a lei and a weird hat like that. If I had noticed him I would probably remember. Of course, it's hard to see the far lane from the teller window. There's usually a car or two in the way and the poles block the view, too. Sometimes I can't even see the person I'm dealing with."

Her explanation seemed viable. Heck, when I went through my bank's drive-thru, I often couldn't tell who I was dealing with, either. But I'd driven all the way here, I might as well be thorough, right? "Do you have certain procedures for handling withdrawals at the window?"

"Yes." She sat up even straighter in her seat, like a kid being quizzed by a teacher. "We always ask for identification. Then we compare the signature on the driver's license or ID card to the signature on file for the account to make sure they match."

I mulled that piece of information over for a moment. "What about the number on the license? Do you compare that to the number you have on file?"

"No," she replied. "The driver's license number doesn't appear on our computer screen."

The manager interjected a comment here. "For our account holders' security, we don't give tellers access to any more of their personal information than necessary."

"That makes sense," I said. When personal information was compromised, businesses ended up with a major PR problem, especially if the breach came from within.

Tammy looked at her boss and, when the woman nodded, continued. "When the customer sends us their license, we double-check that the name on the license is the same as the name on the account."

I mulled a little more. "Is there a limit to how much cash a customer can withdraw at the drive-thru?"

"Three thousand dollars," Tammy informed me. "If they want to withdraw more than that, they have to come into the lobby."

The manager chimed in again now. "Three grand is the standard limit in the banking industry for drive-thru withdrawals."

No doubt the thief knew of the withdrawal limit. That would explain why he kept all of his withdrawals under three grand even when many of the accounts contained far more money. He couldn't risk going inside the bank where he'd have a much more difficult time escaping should his nefarious intentions be discovered. Of course he'd been a crafty SOB. Every one of the fraudulent withdrawals he'd made had been on the first or fifteenth of the month, payday for most people, the day when their accounts would be flush.

"Thanks for taking the time to meet with me. Here's my card if you think of anything else." I held out a card to each of them. The way I was running through business cards lately I'd need to request a new box soon.

"If you catch the guy," the manager said, "please let us know as soon as possible. We'd love to recover some of that loss if we can."

I gave her a nod. "Will do."

Most of the banks had reimbursed their customers for the fraudulent withdrawals, though at least one of them was dragging its feet, alleging that the customer was negligent in providing the banking information to the thief and should bear responsibility for the loss.

My visits to the next two banks yielded no new information. Both of them showed me their security videos, and the same dark pickup appeared in both clips. At the bank where Jessica's withdrawal had been made, the video clip showed that the person driving the truck had worn a woman's wig and a flowery scarf around his neck while making the withdrawal. Unfortunately, the teller had no recollection of sending $1,200 through the tube to a cross-dressing thief in a pickup truck.

Not a productive afternoon.

It was after five by the time I wrapped things up. Given that my roommate/BFF was working late and that my boyfriend was undercover somewhere in the dark and dangerous drug underworld, it looked like I was on my own for dinner. Why not treat myself to a nice meal at my favorite French restaurant, Chez Michel?

chapter twelve

Table for One

I pulled into the lot and circled to the front doors, waiting as a couple on a midweek date exited their car in front of me. Once their valet had driven off in their car, I pulled up and handed my keys to the next young man. I was tempted to hand him my briefcase and see what he might be able to accomplish on my investigation. All of my training appeared to be for naught today.

I stepped inside the restaurant, removed my new black-and-white-striped sunglasses, and slid them into the inside pocket of my purse. As I approached his stand, the maître d' glanced up and arched a brow. "How many tonight?"

How many does it look like? I wanted to snap. My lack of success—compounded by my lack of sleep and lack of date—had made me testy. "Just me." *Yep, just me, myself, and I. The three of us will have a great time. Maybe we'll split a bottle of wine.*

The man led me to a table for two in the back corner, as if trying to hide their pathetic, lonely patron away from the eyes of their happier, accompanied customers. After pulling out a chair, he snatched the second set

of silverware from the table as if not to embarrass me
further.

Ugh. Maybe treating myself to dinner had been a bad
idea.

As I began to look over the menu, a man's laugh floated
across the room. *A man's laugh that rang a familiar bell.*
My gaze followed the sound and I found myself staring
at my ex Brett and a pretty woman who had to be his new
girlfriend, Fiona. Or should I say his fiancée? A rock the
size of an escargot graced the ring finger of her left
hand.

No doubt about it now.

Treating myself to dinner had *definitely* been a bad idea.

I contemplated whether I could sneak out without being seen. Brett and I had ended our relationship on good
terms, or on as good terms as possible when you mutu-
ally decide to go your separate ways. Still, I didn't want
him to see me sitting here, without a date or even a friend,
like some pathetic loser. And I had to admit, even though
it was clear the two of us were not meant to spend the rest
of our lives together, it hurt a little to see that he'd moved
ahead so quickly.

Quicker than Nick and I.

Ouch.

I'd just stood to attempt a quiet escape when my phone
went off in my purse, booming "Gunpowder and Lead"
across the restaurant. *Dammit!* Every head in the place
turned my way, including the heads perched on the shoulders of Brett and Fiona.

All of a sudden, my French came back to me. Well, at
least the word I needed now, which was "crap."

Merde. Merde, merde, merde!

I gave Brett a wave and a forced smile as I settled back
into my chair. I pulled the phone from my purse and jabbed
the button to accept Eddie's call. "Hi, Eddie," I said, keep-

ing my voice as low as I could so as not to disturb the other diners any further.

"I've found us an art appraiser," he said. "The art teacher at the twins' school has a masters in fine arts from SCAD."

"Scab? What's scab?"

Despite my attempts to keep my voice to a whisper, a woman at the next table overheard me, quirking her lip in disgust.

"It's *SCAD*," Eddie repeated. "Savannah College of Art and Design. It's one of the top art schools in the country. Mrs. Windsor also spent three years working as a curator at the Guggenheim. She knows her stuff."

"Fantastic. It'll be nice to get a professional opinion."

The waiter approached and I asked Eddie to hold while I placed my order, not only for my wine but for my food, as well. I wanted to eat as quickly as possible and get the heck out of there. My peripheral vision told me that Brett had cast a glance or two my way since my wave.

"She can take the afternoon off next Tuesday," Eddie said. "Does that work for you?"

"That works fine. Thanks, Eddie."

As I ended the call, I noted a waiter approaching Brett and Fiona's table with an appetizer of *boudin blanc*. The instant the server set it down between them, Fiona's face turned green. She leaped up from her seat and dashed to the ladies' room.

Sheesh. You'd think a woman who was a professional chef wouldn't freak out over a little white sausage.

When the waiter left his table, Brett stood and came over. "Hi, Tara."

A warm flush rushed up my neck. I hoped he wouldn't notice. "Hi."

His gaze moved over my face. "You look great."

"I just had a facial." I circled an open hand in front of my face. "All this skin is brand-new."

He chuckled. "How're things going?"

That was a hard question to answer. Hard, at least, to answer *honestly*. Since Brett and I had broken up I'd been nearly run off the road by a thug hired to kill me, shot four men in a strip club, been fired from the IRS, engaged in a shootout at a truck yard, and had my ass burned in a gas well explosion. And that was just for starters. But I'd also fallen in love with Nick, evened the score with my college nemesis, and been rehired by the IRS after a jury found me innocent in my excessive-force trial.

I looked up at Brett. "You know how things always are for me. Totally nuts with a side of crazy."

He offered me that boyish smile that used to turn my knees to mush. "You wouldn't want it any other way."

True that.

"I noticed Fiona's ring," I said. No point in pretending otherwise, right? "Looks like congratulations are in order."

"Thanks." Brett glanced in the direction she'd run. "It's kind of hard to believe I'm going to be someone's husband." He looked down for a moment, then back up at me. "And someone's father."

It took a moment for his words to register. "Fiona's pregnant?" *Wow.* He hadn't wasted any time once we'd split up, had he?

He nodded, looking a little embarrassed. "It was a . . . surprise. But it's one I'm happy about." The soft smile he offered was genuine.

"You'll be a great father," I said. He would be, too. He doted on Napoleon, his Scottie mix, as well as Reggie, a pit bull he'd taken on after Christina and I had arrested the dog's owners. Any child of his was sure to be hopelessly spoiled.

His smile morphed into a look of concern and his eyes

cut to the empty seat across the table from me. "How are things with Nick?"

I debated my answer. Frankly, I was still upset with Nick for taking on the undercover assignment in the cartel. Not that he'd had much choice in the matter, but he didn't have to be so eager about it. Still, I wasn't sure I wanted to air our dirty laundry, especially to Brett, what with his pretty bride-to-be and a baby on the way. Not that it was a competition or anything, but, if it were, Brett would definitely be winning. By a wide margin, too.

"Things are good," I said finally. "He's working a dangerous undercover case that's got me a little worried, though. I came here hoping the crème brûlée would take my mind off things."

"The crème brûlée *is* pretty mind-blowing."

Less than a year ago Brett and I had shared the dessert at this very restaurant. Things had changed so much since then.

"Tell you what," Brett said as my waiter approached, "your dessert is on me."

At one time, he might have meant that literally and suggested I eat it off his naked body. Now, though, a plate would be involved.

He asked my waiter to bring me a crème brûlée and add it to his tab.

"Thanks, Brett."

"Any time."

Fiona reappeared at the other end of the room, looking a slightly lighter shade of green now. Brett bid me good-bye and returned to his table. Fiona glanced my way and said something to him, probably asking who I was. I was curious what he'd said in return.

An old friend?
The girl I left for you?

Just somebody that I used to know?

Choked up with emotion, I had a hard time getting my dinner down. I felt worried and lonely and, admittedly, a little jealous. I'd only recently got an "I love you" from Nick, but Brett had already given Fiona a diamond and a zygote. Not that I was necessarily ready for those things quite yet, especially the zygote. How could I chase down bad guys if I were suffering from morning sickness like Fiona? Adding a kid to the mix would definitely complicate things for me and Nick jobwise, too. It was one thing for a single guy to go undercover inside a dangerous cartel, but it would be another thing entirely for a father to risk his life that way. Given that I was the best shot in the office, Lu often assigned me to investigations where gunplay was likely. Should a mother with a baby at home put her life at risk? If—*when?*—Nick and I decided to settle down and reproduce, we'd face a lot of tough decisions.

But why worry about that now? I forced those complicated thoughts aside and decided to just enjoy the delicious crème brûlée the waiter was placing in front of me.

I jabbed the top with a spoon to break through the hard top and scooped up a piece of the hard glaze along with the creamy goop underneath. I loved the stuff, even if it was a bit like eating glass. I stuck the spoon in my mouth and closed my eyes to savor the delicious flavor. *Yummm.* It was almost enough to make me forget that Christina and Nick could be dead right now.

Almost.

chapter thirteen

*P*hone Calls and Carbohydrates

At three o'clock Friday morning, the sound of rumba music pulled me out of a fitful sleep. My head felt foggy, my eyes droopy, my limbs heavy. But at least now that I was regaining consciousness, the nightmares involving El Cuchillo fled to the dark recesses of my mind. The killer had been running through my head all night, slashing and stabbing indiscriminately, leaving a trail of bloody, dismembered bodies in his wake and leaving my heart pounding so hard it was a miracle blood wasn't spurting out my ears.

As my skinny, creamy cat Anne stirred beside me, lifting her furry white head, the rumba notes kicked in again.

Wait. There'd been no music in my dreams. What's making that sound?

The secret cell phone, that's what!

Snapping fully awake, I sat bolt upright, upsetting the cat, who scampered to the end of the bed. I grabbed the phone from my nightstand and frantically clawed it open.

My mouth started speaking before the phone even made it to my ear. "Nick? Nick, are you there?"

When he spoke, his voice was hushed and hurried. "We can't reach anyone on our outside team. I need your help."

"Anything."

"I need you to follow a car, see where the driver goes." He gave me a color, make, and model—*black Toyota Sequoia SUV*—and a Texas license plate number. "It'll be heading south on Central Expressway from Plano in twenty minutes or so. Can you get up there by then?"

"If I haul ass."

"And what a sweet ass you haul."

"Aww," I replied. "You're making me blush."

"Take your gun," he said, "and don't get out of your car under any circumstances. The guy in the Sequoia is extremely dangerous. He'd slit his own mother's throat if she got in his way."

"Got it," I said. "Take my gun. Stay in my car."

"Don't call me back," he said. "I never know when someone's going to be with me. I'll call you later for the information."

"Okay."

"Tara," he said, his voice tinged with worry. "Be careful."

"Always am," I said.

"That's a lie."

He was right. I'd been known to take some crazy risks. But, hey, I was just doing my job.

"Where are you?" I asked, almost afraid to know the answer. Though we had our share of drug violence here, much of the most gruesome violence took place south of the border.

"Our targets are expanding their network in north Texas. I'm still here in town."

I closed my eyes. *Thank God.* My heart squeezed painfully. "I miss you, Nick."

"Good," he said. "The more you miss me, the better the sex will be when I get back." With that, he gave me a "gotta go" and disconnected.

Leaping from my bed, I ripped off my nightshirt and headed to my closet. I grabbed the first thing I found, a pair of blue scrubs with BAYLOR MEDICAL CENTER printed on the chest. I'd bought the scrubs at a secondhand store months ago when I'd been staking out a post office and needed some undercover disguises. Last time I'd worn the scrubs, people had assumed I was a real nurse and asked me all kinds of personal and disgusting medical questions about warts, and infected tattoos, and issues *down there.* Since I'd be doing surveillance from my car tonight I wouldn't have to worry about that.

I slipped into the scrubs and a pair of sneakers, forgoing a bra and socks. There was no time for undergarments. I scurried downstairs, hurdling Henry, my furry Maine coon, who lay on the rug at the bottom. He tossed me a dirty look.

"Count your blessings, cat," I told him. "You could be a lion in a teeny cage." *Poor Simba.*

Grabbing my father's old field glasses from the coat closet and my purse from the table in the foyer, I ran into my garage, punching the button to raise the door.

"Dammit!"

Alicia's black Audi was parked behind my car in the drive, blocking me in.

Closing the garage door, I darted back inside, once again hurdling Henry, who refused to move. *Pompous cat.* I glared down at him. "You are not the center of the universe."

The look he gave me in return said both that he pitied

my ignorance of astronomy and that I could go straight to hell. Assuming, of course, I filled his food bowl first.

I fished around in my roommate's bag for her car keys and ran out front with them, my nipples hardening in the cool night air. At least there was no one around to see the peep show. I bleeped the Audi's door locks open. I'd driven Alicia's car only once before, when she'd downed a few too many Mexican margaritas, but I knew she wouldn't mind my taking it tonight. It was an emergency, after all. I slipped inside, started the engine, and threw the gearshift into reverse.

Ten minutes later, I sat on the shoulder of the south-bound 75 freeway with the lights and engine off and my dad's oversized field glasses resting on my lap. With any luck, I'd look like a motorist having car trouble. With more luck, Dallas PD and the driver of the Sequoia wouldn't pay any attention to me.

I'd been waiting only three minutes when a vehicle fitting the description drove past. Raising the binoculars to my eyes, I checked the license plate.

Yep. That's the one.

I started the engine but kept the lights off until I'd eased into the traffic lanes. Hanging back a dozen car lengths, I followed the Toyota for several miles before it took the exit for the 635 loop. I took the exit twenty seconds later. Shorty afterward, the driver headed off the freeway and onto the surface streets, eventually pulling into a Waffle House on Jupiter Road.

Five cars sat in the restaurant's lot, two near the front and the other three near the back in what was probably an employee parking section. Two eighteen-wheelers had been parked parallel to the far right curb. The bright yellow restaurant was well lit inside, making it easy to see the half-dozen people seated on the stools and the cook behind the counter flipping eggs and hash browns.

As I turned into the parking lot, taking a spot near the front, a young Latino man with short but messy hair and a dark backpack climbed out of the Sequoia and looked around. Fortunately, he gave the Audi only a cursory glance before heading inside.

Even with the outside lights, it was too dark for me to get a good luck at the man. Could he be El Cuchillo? I had my doubts. The photo of El Cuchillo online had depicted a man with his head shaved bald and a face criss-crossed with scars. Though scars wouldn't be visible from this distance, this man looked too young and had too much hair to be the notorious, violent criminal. Given the backpack, this man looked as if he were a mule, moving either money or drugs. As upper management in the cartel, El Cuchillo wasn't likely to do this type of grunt work.

I watched for a moment or two from my car as the Toyota's driver walked past two men in flannel shirts, took a seat down the counter from them, and placed an order with the counter clerk. She nodded and served him a cup of coffee. He added two sugars, stirred, and took a sip, adding a third sugar when the first two packets proved insufficient.

Was the guy waiting for someone? Or was he simply having an early breakfast? Drug dealers, like nurses, truckers, and undercover federal agents, probably worked odd hours. Maybe he'd simply stopped for a stack of pancakes before heading on to his final destination.

Nick had told me to stay in my car and be careful, but I wanted to be as helpful as possible, too, without jeopardizing the investigation, of course. With my disguise in place, surely I could go inside, keep a better eye on the guy. Besides, I probably looked far more suspicious sitting in the car in the lot.

I whipped my comb from my purse, eyed myself in the vanity mirror, and did my best to comb my bed-head hair into some semblance of style.

"Yikes."

Despite my best efforts, my hair looked puffy on one side and flat on the other, but it would have to do. I shoved the comb back into my purse, climbed out of the car, and headed inside, hunching my shoulders to hide my peaked nipples.

"Sit wherever you'd like," called the waitress, gesturing with an orange-rimmed pot of decaf before refilling a mug for a stocky man seated near the end of the counter.

I slid into a booth in the corner where I could keep an eye on the man at the counter. Looking over the menu, I debated my options. Biscuits. Grits. Hash browns. Toast. Pancakes. Waffles. So many carbs, so little time. *Should I go with greasy carbs or syrupy carbs?* Hmm. Tough choices.

The waitress sauntered up with a steaming pot of regular coffee in her hand now. "Coffee?"

"That would be great." I had no idea how long I'd be tailing the driver of the Sequoia. Might as well make sure I was properly caffeinated lest I nod off driving down the highway and end up in a ditch. Or worse.

When she finished filling my cup, the waitress set the pot down on the tabletop, pulled a pencil from behind her ear, and held her pad poised to jot down my order. "What can I get you?"

"Biscuits and gravy," I said. "Extra gravy. Hash browns. Grits. The cheesy kind. And a pecan waffle." Good thing these scrubs had a stretchy waistband, huh?

She made a note of my order.

I cocked my head. "Any chance you've got lite syrup?"

"*Lite* syrup?" She raised a brow. "You're kidding, right?"

I shrugged. "You're right. What's the point, huh?"

She slid the pad back into the pocket of her apron, retrieved her coffeepot, and went behind the counter to submit my gluttonous order.

Pretending to be surfing the Net on my cell phone, I eyed my target over the top of the device. He looked to be in his early twenties and wore jeans, dark tennis shoes, and a lightweight gray windbreaker jacket, nothing remarkable. With the brighter indoor lighting, I could see that he had a thin mustache and a barely there beard, making him look like a Latino James Franco. He'd set his backpack on the floor in front of the stool next to him where it wouldn't be underfoot.

What's in the backpack?

Drugs?

Cash?

A college algebra textbook?

As I watched, the waitress slid a plate in front of him. He'd opted for scrambled eggs and hash browns all the way. The smells of onions and peppers wafted in my direction. He dug in, glancing around while he ate. In my peripheral vision, I saw him take a look my way. Instinctively, I froze in place, as if that would somehow make me invisible. *Stupid instincts.* Fortunately, his gaze didn't linger long enough to notice my telltale reaction. He'd likely taken me for what I appeared to be, a nurse who'd stopped by for a meal after working the swing shift.

Phew.

Looked like I'd pulled off my disguise. Once again, someone had underestimated me. Usually it pissed me off when someone assumed a petite woman like me posed no threat. But sometimes, like tonight, being small and benign-looking worked to my advantage.

It took the cook only a minute to assemble my simple breakfast, and only a moment more for the waitress to bring it my way. I hoped it would take a little longer for the carbs to turn to cellulite on my thighs.

I gave the waitress a smile as she slid the plate in front of me. "Thanks." Picking up my fork, I took a bite. *Yum.*

Not as good as my mother's homemade biscuits and gravy, of course, but not bad, either.

Headlights outside caught my attention. A dark pickup drove past and made its way to the back of the building. Shortly thereafter, a tall, thin, thirtyish white man in loose-fitting cargo pants and a green hoodie entered the restaurant. He had scraggly reddish-brown hair in need of a trim, with matching stubble on his cheeks and chin. His eyes scanned the room, taking in each of the customers as if he were assessing them. When he looked my way, I tilted my head and tapped my phone screen, pretending not to notice him or at least not to care. In reality, my heart was pitter-pattering in my chest, each of my senses on high alert.

He slid onto a stool two seats down from the man I was watching, my target's backpack resting on the floor between them. As the recent arrival hooked his heels over the stool's footrest, the cuffs of his pants rode up, revealing a pair of knobby ankles covered in dingy crew socks. The sock on his right leg had a suspicious bulge.

Damn.

The man's armed.

Was he simply carrying the gun for protection? Or was he here to try to rob the place?

I was armed, too, of course, my government-issued Glock in quick reach inside my purse, which sat on the seat of the booth beside me. But if the guy tried to rob the place and I whipped out my gun to stop him, my target would realize I was law enforcement and that he'd been followed here.

Ugh.

I'd promised Nick I'd be careful.

I hoped I'd be able to keep that promise.

After a couple of minutes, my target finished his meal and stood from his stool, leaving his backpack resting on the floor while he stepped over to the register to pay his bill. I gathered my ticket from my table, preparing to follow after him. He returned to his spot to leave two singles for a tip, but failed to retrieve his backpack, instead heading toward the door without it.

Hmmm . . .

Something told me he'd left the backpack on purpose. Something also told me it was more important to follow the backpack now than it was to follow the Sequoia.

Though my target and Crew Socks hadn't openly acknowledged each other, the abandoned backpack told me the two could be in cahoots. I sat back in my booth and sipped my lukewarm coffee, surreptitiously watching Crew Socks as he sopped up runny egg yolk with a biscuit and shoved it into his mouth, crumbs dropping from his lips to his hoodie. *Ew.* This guy could stand to learn some manners. Clearly his mother had not sent him to Miss Cecily's Charm School as my mother had done for me.

He leaned to his right, reaching down toward his ankle. *Uh-oh.* I unzipped my purse and slid my hand into the inside pocket, feeling for my Glock. Fortunately, the guy merely scratched at a spot behind his ankle before returning his attention to his meal.

He ate ravenously, shoving an entire sausage patty into his mouth at once. It was a miracle he didn't choke. Good thing since, as a purported medical professional, I might be expected to perform the Heimlich maneuver on him. He washed the meal down with five loud gulps of soda and reached down to grab the backpack.

Yep. Definitely in cahoots.

Quickly, I left a tip and stood, figuring it would be less obvious I was following the guy if I preceded him out of the restaurant.

As I stepped up to the register to pay my bill, he stepped

up behind me, stifling a sausage-scented belch over my shoulder. *Charming.*

"How was everything?" the cashier asked as I handed her my ticket along with a ten-dollar bill.

"Delicious, as usual." Heck, I could feel the fat molecules pooling on my thighs already. *Better do my glute exercises when I get back in the car.*

I took my change, slid it into my wallet, and headed outside. Once I was seated again in Alicia's Audi, I busied myself playing with the buttons on her radio, hoping I'd appear to be trying to find my favorite station. I stopped the scanner on a country station playing a song by Brazos Rivers, a superstar I'd recently busted for tax evasion. Hey, just because the singer didn't pay his taxes didn't mean he couldn't belt out a catchy tune. Besides, the more royalties he earned, the quicker Uncle Sam could recoup the overdue taxes.

I was squeezing my glutes together and singing along—*"baby, if you're willing, let's do some horizontal drilling"*—as the scruffy guy came out of the diner holding the backpack by one strap. He scurried to his pickup in the back lot, opened the door, and tossed the bag inside, climbing in after it. As he drove down the other side of the building and pulled out of the parking lot, I started my car to go after him, driving slowly to the exit so he wouldn't spot me behind him.

I hesitated briefly in the exit, giving him time to get a decent lead. As I paused, I noted a silver Dodge Avenger with tinted windows pull away from a pump at the gas station across the street. Through the windshield, I could see the driver and someone in the front passenger seat, though from this distance and with the tinted glass I could tell almost nothing about them. Judging from their size, they were either men or women tall enough to be supermodels or players in the WNBA.

The Dodge pulled out of the gas station and headed down the road after the truck, its driver following far enough behind the pickup that it seemed he didn't want to be noticed.

Hmm. Looked like I might not be the only one tailing the pickup.

Did the Avenger belong to law enforcement? Maybe someone working for the cartel? Or was its appearance mere coincidence and not related at all to the cartel case?

I stayed a couple of blocks behind the Avenger as we headed in a loose, impromptu convoy back onto 635. Using the field glasses, I took note of the license plate numbers on both vehicles and jotted them down to give to Nick later.

I narrowed my eyes at the vehicles ahead. "What are y'all up to?"

Was the driver of the Avenger some type of backup for the guy in the pickup, making sure he and the contents of the backpack arrived safely at their destination? Or was something else going on?

I had no idea what might happen, but I had to be ready for any eventuality. Reaching over to my purse, I pulled the zipper open, pulled my Glock from the inside pocket, and slid a magazine into the gun. I positioned the gun in the cup holder for quick and easy access.

The truck exited in Mesquite, drove past Town East Mall, and turned into a well-maintained, fully fenced apartment complex. The driver punched a code into the security system and the gate slid open to let him in. After he pulled through, the gate slid shut behind him. A moment later, the Avenger rolled slowly past the entrance to the complex before picking up the pace and heading off.

My tensed muscles relaxed. Though I enjoyed a little action every now and then, the last thing I'd wanted was to get in the middle of a shootout at night with a bunch of drug runners. Looked like any risk of that eventuality had now passed. *Thank God*.

I pulled to the curb and cut the lights and engine. Cracking the door, I eased myself out, shutting it as quietly as possible. Tiptoeing to the fence that surrounded the complex, I peered over a line of bushes. The pickup was visible parked in a row in the center. Putting the binoculars to my eyes, I noted that the truck appeared empty. The driver must have already gone inside. But which unit he'd gone into was anyone's guess. There were five expansive three-story buildings encircling the lot and, despite the late hour, lights on in at least a dozen units.

I crept back to Alicia's car, climbed in, and headed in the direction the Avenger had gone. I drove a full two miles down the road, glancing left and right down the side streets, but there was no sign of it.

Pulling into a convenience store, I parked and used my phone to log in to the DMV records. Per my search, the pickup was registered to a man named Terrence Motley at a south Dallas address six miles or so from the apartment complex where he was now. The Avenger belonged to a Carlos Uvalde who purportedly lived in San Antonio, a large city located roughly halfway between Dallas and the Mexican border. The Sequoia was registered to a Lorenzo Vargas at an address in Del Rio, a small Texas town located west of San Antonio in the Rio Grande Valley, near the international border.

I checked the driver's license records next. The address on each license matched that on the vehicle registrations. Motley's photo proved he and Crew Socks were one and the same. Ditto for Vargas and the Latino James Franco. Because I hadn't gotten a good look at the men in the Avenger, I couldn't confirm whether the photo of Carlos Uvalde in the driver's license records matched either of the men. And, of course, I had no idea who the second person in the Avenger might be.

Assuming the information was current, Motley didn't live here at the complex. But who did, then? Another member of the cartel? A distributor? A dealer?

I ran a quick background check on the men. Vargas had no record. Motley had two convictions for possession of marijuana, but both were in small amounts, enough for personal consumption but not enough to indicate he was dealing in the stuff. Uvalde, on the other hand, had served seven years for dealing heroin and assaulting a police officer. Not exactly a Boy Scout.

I let out a long breath. I supposed I'd done all I could for the moment.

Making an illegal U-turn in the middle of the street, I headed back home.

chapter fourteen

$\mathcal{P}$inch Hitter

Bzzzz. My alarm went off much too early the next morning. Having lost three hours' sleep to my late-night mission, I had to fight the urge to yank the plug out of the wall. Still, though I might be exhausted, I had a job to do. Uncle Sam didn't pay me to loll about in bed. I only hoped he'd reimburse my gluttonous late-night snack.

On my drive into work, I stopped at a gas station and bought a large Dallas map. When I arrived at the office, I aimed straight for the supply room. My eyes scanned the shelves. Manila folders. Legal pads. Nine-by-twelve mailing envelopes. Boxes of ballpoint pens.

Viola, Lu's eagle-eyed secretary, stepped into the doorway. "Finding what you need?"

"No." I pushed aside small boxes of binder clips to search behind them. "I'm looking for thumbtacks. I don't see any."

"Thumbtacks?" Viola cocked her head. "I don't get much call for those. Can't even remember the last time I ordered any."

"Darn."

"What do you need 'em for?"

I held up my map. "I need them to mark points on this map."

Viola reached out and snagged a package of colorful Post-it strips which read SIGN HERE. "Can you make do with these?"

They weren't at all what I was looking for, but they'd have to do. I took them from her. "Sure. Thanks."

When I reached my office, Nick's roses greeted me with their soft, sweet smell and gorgeous blooms. My heart contracted in a painful squeeze as I reached out to finger a petal. El Cuchillo better not hurt the man I loved or there'd be a photo of me on the Internet, licking El Cuchillo's blood from the bullet I'd put in his brain. *Yeah! Take that, El Cuchillo!* The thought first made me feel tough, then nauseated as the reality of it hit me. *Ew.* I guess I'd settle for a photo of me standing over the thug's bullet-riddled corpse.

I tossed my purse into my desk drawer and taped the Dallas map to the wall next to my window. Consulting the information in the phishing scam file, I used my cell phone map feature to locate the bank branches where the crook had made the bogus withdrawals. Using the SIGN HERE slips, I marked each of them on the map. After applying the last sticker, I stood back to admire my handiwork. *Pretty cool.* I'd always wanted to make an evidence board like they do on those detective shows on TV.

The fact that all of the victims were local and the withdrawals were all made at banks in the Dallas area meant that whoever did this likely lived around here somewhere. Most criminals tended to operate within their comfort zone, where they were familiar with the streets and could make an easy getaway. Besides, with the price of gas being what it was, it wouldn't be cost-effective for the thief to drive a long distance to make the transactions.

Eddie's voice came from behind me. "What're you doing?"

I turned to find him walking into my office, his gaze roaming over my Dallas map. As he stepped up beside me, I pointed to each of the strips and explained myself. "These are the locations where a target in one of my cases made fraudulent withdrawals."

Eddie snorted. "You've been watching too much *Homeland.*"

I stuck my tongue out at him, which he took as his cue to leave. I returned my attention to the map and stepped forward, using another SIGN HERE sticker to mark the center of the relevant area. In theory, the center should be the criminal's residence or workplace. The sticker ended up smack-dab in the middle of the Daniel Cemetery, an old family plot situated just north of Southern Methodist University.

A quick Internet search informed me that the cemetery had been in existence for over 160 years. The cemetery contained the remains of a number of Daniel family members, and even the bodies of former family slaves. Most recently, local real estate tycoon Trammel Crow, who had married into the Daniel family, had been interred there.

I stared at the map. What could I glean from this information? That the person who'd sent the e-mails was a ghost who'd sent the communications from the hereafter? That they were *eeeee*-mails?

After thinking things over, the only information I gleaned was that law enforcement was a very inexact science. I also realized that maybe I was going about the phishing case the wrong way. I'd been trying to collect evidence and clues that could help me move *forward,* when maybe the direction I needed to go was *backward.* Maybe the key to solving this case wasn't trying to chase after the person who'd made the withdrawals at the bank, but rather to see whether the e-mails could be traced back to their source. I wasn't sure whether the person who'd made the withdrawals was the same one who'd sent the e-mails, or whether the two (if there were two) were simply working together. But if there was more than one person involved, finding one of them would likely lead me to any others.

File in hand, I did an about-face and headed straight to the office of my fellow special agent Josh Schmidt. I stopped in his doorway and rapped on the frame.

Josh looked up from his computer screen. With his cherubic blond curls, baby-blue eyes, and slight stature, Josh was hardly the most intimidating agent on the IRS payroll. He looked more like a hobbit in search of an all-powerful ring than a federal law enforcement officer tracking down criminals. No matter, though. He hadn't been hired for his physical prowess. Rather, it was his mental acuity and cybersleuthing skills that had landed him the job as the department's high-tech specialist. It was precisely those skills that had led me to his office this morning.

After he waved me in, I stepped inside and plopped down in one of this chairs. "I need your help."

Though Josh and I got along fine now, that had not always been the case. When I first met him, he'd been a sniveling, whiny little weasel, competitive with his co-workers and definitely not a team player. He'd done a 180 once Nick and I had sufficiently stroked his fragile ego and requested his assistance. Of course the fact that he'd since met a woman through an online dating service and finally gotten laid hadn't hurt, either. Perhaps his earlier demeanor had been the result of pent-up sexual frustration. At any rate, he was our go-to guy anytime we needed help cracking a computer.

"Help?" he asked. "With what?"

I situated my briefcase on my lap, clicked open the latches, and pulled out my file on the phishing case. I held the file out to him. "With this."

He took the file, set it on his desk, and opened it. He spent a minute or two perusing the contents before looking up at me. "You want me to figure out where these e-mails came from?"

"Exactly." I explained that none of the victims I'd interviewed had provided any leads, and that my attempts to identify the thief or thieves from the bank surveillance videos had likewise been futile.

"I'll need the victims' e-mail account passwords."

"All of them?"

"Let's start with four or five. That should be a big enough sample."

"I'll give them a call right away," I said.

Josh closed the file and set it aside. "I've got some work on my own cases I need to get out of the way first, but I should be able to take a look at this in the next day or two."

"Thanks, Josh."

With that, I headed back to my office. My eyes noted Will Dorsey coming up the hall. "How did last night's softball game go?" I called.

"We lost," he said as he approached. "Seventeen to zero, to those pencil-pushing dweebs at the Census Office. It was humiliating."

I cringed. "Better luck next time."

He put an arm out to stop me. "I can't seem to get a direct answer out of Lu. Any idea when Nick's coming back? We're getting our asses kicked without him."

I shrugged. "I don't know."

Dorsey cocked his head. "He's out on something big, isn't he?"

Though I knew Lu trusted her staff, it was standard protocol for information on large, highly sensitive cases to be shared on a need-to-know basis only. If I hadn't overheard Lu and Christina speaking with Nick in his office, I might not even know what Nick was involved in.

"Yes," was all I said.

Dorsey nodded, knowing I couldn't share more. "Whatever he's working on," he said, "I hope he wraps it up soon. Otherwise, the Tax Maniacs are going to become the laughingstock of the federal government softball circuit."

"That would be a damn shame."

"Wouldn't it, though?" He cocked his head. "Hey, we're short one player tonight. Hana Kim backed out. Said she's got a hot date. Any chance you could fill in?"

"Sure," I said. Why not? It's not like I had a hot date. Heck, I didn't even have a friend to hang with tonight. The game could be just the thing I needed to take my mind off El Cuchillo and his sharp, shiny blade.

We set off in opposite directions again. I returned to my office, took a seat, and called several of the victims in the phishing case. I had to leave a voice mail for Jessica, who was probably in the middle of another facial, but was lucky enough to catch Roy Larabee, Freddie Babcock, and a couple of the other victims. I sent their passwords to Josh via e-mail, and fished another file from my stack.

chapter fifteen

$\mathcal{U}$nnatural Disaster

The case in this file, like the case involving the Unic and Paradise Park, involved nonprofit fraud. In this instance, the culprit was a "Facecrook," a criminal who ran his scam through the popular social networking site Facebook. The crook had set up a Facebook page very similar to that of the American Red Cross with the obvious intent of misleading potential donors. The copycat page purported to be for the U.S. Red Cross, an organization that didn't actually exist. Just as the legitimate Red Cross collected donations to fund disaster relief efforts, this phony organization purported to be collecting for the same cause.

An observant auditor who'd been performing a routine review of a well-to-do couple found a charitable contribution deduction for $2,500 to the U.S. Red Cross. The wife had made the donation after visiting a friend's Facebook page and seeing the heartbreaking post and photo of a little girl allegedly orphaned after her parents perished in a tsunami. The taxpayers had been none too happy when they'd learned their funds had not gone to a legitimate charity but had instead lined the pockets of a con artist. They'd attempted to get a refund from their credit card company. Unfortunately, too much time had passed since they'd made the donation. Having their tax deduction denied had added insult to injury, and led them to demand that the federal government do something to hunt down the greedy and heartless person behind the scam. Thus, that task became mine.

After visiting my brothers' pages to check out the latest photos of my nieces and nephews—*adorable as always*—I pulled up the Facebook page for the U.S. Red Cross. I hoped something on the page might provide me with clues about who was operating the scam. When the auditor had become aware of the fraudulent charity, she had immediately contacted Criminal Investigations. Lu had contacted the victims and asked them not to notify Facebook until her department had had a chance to look into the matter. After all, if the page was taken down, the criminal could easily disappear into cyberspace, never to be found. But with the page still active, I might be able to use it to track down the perpetrator. Once he or she was in my clutches, I'd inform Facebook of the scam so they could shut down the page.

I perused the screen for information that might lead me to the wrongdoers. Images on the page included heartrending photographs of families with young children left homeless, their meager belongings in their hands, their faces and futures bleak. Huts with thatched roofs half gone leaned at precarious angles, damaged beyond repair by severe wind gusts. Broken and bare palm trees, their leaves carried off in a gale, lined a debris-strewn beach. The text noted that the photographs were taken after the recent devastating typhoon in Andorra. So sad. My heart went out to these poor folks.

Wait.

A typhoon?

In Andorra?

I stunk at geography and knew diddly-squat about meteorology, but wasn't Andorra somewhere in Europe? And typhoons didn't strike Europe, did they?

Viola wandered into my office to deliver a memo reminding us to submit our summer vacation requests ASAP since days off had to be allocated to ensure that at least a skeleton crew remained in the office at all times. She eyed me over her bifocals. "If you want some time off for your friend's wedding, you need to get your request in right away."

"Thanks for the reminder." I'd planned on taking off a day or two the week prior to Alicia's wedding to help her deal with last-minute details.

"Hey, Vi," I asked as she turned to leave. "Do you know anything about Andorra?"

"Andorra?" she repeated. "Isn't that the mean, orange-haired grandma from *Bewitched*?"

Looked like I wasn't the only one who should've paid more attention in school. "It's a country." At least I thought it was anyway. Maybe it was merely a state within a country.

She shrugged and left my office, turning right to continue on her route down the hall.

A quick Internet search confirmed that, yes, Andorra was situated between Spain and France. It was a small, landlocked country with no coastline. My search also confirmed that typhoons did not occur in Europe. Rather, they were prevalent only in the Pacific and Indian Oceans.

Sheesh. Apparently, when Mother Nature failed to wreak havoc upon her inhabitants often enough, the criminal behind the fraudulent charity invented natural disasters to keep donations rolling in. He seemed to realize that not only were people very busy these days, but they were also overloaded with information and their attention spans were very short. They took things at face value rather than questioning the information or its source. When one of their Facebook friends made a donation and posted a link suggesting their friends do likewise, who wanted to be the uncompassionate jerk who couldn't spare a mere ten dollars for the victims of a flood, fire, earthquake, or other natural disaster?

The fact that this particular con artist preyed on people by taking advantage of their empathy and generosity seemed especially egregious. If I had to hazard a guess, the culprit had probably copied the horrific photographs from some other Web site.

I wrangled the victims' credit card statement out of the file and placed a call to their bank. After twenty-seven minutes waiting on the phone and three transfers, during which I was cruelly subjected to three different songs by Cher, I was finally connected with an assistant in their legal department.

"What can you tell me about U.S. Red Cross?" I asked, after giving her the preliminary details.

"The organization is based in the Bahamas," she said. "Nassau, to be precise."

Damn. Another con artist hiding out in the Caribbean, beyond the reach of U.S. law enforcement.

"Would you like the contact information?" she asked.

I doubted the information would be valid, but said yes anyway. As she rattled off an address and phone number I jotted them down. "Thanks."

As soon as we ended the call, I plugged the address into a mapping program on my computer. Just as suspected, the computer told me that no such address existed. When I tried the phone number, it merely rang and rang and rang with no answer and no voice mail message. *Rrring . . . rrring . . . rrring . . .*

I jabbed the button to end the call and stared at my computer screen. "Who are you, you bastard?"

Perhaps it was sexist of me to assume the con artist was a man but, hey, if the shoe fits, right? Though the occasional stiletto was involved, most of the shoes tended to be male where these types of white-collar crimes were concerned.

I knew from experience that just because a business had offshore accounts and purported to be based in the Caribbean, it was unlikely that the operators of the business actually lived or worked on the islands. While European con artists traditionally used Swiss bank accounts, those who utilized offshore accounts tended, by and large, to be American. Again, criminals staying as close as possible to their comfort zones.

I put my phone down on my desk and sat back in my chair, eyes closed, trying to think like a criminal. If I were going to run a Facebook charity scam, how would I do it? *Hmmm . . .*

First, I'd set up an offshore account, just as this crook had.

Next, I'd set up a Facebook page that looked legit, just like this crook had.

Finally, I'd set up a dozen or so artificial online personas, "like" the fraudulent charity's Facebook page, and start making connections with random people to whom I claimed some loose, difficult-to-verify relationship, perhaps that I'd briefly attended their high school and remembered them fondly. *It was so nice of you to invite me to sit with you at lunch that time!* I'd make a few friendly comments on their posts.

Your children are adorable!

I've never seen such a cute cat!

Wow, that dress makes you look so thin!

Once I'd gained the trust of my victims, I'd post emotional pleas on my personal pages expressing grief over the loss of life and destruction of homes in the latest natural disaster, note that I'd made a donation to my fraudulent charity, and implore my fortunate, caring, and compassionate friends to make a donation via a quick and easy link on the charity's page. While they were there, I'd suggest, why not "like" the charity page to help spread the word? If this indirect appeal fell short, I'd send personal messages to my new cyberbesties and ask them directly to please support the cause with ten dollars or so. *Heck, that's hardly more than a morning latte,* I'd say. *Together we can make the world a better place!*

Yep, it wasn't hard for me to delve into the criminal mind. I'd concocted many a sordid scheme myself back in high school when I'd been grounded for one infraction or another yet didn't want to miss some kegger being held in a barn or pasture somewhere. *You've got to let me out of the house, Mom. My English teacher is giving us extra credit if we go see the drama department's performance of* Macbeth *tonight.*

As if.

Turning my attention back to my computer screen, I scanned the photos of those who had commented on the U.S. Red Cross page. The vast majority of them were women, though there were a few men in the mix, too. It didn't surprise me that the con artist had targeted women, who were more likely to be drawn in emotionally by the photographs. While it took only a child's sad face to get a woman's attention, when it came to men it generally took a beer bottle or a set of oversized boobs.

I leaned closer in toward my screen. *Who of these people are real and who are mere illusions?*

I clicked on a photo of a smiling blonde wearing a pink cowgirl hat. Her page indicated that she lived in Tucson, Arizona, and contained photos of cactus flowers, the Painted Desert, and the woman and three friends in a Mexican restaurant with margarita glasses lifted. She'd made

everything on her page public. At least a dozen recent posts
told me she was legit. Criminals worked only as hard as
necessary to keep up their ruse. I doubted this perpetrator would take the time to make so many posts.

The second photo I clicked on was an Asian woman in
a black turtleneck. All I could tell about her was that she
lived in Manchester, New Hampshire, and worked as a
sommelier at some fancy-schmancy restaurant.

I maneuvered my mouse to click on a third photo. The
Facebook photo for "Laurel Brandeis" showed a woman
with curly dark hair hovering airborne over a trampoline,
her legs extended out to each side and her fingers touching her toes in a jump the cheerleaders at my high school
had called a Texas T.

Something about this photo seemed familiar. *Do I know
Laurel Brandeis?* It was hard to believe. The odds of me
being personally acquainted with one of the scammer's
victims had to be very low. My gaze shifted to her personal data. She lived in Boise, Idaho, and had attended
Brigham Young University. The likelihood of our having
met seemed infinitesimally small. Yet the woman seemed
very familiar somehow . . .

Dang.

Try as I might I just couldn't place her. The lack of REM
sleep was seriously hampering my work performance.

Given that I had no way of determining which of the
people were real and which were fictitious, I decided not
to waste any more time reviewing the pages. Even if I could
tell the made-up people from the real ones, there'd be no
way to identify who had created the pages for the nonexistent people. I figured my best bet was to beat this scammer at his or her own game. I'd worm my way in, earn
the culprit's trust, and see if I could get the con artist to
willingly or inadvertently give me clues to his identity.

In an earlier case, I'd pretended to be a freelance bookkeeper and used the alias Sara Galloway. I'd made an authentic-looking Facebook page for her in case anyone suspected I wasn't who I said I was and went snooping online to see if Sara G was legit.

I pulled up the page, finding myself face-to-face with a simple headshot of myself taken a couple of years ago at my desk at the CPA firm. "Oh, Sara," I told myself. "You were so young and naïve then." And so free of worry wrinkles.

I hadn't updated the page in a few months, but no problem there. I thumbed through the photos on my cell phone until I found a picture of me taken last summer in my parents' backyard. I wore cutoff shorts, a wrinkled T-shirt, and sneakers, and was feeding peanuts to one of the family goats. I uploaded the photo to my computer and posted it to my Sara Galloway Facebook page along with text that read *I'm finally back from my missionary trip to Africa. Here's me with one of the village goats. I'm so glad I had a chance to give back to the less fortunate. I am truly blessed! I only wish I could do more for those in need!*

My fake photo and story now online for the world to see, I ventured forth and clicked the "like" button on the pages of several legitimate charities before proceeding to the page for the U.S. Red Cross and "liking" that one, too.

Rather than overplay my hand, I did nothing else for now. But over the next few days, I planned to edge closer and closer to my prey. I had no idea how things might play out, or exactly where I would go with this, I simply knew it was the only way of nailing this virtual villain.

chapter sixteen

$\mathcal{G}$et Your Head in the Game

At four-thirty that afternoon, I went into Nick's office and grabbed his baseball bat, hoping it might bring me luck in tonight's game. I left his sports bag alone, having no need for an extra-large T-shirt, men's tennis shoes, or a protective cup.

I tucked the bat under my arm and snuck out of the office. Not that I had to try too hard to be inconspicuous. Lu had an unwritten rule that anyone playing on the IRS softball team could cut out a little early to get ready.

I drove home, changed out of my suit and into a pair of shorts, sneakers, and a T-shirt. I tied a lightweight hoodie around my waist and pulled my hair up into a ponytail. After feeding my cats an early dinner, I grabbed my old baseball glove and a bottled water from my fridge, and headed back out to drive to Exall Park, which sat slightly northwest of downtown, on the east side of Central Expressway.

On the drive over, my thoughts returned to El Cuchillo and his knife, making me feel scared, helpless, and frustrated once again. Not exactly the best mood for facing down the ironically hard-hitting team from the local Peace Corps office.

"There she is!" Will Dorsey called as I approached the open field next to the softball diamond where the Tax Maniacs milled about, beginning to warm up.

I held up the bat. "I brought Nick's lucky bat."

"Well, then," Will said. "I'll be expecting you to hit a home run."

Gee, no pressure, huh? I was a decent enough athlete. I'd played on my high school volleyball team, even earned the title of MVP on a couple of occasions. In college, I'd played intramural softball with a group of accounting majors. We called ourselves the Bean Counters. We'd had some skill, but even more luck, winning the season championship with a score of 9 to 8 when we'd vanquished the Irresistible Force, a team of surprisingly agile nerds from the physics department. I even worked out regularly to keep in shape. But it had been a while since I'd played softball on any regular basis. I couldn't even remember the last time I'd swung a bat. I'd sort of hoped Will would just have me warming the bench.

The Peace Corps team, a group comprised primarily of middle-aged hippies sporting tie-dyed shirts in an assortment of colors, were on the diamond, warming up with some batting practice.

"Tara! Over here!" One of the other IRS team members, a fortyish auditor with prematurely gray hair and a lean runner's build, waved me over to warm up with him.

I put on my glove and we tossed the ball back and forth a few times. His powerful throws impacted my glove with a resounding smack that caused my hand to sting. The balls I threw landed softly in his glove with a soft, unimpressive *plup*.

Damn. I was definitely not on my game tonight.

When it was time for the game to begin, we headed to our dugout. The Peace Corps team likewise headed to theirs.

"Here's the lineup," Will said, holding up a clipboard.

He passed the list to the first guy on the bench, who handed it down for us all to take a look. Hana Kim's name, in the third slot, was scratched out, my name scribbled in beside it.

Will and the captain of the Peace Corps team met up with the umpire, who tossed a coin to see which team would bat first. When the coin landed, the umpire swung his arm, pointing our way.

As the rest of us chanted, "IRS! We're the best!", my warm-up partner headed to home plate.

The Peace Corps' pitcher, a tall, skinny guy with a brown braid hanging down his back, sent a fastball streaming toward my teammate. *Crack!* The ball sailed between the second and third basemen. My teammate ran full speed to first and slid into second.

Will cupped his hands around his mouth. "Nice job! Way to start the game!"

The second batter missed the first pitch, but bunted the second, making an easy run to first base while our other team member advanced to third.

As I stood, Nick's bat gripped tightly in my hand, my team shouted words of encouragement.

"Go get 'em, Tara!"

"You can do it!"

"Show those hippies who's boss!"

I hoped I wouldn't let them down. But, as I stepped into place at home plate, I feared I would. Nervous sweat broke out on my back and upper lip, my hands growing moist, as well.

The pitcher wound up and released the ball, which came

screaming at me. Rather than swing, I stepped back and away.

"Strike one!" called the umpire.

We got it, dude. Did he really have to shout so loud? He was likely to blow out a lung.

The second pitch looked outside to me, so I stood my ground and didn't swing.

"Strike two!" shouted the ump.

Sheesh. No point in arguing the call. What was done, was done.

I needed to hit the next ball. I wiped my sweaty palms on my sleeves and took a deep breath to ready myself. The pitcher released the ball, which came right at my bat. *Ha!* What an easy hit this would be!

I swung with all my might. When I met with no resistance, momentum carried me around in a circle. I nearly hit the umpire and the catcher had to duck to avoid being whacked upside the head with the bat.

"I'm so sorry!" I cried.

The men cast me annoyed looks, but shrugged it off.

"Strike three!" the ump called.

Shoulders slumped, face boiling red, I returned to the bench.

My teammates were less encouraging now, their mumbles of "you'll get 'em next time" sounding weak and insincere and even a little hostile. Clearly Tara Holloway was a poor replacement for the athletic fireplug that was Hana Kim.

The innings went on, our teams neck and neck. The score went from 1 to 1, to 2 to 2, to 3 to 3. I managed to get on base with my next at-bat, but only because I was walked. I was quickly tagged out at second. Better than my first go, but still nothing to brag about.

It was the final inning and the score was tied 9 to 9.

The bases were loaded. And—*dammit!*—I was up to bat.

I hadn't hit a single ball all night. Nick's lucky bat had done nothing for me. Maybe I should've worn his protective cup, after all. Maybe that curved piece of flexible plastic was where he got his mojo. Of course it was more likely his mojo came from the sizable testosterone-producing organ the cup was designed to protect.

I stepped into place, blinking against the setting sun on the horizon. These black-and-white-striped sunglasses were cute, but they did a poor job. I could hardly see the pitcher. He was mostly just a dark shadow outlined by sunlight, what Jesus might look like if he played softball.

I missed the first pitch. *Dang it!*

"Strike one!" called the umpire.

On the second pitch, my poor eyesight confused me and I leaned much too far into the swing, inadvertently aiming for the ball's shadow rather than the ball itself. The ball grazed my face, taking my new sunglasses with it.

The umpire rushed forward. "Are you okay?"

There was a definitive crunch as the man's foot ground my sunglasses into the dirt.

"I'm fine." The same could not be said for my sunglasses, which were in three separate pieces. "My bad."

I picked up my sunglasses, trotted over to toss them in a trash can, and returned to home plate. As I stood there, shifting anxiously on my feet while I waited for the pitch, I realized something. By letting El Cuchillo into my head, allowing him to affect my performance tonight, I was letting that bald-headed, scar-faced, blood-licker win.

Screw that.

My resolve having returned, I squinted against the sun and readied myself.

From the Peace Corps dugout came, "Hey, batter-batter! Hey, batter-batter!"

The pitcher gave me a smug smile.

A smug smile I will wipe right off his face.

He wound up and sent a curveball at me.

CRACK!

The ball flew up and out, over the head of the pitcher, over the heads of the basemen, and over the heads of the outfielders madly running to catch it.

Neener-neener.

As I dropped Nick's bat and took off for first base, my teammates erupted in chants of "Ta-ra! Ta-ra! Ta-ra!" There was no hidden hostility in their voices this time.

I passed second and third base, pumping my fists in victory as I headed home. The IRS team flooded the field, picking me up on their shoulders.

God, this felt good!

I'd needed a win.

chapter seventeen

$\mathcal{F}$resh as a Daisy

My coworkers took me to a sports bar for celebratory drinks after the game. They insisted on paying for my margaritas. Hey, who was I to complain?

When I finally arrived back home that evening, I walked down the block to Nick's place. After collecting his mail from the box, I went inside.

The place seemed eerily quiet, especially after all the noise at the softball game and the sports bar. Grabbing his television remote, I clicked the set on. It was tuned to ESPN, of course. I didn't give a rat's ass which team won which game, but Nick's TV, Nick's station, right? Who was I to change it? Besides, though I knew it was only silly superstition, I felt like changing the channel would somehow jinx things. Nick's place should remain exactly how he'd left it until he came home.

Wandering into his kitchen, I tossed his junk mail into his recycling bin and gathered the rest in a rubber band to take to his mother. My stomach rumbled, reminding me that two margaritas, no matter how refreshing and delicious, do not constitute a meal. I opened his fridge to take a peek. *Score!* A takeout box with two slices of slightly dry, slightly curved-up-on-the-ends cheese pizza sat on the middle shelf. No sense letting good pizza go to waste, right? Or even bad pizza, for that matter.

I took the box out of the fridge, slid the slices onto a plate, and popped them into the microwave for sixty seconds. While they were heating, I wandered upstairs. I wasn't sure what I was looking for, but something compelled me. I stepped into Nick's bedroom and flipped on the light. His bed was unmade, still rumpled from our lovemaking the night before he disappeared into the underground.

I flopped down on the bed and grabbed the sheets, turning over a couple of times to wrap myself up in them like a protective cocoon. Nick's scent remained on the bedding, a crisp, cedarlike smell from his soap and shampoo, with a hint of boot leather. My heart twisted as if wrung by unseen hands. Would Nick and I ever spend another night together in this bed?

When I could take it no longer, I wriggled out of the sheets and went downstairs. I grabbed my pizza from the microwave along with a soda from the fridge and flopped down on Nick's couch. Three bites in I could no longer stomach the bombardment of male-targeted commercials. Viagra. Athlete's foot spray. Beer and more beer. I snatched the remote from the coffee table and dialed up a *Walking Dead* episode saved on his DVR. It promised to be a good one. Michonne, the badass chick with the sword, was out in the Georgia woods, ready to give any zombie who dared approach her what for. Though our weapons of choice were different, hers being a sword and mine being a gun, she was as good with her weapon as I was with mine. Yep, like Michonne, I would totally rule in a zombie apocalypse.

Most people would've likely been so disgusted by the show's gore they would have lost their appetite for pizza, but not me. I hadn't eaten since lunch and was starving. Besides, I had a strong stomach, developed from nearly three decades' exposure to my father's killer chili. Never mind that zombies tore into people on screen, that blood spewed from ragged bite wounds while the zombies chowed down on their victims' intestines, I dug right in.

When the pizza and soda were gone and at least three zombies had been decapitated, I turned off the TV, washed my plate in Nick's sink, and rinsed the soda can, adding it to the mail in the recycle bin. As I headed to the front door, something caught my eye. The samurai sword Nick had brought back from a recent investigation in Japan. He'd hung it, still enclosed in its engraved sheath, on the side wall of his entryway. Quick and easy access should a door-to-door solicitor become a little too pushy.

The sword seemed to be speaking to me. *El Cuchillo might have his sissy little knife,* it said, *but I'm a real blade, made for a real warrior.*

I'm not sure what drove me to take the sword down from the wall. Perhaps it was the overwhelming sense of vulnerability I felt with Nick gone. Or perhaps I just wanted to play zombie slayer. But, whatever the reason, the sword came home with me when I left Nick's place. For safety's sake, I stuck it in my bedroom closet, leaning it up against the custom red gun cabinet Nick had bought me for Valentine's Day.

Bright and early Saturday morning, I heard Alicia taking a shower in my guest bath, getting ready to head off to Martin & McGee. At least tax season was almost over. In two weeks April 15 would be here and she'd finally get to catch her breath. It was a good thing, too. She and her fiancé, Daniel, had a June wedding date and it was time for Alicia and me to start planning her bridal shower and bachelorette party.

My first impulse was to put my pillow over my head and try to go back to sleep, but Henry would have none of that. He climbed up onto my chest and gave me a couple of bitch slaps with his paw. The cat could be a real ass sometimes. Simba, the lion at Paradise Park, had less attitude.

"All right, all right," I told the darn cat, finally opening my eyes to glare at him. "I'll get up and feed you."

He stepped down from my chest, hopped off the bed, and took two steps toward my bedroom door before glancing back to make sure I was following. He twitched his bushy tail a couple of times as if to admonish me to hurry up, then traipsed into the hall. After a quick trip to my bathroom, I scooped up Anne and gave her a kiss on the head. "Time for breakfast, girl."

We headed downstairs to find Henry in the kitchen, standing in front of his bowl, scowling and swishing his tail back and forth. As I passed him, he reached out and swiped his claws across my bare ankle, drawing three thin strips of blood. Forget the zombie apocalypse. Housecats were far more dangerous than any undead human. *Domesticated, my ass.*

I stopped and pointed a finger down at Henry. "You are an ungrateful, spoiled brat."

He gave me a look that said, *No shit. Now quit bitching and get my breakfast.*

I sat Annie on the counter. Unsanitary, I know, but frankly I find people germs far more disgusting. Opening the pantry, I retrieved a can of gourmet cat food and scooped a cup of dry kibble from their bag. I divided the food between Henry's bowl and Anne's.

"Here you go, Henry. Bon appétit." Since he was nearly twice Anne's size, I gave him the lion's share. Of course thinking of lions made me think again of poor Simba, stuck back at that godforsaken hellhole of an animal sanctuary. I could only hope that my efforts to expose Paradise Park for the fraud it was would lead to better digs for the animals.

Henry dug in with gusto, eating noisily, while Anne slid down the cabinet to the floor, tiptoed over to her bowl, and began taking dainty little nibbles. With my cats now occupied with their breakfast, I set about preparing my own. Step one, coffee. Once the pot was brewing, I set the oven to preheat and pulled a roll of refrigerated cinnamon rolls and a bottle of hazelnut creamer out of the fridge. After I got the rolls into the oven, I sat down at the kitchen table with a cup of flavored coffee, my laptop, and my W-2 to prepare my tax return. Yep, I'm a procrastinator. What can I say? Preparing tax returns isn't nearly as much fun as chasing down tax evaders.

Twenty minutes later, my return was complete. I'd be receiving a $67 refund. Not a windfall, but nearly enough to cover a pair of designer sunglasses. I was getting damn tired of the cheap ones. They never seemed to last more than a day or two.

As I double-checked the return to make sure I hadn't missed anything, I found myself wondering how much longer my filing status would remain single. Would the day come when Nick and I would file a joint return together? Hear the pitter-patter of the little feet of our dependents as they ran up the hall to mommy and daddy's bedroom in the morning?

Beep-beep.

The timer went off on my oven, pulling me out of my reverie. I clicked the button to e-file my return and stood to tend to the breakfast.

Alicia strolled in as I was taking the cinnamon rolls out of the oven.

"Hey, stranger," I said. We'd hardly seen each other

in days. I was glad we'd have a chance to catch up this morning.

"Those rolls smell divine."

Though Alicia normally set trends when it came to style and fashion, this morning she wore a simple pair of jeans and a Texas Longhorns sweatshirt. Her platinum-blond hair hadn't been straightened, either, a sure sign she was running out of steam. But who could blame her? She'd been working twelve-hour days nonstop for the past two months. A person had only so much energy.

She aimed straight for the coffeepot and poured herself a steaming mug. "You're up early."

"Couldn't sleep," I told her. Despite the margaritas, I'd slept fitfully, my thoughts alternating between Nick and Christina, the softball victory, and my stack of pending cases.

"You wouldn't know it to look at you," she said, her gaze taking in my face. "Your skin looks amazing."

"I had a facial the other day. Glycolics or something."

She opened the fridge and pulled out the creamer. "So, hard time sleeping. Still worried about Nick?"

"Yes, and I will be until he's back home, safe and sound."

She slid into a seat at the table while I set the rolls on a plate and frosted them. I carried the plate to the table and set it between us to share. We each grabbed a roll and dug in.

I swallowed my bite. "Guess who I ran into the other day?" Before even giving her a chance to respond, I answered my own question. "Brett."

"Oh." She eyed me as if trying to gauge how I felt about the situation.

"And Fiona."

Now she cringed. "Awkward."

"It gets better." I ripped another frosted piece from the roll. "She was wearing an engagement ring."

Alicia's brows rose in surprise. "That was awfully quick, wasn't it?"

I held up a hand. "Wait. It gets *even* better." I shoved the bite of roll into my mouth and spoke around it. "She's *pregnant*."

Alicia set her coffee mug back on the table. "Whoa. That had to be *beyond* awkward."

"Totally." I swallowed the second bite. "It was embarrassing to be there alone. Brett bought me dessert. I think he felt a little guilty or sorry for me or something. He told me about the engagement and the baby and then he asked about Nick and . . ." I shrugged, letting my shoulders finish the sentence for me.

She watched me intently for a moment. "You and Nick will get there, too. You just need more time."

"I'm not in a hurry," I said, and I meant it. Not a *big* hurry anyway. Still, I'd have liked to know for certain that we were headed in that direction. I couldn't imagine anything coming between me and Nick, but it would be nice to have a crystal ball and be able to see for sure that we'd end up together. Then again, Nick had been engaged before, to a pretty schoolteacher who'd taken good care of him. Heck, she even *cooked* for him on a regular basis. Nonetheless, he'd broken things off before they made it to the altar. He'd told me she was overbearing, treated him like a child, and that he simply couldn't take it anymore. But had there been more to it? Had Nick not been ready to settle down then? Would he be ready soon? *Or ever?*

I slugged back a big chug of coffee. *No.* I couldn't let myself get all paranoid. Nick being gone had just made me overly anxious. He wouldn't have moved into a rental on my street if he were afraid of getting too close, right?

Of course not. He and I were soul mates. We were meant to be together. No doubt about it. Right?

Alicia finished her cinnamon roll and poured the rest of her coffee into a travel mug, adding some hot coffee from the pot to fill it to the brim. "I'm off to work. *Again*. Darn tax returns. Darn IRS."

She offered me a teasing grin and I offered her a sympathetic smile. "See ya."

As I watched her grab her purse and head out the door, a sense of loneliness and melancholy seized me. I felt as if I were losing everyone who meant anything to me. Nick was gone indefinitely. Alicia worked such long hours we'd hardly seen each other lately, and once she got married two months from now I'd see her even less. Christina was gone, too, off working the case with Nick. She, too, was engaged, though she and Ajay had yet to set a date. I was beginning to feel like the odd man out. Or odd woman.

But no sense throwing myself a pity party. What would that accomplish?

The rest of the morning was occupied with mopping, dishes, and toilet scrubbing, the trifecta of disinfecting. Once these tasks were completed, I dusted, vacuumed up what seemed to be an inordinate amount of cat hair, and picked up the clutter strewn about the house. I even spent an hour weeding my long-neglected flower beds.

Though I planned to engage in more yard work at Nick's mother's house, I couldn't very well show up already covered in sweat and grime. After a shower and blow-dry, I pulled my hair up into an easy ponytail that would keep my locks out of my face. I threw on a pair of jeans, tennis shoes, and a long-sleeved tee, and drove over to see Bonnie and Daffodil, stopping on the way to buy yet another cheap pair of sunglasses. I got this wraparound pair at a convenience store. They made me look like a cross between the Terminator and Geordi La Forge from *Star Trek: The Next Generation*.

As I climbed out of my car in Bonnie's driveway, the curtains in the front window moved. Daffodil's nose emerged from between the panels as she peeked out to see who dared invade her protected territory. She sounded the alarm, alerting Bonnie to my arrival. *Arf! Arf-arf! Arf-arf-arf!*

Bonnie had the door open before I even reached the porch. "Good morning!" she called. "I hope you're ready to work hard, because I've got ten weeds per square foot out back."

"Hard work'll do me good," I said. I hadn't been to the gym since Nick left, and last night's softball game, most of which I spent sitting on the bench, could hardly qualify as a workout. I could use the exercise.

We headed out back, Daffodil trotting along beside us.

"Here." Bonnie promptly armed me with some type of odd-looking weed-digging device with multiple metal reels and something on the end that resembled a bayonet. "I ordered this from the TV."

I looked the thing over. "How does it work?"

"Heck if I know," she said. "I was hoping you could figure it out and show me."

I spent a minute or two with the device, inadvertently digging several holes in her garden before finally mastering it. I had to admit it worked pretty well. In ten minutes I'd carried out death sentences on three dozen dandelions. No commuted capital punishments for these weeds.

As I passed the white cross in Bonnie's pea patch that marked Nutty's grave, I paused in silent tribute to the dog who was buried beneath it. Losing Nutty had broken Nick's heart. Though Nick would always mourn his first dog, Daffodil had helped Nick's heart mend. It was clear she'd grown as attached to him in the short time they'd been housemates as he'd become to her. She'd brought one of his old shirts with her when Nick had transported her here, and she was still carrying the thing around like a security blanket. She flopped down on the back patio, her face resting on the shirt, and emitted a long, lonely sigh.

I stepped over and stroked her back. "I'm right there with you, girl."

Bonnie and I worked for three hours. After we finished weeding, we prepared her garden for spring planting by pulling out the dead plants, tilling the soil, and adding several bags of stinky composted cow manure, a virtual shitload of shit.

The last thing I did was retrieve her trimmer from the garage. The grass around the perimeter of her yard needed some attention.

I plugged the extension cord into the outside wall outlet and set about my task. *Zzzt. Zzzzzzt. Zzzzzzzt.* As I drew close to her azalea bushes, I bent over to carefully guide the trimmer lest I damage the bushes. As I tilted my head, my wraparound sunglasses slid from my face. Before I could release the trigger on the trimmer handle— *zzzt-crackle-zzt*—the glasses had fallen into the path of the trimmer line and been pulverized. *Jeez.* This pair had lasted me only a matter of hours.

Our muscles tired and sore, Bonnie and I headed inside for a tall glass of peach sangria.

"How's this sound for dinner?" Bonnie handed me a three-month-old copy of *Better Homes and Gardens*. The magazine was opened to a page featuring a recipe for a fried tomato salad.

"Delicious."

While she retrieved the ingredients from her pantry and refrigerator, I flipped through the magazine, stopping to peruse an article on uses for a dead Christmas tree. One of the suggestions was to submerge it in a lake to provide an egg-laying area for bottom-feeding fish. I wondered if the Kuykendahls were aware of this useful little tidbit. It could come in handy in their fishing-guide business.

Three pages after the article was an ad for a feminine hygiene product that promised to keep users fresh as a daisy. The ad featured a photograph of a backyard covered in white and yellow daisies. Atop the daisies was a trampoline, and hovering over the trampoline—defying gravity like the witch from *Wicked*—was none other than Laurel Brandeis in her airborne, spread-eagle pose, proudly exhibiting her flower-fresh lady bits to the world.

Aha!

Now I knew why she'd looked so familiar when I'd seen her photograph on the bogus charity's Facebook page. Still, I found the ad a little overdone. It would take more than a feminine care product to get me so excited I'd leap into the air or spontaneously turn cartwheels. But Nick returning home from the cartel case unscathed? Heck, that would have me doing back handsprings.

I held up the magazine. "Mind if I tear out this ad?"

Bonnie's eyes blinked and a look of concern crossed her face. "Um . . . okay."

I glanced back at the ad, realizing she must have made some very embarrassing assumptions about my girly parts.

"Oh, no. It's not for me!" I said. "I mean . . ." I figured there was no better, and more convincing, way to explain things to her than to show her the Facebook page for the U.S. Red Cross. I retrieved my phone from my purse, pulled up the page, and showed her the image for Laurel Brandeis. "It's the same photo. See?"

"Why, it sure is!" Her surprised expression morphed into one of consternation. "Isn't that copyright infringement for the Web site to use the photo?"

"Good point," I said. If I caught this guy, I'd turn his information over to the Daisy Fresh Feminine Hygiene

Company and let their lawyers take a few swings at him, too.

While Daffodil lay on her bed in the corner and watched us, Bonnie and I worked side by side in her kitchen, slicing and breading the tomatoes, chopping three types of lettuce, dicing olives, and, of course, sipping peach sangria. Bonnie was an easygoing woman, and it was nice to spend time with her. I found myself imagining the two of us baking Christmas cookies along with a rug rat or two. In my daydream, Nick helped our children sprinkle green-colored sugar onto tree-shaped cookies, glancing up to give me a soft, loving smile.

Would it ever be?

If Nick survived the cartel investigation, my fantasies of familial bliss could be a real possibility, right? But if he didn't, I would be left with a broken heart and Bonnie would be left with only a sweet, furry dog.

I couldn't let that happen.

The only problem was, given that I had no idea where Nick was and what danger he might be in, what could I do about it?

Nothing. That's what.

chapter eighteen

*A*rt, Art Thou?

After leaving Bonnie's place, I swung back by my town house to clean up and change clothes for the gallery opening. I slipped into my go-to black dress and a pair of slingbacks. The beautiful ruby drop earrings Nick had given me adorned my ears.

When I finished, I took a look at myself in the mirror. Not bad. But not great, either. Knowing a group of artists were sure to be stylishly dressed, I didn't want to look too bland.

I wandered into my guest bedroom. Alicia was a master fashionista with a constantly changing and evolving wardrobe. I added to mine on a fairly regular basis, but I also tended to hang on to my favorite older pieces. Jeans in my closet had been with me since high school and had seen me through some very fun times. My old pair of ropers were hopelessly out of date now, too, though when Alicia had pointed that out to me I insisted the boots were "classic."

Alicia wouldn't mind if I raided her accessory drawer. She was always generous and willing to share, especially with her bestie. I pulled the drawer open and poked around.

A lime-green headband. *Nope.*

A whimsical female necktie in pale pink satin. *Nope.*

An infinity scarf in a red and white houndstooth check pattern. *Yep, that's the ticket.* The scarf would add some interest and texture, and would also tie in with my ruby earrings.

Fully accessorized and fashionable now, I gave each of my cats a kiss on the head, plucked their stray furs from my lipstick, and went out to my garage. I slid into my car, punched the button on the remote to open the door, and took off.

The gallery sat at the edge of the Bishop Arts District, an electric and thriving area in Oak Cliff, which was a few miles to the southwest of downtown. The district was known for its unusual boutiques, good restaurants, and its regularly scheduled wine crawls, where patrons could purchase an empty wine glass and have it filled with a different wine at each shop they chose to visit. By the end of the night, shoppers often found their wallets lighter, their arms laden with unique purchases, and their minds fuzzy from a blend of merlots, cabernets, and pinot noirs. I should know. I'd attended the crawls a time or two with Alicia. We always invited her old neighbor, a teetotaler who didn't mind being the designated driver, especially since we always sprung for her dinner.

The small lot at the converted church was full, so I had to take a spot at the curb on the next block, near the Dude, Sweet chocolate store. As I approached the church building, I gave it a thorough once-over. Though its steeple and colorful stained-glass windows made it readily apparent that the building had once been a house of God, the robin's-egg-blue exterior let passersby know those days had passed, its congregation having outgrown the relatively small space and moved on to a larger facility. An enormous white stone sculpture in the shape of a dragonfly sat at an angle in the small side yard, a lush bed of kudzu sprawling beneath it.

The night was fresh and cool, and a number of the gallery patrons had spilled onto the front steps with their champagne and hors d'oeuvres. As I approached the open double doors, the sounds of chatter, laughter, and harp music drifted out into the night. The people here were happy, having a good time. None of them had to worry whether their boyfriend was currently being sliced, diced, or filleted by El Cuchillo.

As I stepped inside the building, a waiter with flutes of champagne on a tray approached me. "Would you like some champagne?"

"Don't mind if I do." I accepted a glass and gave him a polite nod.

Drink in hand, I ventured through the shallow foyer and into the more open space of what had at one time been the church sanctuary.

Now this is what an art gallery should be.

The perimeter walls featured painting after drawing after mosaic, spaced far enough apart to enable patrons to assess each piece individually, yet close enough to make good use of the available wall space. Six movable, hinged, zigzagging walls were set up in the center, providing more display space for the works. Pedestals, set off with velvet ropes, featured three-dimensional pieces and sculptures.

Though many of the pieces here could be considered modern, the artists' skill and talents were obvious, even to my untrained eye. The choices of color, shading, shape, material, and texture implied a sense of purpose and direction and theme and mood.

I wandered past the harpist, giving the woman a smile to let her know I appreciated the beautiful music she was making, before moving on. On the raised platform at the front of the church stood three tables loaded with appetizers and finger foods for the crowd to enjoy. Though I'd eaten the delicious salad at Bonnie's house, it would be silly not to sample some of the offerings here, wouldn't it? I eased my way through the crowd to the front of the room and filled a plate with fruits, cheeses, spinach-filled pastry puffs, and more.

A loud, high-pitched titter drew my attention to my right. Aly Pelham, whom I recognized from her photos online, stood with a small group of people. She was every bit as polished and eye-catching as she'd looked in her pictures. Her sleeveless tangerine dress cascaded over her tall, curvy form like water over rocks. Her bleached-blond hair was swept up in an elegant twist, revealing dark roots and a pair of spiraling silver earrings dangling from her ears. The silver color was repeated in her five-inch heels. An enormous diamond nearly the size of a football graced her ring finger.

Behind her stood a man who could only be Rodney Fowler. He looked just like his mother, only with shorter, darker hair tinged here and there with gray. He wore a classic black suit, white dress shirt, no tie. His expression was bored yet tolerant. It seemed clear he was here only to indulge his much younger bride-to-be.

I meandered closer, drawing near enough to eavesdrop on the conversation and observe the couple with more scrutiny. Aly laughed a little too loudly at the others' jokes, leaned in a little too close when they spoke, exclaimed a little too loudly in response to their comments, reached out to touch them a little too often. Truth be told, it was a little hard to watch. She was trying too hard to fit in with the other artists, working too hard to earn their respect, almost as if she knew she wasn't really one of them. The harder she tried, the quicker the others slipped away to join other conversations.

"You must let me show you my exhibit at the Unic,"

she told a woman who'd begun to edge away from the group. "I can arrange for a private viewing. You will absolutely love it!"

"Wonderful," the woman said without conviction. "I'll be in touch."

When Aly's group had dwindled and she was glancing around for a conversation to horn in on, I sidled up to her. "Hello, Ms. Pelham, Mr. Fowler. I'm Special Agent Tara Holloway, from the IRS."

Rodney stepped up closer behind his fiancée in a protective gesture. "What are you doing here?" It was more an accusation than a question.

"Just enjoying the art." I lifted my plate. "And these cheesy, puffy things." *Seriously, what's in these yummy hors d'oeuvres? Crack?*

Rodney looked around for a moment. "It's entirely inappropriate of you to accost us in public like this."

"I'm not accosting anyone," I said. But given that his knickers were already in a twist, I figured I might as well ask them a question or two, see if I could obtain some information. Without waiting for a response from Rodney, I turned to Aly. "You seem to be more interested in art than Rodney. Was it your idea to create the Unic?"

Aly's eyes grew wide and her lashes fluttered. She looked from me, to Rodney, then back to me. "Well, we—"

Before she could finish speaking, Rodney put a hand on her shoulder to silence her. "We don't have to answer your questions."

"That's true." Everyone had the right to claim Fifth Amendment protection, after all. "But if you give me a little information now, I might not have to take your deposition later."

I knew to them I was coming off as an overbearing agent, but truly I was trying to keep this situation more casual and congenial, if such a thing was possible. My case wasn't on entirely solid footing and I knew that. If they'd just give a little, we might be able to reach some type of acceptable compromise. Frankly, I was damn tired of all of my cases ending in shootouts or explosions or fistfights. "So, would you like to tell me now how the Unic got its start?"

Before Aly could get a word out, Rodney answered for her. "We came up with the idea together."

"That's very nice," I said. I looked at Aly again. "I'd love to hear more about your art. What projects are you working on now?"

Her eyelashes fluttered again. "I . . . I haven't done much lately. My muse seems to . . . have taken a long vacation."

"Like writer's block?" I asked. "Or the artistic equivalent?"

"Exactly. That's why I go to events like this, to look for inspiration and be among my fellow artists."

I supposed the muse thing made sense. But if someone truly wanted to make a creative field their profession, didn't they have to hunt down their muse and drag her back, kicking and screaming, if she failed to show up?

At that point, I honestly had no idea what else to ask them that might be helpful. There was one thing, however, that I was curious about. "What do you think the purpose of art is, Ms. Pelham?"

She blinked again, her expression bewildered, as if she'd never considered this critical question. "The purpose of art?"

"Right," I said. "Is it supposed to be a means of personal expression for the artist? To send a message to those who see it? To make us think or feel? To simply give us something pretty to decorate our houses with? Or is it something else entirely?"

She tilted her head, as if considering my words. "I guess art is supposed to connect us with other people somehow."

Not a bad answer. The art I'd most enjoyed were the pieces I could somehow relate to, like *Life's Compost*. Maybe Aly wasn't a total fraud. Maybe she was just insecure and lazy.

"Thanks for speaking with me," I told them. "I'm leaving now. Enjoy the rest of your evening."

I felt their stares bore into my back as I made my way to the door.

chapter nineteen

$\mathcal{M}$istakeout

On my drive home from the gallery, I decided to swing by the apartment complex near Town East Mall where Terrence Motley had gone after picking up the backpack from the Waffle House. Maybe he'd show up again tonight. If I could figure out which unit Motley went into, I could pass that information along to Nick. After all, the more information I could gather, the quicker the DEA could resolve the cartel case, right? And if there was anything I wanted, it was a quick resolution. With my nerves on edge and my mind constantly consumed with worry, it felt as if Nick had been gone forever, the seconds passing like centuries. Honestly, I wasn't sure how much more I could take.

I waited at the curb fifty yards from the entrance until a car turned into the complex. Hurriedly, I started my engine and drove up behind the other car, staying close on its tail as it went through the open gate. I hoped my behavior wouldn't seem suspicious. When Alicia and I had lived at a gated apartment complex after college, people regularly followed other cars through the gate and nobody thought twice about it. As big as the complex was, this kind of thing probably happened all the time.

Having made it through, I circled the parking lot, looking for the pickup but not spotting it, before I settled on a parking space near the exit. From that vantage point, I could keep an eye on the entire lot, plus execute a quick getaway if needed. Throwing my gearshift into reverse, I backed into the space and cut my engine.

I'd been sitting in the dimly lit lot for an hour, keeping a lookout for Motley's truck and watching a romantic comedy on my phone, when my eyelids and head began to feel heavy. Between working virtually nonstop on my cases and not getting enough good sleep, I was beyond tired. Still, I couldn't afford to take the power nap I craved. If I sat out here and missed Motley, my efforts would be for naught, and Nick and Christina would have to spend even more time undercover with the cartel.

I couldn't let that happen.

I *wouldn't* let that happen.

I blinked, performed a dozen seated jumping jacks to get my blood moving, and slapped my own face for good measure. *Ow!* That ought to keep me awake for a while. But just in case things went awry, I set the timer on my phone to go off in fifteen minutes.

Things went awry.

Despite my efforts to stay awake, a thick mental fog rolled in. My head nodded forward, snapped back, and nodded forward again.

Rap-rap-rap.

I jerked awake. *What the heck?*

Glancing frantically around me, I spotted a man in lounge pants and a T-shirt standing next to my car window. When our eyes met, he made a motion for me to roll the window down.

"I'm the onsite property manager," he said. "I got a report that someone was sleeping in the lot."

Looked like *I* was that someone.

"Sorry." I offered him a smile. "It's been a long week."

He glanced at my window. "You don't have a parking decal. Are you a resident?"

Damn.

"No."

"Then what are you doing out here?"

Think quick, Tara. "My . . . uh . . . ex owes me over twenty grand in child support." *Nice lie. Good for me!* "I thought I saw his truck pull in here the other day, so I came back to see if I could find him. He moves all the time. You know, trying to stay one step ahead of me and the process servers."

"A deadbeat dad, huh? What's his name?"

"If I tell you, are you going to tip him off?"

"Hell, no. My father still owes my mom years of back support. If I can help you out, I will."

Thank goodness. "His name's Terrence Motley." I spelled it out for him. "M-O-T-L-E-Y."

"The name Motley doesn't ring a bell," the guy said, shaking his head. "But this is a big place and we've got people moving in and out all the time. Let me take a look at our official tenant list to be sure." He pulled a cell phone from his pocket, tapped the screen a few times, and swiped his finger upward, apparently looking over the list. He shook his head a second time. "There's no Motley on a lease here. Of course he could be shacking up with another tenant. People do that all the time. The tenants are supposed to notify us if they get a new roommate but not all of them do."

"Thanks for checking. Okay if I wait out here a little longer, see if he shows up?"

"Sorry," he said. "The woman who reported you is a total pain in the ass. If you don't leave, she's liable to call the cops and report you for trespassing."

Damn busybody. "All right." I sat up straighter in my seat. "I'll go now, turn the matter over to my attorney."

"Good idea." He backed away from the car. "And good luck."

With one last nod his way, I started the engine, drove to the exit, and left the complex, the gate clanging shut behind me.

At five A.M. Sunday morning, the secret cell phone played its rumba tune, waking me once again. I grabbed it off my dresser, opened it, and croaked, "Hey."

"Sorry to wake you," Nick said, sounding hurried. "What do you have for me?"

I'd left my notes right next to the phone. Sitting up, I turned on my lamp. "The guy in the Toyota went to the Waffle House on Jupiter Road. He set a backpack on the floor and left it behind after he paid his bill."

"You could see that from the parking lot?"

I didn't want Nick to get angry with me, but I didn't want to lie to him, either. "I went inside."

"Dammit, Tara! I told you to stay in your car! These thugs make the dealers in *Breaking Bad* look like characters from *Barney*."

"It was safe. There were a bunch of people inside. Besides, I figured I'd look more suspicious if I was sitting in the lot in my car."

"You weren't supposed to do that, either! You were just supposed to see where the Toyota went."

I exhaled a huff. "You can punish me when you get back if you'd like."

"I just might do that."

I explained that the backpack was picked up by a tall white guy. "He drove a pickup." I gave Nick the pickup's plates. "The truck's registered to a Terrence Motley. He's got two convictions for marijuana possession. I followed him to an apartment complex near Town East Mall." I gave Nick the address of the complex, neglecting to mention my aborted stakeout last night. No sense getting him all riled up over nothing. "The complex is gated so I couldn't tell which unit he went into. But I wasn't the only one following him."

"Are you saying he had another tail?" Nick's voice held surprise.

"Yep. Two men in a Dodge Avenger." I rattled off the license plate number. "The car's registered to a Carlos Uvalde with a San Antonio address. His driver's license data matches the car registration. He's got priors for selling heroin and assaulting a cop."

Nick was quiet a moment, probably processing the information and making notes. "Thanks, Tara. This gives us a couple of new leads."

"Good."

"But I'm still going to punish you."

"I'm counting on it." Hell, I was looking forward to it.

chapter twenty

*H*old the Onion

First thing at work Monday morning, I brushed the fallen rose petals off my desk and added some water to the vase to give the waning flowers a fresh drink. The second thing I did was venture back to Josh's office for an update on the e-mail phishing case. If he'd been able to track down the computer from which the e-mails had been sent, that would go a long way in helping us identify and catch the culprit or culprits.

I stepped into his doorway. "Hey, Josh."

He gestured for me to come inside and take a seat. "Word around the water cooler is that you hit a home run Friday night."

"Yep. I credit Nick's lucky bat." And a burst of motivation fueled by my desire to see El Cuchillo vanquished. I plunked myself down in a chair. "Speaking of luck, did you have any?"

"Oh, I've had lots of luck. All of it bad." Josh slid frustrated fingers into his curls. "I couldn't track the e-mails to their source. Whoever sent them used an onion router."

"An onion router?" *What the heck is that?* I knew my way around guns and could disassemble, clean, and reassemble one with my eyes closed, but where technology was concerned I was a total cavewoman. When my eyes glazed over and drool pooled in the corner of my mouth, Josh realized further explanation was necessary.

"An onion router is a program that sends online communications through multiple, unrelated channels in order to mask its original source."

Huh?

When the glaze and drool did not cease, Josh worked up an analogy to see if that would make things more clear for me. "It's like when a money launderer doesn't want to leave a paper trail and shuffles cash through multiple accounts. Or when someone wants to travel to a foreign country but doesn't want anyone to track him so he makes stops along the way, changes planes and airlines, maybe transfers to a bus or train or hires a private car service to throw pursuers off track."

The glaze cleared and the drool dried. "Okay. I get it now. But what does this mean?"

"It means we're dealing with a tech expert," Josh said. "And it means we're going to have to go about this the hard way."

"Dang." I much preferred the easy way, when a criminal was an amateur or so dumb or arrogant that he made stupid mistakes, underestimated our ability to catch him, and virtually fell into our laps. "Any idea where we should go from here?"

Josh stared ahead for a moment in thought. Finally, he turned his gaze my way. "I guess we could try to figure out how the thief obtained the victims' e-mail addresses."

He spent another moment in apparent thought, this time

staring straight up at the ceiling. Hey, whatever works, right?

He lowered his head and looked back to me. "Maybe the person works for some local company that collects e-mail addresses from its customers," he said. "Stores are always asking for e-mails to send promotions."

I could attest to that. E-mails informing me of one sale or another constantly crowded my inbox.

"Let's say the thief works at a store that collects e-mails from its customers," I said, thinking out loud now. "How would the thief tie the e-mail address to a mailing address? Hardly anybody pays with checks anymore, and there's no way to glean a customer's address from a credit or debit card."

"That's true," Josh conceded. "But what about those store loyalty cards?"

I knew all about those, too. My wallet contained approximate 362 of the stupid things.

"When a person fills out the application for the loyalty card," he continued, "the form asks for both a mailing address and an e-mail address."

"That's right." Hope began to bubble up inside me. "If we can find a common link among the victims, some place that had all of their e-mail and home addresses, maybe we can find our culprit."

Josh just as quickly burst my bubble. "Maybe. Maybe not. Say we figured out that all of the victims had a particular grocery store card. In order to figure out who might have used the information in the phishing scam, we'd have to figure out who all at the store had access to the card records. There'd probably be dozens of people who'd have access, both at the local store and the corporate headquarters offices. Unless one of them confessed, how could we determine who it might be? Besides, for all we know the stores might even sell their mailing lists. Nobody reads the fine print on those applications. It probably gives the store the right to sell the data to other businesses."

Ugh. "And it might have been someone at one of those other businesses who ran the scam."

"Exactly."

I looked out Josh's window as if looking for a solution, a way to move ahead with this case. The only thing I saw was a pigeon dropping a purple load on the windowsill. Someone must have shared a blueberry muffin with the bird this morning. I turned back to Josh. "Got any other ideas?"

He raised his palms. "It's easy to harvest information online. There's a good chance the thief found the victims' e-mail addresses along with their mailing addresses somewhere on the Internet. You can find all kinds of stuff like that on the Web. Businesses give contact information for their staff. Organizations post their membership lists online without implementing proper security protocols to limit access." He motioned for me to come around his desk.

I stood and stepped around beside him.

He angled his monitor so that both of us could see the screen. "Watch. I bet I can get Nick's personal e-mail and home address in less than a minute."

I pulled out my phone and started the stopwatch feature. "Okay. Go."

Josh typed Nick's name in quotation marks, along with the words "Dallas," "e-mail address," and "home address." I'd hardly had time to take another glance out the window before Josh proclaimed his work, "Done."

I stopped the timer. In a mere seventeen seconds, Josh had pulled up a screen listing the members of my neighborhood homeowner's association, along with contact information for tenants who lived in the rental units. Nick's home address, along with his e-mail, were right there for the whole world to see. So were mine.

Josh's expression grew smug. "That's what happens when people are too cheap to hire professional Web-masters."

I expelled a long, frustrated sigh. I'd hoped this case would be a slam dunk. Instead, it looked like we'd be chasing down rabbit trails.

Wait a second . . .

What if instead of chasing after rabbits, we could dangle a carrot and get the rabbit to come to us?

"What if we send a response to his e-mail?" I asked. "We know this guy's MO. We could provide some fake information and nail him when he goes to the bank to withdraw the funds."

"That could work." Josh's eyes gleamed. He had a box full of high-tech spy gadgets and fancied himself some type of secret agent. *James Treasury Bond.*

I could probably handle the stakeout of the bank by myself, but it was clear Josh wanted to be included. What fun is it to work on a case if you can't be part of the final bust?

We pulled some documentation from the file. Several people who had received the suspicious e-mail had realized it was a scam, contacted the IRS, and provided copies of the communication.

Josh put his hands to his keyboard. "I'll create a fake e-mail address that looks like one of the ones the thief contacted. Give me one from the file, either a Yahoo or Gmail account."

I looked over the documentation. One of those who'd recognized the e-mail for the con it was had been Thelma Puckett, a ninety-two-year-old great-grandmother whose e-mail address was grannytpuckett@yahoo.com.

"Here's one," I said, handing him the printout.

"Shouldn't we use a man's information?" Josh asked. "You said the bad guy is a *guy,* right?"

"Yeah," I said, "but where's the fun in that? Let's make him dress up like an old lady to make the withdrawal. It'll be fun to drag his ass off to jail in a gray wig, reading glasses, and a flowered housedress."

"All right." Josh simply added an *s* to the end of Granny Puckett's e-mail address, making it grannytpucketts@ yahoo.com. Chances were the thief wouldn't pay that much attention. Josh copied the text of the e-mail the culprit had sent, and pasted it into an e-mail addressed to our target so that our response would look legit. "What bank should we use?"

I performed some quick research on my phone and determined that Farmers Bank and Trust had a single location in Dallas, and that it was less than three miles from the Daniel Cemetery.

"Use this bank," I said, holding up my phone so Josh could read the information from the screen.

While I called Farmers Bank and Trust to determine their routing number, Josh typed in the name of the bank and made up a fake account number. As I repeated the routing number to the clerk on the phone, Josh typed that in, too.

"Thanks." I ended the call and turned back to Josh.

"What do you want to use for her social security number?" he asked.

"April fifteenth is tax day, so how about 415 for the first three numbers." I glanced down at my phone. "Eight for *t,* as in Tara. Five for *j,* as in Josh. Then end with 1040, like the tax form."

Josh typed in the fake number, 415-85-1040, and hit send. "When are you going to stake out the bank?"

Per the information in the file, the thief normally made

the phony withdrawals only two to three days after receiving information from a victim. He must have realized that he needed to work fast, before the victims could realize they'd been duped and close their bank accounts.

"Wednesday morning." I glanced again at my phone. "Their drive-thru opens at seven-thirty. Meet me there. I'll bring coffee."

"Make mine hot chocolate."

Some James Bond, huh?

chapter twenty-one

*L*unch with the Lobo

Lu peeked into my office around noon, catching me fingering a limp petal on one of the roses Nick had sent me. "You're a pitiful sight." She motioned with her hand. "Come on, lonely girl. I'm taking you to lunch. My treat."

"Okay." Maybe I should look pitiful more often.

I grabbed my purse and followed Lu down the hall. After she rounded up her handbag, we headed downstairs in the elevator and traversed the crowded lobby.

"What's your pleasure?" Lu asked as we stepped out onto the sidewalk.

"How about the Zodiac at Neiman Marcus?" I suggested.

"Good idea," Lu said. "I'm almost out of eye shadow. I can pick some up at the cosmetic counter after we eat."

Neiman's probably hadn't carried Lu's shade of bright blue eye shadow since the 1970s, but no sense pointing that out to her.

After we'd been seated and placed our food orders, I took a sip of my tea. "How are things with Carl?"

Lu had met her boyfriend several months ago via an

online dating service. While Carl's odd comb-over hairstyle, polyester leisure suits, and white bucks left something to be desired, the guy was as nice as they come. And he was clearly crazy about Lu, doting on her nonstop.

"I'm thinking about getting back on that dating site, seeing if there's some fresh pickings."

"Why?" I asked. "You and Carl seem so happy together."

"We are," she said, her orange lips puckering. "But it's getting too serious, moving too fast."

"Too serious? Too fast?" How could that be? It's not like they were high school kids. Heck, they were both in their sixties.

She plucked the lemon wedge from her glass and squeezed a few drops of juice into her tea. "He's starting to make noises about making our relationship permanent."

"Permanent? You mean *marriage*?"

She nodded, her towering pink beehive quivering atop her head. "I'm not interested in washing a man's dirty drawers and cooking him dinner. I did that for my husband for more than three decades, God rest his soul." She looked up and raised a hand as if bidding her deceased hubby hello in the hereafter.

"Many men do their own laundry these days," I said. "Some of them even cook."

"Even so," she said, shrugging, "I just want to have fun. Sow some wild oats."

The only thing most women Lu's age would be doing with oats was baking oatmeal cookies for their grandchildren. But I supposed I couldn't fault the Lobo for wanting to maintain her freedom. I'd hate to see *her* end up the lonely girl, though.

She eyed me intently, her eyes narrowing, her upper and lower false eyelashes gathering to form a thick black fringe. "What about you and Nick? Any talk about tying the knot?"

Heat rushed up my neck to my cheeks. "Nick and I aren't ready to talk about that yet."

Lu harrumphed. "You might not be ready to talk about it, but that blush on your face tells me you've *thought* about it."

I have. More than I want to admit. "Of course I have." I tried to sound nonchalant. "It's only natural for a woman my age to think about it. But just because I don't want to waste my time playing around anymore doesn't mean I'm ready to settle down just yet."

I wasn't, was I? I mean, I couldn't visualize myself ending up with anyone but Nick. He'd been the only guy I'd ever dated who truly understood me and accepted me as I was, tolerating my many annoying habits and hopeless imperfections with little complaint. But could I visualize the two of us sharing housekeeping duties? A bathroom? A closet? Maybe. But the visualization was still a faint pastel, a light watercolor, a paint-by-numbers that had yet to be fully completed.

"I understand where you're coming from." Lu tossed her head one way then the other. "'Course Nick may be a little gun-shy, too, after what happened with his first engagement."

Nick had been engaged years ago to a schoolteacher named Natalie. It hadn't ended well. But surely he wouldn't let their history affect our relationship, would he? After all, Natalie had been rigid and controlling and high-maintenance, like a Mercedes-Benz. I was the exact opposite, the Volkswagen Bug of girlfriends. But just because I didn't have a ring on my finger didn't mean our relationship wasn't solid, did it?

My concerns must have been written on my face because Lu said, "You might have your doubts, Tara, but none of the rest of us do. Hell, we've got a pool going."

My mouth fell open. "You do?"

"Mm-hm. If you've got a ring on your finger by the end of summer, I'll win five hundred bucks."

"Does Nick know about this?"

She offered a sly smile. "He put fifty bucks on September."

Whoa. September was only five months away. While that might seem like a long time from now, Nick and I had only begun dating late last fall and would have yet to complete a full year together by then. Still, like Lu and Carl, Nick and I were hardly children. Besides, as coworkers in addition to romantic partners, our time together had been much more intensive than the typical relationship. We'd been through so much together in such a short time. I'd helped him escape his forced exile in Mexico and together we'd taken down a man running a fraudulent cross-border financial enterprise. We'd gone on to bust a minister who'd fleeced his church and its congregants, a gun nut running a taxidermy and tax-processing outfit, a scumbag running a drug and prostitution ring, and an international criminal ring importing counterfeit electronics, pharmaceuticals, and weapons. We'd survived multiple physical attacks by our targets, emerging battered and broken yet stronger and wiser. And we'd done all of it together, watching each other's backs, sharing the load. It seemed only right that we'd watch each other's backs and share the load on a personal level, too. Right?

When I could gather my cartwheeling wits I rolled my eyes. "Marriage is the least of my concerns right now," I said, though the statement wasn't entirely true and Lu probably knew it. "I just hope Nick comes back *alive.*"

"You and me both, Tara," Lu said as the waitress set her plate down in front of her. "You and me both."

Suddenly I had no appetite.

So much for this lunch cheering me up.

Several bites into her meal, Lu noticed I wasn't eating.

She stretched a hand across the table and patted mine. "Don't worry about Nick. That boy will be fine. He's smart and he's strong. Ain't nobody going to whoop his ass."

I didn't point out the fact that just minutes before she'd expressed concern about his safety and was now contradicting herself. Frankly, I liked this more confident approach. "I hope you're right."

She narrowed her eyes at me. "I'm *always* right. Haven't you learned that by now?"

I raised my hands in surrender. "That you are."

"If I were you," she said, pointing at me with her fork, "I'd head over to the lingerie department and buy a little something special for when Nick gets back. An athletic guy like him, with all those muscles, he's gotta be great in bed."

I raised my hands again, this time to stop her. "I am not discussing my sex life with my boss."

"Well, damn," she said, slumping back in her seat. "This conversation was just getting interesting."

Twenty minutes later, we left the restaurant and headed to the cosmetics counter.

A thirtyish woman with flawless makeup stepped up on the inside of the counter. "May I help you, ladies?"

"Sure can," Lu replied, plunking herself down on one of the stools. "I need some new eye shadow." She closed her eyes and pointed to her blue lids. "Got anything this color?"

The woman cut a glance my way. What could I do but raise my palms?

"We're out of that particular shade," the clerk said politely, "but I can fix you up with something else in a cool tone. Why don't we try a few colors and see what you think?"

Lu opened her eyes and frowned. "I've been wearing this shade all my life. I doubt you'll be able to do better."

"Let's just try, shall we?" The woman proceeded to pull several samples out from under the counter.

Ten minutes and fifteen samples later, the clerk and I had managed to talk Lu into trying a soft mauve that was far more up to date than her usual color. That was as far as she'd go, however. Her bright orange lipstick and clown-ish pink rouge were here to stay.

chapter twenty-two

*A*ppraisal

Yesterday, after having lunch with Lu, I'd sent the fictitious Laurel Brandeis a friend request on Facebook. When I checked my computer on Tuesday morning, I discovered she had accepted my request. *Good.* That put me one step closer to catching the Facecrook.

I typed up a quick message to her.

> *You're the Laurel Brandeis I went to summer church camp with in 1999, right? I think we were in crafts class together. I'm a bookkeeper now in Texas but I do missionary work when I can. How have you been?*

I sent the message, hoping the crook wouldn't see through my ruse. It sounded realistic enough, didn't it? I hoped so.

I spent the rest of the morning wrapping up some paperwork on other, smaller cases. At one o'clock, Eddie and I headed out of the office for a quick lunch. Afterward, we drove to the Unic. We found a parking spot

around the corner, and waited on the front sidewalk for
Eddie's children's teacher to arrive.

"There she is." Eddie lifted his chin in indication.

A white Corolla had pulled to the curb half a block
down. A thin woman with wavy black hair climbed out
of the car. She wore a fitted gray dress with high-heeled
boots and chunky, square jewelry. She looked chic, sophis-
ticated, classy, and artsy. *Perfect.*

Eddie greeted her as she approached, holding out his
hand. "Thanks for your help, Mrs. Windsor."

She shook his hand. "Happy to advise." She turned to
shake mine. "Alexandra Windsor."

"Special Agent Tara Holloway," I said.

The three of us headed inside. Josette looked up from
her desk, her smile fading when she recognized me and
Eddie. "You are back, I see." Her gaze moved to Alexandra, assessing, before returning to me. "You would like
three tickets?"

"We're on official business today," I said. "We don't
need tickets."

I didn't wait for her to object. Instead, I headed into the
exhibit space with Eddie and Alexandra following behind.
The *click-clack* of Alexandra's boot heels echoed in the
room as we made our way in.

I handed her the brochure I'd kept from our last visit.
"This will tell you a little about the pieces and the artists."

She took the pamphlet from me and continued on,
stopping at the first exhibit. She studied the canvas for a
moment or two, read the entry regarding the piece in
the brochure, then looked up at the ceiling. "There's no
light on this piece."

Given that the canvas was blank, what did it matter?
There wouldn't be any more to see if it were illuminated.

My question must have been written on my face,

because Alexandra said, "Museums and galleries typi-cally light the work in some way. It's odd that there's not any special fixtures in here."

I looked up and noted that she was right. The space con-tained only standard light fixtures placed at even intervals.

I watched Alexandra as she eyed *Picking at Scabs.* Her nose twitched in disgust. "The artist seemed to be going for shock value here. It's a cheap way to get attention, in my opinion."

She moved on to *Bad Hair Day,* an amused smile play-ing about her lips as her eyes took it in. "Now this one I can relate to."

"The artist who painted this is engaged to the direc-tor's son," I said, keeping my voice low so that Josette, who was keeping an eagle eye on us from her desk, couldn't overhear our conversation.

"Hmm." Alexandra tapped a finger on her lips as she considered this information. "I do see some expertise with the color in this piece, though."

"She trained in fashion design."

"That would explain it," she said.

As we continued around the museum, Sharla Fowler emerged from her office, no doubt summoned by Josette. She walked briskly toward us, not quite storming but right on the brink.

"Josette tells me you refused to pay for tickets," she spat. "Need I call the police?"

Really, didn't people realize it was stupid to piss off the IRS agents investigating them? Her overly aggressive demeanor was beginning to chap my ass.

"Need we return with a search warrant?" I replied.

That shut her up.

Sharla turned to Alexandra. "Who are you?"

Alexandra offered a quick bio. "I am a former curator of the Guggenheim, a SCAD graduate, and art instructor."

She offered a smile now, too. "My name's Alexandra Windsor."

"Alexandra Windsor," Sharla repeated, as if committing it to memory.

"I'm curious," Alexandra said to Sharla. "How often do you change the exhibits here?"

"We've had the same exhibit since the Unic's inception." Sharla's eyes narrowed. "We are quite proud of the collection we put together."

Alexandra was unfazed by Sharla's behavior. Teaching schoolchildren and dealing with pushy parents undoubtedly made a person thick-skinned and unafraid of confrontation. "If the exhibit never changes, why would anyone come back?"

Apparently unable to cough up a valid explanation, Sharla chuffed in what was likely feigned indignation. "I refuse to put up with these boorish insults." She spun on her heel and returned to her office, slamming the door so hard behind her it was a miracle the glass didn't shatter.

Alexandra turned to me and Eddie. "Do the people you investigate act like that very often?"

"All the time." I shrugged. "Sometimes they even shoot at us. You learn to live with it."

We continued about our business. While Alexandra merely raised a brow at the fan, vacuum, and hair dryer, she laughed outright at the macaroni mosaic upstairs. "It looks like a child made this."

"That's because a child *did* make it." I told her how I'd found Hunter's birth certificate via my online research system. "The Unic paid Hunter forty grand for the piece."

"Ridiculous," Alexandra said, adding an eye roll for emphasis.

My thoughts exactly.

She moved over to the coffin and the syringe rocket. "Wow," she said. "These are fascinating. I can definitely see some talent here. Also a dedication to the work. It would've taken hours and hours to glue all those pills to the coffin."

When we'd navigated the entire space, the three of us nodded good-bye to Josette and stepped outside.

"What do you think?" Eddie asked Alexandra.

Her lips formed a slight frown. "Some of the pieces were quite good. Intriguing. But others? They belong on a fridge, not in an art museum." She straightened her scarf. "Would you like a complete appraisal, or has today served your purposes?"

Eddie and I engaged in a brief discussion, deciding to hold off on an appraisal for now. No sense spending tax-payer dollars on something we might not need.

"Thanks so much for your help," I said, shaking her hand again.

"My pleasure."

Alexandra bid us good-bye and returned to her car. Eddie and I likewise headed to mine.

Once we were seated inside, I reviewed the evidence. "Okay. We know Sharla is way overpaid given that she only works part-time. The payment to Hunter was clearly a sham. I think I can easily prove that. Probably the payment to Jackson, too."

I had my doubts whether any jury in Texas would consider air to be an art medium. If it were, that would mean anyone who burped or made armpit fart noises was creating art.

"But Alexandra thought the other art was the real deal." I mulled everything over another moment. "It's like they're cheating, but in a half-assed way."

I was used to my cases being black-and-white. Either someone was doing something wrong or they weren't. This case was more gray, at least where the women's art was concerned.

I turned to my partner. "Where do I go from here?"

Eddie had been an agent much longer than me and often served as my mentor. When I was in doubt about something, he was my go-to guy.

Though it was only half past three, Eddie tugged at the knot in his tie, apparently ready to call it a day. "Set an appointment with Sharla and Rodney Fowler," he advised. "Tell them to have their CPA or attorney present if they wish. Then negotiate."

"Okay. The payment to Hunter has to be reclassified as a gift, no question," I replied, expanding on Eddie's suggestion. "Same for Jackson. Rodney had no right to claim a charitable deduction for gifts to his family."

"Right," Eddie said, "so work up a figure for that. The payments to Aly Pelham will be your bargaining chip. Tell Rodney you won't reclassify the payments to Aly if they agree to pay tax on the others. Then tell Sharla she either needs to start earning her outrageous salary by running a real museum, keeping it open longer hours and changing the exhibits, or you'll treat her salary as a gift, too. If they don't meet you halfway, send Rodney a bill for the whole shebang. If he still doesn't pay, you'll have no choice but to see that criminal charges are filed."

"Good plan. Thanks, Eddie."

"Thank me by buying me a beer," he said, unbuttoning the top button of his dress shirt now. "It's close enough to quitting time."

chapter twenty-three

You Can Bank on It

At seven the next morning, I waited at the door of Farmers Bank and Trust in the moist morning air, my hair expanding like a sponge. The sun was just beginning to peek over the horizon, reminding me that I had yet to replace the sunglasses I'd inadvertently weed-whacked. A fiftyish woman in a pantsuit approached, eyeing me warily. Given that the bank wouldn't be open for business for another half hour, I couldn't blame her. For all she knew, I was here to rob the place.

"Are you the bank manager?" I asked.

"I am." She took the business card I held out and glanced down at it.

I extended my hand. "I'm Special Agent Tara Holloway with IRS Criminal Investigations. We're trying to catch an identity thief who's targeted several banks in the area. I'm hoping you and your staff might be able to help us."

"I'm glad law enforcement is doing something about this problem." She gave my hand a firm shake. "We'll certainly do what we can to help your investigation."

It was nice to have an ally. Most people weren't all that happy when the IRS showed up on their doorstep.

She dug around in her purse for her keys. "This kind of fraud costs us dearly, and frankly, I'm sick and tired of customers acting like it's our fault their bank account got emptied. Everyone knows they shouldn't share their personal information online. They're the ones who give away the key to the candy store."

I could see her point. Still, it was hard to fault the victims too much, especially in this case. The e-mail did look pretty darn convincing.

"My partner and I will be waiting in the parking lot." I handed her a copy of the reply e-mail Josh and I had sent to the con artist in which we purported to be Thelma Puckett. Pointing to the fictitious account number, I said, "When someone tries to make a withdrawal from this account, the teller needs to call me on my cell phone number immediately. The tellers also need to be very careful not to give the person any hint that something's up or they could blow the case."

The last thing we needed was to sit here all day, then have the thief become suspicious and make a quick getaway before we could follow him.

I wrapped up my directions. "After I've been notified, the teller should inform the person that the account is already overdrawn so the withdrawal can't be made."

The manager took the page from me and nodded. "I'll make sure all of the tellers receive proper instruction."

"Thanks."

While she unlocked the door to the bank, I returned to my car. I'd backed into a spot that faced the drive-thru lanes where I'd have a good vantage point on the activity. So as not to arouse the thief's suspicion, I put up an accordion-style reflective sunshade in the window that would hide me and Josh and make it look as if my car belonged to an employee and was parked for the day. I situated my cell phone in easy reach on the dashboard, ready to grab it when it rang.

I lowered my visor, took one look at my hair in the vanity mirror, and tried not to scream. Thanks to the morning moisture, it had grown even bigger and spongier than I'd expected. Whipping my comb from my purse, I did my best to stretch and flatten it back into place, but it stubbornly refused to cooperate. *Ugh.* Oh, well. It wasn't like I was running for beauty queen here. If anything, my kinky hair made me look more wild and tough. That could be an advantage when we took down the thief later.

I was halfway through my latte when—*rap-rap!*—Josh tapped on my passenger window. I pushed the button to unlock the door. "Howdy, pardner."

His baby-blue eyes went wide. "What happened to your hair?"

"Humidity." *Sheesh.* Way to make a girl feel good. No wonder it took him so long to lose his virginity.

He slid into the seat, plopping a small duffel bag onto his lap. "This is too early. The roosters haven't even crowed yet."

"Cock-a-doodle-doo," I sang. "Does that make you feel better?"

He cast me an irritated glance. "No."

"How about this?" I held up the large hot chocolate I'd ordered for him.

His face brightened. "Oh, goody! You got me a big one!"

Oh, goody? What a man-child.

Josh took the cup from me and proceeded to drain half its contents in one long gulp.

I gestured to the bag on his lap. "What's in there?"

"Some gear that might come in handy." He plunked his drink back into the cup holder and pulled a bunch of spy cameras from the bag. A small teddy bear, standard nanny-cam fare. Another tiny camera made to look like a ball-point pen. Another hidden inside a wristwatch. A fourth in a decoy smoke alarm. He also had a model built into a key-chain remote and another inside a fully functioning flash drive.

"What's the plan?" I asked.

"I figured I'd situate one of these on top of the box for the canister vacuum so we can get a better look at the thief. We can take video and pictures, too. For evidence."

I looked over the selections. "The bear's too obvious," I said. "Besides, somebody might pick it up and carry it off. The smoke alarm would look out of place outside. With the pen, the watch, and the flash drive, there's the risk that somebody will take it, too. They might keep it for them-selves, or they might try to turn it in to the bank. Got any-thing else?"

"No." Josh scowled.

I could hardly blame him. I'd pooped all over his party. I thought for a moment, then snapped my fingers. "I've got an idea."

I reached into my purse, pulled out a pack of gum, and proceeded to shove five sticks into my mouth. When the wad was soft and pliable, I pulled it out of my mouth, grabbed the pen off Josh's lap, and laid it on the wad. I squeezed until the gum surrounded the pen. "See? It'll just look like some jackass vandalized the machine. Nobody will pick the pen up if it's covered in gum."

Josh cringed. "That's disgusting."

"No. It's clever."

"It's disgusting *and* clever."

"Conceded."

Climbing back out of the car, Josh and I trotted over to the last drive-thru lane. I laid the gum-engulfed pen on top of the box, aiming the camera lens so that it would look directly into the driver's window.

Josh tapped the screen of his tablet. "I need to check the live feed. Go stand where the car would be."

While Josh looked down at his screen to make sure the live signal was functioning, I took a few steps to the right, positioning myself in the drive-thru lane. "How's it look?"

He held up his tablet to show me. I could see myself clearly on the screen which, given that I'd downed a twenty-ounce latte and had energy to spare, meant I had to do some dance moves. I started with the classic John Travolta *Saturday Night Fever* finger point, segued into moves from the Michael Jackson *Thriller* music video, and wrapped up with some *Napoleon Dynamite* maneuvers.

Josh merely cast me a look, turned, and walked away. *Now whose party is being pooped on?*

I followed him back to the car. "Could you get me one of those antiseptic wipes from the glove compartment?"

Josh opened the glove box, retrieved a wrapped wipe, and tossed it to me. I used my teeth to tear the foil packet open, pulled out the wipe, and cleaned my sticky hand.

We took our seats once again, making small talk as we sat there. In the narrow space between the window shade and the edge of the windshield, I noticed the green lights come on over the drive-thru lanes. My eyes checked the clock on my dash. *Seven-thirty. Right on time.* The bank manager ran an efficient ship.

Though I'd started this stakeout early to ensure we didn't miss the thief, I didn't really expect him to show up until the afternoon. The records in the file indicated he'd made all of his previous withdrawals between two and four P.M. Still, criminals weren't exactly reliable. Better to spend some extra hours in the car than to miss him entirely. Besides, Josh and I could take turns watching the video feed while getting other work done on our computers.

Josh took a potty break at nine-thirty, and I followed suit once he returned, spending the rest of the morning squinting against the sun as I watched the drive-thru lanes. At noon, my stomach began to rumble.

"Hungry?" I asked my partner.

"I could eat," Josh replied.

I glanced out the car window to see what lunch options were in walking distance. There was a Taco Bell, a Burger King, and a Hooters.

"I'll buy us some lunch." I gestured out the window. "What sounds good? Burritos or burgers?"

Josh's gaze locked on the Hooters sign. "I'm in the mood for wings. I'll go get them since you bought the coffee this morning."

Wings didn't sound appetizing to me at all. The thought of chicken bones reminded me of that filthy, fly-covered grill at Paradise Park.

Before I could argue, Josh had hopped out of the car. I unrolled my window. "Bring me a Cobb salad!" I called after him. "With ranch dressing!"

He didn't return for nearly an hour. Judging from the smudges of sauce on his cheek, he'd decided to eat at the restaurant rather than bring his wings back to the car. The salad he handed me was warm and soggy, but I chose not to complain. It had taken the guy a decade and a half longer than anyone else to reach puberty. I couldn't fault him too much for wanting to eat inside and ogle the girls in their tiny orange shorts and tight T-shirts.

My tummy now full, I fought the urge to close my eyes and take a nap in the warm car. *Focus, Tara,* I admonished myself, forcing my eyes to stay open and lock on the feed on the tablet. I watched as a minivan drove through.

A Passat. A Scion. A short, skinny guy on a Harley that looked too big for him.

A couple of hours later, the screen provided a partial view of a dark pickup pulling up behind the Prius currently in the farthest of the drive-thru lanes. I watched while the middle-aged woman in the Prius finished her transaction, slid her car into gear, and pulled out of the lane. The truck edged forward, its driver coming into sight.

Bingo.

The person at the wheel wore a gaudy floral shirt, enormous round-lens sunglasses that covered half his face, and what was clearly a mop head on top of his skull. Obviously, he'd made only a half-assed effort at disguising himself. Then again, with all the success the criminal had enjoyed so far, he'd probably grown lax, thinking the withdrawal was in the bag. *Idiot.* The only thing about to be bagged was *him.*

I nudged Josh, who had dozed off in his seat, spilling drool tinged with barbecue sauce down his chin. "Wake up, buddy. Our thief is here."

Josh came to, sitting up and wiping his chin on his sleeve. "The thief? Are you sure?"

I pointed at the screen. "Take a look for yourself."

Josh pushed some buttons on his tablet and zoomed in on the face in the truck window. "That is one ugly grandma."

With the huge glasses and mop-wig, it was difficult to tell the man's age or what he might look like without the getup. About the only thing I could tell for certain was that granny had an Adam's apple and a five o'clock shadow. Perhaps granny should consider hormone treatments.

We watched as the man stretched an arm out the truck's open window, removed the plastic canister from the machine, and opened it, sliding the withdrawal slip inside. The buzz of a pending bust began to tingle inside me. If he thought he'd be driving away with several hundred dollars, he'd be sorely disappointed.

The vacuum sucked the canister up through the tube. Sure enough, not ten seconds later, my cell phone rang.

I jabbed the button to accept the call. "Special Agent Holloway."

"Hi," came a female voice. "We've got a customer in the far lane who just sent a withdrawal slip for the account you referenced."

"Thanks," I told the woman. "I've got him in my sights. You'll tell him the account is overdrawn?"

"Right," she said. "That's what our manager told us to do."

We ended the call, and I carefully removed the sunshade from my windshield and started my car, ready to follow the truck as soon as he pulled away. Josh and I continued to watch the zoomed image on the tablet. Though the pen had no audio and we couldn't hear their interaction, it was easy to follow what was going on. The guy's mouth turned down in a frown as the teller told him she couldn't honor his withdrawal request. He said something back that, not being a lip reader, I couldn't decipher. He then rolled up his window, banged a hand on his steering wheel, and mouthed a word that was unmistakable.

Fuck.

"Think you're going to rip off Granny Pucketts?" I let loose a laugh. "Not on my watch, buddy."

Neener-neener.

chapter twenty-four

$\mathcal{I}$t's All Greek to Me

The guy punched the gas and pulled out of the drive-thru with a squeal of his tires. *Screee!*

I pulled out of my parking spot and began to follow him, holding back half a block so he wouldn't get suspicious.

A quarter mile down the road, he pulled into the parking lot of a grocery store. He stopped the car in a remote area beyond the scope of the security cameras mounted on the front of the building. Josh and I drove on, pulling into a spot between two cars closer to the store. I reached into my purse and whipped out the old pair of field glasses I'd sponged off my father.

As I watched, the guy yanked the mop off his head. He climbed out of the truck, reached behind the seat, and pulled out two license plates and a screwdriver. He proceeded to screw one plate onto the front bumper, the other on the back.

Josh squinted through the windshield. "Is he putting license plates on the truck?"

"Yep. Write the number down for me."

As I rattled off the numbers, Josh typed them into his

notes app on his tablet. I had him repeat the license number back to me to make sure we got it right.

When the guy climbed back into his truck, I eased out of the space to continue following him. Not an easy task. Once he'd cleared the parking lot, he drove like a rabid bat out of hell, weaving in and out of traffic, nearly clipping a mother in a minivan and tailgating another truck until that driver turned, holding his middle finger up out of the window.

"Hurry up!" Josh said as we approached a light turning yellow. "You'll lose him!"

I floored the gas and went through the intersection just as the light cycled to red.

Despite my best efforts, the thief continued to move farther and farther away. He turned down Airline Road and made his way past the Daniel Cemetery I'd earlier identified as the center of his criminal realm. When he made a left two blocks later near the Southern Methodist University campus, a gaggle of coeds stepped into the street right in front of my car, forcing me to hit the brakes and make a quick stop. Not only were they lucky I hadn't run them over, they were also taking their merry time to cross.

"Hurry up!" I shouted, giving a tap on my horn. *Honk.*

The girls took my honk as their cue to cast me nasty looks and move even slower. One even looked right at me through the windshield and mouthed the word "bitch." Exasperated, I yanked the wheel and pulled up onto the sidewalk to get around them. Not exactly exemplary driving behavior but, hey, it's not like Dallas PD would issue me a ticket.

By the time I could make the turn, the truck was nowhere to be seen.

Now it was my turn to bang on my steering wheel. "Dammit!"

"We've got the plate," Josh reminded me. "I can run it and figure out who the truck belongs to."

As I cruised down the block, my eyes peeled for the truck, Josh looked up the information on our DMV search link.

When he'd obtained the information, he relayed it to me. "According to the DMV, the truck belongs to a Thomas Peabody who lives in Longview."

Longview? The town lay two hours' drive east of Dallas. Would someone drive all this way to make bogus withdrawals? Maybe I'd been wrong to assume the crook lived here in the city.

"Check Peabody's driver's license information," I suggested. It was possible that Peabody had recently moved to Dallas but failed to update his car registration.

Josh ran that search next. "His driver's license gives the same address in Longview."

"What else does it tell us?"

"Peabody was born in nineteen sixty-eight. Brown hair, green eyes. Weighs a hundred and sixty pounds."

My eyes continued to scan the parking lots and street for the truck. "Check to see if he's got a criminal record."

Josh ran a search through the criminal information clearinghouse. "No record."

Crap. Crap, crap cra—*Wait. Is that the truck parked in front of that frat house?*

I hadn't been in a sorority, though I'd attended a number of open frat parties during my days at UT. Still, I'd been out of college too long to remember the Greek alphabet. What were those letters? Was that a phi? A thi? A chi? A beta? A theta? A zeta? Oh, well. I supposed it didn't really matter.

I pointed to the house, which in typical SMU fashion, was traditional red brick with tall white columns. "That's the truck, right? In front of that frat house?"

Josh looked at the plates to confirm. "That's the one."

I put two and two together and hoped it would lead to four. "You think Thomas Peabody had a son who lives in the frat house?"

It would make sense, after all. Parents often put a car in their own name, even when they purchased the car for their children. I doubted Thomas Peabody himself was living here. Even if he was one of those students who changed his major fifty times and only took six hours of classes per semester, he'd probably have earned a degree by now. Besides, even if Peabody had joined the frat years ago, I doubted the fraternity rules would allow a man in his upper forties to live in the house. Plus, he was the right age to have a kid in college.

"Want me to check the vital records?" Josh asked. "See if Thomas Peabody has a son?"

"Or we could just go to the door and find out." That sounded like a better idea to me. It would be much more efficient. Besides, I was dang tired of sitting in this car and would have loved to stretch my legs.

We exited my car and walked to the door. After knocking five times and getting no answer, I tried the handle. The door was unlocked.

I swung the door open and stuck my head inside. While the outside of the house had been decently maintained, the inside seemed more like a typical bachelor pad. Or should I say *bachelors'* pad? Like Kevin Kuykendahl's truck, the place smelled like beer and urine, though the frat house also had an overlay of bacon, pizza, and pine-scented sanitizer.

"Hello?" I called. "Anybody home?"

A young man in jeans came up the hall, a backpack slung casually over one shoulder, a cell phone in his hand. His T-shirt featured a bastardized cartoon of a *My Little Pony* character rearing up to show off his enormous equine genitalia. Under the image were the words WILD PONY PARTY '14.

"Hi," I said as the boy approached. "Can you tell me who owns the black truck parked out here?"

The boy took a glance out the door. "That's Peabody's."

"He got a first name?"

"Devon."

The boy attempted to squeeze past me to get out the door, but I put a hand on his arm to stop him.

"Could you get him for me?"

"I'm late for class. You can go on up. His room's on the second floor. Third door."

I released the boy and he made his way out the door, past Josh, and down the steps with a bouncing gait.

The rules regarding search and seizure allowed an agent to search a residence or business if the owner or resident agreed. Although the boy who just left could not legally give me permission to search any bedroom other than his own, I figured that since the common areas were shared his invitation for me to go inside would legally allow me into the foyer and hallways.

I waved Josh inside. To the right of the foyer was a large, open room with a couple of worn, stained couches pushed up against the walls. To the left of the foyer was a set of stairs. We took them up to the second floor, and made our way to Peabody's room. I rapped loudly on the door.

A groggy, froggy voice came from inside. "Come back later. I'm sleeping."

"Hi, Devon," I said. "Can I talk to you?"

He hesitated a moment, probably trying to identify my voice.

"Who is it?" He sounded slightly more awake now.

"Tara." No sense giving him my last name or adding my title of special agent and risk him jumping out his

window to escape. Though it felt good to stretch my legs,
I wasn't in the mood for a foot chase.

A moment later the door opened. A beefy boy stood
there, a vacuous expression on his face. His dark blond
hair was flat on one side, unruly on the other, in typical
bed-head fashion. He wore only a jockstrap and a pink
plastic clothespin on one nipple.

"Ouch." I gestured to the clothespin. "That's going to
be one hell of a purple nurple."

Devon looked down and issued a grunt. "Looks like I
had even more fun last night than I remember." He removed
the plastic clothespin, tossed it over his shoulder, and proceeded to rub his bruised nipple.

I exchanged glances with Josh. Given Devon's state of
undress and barely conscious brain, he couldn't be the man
who'd attempted to make the withdrawal at the bank. But
surely he could tell us who was, right?

"I was told by another boy that you own that black truck
outside," I said.

"Yeah? What about it?"

His defensive tone told me that he might not be forthcoming with the information if he realized I planned to
bust his friend.

"Um . . ." I racked my brain, trying to come up with
an excuse to be here asking about his truck. "I just saw
the guy driving it and followed him here. And, well . . ."

Well, *what,* Tara? I tried to rewind my brain by several
years and access the girl I'd been back in my college days.

"I think he's the same guy I met in a bar a couple of
weeks ago. He asked me to call him but I lost his number.
I'd sure like to see him again. We really connected." I
hoped that excuse sounded plausible.

Devon simply stared at me. "What was that guy's
name?"

"Um . . . I don't remember that, either." I took a cue

from him, rolling my eyes and faking a giggle. "It was a crazy night."

Devon tugged on the waistband of the jockstrap and let it go with a snap. "I don't remember anyone saying they hooked up with a cougar."

A cougar! I was only in my late twenties, hardly old enough to qualify as a cougar. But given that I was dressed in work clothes, I probably looked a lot more mature than the college girls. At least that's what I told myself. I sure as hell didn't want to admit I was beginning to age.

"Look," I said, my patience running thin. "Can you just tell me who's been driving your truck?"

Another tug, another snap. "Hell, I don't know," he said. "I leave my keys right here." He opened the door farther, showing me a hook on the wall just inside the door with a set of keys hanging from it. "The guys just come and borrow the truck when they need to move things or whatever."

I was tempted to ask whether his parents knew he was lending his truck out willy-nilly, but that was a mature, adult thing to say. It would get me nowhere and would raise his suspicions that I wasn't the love-struck bar-hopper I claimed to be.

Devon cocked his head. "What did the guy look like?"

"Brown hair," I said. "A little bit of beard stubble." A paltry amount, really, when compared to those crazy-eyed Kuykendahls. "Average height."

"Brown hair? Average height?" He grunted again. "That doesn't really narrow it down much."

Damn. He had a point. I wasn't sure I'd be able to identify the thief even if he was standing right in front of me. "He mentioned something about being into computers," I said, assuming anyone who'd be able to pull off the phishing scam and use that onion router thingy Josh mentioned had to be a computer geek. "Does that help?"

"Not really." Tug, snap! "Everybody around here's got computers and laptops."

Turning my head, I glanced down the hall. There appeared to be five rooms on this floor, and there were likely just as many on the third floor. I didn't have probable cause to go into all of the rooms, yet I still didn't know which one belonged to the driver. Walking down the hall and knocking on doors would likely get me thrown out. If any of these boys figured out I was law enforcement, they'd surely demand that Josh and I leave. With all the hazing pranks and underage drinking that went on at frat houses, these boys learned quickly how to keep cops out of their hair, demanding to see search warrants before they'd let law enforcement officers inside. It was also possible that the driver was a member of the frat, but lived elsewhere. He might have returned the truck and left the house.

I was trying to figure out where to go next with my questions, when—tug, snap!—Devon solved the problem for me.

"We're having an open party here Friday night," he said. "Classic toga theme. All the guys will be here. Why don't you come back then?"

Why not, indeed?

chapter twenty-five

Come Out, Come Out, Wherever You Are

On the drive back to the office, I zipped into a car wash, hoping the place might sell sunglasses along with the pine-scented air fresheners and polishing cloths. With all the squinting I'd been doing all day, it was a wonder my eyeballs hadn't popped out of their sockets. I was in luck. A display on the counter by the register offered six or seven styles, though all were in standard black or brown. The sunglasses were even on sale, two pairs for twelve bucks. I selected a black pair with large, round lenses, along with a brown rectangular pair. As many pairs as I'd gone through lately, I figured it couldn't hurt to double up.

"Need any oil?" the male clerk asked. "Maybe some wiper fluid?"

"Nope," I replied. "Just the sunglasses."

He rang up my purchase, I swiped my debit card, typed in my PIN, and was on my merry way.

After Josh and I returned to the office Wednesday afternoon, Eddie stopped by my office.

"I cashed in that lottery ticket." He held out a twenty-dollar bill and five singles. "Here's your share."

"Thanks, buddy." I took the bills from him. As soon as my schedule slowed down—if it *ever* slowed down—I'd swing by the Brighton store and treat myself to the designer pair of sunglasses I'd earned.

As Eddie left the room, an idea popped into my mind. I hopped onto Facebook and typed up a post.

Woo-hoo! I just won $15K in the lottery! This is my chance to do some real good. Trying to decide which charity I should donate the proceeds to. I'm considering an animal sanctuary, but I'm not sure. Anyone have a suggestion?

I hit the enter button and the post popped up on my page for all the world, *and especially the daisy-fresh "Laurel Brandeis," whoever she really was,* to see. I hoped Laurel would come to me with the suggestion that I donate the proceeds to the nonexistent U.S. Red Cross. If that didn't work, I'd approach the U.S. Red Cross directly via a Facebook message. I didn't want to go that route unless I had to, though. The more direct I was, the more likely the Facecrook was to become suspicious. It would be much better if I could lie low, subtly draw the bad guy out of his cyber hidey-hole.

I stayed late at the office that night, ordering dinner in for myself and the night watchman perched on his lonely stool in the building's lobby. Josh had downloaded the video clip of the thief at the bank. As I ate, I watched it all the way through five times, freezing it several times to take a closer look at the young man. No matter how closely I looked, though, no distinguishing characteristics popped out. All of his features were proportional and average-sized. No scars. No birthmarks. No tattoos that I could see. Straight teeth.

Remembering Josh's earlier point about organizations posting membership rosters online, I Googled the address of the frat house and learned that it belonged to Gamma Gamma Theta. Logging on to the fraternity's Web site, I was able to search by school and find the SMU chapter's roster. Sure enough, it included not only a list of the members' names but also a color headshot of each boy.

My eyes slowly made their way down the column of photos. The first photo depicted a white guy with brown hair. He was a definite *maybe*. The next photo was an African-American guy. *Nope*. The third was another white guy with brown hair. Another *maybe*. White guy with blond hair. *Nope*. Another white guy with brown hair. *Maybe*.

The problem was, any guy who belonged to a frat came from a family with enough money to fix things like oversized noses or crooked teeth. You know, the things that made people unique and identifiable and even interesting. Seriously, these frat rats might as well be clones.

Nonetheless, I continued on down the list, past Devon Peabody. When I'd reached the end of the listings, I had only eight *nopes* and thirty-two *maybes*. Not a good ratio. So much for the process of elimination.

Since I'd gone as far as I could on the phishing case for now, I moved on to the Unic case. It took me until eleven P.M. to work up the numbers, but once I'd computed taxes, interest, and penalties, Rodney Fowler would owe over a hundred grand on the payments made to Jackson, Hunter, and Aly. Being in the highest tax bracket sure did suck when you got hit with an underpayment. I added another line showing the additional ninety grand that would be owed if Sharla's salary were adjusted downward to the average for directors of art museums. I'd found the salary data online. *Seriously, what did people do before the Internet?*

I typed up a cover letter to go with the spreadsheet I'd drafted. In the cover letter, I noted that, per our professional art consultant with the fancy degree and Guggenheim pedigree, the Unic did not quack like the duck it purported to be. If the Unic didn't want to lose its tax exemption, it had ninety days in which to start quacking. In other words, it needed to buy more art pieces, rotate its exhibits, and serve as more than just a tax-exempt space in which Aly Pelham could throw parties and Sharla Fowler could plan her next vacation. Yawning, I e-mailed a copy of the letter and spreadsheet to Rodney and Sharla, then dropped another copy in the mail to each of them as per IRS policy.

I raised a hand to the security guard as I exited the building. "Good night, Gordon."

"Stay safe, Agent Holloway!" he called, raising his hand as well. "And thanks again for dinner."

I woke Thursday morning and did what I'd done first thing every morning since Nick had gone undercover. I checked the secret phone for a message.

Nothing.

The screen was blank.

My heart slumped inside my chest. They say sometimes that no news is good news, but such was definitely not the case here. No news was definitely *bad* news. At worst, it meant that Nick was dead. At best, it meant that Nick was so imbedded with the bad guys that he couldn't find a moment of privacy to contact me. The thought that he was working so closely with El Cuchillo made my blood freeze in my veins. If El Cuchillo wanted to lick my blood off his knife, he'd have a plasma Popsicle.

I went into the bathroom and took a look at myself in the mirror. *Urk*. Big mistake. Whatever good the glycolic treatment had done had since been undone by stress and worry. The bags under my eyes were back, carrying their own second set of bags. The worry lines on my forehead were so deep and pronounced it looked like my eyebrows were playing a skin accordion. Poor Nick. If he came back, he'd come back to *this*? I decided then and there to schedule another glycolic treatment. Maybe I'd buy some of those teeth-whitening strips, too. With all the coffee I'd been drinking lately to fuel my late hours, my teeth had lost their sparkle.

After cleaning out the litter box and picking up the stray turds Henry had kicked across the bathroom floor, I took a shower, fixed my hair, and dressed for work. Downstairs, I set the coffee to brewing and fed my cats. Anne expressed her appreciation for the meal by performing figure eights around my ankles, while Henry expressed his disdain by sniffing the wet food, flicking his tail to indicate his disgust, and waltzing off.

"You'll be back!" I called after him.

I fixed myself a bowl of Fruity Pebbles and decided to take it into the living room so I could catch up on local and world events by watching the morning news. I'd been so busy lately I hadn't had time to glance at a newspaper or watch TV. Finagling the remote out from between two couch cushions, I clicked on the television and plopped down on the sofa.

A handsome male anchor filled the screen. "In international news this morning, the bodies of three people who disappeared in the Mexican city of Culiacán last month have been found in shallow graves twenty miles outside the city. Though the bodies were largely decomposed, medical examiners were able to determine from marks on the victims' bones that the throats of all three had been slit. All three victims were suspected members of the Sinaloa drug cartel, which has experienced a power vacuum since the arrest of its leader in early 2014. Mexican police believe the killings were carried out by a well-known member of the cartel known as El Cuchillo."

My cereal stuck in my throat, refusing to go down. My hands shook so violently that milk sloshed over the edge of the bowl and onto my pants, the sofa, and rug. I forced the cereal down, set the bowl on the coffee table, and put my head between my legs, trying not to hyperventilate.

If El Cuchillo had no qualms about slitting the throats of fellow members of the cartel, what would he do if he suspected Nick and Christina were undercover agents out to nail him? That Alejandro, his trusted ally, had double-crossed him? I didn't even want to consider the possibilities.

Thankfully, before my mind could go too far down that horrific trail, a buzz sounded from the coffee table. *Bzzz.*

The secret phone!

I grabbed the device from the table. My heart soared when my eyes took in a text.

Hope to see you soon. XO.

What?

See me soon?

Was that Nick's way of telling me they'd made quick progress on the case and he'd be returning shortly? Dare I hope that was the case?

Though it was only seven A.M., I immediately phoned Bonnie and gave her the news.

"'See you soon,'" she repeated. "Do you think that means he's coming home?"

"I don't know," I said. "I hope so."

To be honest, I was afraid to get my hopes too high lest they be dashed. And the last thing I wanted to do was give Bonnie false hope. If something went wrong, it would only be that much harder to take.

"These investigations can change on a dime, though," I cautioned. "You might think you're making progress, then *bam,* you hit a wall."

"My, aren't you a killjoy?" she snapped.

I hated to be negative, and I hated to renege on my promise to Nick that I would remain strong for his mother, but anything could happen. We should hope for the best but expect the worst. We had to be prepared for anything.

"I'm sorry," I replied. "I'm just trying to be realistic."

"I know, honey." She sounded deflated now, which made me feel guilty. "I shouldn't have snapped at you. I'm sorry about that. I just—" Her voice broke and it nearly broke my heart. "I want my boy home."

Tears rimmed my eyes. "I want him home, too."

Hell, I didn't just *want* him home, I *needed* him home.

Despite my attempts to maintain my independence in our relationship, I realized then that I'd become dependent on Nick in so many ways. While my parents had once been my rocks, that role had shifted to Nick over the past few months. He was the person I counted on to be there for me no matter what crazy things were going on in my life. He provided me with an emotional release, letting me vent on him like an active volcano. While I used to take my problems to Alicia, since she'd become engaged to Daniel I'd done so less and less, instead taking those problems to Nick. On a more base level, when the stress of my job and life in general needed an outlet, Nick provided me with a physical release. The stair-stepper at the Y was a poor substitute, though it did provide a similar up-and-down motion and used many of the same muscle groups, such as my quads and glutes.

The epiphany that I needed Nick in my life made me feel vulnerable and frightened and alone and incomplete. He was no longer simply my favorite toy and a sexy accessory, he was as vital to me as one of my organs. Not a kidney, though, because apparently a person can live with only one of those. He was more like a heart or a liver, something you only have one of and will certainly perish without.

Ugh. The thought of organs led me back to El Cuchillo and the numerous victims he'd gutted. What kind of person could kill with a blade like that? I'd been forced to shoot people before, but firing a gun at a human target from a distance was much less personal than shoving a blade into another human being at point-blank range while looking them in the eye. Besides, even when I'd fired my gun previously, I was a good enough shot to know that none of the bullets would be lethal. Pulling a trigger was much easier when you knew it would only stop someone temporarily, not end their life.

I did my best to force those disturbing thoughts from my head as I bid Bonnie good-bye. As soon as we ended our call, I texted Ajay and told him I'd heard from Nick. Ajay texted me back in less than ten seconds.

Thanks. When they get back let's do something special.

My first thought was to get tickets for opening night of the Texas Rangers baseball season. Nick and Ajay would enjoy the game and the bratwurst, while Christina and I would enjoy the frozen strawberry margaritas. But opening day was next week. I doubted they'd be back by then.

Rather than suggest the baseball game, I simply typed back *Great idea.*

Though I parked in my usual spot in the federal lot, instead of heading into the Federal Building I trotted over to the Department of Justice to see if I could round up an attorney. Even if I went to the toga party Friday night, the chances of me recognizing the guy who'd dressed in the mop and flowery shirt at the bank were slim to none. After all, the photographs of the frat rats I'd reviewed online hadn't narrowed things down any. What was I supposed to do? Make my way around the party, sidle up to the guys and say, "Hi, I'm Tara. I'm a Sagittarius. Which one of you drunks is the A-hole who ripped off a bunch of people through a phishing scam?"

Not likely.

Fortunately, Ross O'Donnell, our usual counsel, was in his office. The stack of files on his desk was high enough to rival my own, though Ross never seemed to get flustered. He was either naturally calm or hooked on quaaludes. Given that he managed to get to work every day and successfully prosecute the majority of his cases, my money was on naturally calm.

I rapped on his door frame. "You busy?"

He glanced at his watch. "I've got to be at the courthouse in half an hour to argue a pretrial motion, but I've got time for a quick chat."

In other words, he'd appreciate it if I got right down to business.

"I need a search warrant." I gave him a fast rundown of the phishing case and how Josh and I had tracked the pickup truck to the frat house. "The thief might live in the frat house. We just don't know his name or which room is his."

Ross tilted his head one direction, then the other, as if tossing ideas back and forth in his mind. "It's going to be a hard sell. You know how Judge Trumbull is. But I'm willing to give it a shot. The worst she can do is say no, right?"

An hour later, Ross and I were standing in front of Judge Alice Trumbull, arguing why she, in her infinite judgely wisdom, should give me a search warrant for the Gamma

Gamma Theta house. Judge Trumbull was a diehard liberal, a leftist who'd engaged in war protests and bra-burning back in the 1960s. Though I knew she took her duties seriously and respected her for that, I had to admit that her refusal to rubber-stamp our requests made our jobs infinitely more difficult.

"I'm not asking to search the entire frat house," I told her, hoping to make my request appear limited in scope. "Just the bedrooms."

After all, the thief was likely to keep his computer and other evidence of the crime in his bedroom. I doubted he'd leave such things around in their common living area or kitchen.

"Just the bedrooms?" Judge Trumbull snorted, causing her loose jowls to jiggle. "Honey, there are numerous bedrooms in that house that belong to boys who are not under suspicion in this case. You're not even sure your target lives in the house. No way am I going to let you engage in an all-out panty raid. The IRS is not going to become the NSA, stomping on the rights of American citizens. You want a search warrant? Narrow down your list of suspects, determine where he resides, and give me more evidence."

Though I was tempted to stomp my foot and throw an all-out hissy fit, I knew it would do no good. Once Judge Trumbull made a decision, she didn't waffle. She banged her gavel—*bam!*—and called her next case.

I thanked Ross for making an effort and headed outside to walk back to my office. On the way, I thought things over some more. I'd attend the frat party tomorrow night. Not that I had high hopes anything would come of it, but what could it hurt? Besides, I needed some fun. And if going to the party didn't help me better identify my suspect, I could always try to draw the culprit out again, send him another fake bank account number, take a second stab at nabbing him.

Second stab. *Ugh*. Once again, I found myself thinking about El Cuchillo.

At the office later that morning, I followed my usual routine. Check my phone messages. Check my inbox. Log on to my computer and read my e-mails. There was one from my mother saying she and Dad couldn't wait to see me, along with a question from my father: *What gun is best for pretending to shoot a lion? I can't decide which rifle to bring.*

I sent a reply. *Bring them all. We'll look them over tomorrow and decide.*

Once I'd finished with my e-mails, I pulled up my Sara Galloway Facebook page.

Bingo.

Laurel Brandeis had sent me a personal message. *Congrats on winning the lottery! If I were you I would donate the money to the U.S. Red Cross. They help so many people.* Heck, she'd even sent me a link to the phony charity's page with instructions on how to make a donation.

But this little cat wasn't quite done playing with her mouse just yet. Besides, I had to act like a reasonable person would under the circumstances. If I'd actually won the lottery and was considering donating money to charity, I wouldn't necessarily donate the funds to the first charity someone suggested to me. I'd put some thought into the decision before making a move.

I sent Laurel a reply message. *Thanks for the suggestion. I'm leaning toward a local charity, though. My mother wants me to get a photo with someone from the organization to put in the newspaper back home. Mothers, huh? :)*

With any luck, that message would draw the crook out from his lair in cyberspace into the real world. And if and when it did, IRS Special Agent Tara Holloway would lower the boom.

chapter twenty-six

*Y*ou Win Some, You Lose Some, You Settle Some

Later that morning, my cell phone rang. My readout indicated the call came from Anthony Giacomo.

Anthony was a tough-as-nails attorney who, despite being only slightly bigger than me and dressing primarily in lavenders and soft pinks, could put the fear of God in his opposing counsel. His brain was so nimble it could perform a round-off back handspring triple flip and stick the landing every time.

I jabbed the button to take his call. "Hi, Anthony."

"Hi, yourself. You got lunch plans?"

"Nope."

"Well, you do now. What's your pleasure?"

"How about the Pyramid in the Fairmont Hotel?" The place was one of my favorites. It was quiet and private and served good food. They had a new kale and watercress salad, as well as a wedge salad. Perfect lunch choices. Yummy, but not so heavy they weighed you down for the rest of the day.

"Half an hour?" he asked.

"See you then."

I worked a few more minutes until I reached a good stopping point. I grabbed my purse and headed out the door. The Fairmont was only a short walk away. It felt good to get out into the crisp spring air and clear my head. It had been much too smoggy in my skull lately.

I pulled open the door to find Anthony waiting for me in the lobby. He looked as dapper as ever in a gray suit with a peacock-blue dress shirt and silvery tie with matching pocket square. His dark hair was perfectly coiffed and a sapphire gleamed from his earlobe.

He gave me a hug, then stood back, one hand on each of my shoulders. "I'd like to say you're looking well, but we both know that would be a lie. You look like something the cat dragged in. And then chewed on. And then coughed up. And then took a crap on."

I might have been offended if I didn't know he meant to express concern, not insult. "Things are a little tough right now." I forced a smile. "But it's great to see you."

He tsked. "Oh, you poor, naïve, innocent little soul."

"Excuse me?"

"This isn't a social call, my dear. I've been hired to represent the Unic Art Space and the Fifty-Yard Line Foundation."

Oooooh, shit.

Anthony Giacomo was someone you wanted on your side, not across the table. If I'd thought things were tough before, they'd be beyond tough now.

"Wait," I replied. "Isn't it a conflict of interest for you to represent them after you represented me?"

Anthony had recently saved my ass after I'd put several bullets in a target's leg and been brought up on felony excessive-force charges. He'd defended me in my criminal trial. Thank God he'd been successful. If it weren't for him, I might be sporting an orange jumpsuit today and eating lunch with my new prison girlfriend, Blunt Force Betty.

"It is a potential conflict," he agreed. "but I've informed the Fowlers of my former relationship with you and they were okay with it."

"Is that legal?"

"Of course. As long as the conflict is disclosed, a client can waive any objection. They know I'll fight as hard for them as I fought for you."

I knew it, too. *Damn.*

"Two?" the hostess asked, retrieving menus from her stand.

Anthony nodded and the woman led us to our table.

Anthony pulled out my chair like the gentleman he was, then took a seat across from me, opening the menu to peruse the options. "Order whatever you like," he said. "I'll pass all the costs onto my client."

"You're awful," I told him, at the same time eyeing the steak frites, the most expensive item on the menu. I supposed that made me awful, too. Still, as much as I'd like to stick it to the Fowlers, I couldn't. Agents were not permitted to be wined and dined by taxpayers they were investigating, nor by their attorneys.

The waiter arrived and took our drink orders. While I stuck with iced tea, Anthony asked for a double scotch.

When we were alone again, he shot me a pointed glance across the table. "You know I've never lost in court, right?"

I shot him a pointed look right back. "Neither have I."

"Touché."

As our drinks arrived, I took a sip of my tea, trying to figure out exactly where Anthony intended to go with this conversation.

After setting our drinks down, the waiter took my order and turned to Anthony. "What may I get you, sir?"

Anthony put a hand on his belly and eyed me across

the table. "Not sure what I'll have room for once I finish eating you alive."

"Ha-ha," I said. "You're a regular Eddie Murphy."

Chuckling, he held out his menu to the server. "I'll have the steak frites."

The waiter nodded, took the menu, and left.

Anthony tossed back a gulp of his drink and grimaced. "This stuff is liking drinking fire."

"Then why do you do it?"

He shrugged and grinned simultaneously. "Maybe I like the taste of fire."

I grabbed a roll from the basket the waiter had left on the table, slathered it in butter, and tore off a piece. "If I have surmised correctly, you brought me here to discuss a settlement?"

He winked at me. "You always were a smart cookie."

If I were a cookie, I'd be full of nuts.

He reached into the inside pocket of his suit jacket and retrieved a copy of the e-mail I'd sent to Sharla and Rodney Fowler the night before. He held it up. "These are some mighty big numbers. My goodness! They even have commas."

"I don't deal in decimals," I replied. "My time is too valuable."

"I know that's right." He set the papers on the table and sat back in his chair, crossing his arms over his chest. "Lay out your case for me."

"Why don't you lay out your defense?" I knew from both experience and training that the first to speak in a negotiation often ended up at a disadvantage, inadvertently disclosing too much or suggesting settlement terms without first getting a good read on their opponent. Of course if this case went to court the IRS would have the burden of proof and thus would have to set out all its evidence and arguments. But I wasn't about to let Anthony know

I'd be willing to waive the taxes on the payments to Aly and the part of Sharla's salary deemed excessive if he'd agree to the rest of the demand. I knew there was no guarantee the IRS would win if the issue were tried before a jury. Although the number I'd used in preparing my spreadsheet had been an average, compensation for museum directors varied widely and a number of them earned substantially more than Sharla. Who knows? A jury might find that she was entitled to her quarter-million-dollar salary.

Anthony grinned. "So you'll show me yours if I show you mine?"

I grinned right back. "Sure. I'd love to hear how you'll justify Sharla and Rodney paying forty grand for that macaroni piece. I mean, really. It didn't even come with cheese. And you know the artist was Sharla's grandson and Rodney's nephew, right? And that he's like two months old?"

Okay, so that was an exaggeration. But what fun was a negotiation without a little hyperbole?

"I'm aware of the facts," he said. "But I'm surprised at your lack of taste. That piece was a work of genius. Hunter Gabbert is a prodigy in pasta, the Michelangelo of manicotti, the Renoir of rigatoni."

"You don't believe that for a minute."

"Don't I?" He batted his eyes at me.

"What were your thoughts on Jackson's works?" I asked.

"The fan and hair dryer?" he replied. "They blew me away. Literally."

"Now you're telling the truth."

"You're right. But what do I know about art? And what do *you* know, hmm?" He arched a shaped brow.

"Not much," I acquiesced. "Which was why we had an expert come in and take a look. An expert with a degree from Savannah College of Art and Design," I added. "She also worked for several years as a curator at the Guggenheim."

"Her pants sound quite fancy." He intertwined his fingers and propped his chin on them. "What were her conclusions? Do tell."

I realized I was giving Anthony a peek at my cards here, but this discussion wouldn't move along unless each of us gave a little. "She thought Jackson's and Hunter's pieces were a joke."

"What about the rest?"

"She agreed they showed some talent," I said, "or at least some artistic inclination. But the fact remains that Aly is engaged to Rodney and was paid quite a bit for her work even though she had no prior sales. She hasn't sold a piece since, either. The Unic is her only claim to fame. If you ask me, she's an art groupie, a wannabe who wants to float around in art circles and pretend to be in the game, but who's not willing to put in the time and effort it would take to become a real artist."

Anthony seemed to mull that over for a moment. "Fair enough. Maybe instead of debating the value of her art, we should just talk numbers. What's the smallest figure that would make you happy?"

"What's the largest sum your clients are willing to pay to settle this?"

We sat in silence, staring each other down, neither of us willing to divulge our secret number as of yet.

I finally broke the standoff. "I'll tell you this much. Any number they offer has to come with a laundry list of changes at the museum. They need to be open reasonable hours, maybe even offer an occasional class or something. They need to buy more pieces from legitimate artists and change their collection more often. They also need to install proper lighting."

"All right," he said. "Let me speak with my clients and get back to you."

"Okeydokey."

The food arrived then. Anthony picked up his fork, reached across the table, and snagged a cucumber slice from my plate. He held it aloft. "Always nice doing business with you, Tara."

chapter twenty-seven

$\mathcal{P}$early Whites

When I returned to the office after my lunch with Anthony, I checked my Facebook page. Laurel Brandeis had sent me another message.

I hope you don't mind that I contacted the U.S. Red Cross on your behalf to see if they could send someone to pick up your contribution check. They should be getting in touch with you directly to set something up. You're so generous!

A second message had also arrived, sent by purported U.S. Red Cross fund-raising chairperson Peter Stanovich.

We appreciate your interest in our charity and supporting our efforts to help those who have suffered a natural disaster. I would be glad to meet with you ASAP to accept your donation.

Boy, this con artist didn't waste any time, did he? He probably knew he had to strike while the iron was hot, or at least while my alleged lottery winnings were burning a hole in my pocket.

I sent a return message to the purported Peter Stanovich. *Since you got in touch with me so quickly this seems meant to be! Can you meet me at three tomorrow after-noon in front of the Dallas downtown library?*

He sent a reply in less than fifteen minutes, obviously keeping a close eye on his inbox. *Works for me! Looking forward to meeting you.*

That sentiment would surely reverse itself once I slapped cuffs on his wrists.

I messaged him back immediately. *How will I know you?* With any luck, the guy would send me a photo of himself.

Alas, luck was not with me. He responded with *I'll hold up a sign with your name.*

Darn.

I phoned around the office, trying to find another agent who would be available to come with me tomorrow to bust this crook. Eddie was busy with a deposition, and Josh had already been corralled to help another of our fellow agents delve into the mainframe at a local company that had refused to turn over any physical records.

"We're still on for the toga party tomorrow night, right?" he asked, excitement in his voice.

Poor guy. He'd probably been barred from frat parties when he was in college. He'd clearly never been one of the cool kids. Until *now,* I supposed. Our badges and guns provided instant street cred and a definitive cool factor.

"Sure," I said. "We're still on."

"Can Kira come along?"

"Why?" I asked. "Do you two have a date planned for afterward?"

"No," Josh replied hesitantly. "It's just that she's never seen me in action."

Sheesh. Trying to impress his girlfriend, huh? I supposed I couldn't blame him. It was pretty damn sexy to see your guy successfully wrangle a target. As ashamed as I was to admit it, I'd been totally turned on recently when Nick had engaged physically with Brazos Rivers, the country-western singing sensation and tax cheat. *All that raw muscle and masculine power . . .*

"Tara?" came Josh's voice through the phone, ripping me out of my muscle-ripped memory. "Are you still there?"

"Yeah," I said. "No problem. You can bring her."

Heck, having Kira along would probably make us look more like legitimate college students. With her bleached hair and tendency to go heavy on the eyeliner, she'd fit right in.

I ended my call with Josh and tried William Dorsey, the newest agent in the office, next. Luckily, Will would be available tomorrow to help me bust the Facecrook.

"I'll bring my Nikon," he said. "Make it look authentic."

"Great. Thanks."

This would be the first chance Will and I had to work a case together, at least officially. Not long ago, I'd held a number of smugglers at bay in a truck yard while Nick, Eddie, and Will climbed atop an eighteen-wheeler for cover. Seemed I was always having to rescue my male co-workers. I turned that whole damsel-in-distress thing on its head.

My cell phone rang. The readout told me it was Anthony on the line. I accepted the call. "That was quick. Got an offer for me?"

"Sure do."

"Better be a good one."

"Oh, indeed it is," he said. "Hold on to your hat."

"I'm not wearing a hat."

"Then hold on to your ass," he snapped.

"All righty."

"To make all of this ugly little business go away, the Fowlers are willing to pay a full twenty grand."

"Twenty thousand?" I let out a laugh. "You must be

joking. That's chump change. The Fowlers probably have that much in their couch cushions."

"Tara, my dear," Anthony retorted, "being a nasty little bitch doesn't become you."

"It doesn't become you, either."

He chuckled. "Touché, once again."

"My time is valuable," I told him. "Don't call me back unless you've got a serious offer to put on the table."

"Au contraire," he replied. "I suggest you consider the fact that if you refuse this offer you could end up with nothing. I'll give you until the end of the day to accept." With that, he bid me adieu and hung up.

"Kiss my derrière," I said to the phone before slipping it into my pocket. Hey, if he could speak snotty French so could I.

On my way home from work that evening, I decided to swing by the address listed for Terrence Motley in the DMV records. I don't know what I expected to glean from my surveillance, but I hoped I might find another clue that could be helpful to Nick and Christina. At worst, the trip would just be a waste of gas, right?

The house was in south Dallas, in a slightly rundown yet conveniently located neighborhood that would probably be "discovered" by the gays or professionals soon and be cleaned up, remodeled, and gentrified, tripling home values. For now, though, the yards were unkempt, the shutters were missing or cockeyed, and the driveways bore evidence of oil leaks.

I cruised slowly by. There was no car in the driveway of the small blue house purportedly occupied by Motley. No vehicle at the curb, either. The front curtains were pulled shut. I spotted a tricycle on the front porch, though, along with three colorful plastic dinosaurs strewn about.

What kind of father would deal drugs? The thought both disgusted and disturbed me. It also made me grateful my parents had made their money the old-fashioned way, through hard work that they complained about every evening over dinner.

As I circled back at the end of the block, an older model green Kia Sportage pulled into the driveway at Motley's address. I watched as a blond woman climbed out, opened the back door, and wrangled two young children out of car seats. As the kids made their way to the front door, the woman stepped over to the mailbox and pulled out a stack of mail. She turned to head to the porch, failing to notice as an envelope fell from her hand to the ground. Waving her arm, she motioned the children inside, followed them in, and shut the door behind them.

I continued back toward the house, pulling over to the curb and eyeing the errant envelope. It was addressed to a Denise Newsom.

Performing a quick search on my phone, I confirmed that a twenty-eight-year-old woman named Denise Newsom lived at this address, along with a thirty-year-old man with the same last name. The marriage license records confirmed the two were husband and wife.

Why would Terrence Motley be living with this family?

Or *was* he?

It took me a minute or two to find a home phone listing for the Newsoms, but when I did I drove to a nearby strip mall and stepped into a mom-and-pop Indian restaurant, the smell of curry greeting me.

A round, middle-aged Indian woman in a yellow sari stepped out from behind the takeout counter with a stack of menus in her hand. "Just one?"

"Actually, I'm not here to eat." I offered a cringe of regret. "I'm having car trouble and my cell phone battery is dead. May I use your phone to make a quick local call?"

I didn't want to use my personal cell or work phone and risk anyone on the other end identifying me as law enforcement.

The Indian woman frowned, but gestured to a phone mounted on the wall behind the counter. "Make it quick. We are busy now."

Busy? There were only two people in the place. Then again, there were five paper bags lined up on the counter, waiting to be picked up. Looked like their primary business was takeout.

"Thanks." I dialed the Newsoms' number.

A female voice came over the line. "Hello?"

"Hi," I said. "Could I speak to Terrence, please?"

"Who?" she replied, sounding confused.

"Terrence," I repeated, adding "Motley" just in case he might go by the nickname Terry or maybe by his middle name.

"There's nobody here by that name," the woman said. "I think you've got the wrong number."

"Sorry." I hung up, thanked the Indian woman again, and perused the menu board behind the counter, placing a to-go order for the vegetable pulao. Fifteen minutes later, dinner in hand, I headed back out to my car.

As long as I was out, I figured I'd stop by Nick's mother's house to check on her and Daffodil. Nick's mother looked worried, two deep lines etched between her brows. Daffodil, on the other hand, looked fat and happy. Especially fat.

"Wow," I said. "She looks nothing like that skinny stray Nick brought home from the pound."

"What can I say?" Bonnie said. "When I'm anxious, I cook. I was just sitting down to supper. Why don't you stay and eat with me? I'd love the company."

My pulao was waiting in the car, but how could I refuse Nick's mother? Heck, I'd been lonely, too. Lately it had been just me and my cats at home. Kinda pathetic, huh? "I'd love to stay. Thanks."

While Bonnie grabbed a second plate from the kitchen cabinet and a fork from the drawer, I poured myself a tall glass of the homemade peach sangria she kept in constant supply in her fridge. Glass in hand, I took a seat next to Bonnie at her kitchen table. A platter of fried chicken sat in front of us. I fished a leg off the pile, then helped myself to some mashed potatoes and green beans.

Neglecting her own meal, Bonnie pulled chicken meat off the bone for Daffy and hand-fed her the pieces. "Here you go, girl."

Daffy took the bites, then gave Bonnie's hand a long-tongued lick. Though I suspected the dog had been merely licking chicken juice off her hand, Bonnie said, "Aw, thanks for the kiss, girl."

When Daffy had eaten her fill, she waddled over to her bed and plopped down, heaving a big sigh. Pigging out had evidently exhausted her.

"How's work going?" Bonnie asked.

Though IRS policy prevented me from naming names, I told Bonnie as much as I could about my pending cases.

She shook her head. "There has to be a special place in hell for people who pretend to be collecting for the poor and keep the money for themselves."

I felt the same way.

"You be careful at that hunting place," she warned. "All those people with guns. That could get dangerous."

Oddly, guns didn't scare me nearly as much as knives. I supposed that was because I'd grown up around firearms and carried one myself.

When we were through with dinner, Bonnie served up two dishes of cherry cobbler and we took them onto her back patio. It was a pleasant evening, cool enough to be refreshing but not so frigid that we felt the need to go back inside. As we ate our cobbler, I gazed at the stars, wondering if Nick, wherever he was, saw these same stars right now.

Bonnie looked up, perhaps having the same thought. With her eyes still on the sky, she said, "I'm so glad Nick found you, Tara. I've never seen him happier than he's been since you two got together."

My heart squeezed. This was nice to hear. "Thanks, Bonnie."

She turned to me. "You are just what that boy needed."

Nick was just what I needed, too.

We sat in companionable silence for a few more minutes before I rose to go. Henry and Anne's dinner was already late, and I needed to make a stop at the grocery store for the upcoming week's provisions.

Bonnie walked me to the door, Daffodil trotting along behind us. We stopped on the porch and Bonnie gave me a warm hug. "Come see me again," she said. "Soon as you can."

"I will," I promised. I knelt down and gave Daffy a kiss on the snout and a double-handed scratch behind the ears. "Be a good girl, 'kay?"

She woofed once as if in affirmation. *Woof!*

I stopped by WalMart on my drive home and stocked up on my usual staples. Bananas. Fruity Pebbles. Cat treats. Frozen vegetables. Bread. Those bright orange slices of processed something-or-other pretending to be cheese.

As I passed the health and beauty section, I made a turn down the toothpaste aisle, my eyes scanning the shelves for whitening strips. When I found them, I compared the name brand to the store brand, mentally debated the pros and cons of the high-powered three-day strips versus the slower-acting but purportedly less irritating seven-day program, and went, of course, for the strips that would get the job done the quickest. No sense making things more difficult for myself, and efficiency was a virtue, after all. Or if it wasn't, it should be.

When I arrived home, the first thing I did was scurry to the kitchen to feed the cats. Both of them were sitting expectantly in front of their bowls.

"Sorry, you two!" I called as I scooped a cup of kibble from their food bag in the pantry.

As I poured the food into Henry's bowl, he took another swipe at the back of my hand, letting me know he was none too happy with my substandard service.

I snatched him off the floor and cradled him to my chest, holding him by the scruff of his neck, looking him in his angry eyes, and calling him my "poopie-poopie-poo!" He hated it when I did that. *Ha!* That would teach the furry little asshole to mess with me.

Henry struggled to get loose. Experience taught me I had precisely three seconds to release him before risking the loss of an eye.

Having evened the score, I set him in front of his bowl. "Down you go, my poopie-poopie-poo!"

He twitched his tail twice, the cat equivalent of giving me the finger, and set about noisily crunching his dinner.

As I poured the rest of the food into Anne's bowl, she rubbed her face on my calf and purred, my sweet little suck-up. Unlike Henry, Annie loved being my poopie-poopie-poo.

After changing out of my work clothes and into my pj's, I brushed, flossed, and applied a set of the whitening strips to my teeth, pushing firmly on them to cement them to the enamel. *There. That should do it.*

While the strips worked their whitening, brightening magic, I lugged my hamper downstairs and started a load of laundry. Wandering into the living room, I clicked on the ten o'clock news, catching it in the middle of the weather report. Looked like we were in for more of the same the next few days. Mild temperatures. Sunshine. Pollen counts high enough to cover our cars in yellow powder and cause a rash of sinus infections. No doubt Ajay would be busy prescribing nasal sprays and antibiotics the next few days.

My eyelids began to sag, but I still had ten minutes to go on the strips. No matter. I'd just lie down on my couch and rest my eyes for a moment until the time was up.

Just a quick rest.

Just . . .

a short . . .

Zzzzzzzz.

I woke at three A.M. to Matt Damon on my television screen, running either from or after somebody. One of the *Bourne* movies. Annie was curled up next to me. Henry lay on his side atop the TV armoire, one paw thrust out in front of him, snoozing.

A dry, white crust had formed around my mouth. *Uh-oh. The whitening strips.* The strips that were supposed to be on my teeth for no more than thirty minutes.

As I sat up, I ripped the strip from my upper teeth. *Zing!* Holy crap! The sensation felt like my teeth were being electrocuted.

"Ow-ow-ow!" My nerves felt exposed and raw. I knew it would hurt to rip off the bottom one, but I couldn't very well leave it on any longer. I grabbed the edge of the strip and ripped that one off, too. "Ow-ow-ow!"

Alicia's sleepy voice came from upstairs. "You okay down there?"

"I fell asleep with whitening strips on my teeth!"

She appeared on the stairs a moment later, disheveled from sleep. "If I'd known you had them on, I would've woken you when I got home."

I picked up the strips and took them into the kitchen to

throw them away. The two of us walked back upstairs together.

"My parents are driving in tomorrow for the weekend," I told her.

"No problem," she said. "I'll go stay with Daniel. His place is closer to the office anyway."

She was in the final stretch of tax season, thank goodness. I missed spending time with my best friend.

She stopped in the door to my guest room. "You doing okay?"

"Other than feeling like I'm biting down on a live wire?"

"Yeah," she said.

I knew what she was asking. She was asking how I was holding up with Nick working undercover within arm's reach of El Cuchillo. The answer? "I'm terrified, Alicia. His most recent text said 'See you soon,' but I don't know if he meant that literally or if he was just sending a vague message in case anyone got hold of his phone. I have no idea when he'll be back or . . . or even if he'll ever be back. It's like my life is on hold."

She stepped over and gave me a hug. "If he's not back by the time tax season is over, you and I are going to take a vacation. We'll go stay at a B and B in Granbury and shop on the square and eat at that cute little teahouse you like."

"That sounds perfect."

With one last hug, she released me and we parted ways to go into our bedrooms. My teeth throbbed, and my gums felt as if all of the skin had been scraped off with a wire brush. I went to the bathroom for an aspirin. I found a bottle in my medicine cabinet. They'd expired two months ago, but with any luck were still potent enough to dull the screaming pain in my mouth.

I popped two onto my tongue, filled a glass with water, and put it to my lips.

Aaaaagh!

The cool water coursing over my teeth caused fresh agony. I spat the water into the sink, the two aspirin going with it. *Damn.* I'd done a lot of stupid things in my life, but this really took the cake. *Ugh, cake.* Just the thought of it in my mouth made me cringe. I'd never eat or drink again.

I flopped down on my bed and grabbed my pillow with two clenched fists, trying to channel the pain. A minute later, Anne jumped up onto the bed, stepped over to sniff my scaly lips, then jerked her head back as if disgusted. My lips probably looked as dry and disgusting as Quent Kuykendahl's.

She settled in the curve of my hip and went back to sleep. I closed my eyes and tried to do the same.

chapter twenty-eight

$\mathcal{S}$ ay Cheese!

When I woke the next morning, my teeth still felt sensitive. I glanced at them in the mirror. They might hurt like hell, but they sure were white and shiny. Especially in contrast to my raw, red gums.

I showered, dressed, and went downstairs. Alicia had left the coffeepot on for me, but there was no way I'd attempt to drink a hot beverage. Heck, I wasn't sure I could drink any beverage at all. Maybe I should stop by the medical clinic and see if Ajay could hook me up to an IV filled with orange juice or espresso.

Just as I plopped my butt into my office chair at work that morning, my cell phone rang again. *Anthony.* I took the call. "Good morning, sunshine."

He wasted no time, getting right down to business. "The Fowlers will go up to forty grand. Final offer. You'd be a fool not to take it, Tara."

They'd doubled their offer after I'd ignored their low-ball bid yesterday. I wondered how much they'd come up if I turned them down again? I realized the case wasn't a sure thing, but forty grand wasn't even in the ballpark. I wanted at least seventy-five.

"No, thanks," I said.

"So you're a fool then?" Anthony snapped.

"The fooliest."

"That's not even a word."

"I'll settle at one hundred and twenty-five thousand," I said, building in some room for negotiation.

"This is the part where I issue a derisive scoffing sound," Anthony said, following his words with the forewarned derisive scoff. "And now is the part where I say 'we'll see you in court' and hang up, leaving you feeling worried and anxious and second-guessing yourself."

"If you're going to warn me that you're hanging up on me, doesn't it lose all effect?"

"You tell me."

Click, he was gone. And damn if I didn't begin to worry and feel anxious. *Had turning down the offer been a bad decision?*

Oh, well. Too late now. I wasn't about to call Anthony back and grovel. I was tired of feeling powerless and scared. People like the Fowlers and the Kuykendahls and El Cuchillo would keep committing their crimes until someone had the balls to stop them. I was going to be that person with the balls. Metaphorically speaking, anyway.

I was antsy all day, finding it hard to work on my files, eager to move ahead on my bust of Peter Stanovich—or whoever he really was. The anticipation had me buzzing with nervous energy. Several times I found myself looking across the hall to Nick's office out of habit. If he were here, I'd be sharing my excitement with him, doing fist or chest bumps, engaging in a prebust pep rally of sorts. *Go, team, go!* With him gone, I had to sit here with all of my pep locked inside me, unrallied. The other agents, though certainly supportive, didn't have time or patience to listen to me chatter on about the pending arrest, speculating how things might go, formulating game plans and backup game plans.

This sucked.

It was a reminder of yet another role that Nick filled in my life, that of cheerleader, though minus the short skirt and pom-poms. When had I become so dependent on the guy? It had snuck up on me, bit by bit, before, without my knowing it, he'd become an integral, critical, *necessary* part of my life.

· Perhaps it was selfish of me to think about it, but if he didn't come back from the cartel case alive, what would become of *me*? I'd have to join the Big D Dating Service and troll for a replacement boyfriend online. But I knew with absolute certainty that I could never, *ever* find anyone as right for me as Nick.

We had our problems, sure. We were both incredibly stubborn and butted heads sometimes. He could be a bit overbearing, while I could be a bit defensive. He didn't understand my love of ethnic foods and British sitcoms when there were perfectly good meat and potatoes to be eaten and American shows with actors whose speech was easier to understand. I, on the other hand, would never understand how he could watch fishing shows on TV and live on a virtually vegetable-free diet of hamburgers, barbecue, and steak.

But what we had in common was so much more meaningful. We shared a strong work ethic, a sense of justice and purpose, an innate understanding that we'd been given an unusual skill set—the ability to comprehend numbers and handle weapons—and that we were duty-bound to put those skills to use for the American people. We weren't apathetic procrastinators, simply letting life carry us along wherever its currents decided to take us.

We were people of action, riding life's rapids, sometimes paddling frantically against the flow or slamming into boulders, taking only the forks that we chose.

Yep, if Nick didn't return, a piece of myself would be forever missing.

I'd never be the same.

Ugh.

I reached into my purse and pulled out my rarely used checkbook. Tearing a check from the pad, I dated it for the twelfth of Never. I made it out for $15,000, payable not to the U.S. Red Cross, but rather to U. R. Busted. In the memo section, I wrote "Neener-neener." I signed the check with a flourish, thus completing my prop. Hey, if you can't be a smart-ass on the job, you should get a new job.

I was checking the secret phone for the millionth time that day when Will Dorsey stepped into my office, a fancy camera hanging around his neck. "Ready to go nab that Facecrook?"

I stood, stuffed my handcuffs into my pants pocket for easy access, and slid my gun into the hip holster hidden by my blazer. I might be missing my cheerleader, but it was nonetheless time to *go, team, go.* "I'm ready now."

It was only five blocks to the central library, so Will and I decided to walk it. On the way, I asked how his three boys were doing.

"They're great," he replied. "Thanks for asking. They sure do wear me out, though. Between potty training and homework, my wife and I don't get a minute to ourselves."

Although his words made it sound as if he were complaining, his tone made it clear he didn't really mind his situation one bit.

As we approached the library, we glanced around for Peter. There was no man holding up a sign with my alias written on it. The only men we saw were making their way in or out of the building. None appeared to be waiting for do-gooder Sara Galloway to show up with a $15,000 check.

We stopped at a spot about thirty feet from the front doors, far enough from the bustle that we wouldn't impede traffic flowing in and out of the building and where we could execute a bust without interference. As we stood there, I glanced around, searching the moving masses for a man who appeared to be looking for a free meal ticket. Unfortunately, I had trouble seeing much through the black pair of sunglasses I'd purchased at the car wash. The shades were excessively dark, making the entire world appear to be at dusk. Frustrated, I ripped them from my face, marched over to a nearby trash can, and tossed them inside. I really needed to find time to get over to the Brighton store for a good pair.

As we continued to wait, I pulled the check from my purse and held it in my hand as if ready to hand it over. I glanced around, noting nobody of interest except, perhaps, a stocky man in a nice suit leaning back against a light post half a block down, smoking a cigarette and talking on his cell. His gold watch glinted in the afternoon sun as he put the butt to his lips and took a puff.

"Think that's him?" Will asked.

"The guy in the suit?"

"No. The nerdy-looking dude heading our way."

I followed his gaze to a man in khaki pants and a pink button-down who proceeded slowly toward the building, glancing left and right, clutching something tightly to his chest as if to hide it from passersby. It was flat and rectangular. *A book?* I shrugged. "Maybe."

As we stood there watching, the man scurried up to the book drop, took one last, quick glance around, then shoved the book he'd been holding inside. Just as quickly, he scurried off.

Will stifled a laugh. "I bet I know what kind of book that was. He's looking fifty shades of pink right now."

We continued to wait, the minutes ticking slowly by.

3:04.

3:05.

3:06.

The man in the suit ended his phone call, but continued to puff away on his cigarette. He glanced our way a couple of times, but I supposed that was to be expected. We'd been standing out here quite some time. He was probably curious why.

3:07.

3:08.

3:09.

When my cell phone showed 3:12, my anticipation turned to annoyance. "Where is he? Do you think he figured out this was a ruse?"

Just as the words left my mouth, the man in the suit tossed his cigarette butt aside and aimed directly for us. I realized now that he'd been performing his own surveillance, watching me and Will to figure out if we looked like some benevolent bookkeeper and her friend along to snap a photograph. Looked like we'd passed muster.

"Here he comes," I said under my breath to William.

As the man approached, I opened my eyes wider, hoping to look innocent and excited.

"Sara Galloway?" the man asked when he was twenty feet away.

"That's me!" I called, walking toward him with my hand extended. "You must be Peter Stanovich."

He nodded as he shook my hand. "That I am. Sorry I'm late. Had a phone call I had to take. Seems there's a mudslide in Blefuscu."

Blefuscu? Wasn't that one of the fictional islands in *Gulliver's Travels?*

Still holding on to his hand, I cocked my head, forcing a smile. "I thought you said you'd be holding a sign with my name."

"Forgot paper and a pen." He shrugged nonchalantly and gave my hand a final squeeze before releasing it. "It's so nice to meet you, Sara."

Nice?

Ha!

He'll soon be eating his words.

Stanovich glanced at Will, his expression questioning. "I'm Sara's friend. LeBron Tee."

What the—

Will held up his camera. "She asked me to take a photo for her."

Peter, or whoever the heck he was, smiled a stiff smile. "How nice."

Will waved his hand. "Scootch together while she hands you the check. That'll make a nice shot."

Stanovich turned to face the man he knew as LeBron Tee. I turned, too, and sidled up to Stanovich on the left, holding the check face out in front of us. He reached out and grasped one end, as if afraid I might change my mind and decide not to give it to him.

Will raised his Nikon to his eyes. "Say cheese!"

"Cheese!" called Stanovich.

Sucker.

Before Peter could figure out what was happening, I pulled my cuffs from my pocket and snapped one of them onto the wrist of his hand that was touching the check. *Click.*

"What the—" His brain apparently worked faster than his mouth. He yanked his cuffed hand aside, yanking the check with it.

Before I could get the other cuff snapped he took off running. Luckily for me, those cigarettes had taken their toll, and within a few yards the man was huffing and puffing like a big bad wolf trying to demolish real estate owned by swine.

I ran around in front of him, put my arms out like a basketball player blocking a shot, and yelled, "Federal agents! Hands up!"

He, too, was ready to play ball, faking a left but then heading right, getting an advantage as my momentum carried me several steps in the wrong direction.

"Get him!" I yelled to Dorsey.

Will ran after Stanovich and circled around in front of him. As we closed in from both sides, Stanovich walked backward now, his hands half raised, the cuffs dangling from his wrist. In a panic, he glanced left and right. Realizing there was no escape, he turned and ran toward the library. In a split second he'd yanked the door open and run inside.

Dorsey and I were after him in a flash, careening into each other as we both tried to go through the same door at the same time.

I pulled my gun from its holster. I had no idea whether Stanovich was armed, but it never hurt to be safe rather than sorry. "Everyone down!" I called to those in the vicinity. "Federal agents in hot pursuit!"

Rather than ducking, the bewildered woman working the circulation desk put her hands in the air instead. Instinctive reaction when seeing a gun, I supposed. Several others nearby followed suit, surrendering rather than taking cover. Oh, well. I supposed it didn't much matter. By that point our target had run farther into the room. These people were safe.

My eyes spotted Stanovich rounding the reference desk up ahead and bolting into the monolithic shelves of the nonfiction section. Running after him, I darted past biographies of Hillary Clinton, Jim Henson, Desmond Tutu, and at least eight different offerings on the band One Direction. Heck, those boys hadn't been alive long enough to fill a book with their life stories, had they?

I continued to chase Stanovich into the children's section.

"Stop!" I hollered.

A woman and her daughter who were seated at one of the child-sized tables nearby looked up and scowled. They put their index fingers to their lips. *Shhh!*

Sheesh, people! 'Scuse me for trying to bust a criminal here!

Stanovich ran deeper into the kids' area. Just as he passed a bookshelf, a stroller appeared right in front of me, blocking my way. With all the momentum I had going, I knew I couldn't stop myself in time. My options were to slam into the stroller at full speed and risk injuring the child, or to dive over the thing, execute a rolling somersault, and leap to my feet to continue my pursuit. Hey, they did it in the movies all the time. I'd even seen Keanu Reeves do it once. And if that guy could do it, surely I could, too.

I leaped into the air to execute the dive maneuver. As I flew through the air, realization struck, telling me that my visualization had been overly ambitious. I had neither the flexibility nor the coordination to pull off such an acrobatic maneuver, nor did I have a stunt double to execute the feat for me. I managed to clear the baby stroller and curl myself into a ball, but rather than bouncing to my feet I careened like an off-kilter bowling ball across the floor and into a waist-high bookshelf.

Graceful, huh?

Fortunately, the shelves were bolted tight to the floor so they didn't fall over onto the trio of schoolgirls perusing the Laura Ingalls Wilder books on the other side. The impact did, however, release an avalanche of heavy hardcover Harry Potter books, which pelted me with bruising force as if they were, indeed, sorcerer's stones.

While I lay buried under multiple copies of all seven books—*seriously, J.K., wouldn't a trilogy have sufficed?*—Will ran past me, chasing Stanovich into the fiction section.

Grabbing the top of the bookshelf, I leveraged myself to my feet, kicked the *Half-Blood Prince* and *Prisoner of Azkaban* aside and ran, fast and furious, to the fiction area. I could see Stanovich running down the aisle between the two sets of tall shelves. Sprinting along the outer corridor, I overtook his pace and turned down an aisle to intercept him.

We collided at the intersection of romance and mystery. Thanks to my recent softball game with the Tax Maniacs, today I had the forethought to slide, taking Stanovich out at the ankles. His arms windmilled, the loose handcuff clanking against the bookcases as he grabbed at the shelves on his way down.

Thum-thump!

He hit the ground, his hip making the first impact, his shoulder the next. Will and I pounced on him in an instant. Will rolled Stanovich onto his back, grabbed the man's free hand and held it still, while I wrestled the other into place and secured the loose cuff with a click.

My quarry now cuffed, I sat back on my haunches to catch my breath. Chasing this idiot had winded me. Phew.

"Let me go!" Stanovich screeched at the top of his lungs. "Let me go!"

I levered myself to a stand and looked down at him. "Not gonna happen, buddy."

From all around us came shushing sounds. A quick and efficient *Sh.* An elongated *Shhhhh.* An emphatic *Shh!* One bibliophile even offered a melodic and rythmic *sh-sh-sh-sh-sh,* like a human lawn sprinkler.

Keeping my voice low lest I be shushed to death, I read Peter Stanovich his rights.

"You have the right to remain silent," I whispered. "I suggest you take advantage of it."

The moron didn't listen to my advice. "Let me go!" he shrieked again. "Let me go!"

A fresh medley of shushes came from all around.

"Let me go!"

Jeez. If this guy didn't have the sense to shut up, I'd just have to shut him up myself, wouldn't I?

I grabbed a book from the shelf, a juicy Scottish romance featuring a man in a kilt with six-pack abs and a bare, waxed chest on the cover. I wouldn't mind eating some haggis off his firm tummy.

"Good choice," Will said, gesturing to the cover.

I cut him a questioning look.

"What?" he said defensively. "My wife reads those books and leaves them lying around."

"Help!" hollered Stanovich, trying a new tactic. "I'm being attacked! Someone help!"

The library patrons were far less concerned with this man's safety than they were about the noise level.

Sh!

Shhh!

Sh-sh-sh!

Opening the book, I ripped out page 56. *Rrrip!* I crumpled the paper and bent down to shove it in Stanovich's mouth. *Ha!* Not only had I made him eat his own words, he was now eating those of author Rose N. Bloom, a pen name if ever I'd heard one.

Rrrip! I ripped out page 57 and repeated the process, having to push a little harder to get this page into his mouth given that he was working his tongue, trying to expel the previous one. I continued to recite his rights. "Anything you say can and will be held against you in a court of law."

Rrrip! "You have the right to an attorney," I said, shoving page 58 into his mouth now. "If you cannot afford an attorney, one will be appointed for you."

By the time I was done reading his rights, Stanovich's mouth was filled to the choking point with all of chapter 4 and a portion of chapter 5. His gag reflex activated. *Hork! Hork! Hork!* The sound was followed, of course, by a chorus of *Shh! Shh! Shh!*

A petite librarian wearing a pastel yellow dress, reading glasses, and a shocked expression sprinted up the aisle. "What is going on here!"

Her gaze traveled from the choking man on the floor to the book in my hand, a gasp leaping from her throat as she took in the evidence of my horrific act of bibliocide.

A warm blush spread up my cheeks, just like the time my elementary school librarian had caught me looking up the word "erection" in the dictionary. Prior to what I had just learned on the playground, I'd only heard a derivative of the word used in conjunction with the word "set," as in "erector set." "Um . . . is this available for checkout?"

Shh!

Shhhhh.

Sh!

Disregarding the pleas for silence, Stanovich turned his head to the side and—*hwaaak*—expelled what had to be the world's largest spitball.

Will looked down at it and snapped a photo. "I'm sending this in to *The Guinness Book of World Records.*"

I pointed down at it. The words "swollen, engorged manhood" stared up at us. "You might want to shoot from a different angle."

Will nudged the wad with his toe, rolling it until the words disappeared over the horizon, and snapped another shot.

Bending down, I pulled a wallet from the back pocket of Stanovich's pants. He had nearly seven hundred dollars in cash inside, as well as a Michigan driver's license identifying him as Stanley Peters. Like me, he'd chosen an alias not too different from his real name.

"Jig's up, Stan my man," I said. "That's what happens when you let your greed get the best of you."

While we waited for the marshals to arrive and haul Peters off to the klink, I sorted things out with the librarian. When she learned I was a federal agent, she waived the damage fee for the book. She didn't spare me the disapproving look, however. "Next time might I suggest you choose a less popular genre with which to disable your perpetrators. A reference book, perhaps."

"Yes, ma'am." I did my best to look contrite. Actually, I was feeling pretty darn proud of myself. Not every agent would have been so resourceful. Luckily for me, I was a person who could think on her feet.

Once the marshals had taken Peters away, Will and I started our trek back to the IRS offices.

I turned to him as we waited at a stoplight. "*LeBron Tee?* What the heck was that?"

"It's a cross between LeBron James and Mister T," he replied matter-of-factly. "I wanted to sound like a badass black dude."

"You *are* a badass black dude. Just because you don't wear gold chains or a sports jersey doesn't mean you aren't as tough as they are."

He sighed. "I suppose you're right. But when I transferred over from the collections department, I guess I thought special agents would look different somehow. I'm wearing the same suits I wore then."

"Being a badass isn't about how you look on the outside," I said. "It's about who you are on the inside. But maybe you're on to something. We could propose a uniform to Lu. Maybe something with tights and a cape printed with dollar signs?"

"Tights?" Will cringed. "I have a hard enough time with briefs."

chapter twenty-nine

*T*oga! Toga!

I returned to the office to find that the very last rose petal had fallen off the stem, dropping to its death on top of my Fifty-Yard Line Foundation file. Even though the only thing that remained in the vase were thorny, mold-covered stems, I couldn't bring myself to throw them out. They might be the last flowers Nick ever sent me.

It was after five o'clock, well past quitting time, but I decided to take one last glance at my inbox. Good thing I did. To my surprise and delight, I found a manila envelope from Anthony Giacomo. The stamp on the outside indicated it had been hand-delivered by a courier.

Inside I found a certified check from Rodney Fowler in the amount of $100,000, less than my last, padded demand but far more than I'd hoped to settle for.

I threw a victorious fist into the air. "Score!"

The attached letter from Anthony, typed up on his law firm's letterhead, read:

You drive a hard bargain, Agent Holloway, but I've managed to convince the Fowlers to bend, at least partially, to your will. Of course my upstanding clients admit nothing, other than that you were an immense nuisance, comparable to a bit of toilet paper stuck to one's shoe, as well as an artistic neophyte with a pathetic and unenviable lack of discernment. However, it was worth the check's sum simply to put this matter to rest.

As far as your list of suggestions regarding the operation of the Unic, the staff will implement them as soon as reasonably possible, but in no event later than two months from the date of this letter.

If you agree to these generous terms, please send us a settlement agreement for signature. If you do not agree, be advised that I will take you to court, shred you like an Enron financial report, and eat your remains for dinner, paired with an endive and radicchio salad and a lively, but not overly sweet moscato. Dessert as yet to be determined, though I'm leaning toward a hazelnut mousse.

Sincerely, lovingly, fondly, and platonically yours, forever and ever,
Anthony Giacomo, Esq.

I pulled out my cell phone and called his office, leaving a one-word response on his voice mail. "Deal."

Two cases down, two to go. Things were looking up. All I needed now was to nail the frat rat running the phishing scam and catch the Kuykendahls selling animals for cash under the table. Then my work would be done.

Of course things always sounded so easy in theory . . .

I arrived home from work to find that my parents were already at my house. My mom, who was petite and chestnut haired like me, stood in the kitchen making chicken-fried steak, stewed okra, and mashed potatoes with gravy. *Yum!* My broad-shouldered, leather-skinned father wrangled a new air filter into my living room intake vent, God bless 'im.

I gave them both a hug and a kiss on the cheek. "Thanks for coming."

My mother tossed a piece of breaded meat into the sizzling frying pan. *Tsssss.* "Anything for our little girl," she said. "Though one of these times I wish you'd just ask us for something normal, like a loan. This whole lion-hunting business has got me all in a dither. What if those folks realize you're out to get them? They'll all be armed. Heck, they could fill you full of lead and feed you to that lion and nobody would be the wiser."

"We'll be fine." Dad screwed the metal grate back into place and stood. "I'm the best shot in east Texas and I taught Tara everything I know."

True, and at some point the pupil had surpassed the master, though my father wasn't likely to admit it. Far be it from me to rub it in his face, either. Especially when doing so would mean I'd have to figure out how to change my air filters.

"Dad's right, Mom," I said. "We can take care of ourselves."

She grabbed the potato masher and began pulverizing the spuds, probably as much to work out her anxieties as to prepare dinner. "You two think you're so tough. I have half a mind to let you cook dinner."

She'd never do that and we all knew it. I couldn't cook to save my life, and the only thing my father could make was chili or grilled meat on his backyard barbecue.

I went upstairs and changed out of my work clothes and into a pair of shorts and a tank top I could wear under the toga later. When I returned downstairs, my mother handed me a glass of sweet tea.

"I'm almost afraid to ask." She took my hand. "Have you gotten any word from Nick?"

I'd told her about the secret phone, too. My mother had a way of wheedling information out of me. "His last text said he hoped to see me soon."

Her eyes brightened with hope. "He's coming home?"

"I don't really know," I said. "I wasn't sure how much to read into it. He might have meant they were about to wrap up their investigation and make arrests, or he could have simply meant that he hoped things would move quickly. Who knows?"

She gave my hand a squeeze before releasing it. "Nick's tough. He'll be back before you know it."

I knew my mother only meant to be supportive, but her words made me want to scream. My hands formed involuntary fists, my nails digging into my palms. Nick might *not* be back before I knew it. He might not ever be back again. I was sick of everyone trying to cheer me up and act like this wasn't a big deal, because it was. It was the biggest deal that had ever happened to me. I couldn't just whistle "Zip-a-Dee-Doo-Dah" and pretend that it was a wonderful day, because my, oh, my, it sure as hell was not.

But I supposed I couldn't fault my mom. I'd have been just as annoyed and upset if she'd done the opposite, pointed out the danger he was in and the real possibility that he, like other undercover agents before him, could lose his life to the cause. I should cut her some slack. There was nothing anyone could say to me that would be right.

My parents and I ate dinner on my back patio. Mom caught me up on the gossip from back home in Nacogdoches. "You remember Esther and Vernon Littlefield?"

"That old couple who owned the farm down the road?"

"That's them. The sheriff found two acres of wacky weed growing on their back forty. Arrested 'em both. 'Course they claim they had no idea what it was, that it just cropped up naturally. But Linda over at the post office says she heard from Juanita at the doughnut place who heard from Gwendolyn at the hair salon that the Littlefields were selling it to one of those medical marijuana stores in Seattle."

"Growing a crop of Mary Jane." Dad jabbed his fork into a bite of meat. "I suppose that's one way to supplement your social security."

Mom went on to tell me that she'd run into one of my old high school friends at the grocery store. "I remember when you two used to have those sleepovers. You'd stay up all night giggling and carrying on."

Life sure had been easy and worry-free back then. *Sigh.*

"Clara Humphreys sends her regards."

"How nice," I replied. I'd always liked Clara, even if she tended to prattle on about her health problems for hours on end. "Send my regards right back to her." And, while I was at it, why not send some to Broadway and Herald Square, too?

When we'd finished our meal, my mother served us heaping helpings of her homemade blueberry pie for dessert. When I finished, I felt as swollen and engorged as the "manhood" referenced in Rose N. Bloom's romance novel.

Later that evening, as my parents settled in front of my TV downstairs for the night, I went upstairs to get ready for the toga party at the Gabba Gabba Hey house. I loaded on the makeup, hoping the excessive eyeliner and blush might make me appear more like a coed vying for male attention than a federal agent who'd graduated from college more than half a decade prior and was attending the party only with the hope of nailing a suspect, not looking to get nailed.

When I went to fashion a toga from my sheets, however, I realized that the dark green color wouldn't look quite right. The sheets on my guest room bed were no better. They were light blue with a striped border. Looked like I'd have to make a quick stop by a department store on my way to meet Josh and Kira.

I bid my parents good-bye and headed out. Making a quick detour at Target, I grabbed the first white sheet I saw and proceeded to the checkout.

I met up with Josh and Kira a couple of blocks from the frat house. They climbed out of Josh's car as I drove up. Kira, who was as painfully thin and long-limbed as a Tim Burton character, wore a shiny black satin sheet that perfectly complemented her white-blond hair, hanging in dreadlocklike chunks around her face. On her feet were a pair of black gladiator-style sandals that laced halfway up her calves. Her shoes were far more authentic than my sneakers. But I was more concerned with having enough traction to wrangle with our target than with looking like an authentic Roman.

Josh was wrapped in a pink sheet printed with images of the Disney princesses. *What the heck?* Were the sheets his way of sleeping with several women every night, engaging in a cartoon orgy? Did he dream of slipping his glass slipper to Cinderella? Did he want to get his hands on Snow White's apples? I forced the thoughts from my head. Better not to think too much about it.

I stepped out of my car, grabbed my new sheet from the bag, and tore off the plastic wrap. "Oh, crap," I said as I noted the gathered, elastic edge. "I bought a fitted sheet."

It was too late to go back to the store to exchange it. I'd just have to make the best of it.

With Kira's help, I did my best to wrap the sheet around myself toga style. When we finished, she stepped back and looked me up and down.

"How does it look?" I asked.

Her lip quirked. "Honestly? You look like you're wearing a diaper."

Great. "With any luck everyone at the party will be too drunk to notice."

The three of us made our way to the frat house. It was easy to find tonight. All we had to do was follow the smell of beer, the thrum of techno bass, and the sounds of indecipherable shouts and raucous laughter.

We arrived to find two freshman pledges standing on the front porch, apparently performing door duty. Both of them wore metal whistles hanging from chains around their necks.

I gave them what I hoped was a flirtatious smile. I was more inclined to pat them on the head and hand them a cookie and a glass of warm milk. "Hi. What are you two doing out here?"

"Watching for cops," said one.

The second one looked us over, his eyes narrowing suspiciously.

Uh-oh.

He stiffened and made a face, the kind a mean kid makes when he doesn't want you to sit at the lunch table with him. "You look like you're wearing a diaper."

I tossed my hair and giggled. "I know, right? I accidentally bought a fitted sheet."

His face told me that even though this party was supposed to be open, we might be denied entry if we couldn't convince him we were worthy. Anger boiled up inside me. This had never happened back when I was at the University of Texas. Of course I'd been younger then, and I would've put more effort into my costume.

"We're friends of Devon Peabody," I said. "He invited us."

"Oh." Mr. Suspicious relaxed and nodded. "Okay, then."

Mentioning one of the frat members by name seemed to act like a secret code word.

The boy turned to Josh. "If you hear this blow," he said,

holding up his whistle, "drop your drink and run. If the cops don't catch you with a cup in your hand they can't arrest you."

I knew the laws regarding underage drinking weren't quite as simple as that, but I wasn't about to correct the kid and have him find out I was a cop. Well, a cop of sorts. Besides, he only seemed to be addressing Josh, not me and Kira. I supposed it was clear that Kira and I were over twenty-one. Josh, on the other hand, could pass for fourteen. Maybe even twelve if he were holding an ice cream cone or wearing a beanie cap.

The boys opened the door and let us inside, quickly closing it behind us.

Inside, the place was lit only by colored lights mounted in the corners of the ceiling. Techno dance music blared from enormous stacked speakers at a deafening level, the vibrations shaking the floor and reverberating off our bodies. Hundreds of people milled about, each of them holding at least one red Solo cup, some of them double-fisting their drinks. They weaved around or stumbled into each other like drunken ants in an ant farm, laughing and hooting and hollering. In less than five seconds, I'd been jostled or bumped or groped by a dozen or more people. The crowd and noise created an environment that was near claustrophobic but, despite the sensory overload, we had to venture on.

As we wound our way through the crowd, I spotted Devon Peabody next to a large plastic trash can filled with red liquid. Whooping, he held up a bottle of vodka in each hand and poured them into the open garbage bin, dancing all the while. One of the girls stuck her tongue into the stream, drinking the vodka straight, giggling like a hyena when it ran down her chin and dripped into the can. Partygoers dipped their plastic cups into the liquid, scooping up cupfuls of the punch. One of the girls got some punch on her fingers and stuck them in her mouth to suck it off. A boy submerged both his cup and his hand, shaking the punch from his hand once he'd pulled it out of the can.

Ick.

Where was a health inspector when you needed one?

My stomach roiled and I turned to Josh and Kira. "That's so unsanitary."

"What?" they yelled in unison over the music.

"It's un-san-it-ary!" I hollered back, doing my best to enunciate clearly.

"Sincerity?" Kira shouted, raising her palms in a *WTH?* gesture.

"Yeah!" Josh cried, smiling, performing some wiggly dance moves and raising his hands in the air. "I like this music, too!"

Josh seemed to be reliving a college moment he'd probably never actually had. Poor guy. He'd only recently learned how to play nice with others.

The next thing I knew, he and Kira had cups of punch in their hands. Okay, I guess. We needed to blend in, after all. But if they actually drank that punch I'd insist they go see Ajay for a tetanus shot and antibiotics once the party was over.

The vodka bottles now empty, Devon stepped away from the trash can to toss the bottles into a cardboard box in the corner. As I turned around to scan the crowd, I was swept up in a stream of bodies migrating to the keg out back. "Hey!" Unable to backtrack against the solid flow, I did the only thing I could. Go with it.

A moment later I found myself in the backyard of the frat house. A huge oak tree stood in the middle of the yard, a silver keg of beer underneath it. A couple leaned against the tree, making out with such vigor they appeared to be zombies attempting to eat each other's faces. A half-dozen

guys stood around the keg, laughing, drinking, and filling their cups from the spigot. Five of them had brown
hair.

Was one of them the thief?

Time to find out.

I eased up to the keg. "How's it going?"

One of the boys snorted. "Are you wearing a diaper?"

Ugh. "It's a fitted sheet."

"Are you sure?"

The whole group of them laughed as if he'd said the
wittiest thing possible. I'd been here all of ten minutes and
already this wild party was getting on my nerves. I supposed I'd outgrown this type of entertainment once I'd
graduated, earned some money, and learned the calm,
quiet pleasure of a nice meal and a movie. I wasn't sure
how much more of this I could stand.

"So," I said, gesturing to the cups of beer in their hands.
"You guys upperclassmen?"

"Freshman pledges," replied one of them, polishing off
his cup and leaning in toward the keg to refill it.

Freshman, huh? That meant they were only eighteen
or nineteen years old, under the legal drinking age in Texas.
Not exactly model citizens, but who was I to condemn
them? I'd done my fair share of minor lawbreaking, too.
Underage drinking. Toilet-papering houses. Wrapping duct
tape around a friend's ex-boyfriend's car after he dumped
her. Took the guy half an hour to get his door open. *Good
times.*

"Are any of you good with computers?" I asked,
attempting to segue into a discussion that might lead me
to the thief. "I've been having a problem with my e-mail."

The boys ignored me, instead entering into a shoving
match when two girls with low-draping togas wandered
by. *Jeez.* How bad did I look? I mean, I knew I had bags
under my eyes and worry wrinkles and inflamed gums,

but I used to be able to hold my own at parties like this. These boys were making me feel old and unattractive. Then again, this diaper did nothing for my figure. Not that I had much figure to begin with.

I grabbed a cup from a bag on a picnic table nearby and served myself a beer. I wasn't a huge beer fan, but at least the keg wasn't full of germs like the trash can inside. I wandered around, trying unsuccessfully to insinuate myself into conversations with brown-haired boys but having no luck. As I wandered away from one group, I heard a girl say, "Since when do the housemothers come to parties?"

Housemother?

Ugh.

chapter thirty

*P*arty Crashers

I tossed back the beer, though it did little to ease the sting of the girl's nasty comment. Pretending to be checking a text, I pulled up the camera app on my phone and reversed it so I could see myself. *Yikes!* The image told me why none of the young men at this party had given me a second glance. I looked like crap. Exhausted. Strung out, even, like an addict overdue for a fix. Definitely time to schedule another glycolic treatment. Maybe a double dose. Perhaps Jessica could string me up by my feet and dip me in a vat.

My mind worked, trying to come up with a fresh tactic to elicit information from these boys. In my experience, if a girl had a sizable chest, she could get a guy's attention even if she had the face of a donkey. I wandered over to the beer keg, grabbed a second cup, then skittered around the tree and slid the two cups into the top of my toga. The fitted sheet came in handy now, the elastic edge helping to hold the cups in place on my chest. I scrunched the fabric up around the plastic so the ends of my new twelve-ounce breasts wouldn't look so flat.

Properly equipped now, I went back inside and headed

down the hall, hoping that some of these boys would be willing to give me some information on their fraternity brothers. I'd taken only seven steps when a boy stepped in front of me. His toga was a dingy yellowish gray. *Ew* Hadn't the guy heard of Clorox?

"Hey, there!" he yelled over the music as he stared down at what he thought was my chest. "Let's go dance!"

He grabbed at my hand to lead me to the dance floor, but I stood my ground. "Actually, I'm looking for someone!" I yelled back, the loud bass notes causing my plastic boobs to quiver. "He's a computer science major, I think! Brown hair! You know him?"

I didn't get an answer. Apparently my fake breasts were too distracting.

A jiggle inside the pocket of my shorts told me a text had come in on my cell phone. I pulled it out to find a message from Josh.

3rd floor 4th room! Now!

"Sorry! Gotta go!" I shoved the cell phone into my purse, pushed past my new admirer, and turned sideways to better slip through the crushing crowd. The group thinned as I ascended the stairs to the second floor, thinning even more as I reached the third. I counted the doors, sprinting down the row, my hand feeling for my holster through my toga.

What will I find when I get to the fourth room?

Has Josh found our target?

Or is Josh in trouble?

If I ran all the way up here only to discover that Josh needed help extricating an atomic wedgie from between his butt cheeks I'd be sorely disappointed. I was ready to bust this thief and get the heck out of this loud, smelly house *now*.

The door to the fourth room stood slightly ajar, open an inch or two, just enough to give me a glimpse inside. I could see a floor covered with dirty laundry, beer cans, and fast food wrappers, and heard the sounds of a video game. A *clang* as metal weapons met. A *whoosh* as another weapon missed its target. *Oofs* and *grunts* as the characters engaged in combat.

I knocked on the door.

"It's open!" called a male voice from inside.

I pushed the door open, having to shove fairly hard to move it past a pair of jeans balled up on the floor behind it. Josh lounged in a bright red beanbag chair patched with swaths of silver duct tape. He wore a headset and had a laptop in his lap, leaning first one way then the other as he worked the keys. Another boy, an average-sized, average-looking one with brown hair, reclined in one of those specialized, curved gaming chairs on the floor. On his bicep was a tattoo of a horned, redheaded woman with golden eyes and big boobs. She wore a dark red and gold bikini complemented by thigh-high boots and a cape. Talk about *what not to wear*. Like Josh, the boy had a keyboard in his lap, as well as a mouse pad and mouse situated on top of a stack of greasy pizza boxes next to him. Next to the mouse pad sat a cup full of punch. Judging from the boy's blurry-looking eyes and slack jaw, it wasn't his first.

The boy glanced up at me. "Is that a diaper?"

"Yes." There was no more fight left in me, at least as far as my half-assed toga was concerned. "It's a diaper. A big ol' adult-sized diaper."

Kira lay facedown on the disheveled bed, her top half supported on her forearms, her legs kicked up girlishly behind her. She watched the video game action, displayed on a huge wide-screen flat-panel monitor sitting on a computer desk. Next to the computer sat a high-quality laser printer. This guy had some nice, top-of-the-line equipment.

Josh and the boy talked trash into their headsets.

"Don't invite the noob!" the boy cried into his mic. "He doesn't even have purples!"

Purples? What the heck was he talking about?

"Heal me!" Josh demanded, appearing to be yelling at the screen.

Whuh???

The boy was less civilized. "You're a pussy, Bellmead!" He followed his declaration with a hooting laugh and a sloshing swig of punch that left three red drip stains on his toga.

Josh glanced up at me, his brows angling inward when he noticed my unusual curves. I reached into my toga and pulled out the cups, tossing them aside onto a pile of damp, musty-smelling towels. He angled his head to indicate the desk. I stepped over the laundry and garbage, peeled a sticky burrito wrapper from the bottom of my sneaker, and took a closer look.

In a haphazard pile on the desk lay response e-mails from some of the thief's victims and potential victims. One of the responses said *Screw you and the horse you rode in on, cyberscum!* That person had obviously recognized the e-mail for what it was, an attempt to scam him out of his personal financial data.

The response we'd sent under the guise of Thelma Pucketts lay on top, the withdrawal slip, torn in two, next to it. A mop head perched on top of a basketball on a chair next to the desk.

My heart beat faster than the techno bass.

We've found our guy.

Now all we had to do was take him in.

Given his drunken state, corralling him could prove either much easier or much more difficult than usual. A drunk might give in, too sloshed to put up resistance. On the other hand, drunk people could sometimes become belligerent. With any luck he'd be the former type. After the chase at the library today, I wasn't up for another prolonged arrest.

I flopped down on the bed next to Kira and softly asked, "How'd you and Josh end up here?"

She kept her eyes on the screen as she replied under her breath. "Josh noticed this guy had an Alexstrasza tattoo."

"A *what*?"

"An Alexstrasza tattoo." She kicked her legs casually in the air behind her. "She's a character from World of Warcraft. The Life-Binder. She's one of Josh's favorites, too. I pretend to be her sometimes when we—"

My palm shot up, stopping her before she gave me a visual my mind wouldn't be able to erase. "I get it. You two are into role-play."

"Right. Anyway, Josh told this guy he liked his tatt and the guy challenged him to a game. So here we are."

"What's the kid's name?"

She shrugged. "I don't know what his real name is, but his character name is Lieutenant Longwiener."

Classy. Mature, too. This kid was sure to go places.

I let myself relax for a moment. This party plan had worked out perfectly. No search warrant was required if law enforcement working undercover was invited in by a suspect. The deception didn't matter. Anything we collected here tonight would be admissible in court. This frat rat was going down. Heck, he'd practically served himself up on a silver platter. The deceiver was now the deceived.

Neener-neener.

"What's your name?" I asked the boy.

"Chase," he said.

"Chase what?" I asked.

"Chase Burkhalter. Why?"

I shrugged. "No reason. Just curious." *Just curious,*

my ass. I liked to know the names of the targets I took down.

I stood and pulled out my phone to snap some photos of the evidence before we collected it. First, I took a snapshot of the entire room from the doorway. Next, I photographed the withdrawal slip on the desk. Lastly, I took a pic of the stack of e-mails from victims. I slid the phone back into my pocket and retrieved my cuffs from the belt I wore under my toga. I put them behind my back when the guy glanced up at me.

"What are you doing?" he asked. "Why were you taking pictures of my stuff? That's so not cool."

"No reason," I said, slowly, carefully approaching my prey.

"There's gotta be a reason," the guy spat, his brow furrowed, clearly angry now. He rocked forward in the chair to stand, nearly falling sideways as he tried to get to his feet. That trash can punch sure could do a number on a person's equilibrium.

I decided to strike while he was off balance and at a disadvantage. Grabbing his left arm, I clicked the cuff in place on his wrist. Click.

"What the fuck?" he hollered. "That's so not cool!"

"I'm not trying to be cool," I snapped. "I'm trying to cuff you."

As I attempted to take hold of his other arm, he swung it into the air over his head and waved it all around, keeping it out of my reach as I grabbed at it.

"We're federal agents," I snapped. "You're under arrest for your e-mail scam. Give me your arm. *Now.*"

"No way!" He continued to wave the arm, bending this way and that randomly to make my attempts to catch it even more difficult.

"C'mon, kid," I said. "Quit being an ass. You'll only add resisting arrest to your charges."

He continued waving his arm around.

"Little help?" I said to Josh, who had continued to play the video game.

Josh rocked back and forth a couple of times until he could leverage himself out of the beanbag chair. Once he was on his feet, he jumped as high as he could, trying to grab the kid's arm, but had no better luck than I had. Kira stood on the bed, knees bent for better balance, and attempted to assist us. Despite her long arms, she had no luck, either. This kid was the king of evasive maneuvers. He must've been great at dodge ball back in grade school.

As I held on to his cuffed arm, Chase began kicking out at us while moving toward the door to his bedroom, probably to attempt an escape. After the escapade at the library today, I was in no mood for another chase, especially one in which I'd be chasing someone named Chase. It would be too ironic. Besides, trying to catch this boy if he managed to get out into the thick crowd would be difficult and dangerous.

What to do?

I realized that, though I might not be able to get the second cuff on this jerk, I could put it on myself. *Let's see the turd try to run when he's got a federal agent shackled to him.*

"Fine," I said. "You won't give us your arm? We don't need it anyway." I clicked the cuff onto my wrist and held up my hand, his shackled arm raising with it as if I were some type of puppet master. "Try to get away now, jackass."

My words had been intended as bluster, not an actual suggestion. Chase, however, seemed to take them as a challenge. With his free right arm, he swept Josh aside and took off running, dragging me along with him, the puppet master now the puppet, like Pinocchio in reverse.

Chase yanked me out through his bedroom door and began pulling me down the hall after him. He ran to the railing that looked down three stories to the open foyer and grabbed it with both hands. *Dear God! Is he going to jump over the banister and take me with him?*

"Narcs!" he screamed at the top of his lungs. "Narcs!"

The cry was picked up by kids on the second floor. "Narcs!"

The students on the first floor took up the battle cry. "Narcs! Narcs!"

The house exploded in noise. Girls shrieked. Boys hollered. Warning whistles blew. *Tweet-tweet-tweeeeet! Tweet-tweet-tweeeeet!* The music ended abruptly as someone pulled the plug on the stereo.

"Narcs!" Chase yelled again. "Narcs!"

Red solo cups hit the floor with rapid-fire *thunk-thunk-thunks* followed by wet *splish-splish-splishes* as kids fled in every direction, colliding into each other as they slipped and slid on the punch-drenched floor.

I grabbed at the railing with my free hand as Chase started down the stairs, but my grip was no match for his momentum. My shoulder wrenched as he yanked me after him, and my purse, which contained my gun, badge, and cell phone, dropped to the floor out of my reach. As Chase rushed down the steps, I leaned back, hoping my weight would slow him down. Unfortunately, the motion only managed to trip me up, landing me on my ass. Chase dragged me backward down the stairs, my butt thumping hard down each step—*bump-bump-bump!*—as I tried futilely to get back to my feet. Josh and Kira rushed after us but were a half flight behind.

The cries of "Narc! Narc!" continued as Chase dragged me down both flights, bruising my butt and—*OW!*—quite possibly breaking my tailbone. When he reached the bottom landing, he swung his shackled arm and yanked me off the steps and onto the wet floor. He proceeded across the floor, dragging me behind him.

"Look out!" I screamed as frantic partygoers nearly trampled me.

One of the blond girls from earlier tripped over me and fell, her knee like a cannonball in my stomach. *Oomph!*

Forging his way to the trash can, Chase grabbed the rim with both hands and turned it over on me. "Narc! Narc!"

A rush of red, sticky liquid cascaded over me, filling my eyes and ears and nose. I gasped and sneezed and sputtered, trying to clear my orifices. My toga might as well be a diaper for all of the liquid it absorbed.

Josh finally caught up with us and pulled out his pepper spray, aiming an acrid stream at Chase's face. *Pssssh.*

"Fuck!" yelled Chase. His hands went to his eyes, jerking my shackled arm upward.

At this point, real narcs arrived, a force of seven police officers streaming in the front door, shouting at everyone to "Stay right where you are!" Another added, "And shut your mouths!"

Those in the vicinity froze, while the scraping and shouting noises coming from out back told me that others were attempting to escape over the eight-foot wooden privacy fence that surrounded the frat house's backyard.

Chase attempted to run away but, anchored by me and blinded by the pepper spray, managed only to run nose-first into the wall two feet away. His hands moved from his eyes to his nose as he fell to his knees. "Shiiit!" he cried, his voice muffled by his cupped fingers.

Apparently, some type of sting was taking place. The police rounded kids up left and right and marched them outside to waiting paddy wagons.

When a middle-aged officer stepped our way, I wrangled myself to a stand. I looked around for Josh, but he was nowhere to be seen, the two of us having been separated in the mayhem. I turned to the cop. "I'm a federal agent. I came—"

The cop put his face in mine. "What part of 'shut your mouth' do you not understand?"

A drop of spittle flew from his lips and landed on my cheek. I wiped it away with my free hand. "Sir, if you'll let me find my purse I—"

"You don't know when to stop, do you?" He looked down at the handcuffs. "What's with the cuffs? Some kind of kinky sex thing?"

I gritted my teeth. "Not at all."

He grabbed my free arm and dragged me and Chase to the door, hollering to a younger officer outside. "Get these two in a wagon!"

Despite my vociferous protests, I spent the next two hours locked in a jail cell with one bunk bed, one toilet, and thirty-seven inebriated sorority girls who'd drunk a collective five hundred gallons of trash can punch. I had to give them credit, though. A group of the more sober girls managed to fashion a private tent around the toilet by situating one girl on each side of the commode, another in front of it, their toga sheets stretched between them. Between peeing and throwing up, the girls kept the toilet flushing constantly.

I feared the girls might turn on me if they realized I was the "narc" who'd started the brouhaha at the frat house. I might be tough, but without my gun or pepper spray there was no way I could fight off this many girls. They'd rip me limb from limb before the wardens could stop them. Luckily for me, the scene at the frat house had been such chaos that nobody quite understood what had happened. When the girls had noticed the handcuffs connecting me to Chase, they hadn't realized I'd been trying to arrest the punk, instead, like the cop, assuming it was some type of kinky *Fifty Shades* situation.

The time was a blur. Several of the girls cried. When they'd run dry of tears, they lamented the condition of their mascara. A couple theater majors turned the bunk bed on its side and improvised a sock puppet theater, putting on a remarkably good performance of *Barefoot in the Park*. A group of music majors serenaded the guards with prison-themed songs, including "Jailhouse Rock" by Elvis, the Righteous Brothers' "Unchained Melody," and "Prison Song" by System of a Down. When they'd exhausted their playlist, I taught them the lyrics to Johnny Cash's "Folsom Prison Blues."

One by one, the girls were released. Those with parents who lived in the area were sprung first, while those from out of state had to wait until their parents had been able to contact a local defense attorney and provide a retainer via credit card. Lucky them. I hadn't even been allowed to make my phone call yet. The guard had said, "Someone your age shoulda known better than to get mixed up with these out-of-control kids." He'd followed this declaration with the suggestion that I "shut my pie-hole" and "use this time to think about what I'd done." *Sheesh.* Nobody had said that to me in years. It made me feel irritated. On the bright side, it also made me feel young. *Housemother,* my ass.

I sat on the floor, rested my head against the wall, and closed my eyes, trying to catch some shut-eye. It wasn't easy. The adrenaline was beginning to wane and my buttocks and lower spine throbbed painfully.

"Tara?" came a male voice. "Is that you?"

I opened my eyes to see Anthony Giacomo standing outside the cell. Though not in his usual business suit, he looked nonetheless perfectly stylish in his silky green shirt, designer jeans, and Italian leather loafers. I was surprised the guy recognized me. By then the punch had dried, turning my skin into sticky flypaper. My hair was matted and stained with punch.

I raised a hand. "Hey, Tony."

He cocked his head, his eyes narrowing in question. "What are you doing in this cell with all these college kids?"

"That's a damn good question."

Anthony turned to the guard. "You know you've got a federal agent locked in there?"

The guard, who happened to be the same one who'd told me to shut my piehole, glanced my way. "You mean she wasn't shittin' me?"

"Au contraire," Anthony said. "Unless you want to find yourself without a job, I'd suggest you release her immediately."

It was four A.M. by the time I'd been able to speak my piece, prove my identity, and treat the guard to a well-deserved raspberry. *Pffft.*

I turned to Anthony. "Can I use your phone?"

"Sure." He pulled his cell phone from his pocket and handed it to me.

I dialed Josh.

He answered on the fourth ring, his voice hoarse from sleep. "Hello?"

"What the hell!" I yelled, fueled by fresh fury. "Why didn't you get me out of jail?"

"Wait. You were taken to jail?"

"Yes!" I hissed. "I've been sitting in a cell for hours!"

"Sorry," he said. "It was total chaos at the frat house. I showed my badge to one of the cops, and told him to turn Chase over to our marshals once they were done with him. The cops let me and Kira leave. I figured they'd let you go, too."

"Well, they didn't!"

His voice took on a defensive tone. "That's not my fault."

It *wasn't* his fault, of course. But still, he could've stuck around, made sure I got out okay. Lest I verbally rip him a new one, I simply growled, hung up, and returned the phone to Anthony.

On our way out, we passed federal marshals on their way in to round up Chase and take him to the federal lockup for processing. Chase was apparently out of fight by then, his meager protests of "this isn't cool" lacking volume and conviction.

Anthony was kind enough to give me a ride from the police station, though he insisted I sit on top of a plastic body bag he'd provisioned from the police department's evidence supply. His Jaguar was his baby.

He drove me back to the frat house to round up my purse, then took me on to my car, which was still parked nearby.

"Take care, now!" he called as I climbed out of his car. "And take that sticky body bag with you."

I dragged the bag out of his car, bleeped the locks open on my G-ride, and situated the body bag over the seat. I didn't care much about the fleet car, but I didn't want the seat to be sticky next time I drove it. I drove home, parked the car at the curb in front of my town house, and went inside.

"Holy hell, Tara!" my father cried as I came in my front door.

"My goodness!" My mother rushed over to meet me at the door. "What do they do at fraternity parties these days?"

Though my parents were both up now, their disheveled hair and droopy eyes told me they'd been asleep in bed at some point. Both were in their robes and slippers.

My mother's face contorted in anxiety. "Dad woke up at two to use the bathroom and realized you hadn't come home yet. We've been so worried! What happened?" Before I could answer, she looked down at the bag in my hand. "Dear Lord! Is that a body bag?"

As Annie eased out from under my couch and stepped over to cautiously sniff my leg, I begged their forbearance. "I'm wiped out and all I want to do right now is clean myself up. Can I give you the details in the morning?"

My mother frowned but acquiesced. "I suppose that's all right. At least we know you're okay now." She took the body bag from my hands. "I'll take care of this. You run on up and get a shower before you start attracting bees."

My dad raised a hand to stop me. "At least tell us whether you got the guy you were going after."

"Of course." I offered him a smile. "Tara Holloway always gets her man."

chapter thirty-one

$\mathcal{R}$edneck Rendezvous

Despite shampooing, rinsing, and repeating three times, my hair still bore a pinkish tinge the following morning, courtesy of the Red Dye No. 2 in the punch. My skin hadn't fared much better, looking pink and blotchy in places. I could use a full-body glycolic treatment. Or perhaps a power wash.

But these aesthetic concerns were nothing compared to my buttocks, which had turned black and blue over the last few hours. I couldn't even sit at breakfast. I'd had to eat my banana pancakes lying belly-down on my couch and drink my coffee through a straw.

My mother stood with one hand on her hip, looking down at me. "I can't stand to see you like this, honey. I'm taking you to see the doctor."

With all the pain I was in, I wasn't about to argue. I lay down stretched out in the backseat of my father's king-cab pickup with a bed pillow. My mother insisted I be buckled in and somehow managed to get all three seat belts strapped around me. Frankly, it seemed the belts posed a greater risk of breaking my neck or choking me than saving my life should she have to brake suddenly, but there was no arguing with my mom. She drove me to the emergency clinic.

The receptionist looked up as I came in. "Uh-oh. From that look on your face I'm guessing your lucky streak is over."

I gingerly edged up to the counter. "My butt is bruised. I got dragged down two flights of stairs last night."

Kelsey stared at me a moment, turned to her computer screen, then turned back to me and blinked. "I don't even know how to code that for insurance. There's a code for sprained ankles, broken toes, burns. But there's no number for butt bruises. The closest thing I have is hemorrhoids. Guess I'll go with that."

One pain in the ass was as good as another, I guessed.

Unable to sit, I stood in the waiting room while my mother perched on a chair and perused a six-month-old issue of *National Geographic*. A woman sitting nearby kept cutting glances at me over the top of her mystery novel, probably wondering if my pink tint was due to some type of flesh-eating bacteria. As unsanitary as that trash can punch had been last night, there was no telling what I might have contracted. Mononucleosis. Herpes. Ebola. Syphilis.

The door to the examination rooms opened and Ajay poked his head out. "I hear there's a pain in the butt out here," he called, a smile playing around his lips. "Come on back."

I ambled to the door, my mother following along behind me. Ajay closed it behind us and led us down the hall to an exam room.

"Any word from Nick?" he asked quietly as we walked down the hall.

"Not since last time."

"Damn."

He opened the door to the exam room and held it for me and my mother.

"I'd say take a seat," he said to me as he shut the door behind him, "but I'm guessing that's not an option right now. What happened?"

As he stood there, his hands resting on either end of the stethoscope draped around his neck, I told him about last night's events. The frat party. My attempt to cuff Chase in his room. Chase subsequently dragging me around behind him as if I were a Radio Flyer wagon.

When I finished, Ajay nodded. "All right. Turn around, drop your pants, and put your hands on the table."

Embarrassing as it was, I did as I was told. I cast a warning glance at him over my shoulder. "You better not enjoy this."

"If I can't enjoy it," Ajay shot back, "why do it?" He stepped over and bent down slightly for a closer look. "Ouch. Your butt is solid black-and-blue. On a positive note, it's awfully cute. Firm, too. I'd call it perky, even."

My eyes rolled on their own accord. "Gee, thanks."

Ajay punched a button on the intercom mounted on the wall. "Bring two ice packs to room four please."

The doc pushed gently on my tailbone.

I turned my head and tossed him a scowl over my shoulder this time. "Ow!"

He pushed a little harder. "On a scale of one to ten, how bad is your pain?"

"Fifty-three," I grunted out, "point six."

"Better get an X-ray."

A nurse took me to another room, where a technician took an X-ray of my lower half. While I waited for the images to process, I rested facedown on an exam table with an ice pack on each of my buns. So much for my dreams of having a smokin' hot ass. My butt was as frozen as an Eggo waffle.

I must've fallen asleep, because the next thing I knew Ajay had his hand on my shoulder and was gently shaking me awake.

"Bad news," he said. "Your coccyx is fractured."

Damn that Chase! I had half a mind to march on down to his cell at the federal holding facility and give him a kick in the nuts to even the score. "What's the treatment? Are you going to put me in some type of cast?" How would that even work? Would it be like some type of plaster girdle?

"No," said the doctor. "There's not much we can do for a broken tailbone. You just have to take it easy for a while, try to keep weight and pressure off your lower back."

That would be difficult. My job involved a lot of driving around and sitting and wrangling unruly tax evaders. Then again, maybe the injury would convince Lu to provide me with a Segway for getting around the office. That could be fun. Did they make a model with a cup holder and a built-in television?

Ajay held up one of those doughnut-shaped hemorrhoid pillows. "This will help." He pulled a small brown bottle of pills from the pocket of his lab coat and shook them like a maraca. "So will these."

He handed me the pillow and pills. I looked down at the label. Vicodin, a common, and sometimes abused, painkiller. As much as I would love to have some relief from my sore buns and tailbone, I didn't want to take anything that would prevent me from doing my job. In just an hour or so, my father, Eddie, and I would be heading out to Southern Safari to see about bagging a lion, doctor's order be damned.

"Will these pills impair my judgment?" I asked.

"Not any worse than it already is."

I cast Ajay a look. The look said "shut your piehole." My look sounded suspiciously similar to that cop at the jail last night.

"You shouldn't drive or operate machinery," he said. "So no heading over to the GM plant in Arlington to build cars. No driving a forklift at Home Depot. No filling potholes with a steamroller. Use extra caution when using your vibrator."

My mother eyed Ajay over the top of her magazine and emitted a disapproving *"A-hem."*

"What about my guns?" I asked.

"Guns?" Ajay waved a hand dismissively. "For you, no problem."

I paid my copay and left the clinic with my party favors— the pillow, pills, and ice packs.

When my mother and I arrived home, we found my father decked out in his standard hunting gear. Camouflage pants. Camo shirt. Camo ball cap. He looked every bit the trophy hunter.

I went upstairs and put on a pair of khaki pants and a green T-shirt, makeshift camo. My best sneakers were a trendy Day-Glo orange. Not exactly the thing you want to wear on a hunt, even if it wasn't going to be a real hunt. I gingerly got down on my knees and dug around in the bottom of my closet until I found a navy blue pair.

My doorbell rang a half hour later as Mom and I were packing a cooler and picnic basket in the kitchen. Though I'd assured her that a couple of water bottles and a sandwich apiece would be enough, she'd insisted on making half a dozen sandwiches. She put them in the basket along with an enormous jar of dill pickles, a thermos of warm baked beans, and a tin of her homemade pecan pralines.

"That'll be Eddie." I left my mother to finish stocking the ice chest and went to my front door. I opened it to find Eddie standing on my doorstep. Like my father, he was fully decked out in camouflage, though Eddie's was clearly brand-new. He'd put a cap with the Lone Star Beer logo on his head and tied a red bandana around his upper arm.

I couldn't hold back a snicker. "I do believe you're the first black redneck I've ever seen."

"I feel like an idiot." His eyes moved to my father, taking in Dad's gear as he stepped up behind me. "No offense, Mr. Holloway."

"None taken," Dad replied. He meant it, too. He didn't give a rat's ass whether anyone approved of his clothing. He didn't give a rat's ass whether anyone approved of his simple, country lifestyle. And he didn't give a rat's ass if anyone voiced their opinion, whether or not it matched his own. Dad did nothing to promote movement in the rat-ass market sector.

"Come pick a gun or two," I told Eddie, motioning for him to follow me to my dining room table where my father's gun collection, as well as my own, were laid out.

"Jesus!" Edde cried when he took in the veritable arsenal displayed there. "You've got an entire armory here."

My father picked up one of the rifles. "This one's not bad. The range isn't as long as some of the others, but it's lighter weight, which makes it easier to handle."

He handed it to Eddie, who moved it up and down, testing its heaviness.

Dad picked up a second rifle. "This one's a bolt-action muzzle loader."

The two exchanged weapons.

Eddie held the new rifle to his eye and pretended to take aim at the wall. "Not bad."

Dad showed him a third. "This one's a semiautomatic carbine."

By this time I'd grown impatient. "Just pick one, Eddie. It's not like we're actually going to be shooting anything. Not unless it attacks us first."

Dad cut me a narrow-eyed look, annoyed that I'd interrupted him showing off his collection. You get the man started on his guns and he was like a grandmother bragging about her grandchildren.

"Sorry, Dad," I said. "I'm just anxious to get moving. And my butt hurts so I'm cranky." The pain in my ass was turning me into one.

We packed several rifles in a carrying bag. As Dad went to zip it, I told him to wait a minute.

Hustling upstairs, I retrieved Nick's samurai sword and brought it back downstairs.

"What the heck is that for?" Eddie asked.

I shrugged. "I don't know. In case we run into another rattler or something."

He made a face that told me he thought I was being ridiculous, and he was probably right, but he knew better than to argue with me. I added my night vision scope to the bag, too, as well as my father's. This bust should be wrapped up before nightfall, but it never hurt to be prepared for any eventuality.

Mom emerged from the kitchen with the cooler in one hand, the picnic basket in the other. She set them at our feet. "Don't want y'all going hungry while you're out there."

My father picked up the picnic basket and immediately set it back down. "This thing weighs a ton."

My mother put her hands on her hips. "You complaining?"

Dad raised his hands in surrender. "Wouldn't dream of it. Just making an observation."

Mom walked us out to Dad's truck. "Y'all be careful." She turned to me. "Call me the minute you get things taken care of. I don't want to be sitting here worrying over nothing."

Worrying over nothing was what Mom did best, but pointing that out wouldn't earn me any brownie points. Instead, I promised, "We will."

Dad and Eddie took seats in the front of the cab, while I lay down in the back with the bed pillow under my head, the ice packs on my rear end, and the picnic basket and cooler on the floorboards beside me. Eddie told my father which way to go, and we headed out.

While Dad and Eddie talked sports and ate sandwiches and pickles, I dozed, still exhausted from my late-night escapades. Sometime later, the *plink-plink-plink* of gravel hitting the truck's undercarriage woke me. I lifted my head to see that we'd turned down the county road that led to Southern Safari.

Blinking to clear my eyes, I wriggled gently until I was sitting on the bed pillow with my hemorrhoid doughnut cradling my fractured coccyx.

Dad looked up at the high fence and shook his head. "That's just plain wrong. This place is nothing more than an oversized cage. No self-respecting hunter would shoot anything here."

We passed the sign for the hunting ranch and pulled up to the automated gate, which swung inward to let us onto the property. We drove down a short road also lined with the high fences until we reached a building with a sign designating it as *SOUTHERN SAFARI SPORTS-MEN LODGE*. Though the outside was made of rustic wood, it was clear from the fancy light fixtures and heavy, high-end furniture on the porch that this was no typical hunting shack.

Parked in front were several vehicles, all top-of-the-line SUVs. A gray Toyota Land Cruiser, sticker price upward of $75,000. A silver Lexus LX 570 SUV, which came standard for around eighty-two grand. A Range Rover, which, brand-new, cost around $180K, as much as a nice house in the Dallas suburbs. Nope, these were no soccer-mom SUVs. If I had to hazard a guess, I'd say these cars belonged to corporate bigwigs from Dallas who'd come out here to hunt as some sort of team-building exercise or to get in touch with their Paleolithic side. City slickers trying to act tough, test their mettle—so long as it was in a safe, controlled environment.

A Polaris multipassenger hunting vehicle pulled up. A thirtyish guide was driving, while the other seats were occupied by men with perfect haircuts, expensive sunglasses—no cheap frames for these guys—and de-signer camo gear they'd likely purchased at Cabela's. WalMart T-shirts might be good enough for my father, but not for this crew.

On the flat bed behind the seats lay a dead-eyed scimitar-horned oryx, its white fur stained with blood. My heart writhed in my chest. I fought the urge to turn my gun on the men, yell "on your mark, get set, go!" and chase them until they were backed up against a fence with no means of escape.

Chattering excitedly, the men climbed out of the vehicle, leaving the guide to take care of the carcass. No sense getting their hands dirty, right? The men climbed the two steps to the porch of the lodge and went inside.

As my father parked, a man stepped out from inside the building. He wore a khaki outfit with a tall khaki hat and brown boots. I half expected Curious George to peek out from behind him.

Eddie had a slightly different take on the man. "If he starts singing that 'Happy' song, can I shoot him?"

"You don't like Pharrell Williams?"

"I did," Eddie said, "the first ten thousand times they played that song on the radio. But ten thousand and one sent me over the edge. Besides, my girls keep singing it in the car on the way to school. It gives me an ear worm all day."

"Is that why I saw you skipping to the copier last week?"

"Yeah."

"I'd just thought you'd had too much of Viola's coffee." The stuff was like caffeinated tar.

The man in the hat raised his hand high in a friendly greeting. "Welcome, folks!" he called. "You must be the Galloways."

Dad, Eddie, and I climbed out of the truck.

"Gary Galloway," Dad said, sticking out his hand.

The man took it and gave it a firm shake. "I'm Norman Peele. I'll be your hunting guide today."

Good. My earlier research told me that Peele was the sole owner of Southern Safari Game Reserve, Inc. If there had been any financial games, this guy would have been in the middle of them, right up to his boot tops.

Dad turned to introduce me. "This is my daughter, Sara."

"Right," the man said. "You're the one I spoke to on the phone."

I'm also your worst nightmare, I thought, giving myself a silent pep talk. Probably that wasn't true. I mean, having an undercover IRS agent show up and try to implicate you in charity fraud was no walk in the park, but having your throat ripped out by rabid wolverines would be a worse nightmare. So would being anally probed in an alien invasion. And I had that terrifying, recurring nightmare where I was suddenly standing in a spotlight on a stage, not a stitch of clothing on. Okay, so clearly I wasn't the worst nightmare he could have. But I still bet I could put the fear of God in this guy.

Dad turned to introduce Eddie. "This is my hunting buddy."

"Teddy," Eddie said, also shaking Norman's hand.

Introductions now completed, Norman clapped his hands together. "I've got a great afternoon on tap for you folks. But first there's a little matter of payment." He turned to me. "Let's go inside and run your credit card."

chapter thirty-two

$\mathcal{M}$eow

Norman Peele led us into the lodge. The place had wooden walls, a wooden ceiling, and a wooden floor. It was like being inside the hollow of a tree or a beaver dam.

The open foyer resembled a pro shop. Rounder racks of camo gear and T-shirts. A display of hats, including a souvenir cap with plastic antlers that said I SHOT MY TROPHY AT SOUTHERN SAFARI! A bookshelf with various nonfiction offerings on hunting-related topics, as well as several novels with hunting themes. *Green Hills of Africa* by Ernest Hemingway. *Moby Dick. My Side of the Mountain.* But, sadly, no *Abraham Lincoln: Vampire Hunter.* One of my favorites, *The Girls' Guide to Hunting and Fishing,* was also absent.

An open doorway on the left side of the room led to a cozy lounge where the men I'd seen outside now sat in leather barrel chairs around a circular table, toasting each other and their successful hunt with amber liquid in highball glasses, just as Paleolithic men toasted each other with cholera-laced river water. *Clink! Clink! Clink!*

Peele stepped behind the sales counter. The wall behind him was hung with photographs of trophy hunters and their dead prey. A couple of beefy men with another of the scimitar-horned oryx. A tall, thin woman holding on to the antlers of a barasingha deer. A smiling young boy, who appeared to be no older than ten, with his arm draped over the gaping mouth of a bear with lifeless eyes. The images were disturbing enough, but knowing the animals had been trapped inside the fences with no possible means of escape made their deaths seem unacceptably unfair.

Peele looked at me expectantly. "Got your card handy?"

In preparation for today's sting operation, I'd had Viola order me up a credit card under my alias. I pulled it out of my purse and handed it to Peele. He sat down, ran it through a little black scanner, and handed the card back to me. When the screen popped up with the authorization, he pushed the button to print out a receipt for me to sign.

He handed me the receipt along with a pen. "I just need your John Hancock and we'll be on our way."

I looked down at the slip and nearly choked. *Six thousand five hundred dollars? Holy crap!* It was more than the man had quoted me on the phone, but no sense arguing with him. I'd have the charge reversed anyway, so what did it matter? I signed the slip and handed it back to him in exchange for a copy.

He led us back out front. "Wait here. I'll be right back."

He stalked off in the direction of a detached prefabricated building that resembled an airplane hangar. He slid the wide front door open and disappeared inside. There was a roar as an engine fired up and, a moment later, Peele emerged, sitting atop a tall, open hunting vehicle that provided a wide field of vision, giving his customers another advantage over their prey.

"How about I take y'all on a tour of the place?" he suggested, his gaze running from one of us to the next. "You might see something else you'd like to shoot."

Oh, I saw something else I'd like to shoot, all right. *Him*.

My father glanced over at me for direction. I nodded. Might as well get a better sense of the place if I planned to implicate this man in tax evasion.

Dad looked back up at Peele. "Sounds great."

"Fan-damn-tastic!" Peele said, virtually salivating. "I can just add your kills to your bill when we get back."

I quickly retrieved my pillow and foam doughnut from Dad's truck, and the three of us climbed up to the benches. Dad sat next to Peele in front, while Eddie and I took spots on either side of the bench behind them. I slid the pillow and doughnut under my hindquarters and my cheap rectangular sunglasses onto my face.

Peele punched the gas, taking off down a dirt path, seeming to hit every possible hole or bump. We bounced along, sparks of pain shooting up my spine. After several attempts to find a comfortable position, I discovered that if I leaned on the safety bar to my right, it would take the pressure off my tailbone. Of course I risked falling over the edge of the vehicle and breaking my neck, but at least that would be a quick, painless death.

Peele stopped after driving a hundred yards or so, and pushed a remote control to open an extra-tall gate. The two sides separated, swinging inward with a jerking motion until stopping with a clang. After he'd driven through, he turned in his seat and aimed the remote once again at the gate. The gate swung shut behind us, emitting another clang as it closed us in with the animals.

Like Paradise Park, the land here was equal parts open grassland and stands of scrubby trees, mostly cedars and mesquites. From our vantage point atop the hunting vehicle, we could see for quite a ways into the distance. Mostly what I saw was animal scat and haylike grass.

As Peele drove, he gave us some details about the game ranch. "We've got two hundred acres here. Three large stock ponds. Fifteen species of game." He then proceeded to drop names like the deer had dropped their dung. "A number of famous people have hunted here. Dick Cheney. Shaquille O'Neal. That country star, Brazos Rivers. You hear about him? Got his-self thrown in jail for something or other."

"Yeah," I said, exchanging a knowing glance with Eddie. Nick and I had been the ones to take down the singer for tax evasion. Boy, had that case been a fiasco. "I heard about that, too."

Just ninety seconds into our ride, our guide lifted his foot off the gas and let the vehicle roll for a moment before applying the brake. "Looky there." He raised a finger and pointed toward the horizon slightly to our right. "A herd of barasingha at two o'clock."

I squinted. "Looks more like two-fifteen to me."

The man glanced back and gave me an odd look. Not everyone gets my sense of humor. He turned to my father. "What do you say, Gary? Want to take one of them barasingha home with ya'? Hang the head on your wall? I've got one on my wall at home. Makes a nice conversation piece."

How, exactly, would that conversation go?

Norman: Do those antlers on my wall make my dick look bigger?

Hunting buddy: Hell's yeah! Now pass me another beer.

Dad raised his field glasses to his eyes, took a look at the herd, and shrugged. "I don't know. I've hunted deer for years. One species seems pretty much like another. Hard to get too excited about that."

Gary turned back to Eddie. "How 'bout you, Teddy? You look like a man who might enjoy taking down a large deer."

"No, thanks," Eddie said. "I'm with Gary on this one. A deer's a deer."

For a guy who'd never been on a single hunting trip, Eddie played a pretty convincing hunter.

Disappointment darkening his eyes, Peele turned back around and slid the truck into gear.

"You didn't ask me if I wanted to bag a deer," I said to the back of Peele's head.

He slid the truck back out of gear, his face brightening again with the thought of padding my bill. "You want to take a shot?"

"No, thanks," I said. "I'm more of a gatherer than a hunter." It was true. I had quite a shoe collection. "I just wanted to be asked. Women's rights and all that, you know."

The man simply stared at me for a moment, as if trying to get a read. "Right," he said finally before proceeding on.

We drove on for another minute or two, passing a couple of automatic feeders, before we came upon a trio of oryx drinking on the other side of a stock pond.

Peele braked to a stop and cut the engine. "What about one of them?" he said in a whisper as if afraid they'd flee. Little chance of that. Two of them glanced up at us and went right back to drinking, our presence barely registering with them. The third didn't even bother to look up. Obviously, they didn't consider us a threat. They were used to humans coming around, filling the feeders, checking on things.

Dad stroked his chin. "They sure are pretty. I think maybe I could see one of their heads on my wall."

Buoyed by the possibility of more profits, Peele said, "Their hides make a nice rug, too. Wouldn't a skin like that look great in front of your fireplace?"

Dad narrowed his eyes. "Let me think about it. I've kind of got my heart set on hunting that lion. I've never hunted something that might want to hunt me back. That's gonna be quite a thrill, I expect."

"Oh, it will be," Peele said with a certainty that didn't reach his eyes. "'Course my insurance company puts all kinds of rules on me. They don't want any of my clients getting eaten out here." He followed his words with a forced chuckle. "Heh-heh."

He started the engine again and headed straight across the middle of the field to another gate on the far side. An oryx stood right in front of the gate, munching on grass.

Peele gave a quick tap on the horn. *Honk.*

The oryx lifted its head, but continued chewing the grass, which hung out of both sides of his mouth. *Sheesh.* Between the high fences, the tall hunting vehicle, and the prey that was used to humans, this place was like preschool for hunters.

"Shoo!" hollered our guide, waving his arm. "Get out of the way!"

The oryx merely put his horned head back to the ground for another helping of grass.

Peele shoved the gear into park, jumped down from the truck, and stomped over to the oryx, slapping it on the ass with a resounding *whap!* I half expected him to pull a Jennifer Lawrence and holler, "Screw PETA!"

"Norman's a little kinky, huh?" Eddie said under his breath as the oryx bounded away.

I had trouble finding anything funny in the situation. Even with the Vicodin dulling my pain, that slap on the ass hit too close to home.

Back on the truck now, Peele retrieved a second remote from a plastic bin at his feet, opened the gate, and drove through. He pushed the button again to close the gate behind us.

"Everybody keep on the lookout," he said now, scanning the area. "We don't want that savage lion sneaking up on us."

He drove around the perimeter of the enclosure, which appeared to be about ten acres in size. When we didn't spot the lion he circumnavigated the space again, this time in a tighter loop.

On our third go-round, my father spotted the lion. "Is that him at that trough over yonder?"

Sure enough, the lion was drinking from a large metal horse trough. Hardly what anyone could call savage. He looked no different than a housecat drinking from its water bowl, just on a larger scale.

"That's him," Peele said, stopping the truck. "Good eye, Gary."

Good eye, nothing. The lion was out in the wide open.

I put my field glasses to my eyes. *Is this big cat the same lion I'd seen at Paradise Park?* There was no way to tell for certain, though he appeared to be the same size.

As we watched, the lion turned, spotted us, and began walking our way.

"Get your gun ready, Gary," Peele said. "That cat may charge us."

My dad raised his rifle. "I hope he does. I want to look that son of a bitch in the eye when I kill 'im."

A shiver ran down my fractured spine. My father was playing a role here, but he was playing it far better than I'd expected. Hell, he'd sounded downright bloodthirsty. A moment later, though, I saw him cast a cutting look at Peele when the man bent down to retrieve his binoculars. Obviously, the anger in my father's words, though directed at the lion, had been truly meant for our guide.

As we all watched, the lion walked toward us at an even pace. He didn't crouch to ambush us and he didn't run as if to attack. He was simply strolling over to see what was up, probably hoping we had a fresh leg of lamb to toss to him. It was no different than when my cats followed me into the kitchen, hoping for a treat.

The lion was fifty feet away when he sniffed the air, seemed to realize we had no fresh meat with us, and abandoned his plan to come check us out, distracted by a monarch butterfly fluttering past him. He leaped after the bug like a kitten going after a fly. He pounced, but missed. As long as he was down on the ground, he figured it was a good time to roll around in the grass and sunshine. He rolled over onto his back, his big paws in the air, and wriggled happily.

"How the Sam Hill am I supposed to shoot that thing?" my dad snapped, turning away from his scope to put his eyes on Peele. "It would be like killing Garfield."

"You know, Gary," the guide said in a placating tone, "even lions in the wild take some time to nap and play like this."

My father huffed. "I doubt they do it when they've got a rifle aimed at 'em." Dad put his gun down. "Sheez Louise. I don't need a gun to take down that cat. All I need is a lasagna."

The lion wriggled some more and swatted at another bug.

"Where'd you get this lion, anyway?" I asked Peele. "A zoo?"

Before the man could come up with a lie, the lion opened his mouth for a yawn. Sure enough, his lower left fang was missing. This lion was Simba, no doubt about it.

"Look." Peele's face grew red with rage. "What's it matter where this lion came from? A lion's a lion. You wanted your trophy." He motioned to the cat lying on his back, licking its paw. "There he is. If you choose not to shoot him, that's your own business. But I'm not going to give you a refund if you choose not to take a shot. I've kept up my end of the bargain."

Push had come to shove.

"What do you say, Teddy?" I asked my partner. "Ready to do this thing?"

Eddie lifted his chin in agreement.

I pulled my badge out of my purse and displayed it to Norman Peele. Eddie pulled his from his pocket and did the same.

The guide drew back in confusion. "What the—"

"I'm Special Agent Tara Holloway with the IRS," I said, adding an "ow" when a fresh jolt of pain raced up my spine.

"Senior Special Agent Eddie Bardin," Eddie said, tipping his beer hat.

I pointed to Simba. "That cat came from Paradise Park, which purports to be a nonprofit animal rescue charity. Obviously, that is not the case."

Norman sputtered. "You don't know that."

"He's missing the same tooth as a cat we saw just days ago at Paradise Park." I pulled out my phone and brought up the picture I'd taken on my screen. "See?"

"Could be coincidence," Norman spat.

"Could be you're a lying sack of scat," I spat back. "And as long as we are on that subject, you have the right to remain silent. Anything you say can be held against you in a court of law. You—"

"What?" he cried, shaking his head as if the motion could somehow clear it of the words he'd just heard. "You're going to arrest me?"

Eddie pulled out his cuffs. "Looks that way."

"For what?"

"Aiding and abetting tax evasion," I said. "Unless you can take me to your office right this minute and show me that you paid for that cat with a credit card or check or in some traceable manner other than cash, it seems pretty clear you were helping the Kuykendahl cousins cover their tracks. Their so-called sanctuary is nothing more than a way station for animals headed to one or another of these canned hunting places."

Peele stared at me a moment, put his thumb to his mouth, and chewed it. "What if I was to help you? You know, turn state's witness and testify against those two."

I lifted a shoulder, noncommittal. "You have evidence that could help us?"

"I sure do! Those boys breed the deer and oryx. Hell, they provide stock for half the game ranches in Texas. The big cats and bears and stuff is just a side thing for them."

"How do you know this?"

"Heard it from their own mouths."

"You paid them cash for the animals?" I asked.

He nodded. "That's all they'll take. They claim it's because it would be difficult to repossess the animals if a check bounces."

That would probably be true. Still, it didn't negate the fact that they were running a livestock operation, not a rescue operation.

"But they also told me they wanted cash so that they could hide it from the government," he added. He probably didn't realize it yet, but that little tidbit further implicated him in their scheme, made him a knowing participant in tax evasion. "They even laughed when they told me. They said they'd been doing this for years and nobody had caught up with them."

Well, somebody had certainly caught up with them now. And her name was Sara Galloway. Oops, I mean Tara Holloway.

"How many animals have you bought from them, all told?" I asked.

He looked up in thought. "Six or seven bears. Couple

of tigers. A panther. Probably a hundred or more each of the barasingha deer and the scimitar-horned oryx."

"You don't breed those yourself?"

"No," he replied. "People see babies running around, they lose interest in the hunt. It's bad for business."

My father and I exchanged glances now. I could tell he was as disgusted with Peele as I was.

"Look," I told the man. "I appreciate the information, and your continued cooperation will only be to your benefit. A plea deal might be possible. It'll be up to our lawyers and yours to work it out. But I've still got to take you in and we still have to seize the animals as evidence."

Though I was sure about the former, I wasn't so sure about the latter. Nonetheless, if I could save Simba in any way, I would. He looked so cute over there, napping in the sun.

chapter thirty-three

$\mathcal{S}$wamped

An hour later, via a series of conference calls and private conversations, Norman Peele had contacted a criminal defense attorney who worked out a deal with Ross O'Donnell under which Peele would turn himself in voluntarily. Ross had advised that bail would likely be set at a small amount given that Peele wasn't the primary target in the case and had only incidentally aided and abetted the Kuykendahls in their charity fraud and tax evasion scheme. The attorneys also agreed to a moratorium on hunting at the ranch until a judge could more fully consider the legal issues.

When we were done at Southern Safari, we met up with two federal marshals on the side of the road leading to Paradise Park.

"Wait here," I told my father. "We'll be back as soon as we get the kooky cousins rounded up."

Disappointment flickered over my father's face. "You mean to tell me that I drove all the way out here to help you, and you're not even going to let me watch this bust?"

"Southern Safari was risky enough," I said. "Norman Peele had no idea who we were, so we had the advantage of surprise. The Kuykendahl cousins will know exactly why we're here, and they'll be none too happy about it." Especially since I'd let them think we'd reached an understanding earlier. "They both carry guns and hunting knives. It's too dangerous."

Dad snorted. "Too dangerous for *me* but not too dangerous for *you*?"

Ugh. My father could be so stubborn sometimes. It was clear which parent I'd gotten that trait from. "I've got a Kevlar vest and I'm a trained federal agent."

"And I taught you how to shoot a BB gun when you were three years old. You think you'd be where you are today if I hadn't taught you how to handle a weapon?"

It was true. If I hadn't grown up around guns I'd probably have never considered becoming a special agent.

"All right," I said finally, giving in. "But you have to sit between me and Eddie. And if you get hurt, you're the one who's going to answer to Mom."

"Your mother?" Dad said. "Now *that's* scary."

We left my father's truck on the side of the road, climbed into the marshals' cruiser, and proceeded into Paradise Park, our guns at the ready in case these crazies decided to go down in a blaze of glory. Or, in the Kuykendahls' case, a blaze of crazy.

Today, Kevin's pickup sat in front of the trailer, though the Hummer was nowhere to be seen. Was Kevin here and Quent out on the property? Were both men out on the property together? Had both men gone somewhere else? There was no telling for certain.

"That truck belongs to Kevin," I told the marshals. "Quent drives a green Hummer."

The marshal in the front passenger seat cast a glance back at me. "That might mean they're separated right now. That could be a good thing. Might be easier to take 'em down one at a time."

True. One of them would probably think twice before taking on four federal agents. But if they were only outnumbered two to one, these crazy-eyed rednecks might be foolish enough to give it a go.

"They communicate by walkie-talkies," I said. "If we nab Kevin here, we better assume he's let Quent know we're on the property. We'll have to watch our backs."

Rather than take an unnecessary risk, the marshal who was driving circled the cruiser around to face the exit so we could make a fast getaway if necessary. He also parked the car far enough from the trailer that it would take a good shot to hit any of us. Of course if Kevin went for a shotgun rather than a rifle, he could spray us all in short order.

The marshal reached out to the dash and retrieved the microphone for the cruiser's public address system. He squeezed the talk button. "Kevin and Quent Kuykendahl," he said, his voice traveling and echoing across the space like an announcer at a football game. "We are federal agents here to take you in for questioning about your sanctuary. If you are in the trailer, leave all weapons inside and step outside with your hands in the air."

He released the talk button and we all waited in anticipation, our eyes locked on the door.

When twenty seconds had passed with no movement, the marshal repeated the order.

Again we stared at the door.

Again, nothing.

The marshal returned the mic to the dash. "We'll have to move in."

He drove the car a few yards farther from the trailer and situated it sideways across the dirt road to block the exit. Of course if Quent and Kevin came barreling up in the Hummer they could just knock the cruiser out of the way. Those Hummers were like military tanks.

"Stay here," I instructed my dad as we agents climbed out of the car. "Keep your head down."

Dad did as he was told. Well, mostly. I turned back to see him peeking out the window.

"We'll go that way," the driver said, pointing left. "You two go the other way."

Eddie and I darted into the brush on our right. Using the small stands of trees for cover, we ran from one to the next, closing in on the trailer.

One of the marshals ran up to the front door of the trailer, hunkered beside it, and reached for the knob, throwing the door open. When no gunfire erupted through the door, he ran inside, his partner coming in for backup.

Eddie and I circled around the back of the trailer. Though there were four dusty windows along the back, they were all closed. Nobody was climbing out of them to attempt an escape. We continued on around the other side, finding the marshals emerging from the trailer when we reached the front.

"Nobody's here," the driver said. "All I found was pork rinds and Mountain Dew."

After a brief powwow, we decided to take the cruiser and head out farther onto the property to look for the Kuykendahls. We also alerted the local sheriff's department, who agreed to post deputies a quarter mile down the road in both directions from the gate to Paradise Park in case the cousins attempted to flee or returned from somewhere outside the park.

We drove on, passing Simba's now-empty cage. An enormous bone lay inside, small pieces of rancid meat still attached. Flies swarmed over the lion's leftovers, causing my stomach to squirm a little in response.

Eddie, Dad, and I had our binoculars to our eyes.

Dad pointed off to our left into the high-fenced corral containing the Barasingha deer. "There's the Hummer."

I shifted my focus in that direction. The Hummer appeared empty, though it was possible the cousins were crouched down inside, waiting to ambush us as we approached.

Eddie turned his attention back to the marshals. "Any chance you've got a tear gas gun?"

"We do," said the driver, "but I'm not sure how accurate I can be from this far out. The guns don't have distance settings. You have to eyeball it and estimate. And I'd have to aim high to get the canister over that fence."

"It would upset the animals, too," I added. The last thing any of us would want is to cause a stampede and risk one of the baby deer being trampled to death.

Barking to the left drew our attention. Quent's two Brittany spaniels appeared, running around the perimeter of a watering hole in the pasture. The dogs lunged into the water, swam around for a bit, then returned to the shore, barking again. They appeared disinterested in the deer, probably having been trained to leave them alone.

My father pulled his binoculars down, squinted into the distance, then returned them to his eyes. "Something sure has those dogs upset."

The driver opened his door. "Let's go find out what it is."

Eddie, the marshals, and I entered the pasture, closed the gate behind us, and did another slow, wide approach. Though I'd been concerned the dogs might feel threatened and come after us, they were far too distracted by whatever was in the water to pay us any mind.

Was it a snake? A bullfrog? Some type of waterfowl? Hell, could there be alligators out here? I wouldn't put anything past those crazy cousins.

Weapons at the ready, we crept up on the pond, an agent situated in each quadrant.

The pond was approximately a hundred feet in diameter. The depth was difficult to judge given the murkiness of the water but, from the weeds in the center, I surmised it was only two or three feet at its deepest. Green pond scum covered half the surface area, while water bugs darted back and forth across the remainder.

As I stared at the scum near the edge of the weeds, it began to take shape, like one of those Magic Eye pictures that were the rage years ago.

Boots.

Legs.

A torso.

A face covered in scum and hidden by a covering of uprooted plants. *Swamp Thing. The Buffoon from the Green Lagoon.*

I glanced around me. There were a few broken twigs and some deer droppings. *Aha! There we go.* A nice, solid rock as big as one of Mom's corn muffins.

I picked it up, pulled my arm back, and took aim at the submerged man's crotch. Stone met stones with a wet yet forceful *thwuck!*

The two halves of Kevin Kuykendahl rose from the water as if he were folding himself in two. He rolled onto his side, gasping and retching and gagging on the water, then gasping and retching some more before finally sitting up.

"One down!" I called to my team. "One to go!"

Though Kevin surrendered, he did so from the center of the pond, raising his hands and hollering, "You want me? Here I am. Come get me, assholes."

Eddie and the marshals gathered around me.

"Who's going in?" I asked. I mean, I'd found and essentially disabled the guy. One of them should have to wade into the muck to cuff him, right?

Unfortunately, the men didn't see it that way.

"Be our guest." Eddie swept an upturned hand toward Kevin. "You took him out. We wouldn't want to steal your thunder."

Yeah, right.

I tossed the men a disgusted look and started into the watering hole, wishing I'd had the forethought to ask Dad to bring his fishing waders. The muck at the bottom of the pond sucked at my shoes like a giant-mouthed leech as I took each step. *Slurk. Slurk. Slurk.* I only hoped there weren't any *real* leeches in here.

After a few more steps, my foot caught on something under the water, probably a submerged tree limb. I tripped and stumbled forward, trying not to fall face-first into the muddy water. Though I somehow managed to stay on my feet, my sunglasses fell from my face, landing in the water with a splash and a plop. I made no effort to find the darn things. Why bother? They'd sat cockeyed on my face from the get-go.

By the time I reached Kevin, I'd lost not only my cheap sunglasses, but also one shoe and most of my dignity. Without a word to the ass, I grabbed his arms, yanked them up behind his back, and cuffed him. Taking a cue from Norman Peele, I slapped Kevin's muddy ass to set him in motion. *Smack.*

A minute later, we were back on dry land. I left Kevin with the men as I wandered back into the pond, using my toes to feel around for my lost shoe, swinging my leg back and forth like a fleshy metal detector. *There it is.* I reached down, wrangled the shoe out of the muck, and swished it around in the water to remove as much of the mud as possible. When I got back to shore, I put a hand on Eddie's shoulder to balance myself and wrestled the wet shoe back onto my foot.

Fully dressed now, I turned back to Kevin. "Where's your cousin?" I demanded.

Kevin cut me a snotty grin. "Which one? I got thirteen of 'em."

"You know who I'm talking about," I snapped back. "Quent."

"Hell if I know," he said. "When we heard the marshal talking on his loudspeaker he took off. Don't have any idea where he might've ended up."

If Quent had kept running all this time, he could be a mile or two away by now. But we hadn't seen him heading our way as we'd driven onto the property. Even if he'd been running from one stand of trees to another for cover, one of us would have likely seen him. To get off the back of their property, he would've had to cut through the high fence. I glanced around but didn't see any open spots anywhere. Something told me that Quent was holed up here somewhere on the property, too.

While one of the marshals kept watch on Kevin, Eddie, the other marshal, and I headed into the pasture that held the scimitar-horned oryx. A thick herd of the animals milled around, some grazing, some pooping, a couple of the young ones engaging in playful head butting, their nubby little horns unable yet to do any real damage.

As we made our way deeper into the field, the herd dispersed. A distressed bleating sound drew my attention to a small oryx standing immobilized where the herd had just been.

"He's hiding behind that young one," Eddie said.

Sure enough, Quent's arm was visible wrapped around the baby's neck, holding it in place as he bent over behind it, trying to move it along next to him.

"We see you, moron!" I called. "Release that animal and put your hands up!"

Quent did not do as told. Instead, he picked the animal up in his arms, using the poor thing as a shield. "You'll never take me alive!"

"You heard the man," Eddie said from next to me, gesturing with his gun. "Shoot him in the head and let's call it a day."

As tempting as it was to kill Quent, lethal force wasn't justified here. At least not yet. If Quent pulled his gun or knife, I'd have every right to fire my gun. But until he did, I was at risk of another excessive-force trial if I took a shot. Besides, I didn't want to risk shooting Quent and having him drop the baby oryx and possibly hurt it.

We were debating what to do when the problem solved itself. A large female oryx, no doubt the distressed calf's mother, circled slowly yet purposefully forty feet behind Quent. When she'd drawn in line with him, she turned, put her head down in battering-ram position, and launched herself at her baby's captor. There was a thunder of hooves as she rocketed toward Quent's back. Quent just had time to turn his head and spot his pursuer when the mother oryx hurled herself into the air and the moment of impact was upon him.

Crack!

The sound of horns meeting skull caused us agents to express a collective gasp. As poetic as this justice might be, it was nonetheless hard to watch. I, for one, had to cover my eyes with my hands and peek out from between my fingers.

Quent went limp, his arms releasing the calf, who slid to the ground and ran off just in time to avoid being trapped under Quent's falling body. As he lay there, motionless, the mother oryx circled around, trampled across his back, and ran after her frightened calf.

The three of us stood there, staring at the seemingly lifeless body. *Is he dead?* I sure as heck didn't want to go up there and find out. I mean, I'd been to funerals before, but seeing a body nicely dressed and made up and lying in a comfy coffin is one thing. Seeing a man with his head smashed in, lying in pool of blood in a field, was another thing entirely.

The marshal dialed 911. "We need an ambulance," he told the dispatcher. "ASAP. A man just got rammed in the head by an antelope." He listened for a moment. "She wants to know if he's breathing."

"Why don't you go see?" Eddie suggested to me.

"Hell, no!" I said. "I got the last one. It's your turn."

"You're the primary on this case," he said. "I'm only along for the ride."

The two of us looked to the marshal.

"This is *your* tax case," the marshal said, raising his palms. "One of you should have the honors."

I shook my head. "What a couple of wussies."

I marched forward, choking down the fear that I might soon be seeing what freshly spilled brains look like. As I drew close, I shut my eyes, took a deep, fortifying breath, and forced them back open.

Quent's head, though cut open along his right cheekbone and brow, remained intact, even if bleeding profusely. His chest rose and fell slowly, indicating he was still breathing.

"He's alive!" I called back.

The marshal informed the dispatcher and Eddie stepped forward.

He looked down at the man. "Should we apply pressure to stop the bleeding?"

"You do it," I said.

"What if his skull caves in?"

Ugh. The thought had me sinking to my knees.

Eddie cut a look my way. "Now who's the wussy?"

"Me," I admitted, raising my hand. "Totally."

Eddie pulled off his shirt and pressed it to the side of Quent's face.

When I'd conquered my wooziness, I asked, "Do you think he'll have permanent brain damage?"

"How would anyone be able to tell?"

It was nearly nightfall by the time we'd finished dealing with the Kuykendahls and arrangements had been made for someone from the Dallas Zoo to take over care of the animals at Paradise Park, at least until they could be relocated to legitimate sanctuaries. Eddie, Dad, and I piled into Dad's truck for the drive back to Dallas. Once again, I lay belly-down to keep pressure off my lower spine.

I hadn't even realized I'd fallen asleep until the truck came to a complete stop in the driveway of Eddie's house. I lifted my head and rubbed my eyes.

Eddie turned around to address me over the back of the front seat. "Good work today. I bet you're the only special agent on the IRS payroll who can say they've saved a lion and a bunch of bears."

"You get some of the credit," I said.

"Shoot, no. I was just a warm body along for the ride."

That was kind of true. But having his warm body with me had ensured my safety, reduced the risk that the Kuykendahls would gut me, field dress me like a deer, and barbecue me on their propane grill. Still, I'd reciprocated on many of Eddie's cases. That's what being partners was all about.

"Bye, buddy," I said as Eddie climbed out of the truck. "See you at the office on Monday."

As we drove off, I turned to my father. "Thanks again, Dad. I couldn't have done this without you."

"Anything for my girl," he said.

Little did he know that promise was about to be put to the test.

chapter thirty-four

*E*arly Graves

As we turned out of Eddie's subdivision, the rumba ring came from my purse. It took me a moment to realize it was the secret phone Nick had given me.

"Nick!" In my haste to unzip my purse, I inadvertently knocked it off the seat, the contents cascading to the floor of my dad's truck. Given that it was now fully dark, there was no sunlight to help me see inside the truck. "Turn on the light, Dad! I can't see!"

My father turned on the inside light, but by the time I located the phone under the seat the call had gone to voice mail. Knowing I couldn't call Nick back, I had to wait for him to leave his message. I cursed my clumsiness all the while. When the phone finally popped up with the icon indicating a voice mail had been left, I immediately punched the button to listen.

Nick's voice bore what was clearly a forced calm. "The shit's hitting the fan, Tara. Five members of the cartel forced me, Christina, and Alejandro into the back of a Budget Rental truck at gunpoint."

Christina cursed in the background, followed by a sob

she'd probably tried to hold back, followed by another curse as she tried again to be brave.

"We have no idea where they're taking us," Nick continued, "but I was able to kick the back door and dent it enough to see out of the gap. We passed Southfork Ranch on our right about a minute ago. They're turning left. It's too dark to see much now. Oh, shit, they're slowing down! I've got to go. If this is it . . ."—his voice choked up—"tell my mother I love her. And know that you . . ." His voice became soft and deep with emotion. "You were everything I ever wanted, Tara."

With that, Nick was gone.

Possibly forever.

But, no. No! If I lost Nick, it would only be after I'd done everything in my power to save him.

"Go north!" I threw out my arm to direct my father onto I-45, forgetting all about my broken tailbone as I climbed over the seatback and into the front. "Floor it!"

Dad did what I asked without question. While keeping an eye on the highway exits, I phoned Lu. "I just heard from Nick!" I cried. "They're in trouble!"

I told her everything I knew, except how I'd gotten the information. She could make her own assumptions. "I'm headed there now!"

"Are you armed?"

"Am I Tara Holloway?" Of course I was armed!

"I'll contact the DEA," Lu said quickly. "You call 911."

Without good-byes, we ended the call. I dialed 911 and told the dispatcher that units were needed northeast of Southfork Ranch.

"Where, exactly?" he asked.

"I don't know for certain." The octave of my voice rose with my mounting hysteria. "All I know is they passed Southfork Ranch and took a left about a minute later. Tell

the officers to look for a Budget Rental truck. And tell them
to hurry!"

"Got it," the dispatcher said. "I'll send units to the area."

In what felt like an eternity but was in reality less than
three minutes, we reached the Parker Road exit. Dad turned
on his emergency flashers and honked his horn as he flew
down the shoulder of the exit ramp around the slower
traffic. *Honk! Honk-honk! Hooooonk!* When he reached
Parker Road, he turned right, tires squealing as the truck
careened around the corner. *Squeeee!*

We made the five and a half miles to Southfork Ranch
in less than four minutes. As we approached the ranch, I
spotted a Collin County Sheriff's Department cruiser turning left down a residential street just past the ranch. A
Parker PD patrol car came up the next street on the left.

"Go farther!" I shrieked at my father, motioning with
my arm.

It was possible the members of the cartel planned to
take Nick, Christina, and Alejandro to a house, but I had
my doubts. Even though these homes were situated on
large lots with substantial space between them, the violent thugs would probably want more privacy to carry out
their killings. These were professional murderers, not
the type to take unnecessary risks.

We drove on for another twenty seconds when I spotted
a county road on the left, just before Lavon Lake. Something told me this could be the place. "There!" I hollered.
"Turn there!"

Dad took the turn as fast as he dared, taking out the
speed limit sign with a loud *ping* as his truck slid in the
caliche. After zigzagging wildly for a moment, the two
of us being thrown side to side as if on a carnival ride,
Dad regained control of his truck and straightened out.

With no streetlights on this stretch of pavement and only

a thin sliver of moon, the truck's headlights provided the only illumination. It wasn't enough. *It wasn't enough!* In the darkness we could drive right past the rental truck and not notice it. With lives ticking down, we didn't have any time to waste.

I threw off my seat belt, leaned over the seatback, and reached into the gun case for my night vision scope. Putting it to my eye, I scanned the countryside. All I saw were dozing cows, scraggly brush, and an occasional fence post.

We'd driven a mile or so when my eyes spotted a copse of cedar trees in a pasture about a hundred yards off. I was about to move on when shapes began to appear among the limbs and branches.

Is there something hidden in the foliage?

I squinted through the scope.

Yes!

The Budget Rental truck was parked sideways behind the trees, portions of the logo visible. The silver Dodge Avenger belonging to Carlos Uvalde, the convicted heroin dealer, sat next to it, along with the Sequoia I'd followed to the Waffle House and Motley's pickup truck. Keeping the scope to my eyes, I pointed through the windshield. "The truck's over there!" I informed my father. "In those trees!"

I didn't see Nick or Christina, but they couldn't be far away. The only question now was, *Are they still alive?*

"Cut the lights," I told Dad. With the headlights on, we'd be easy to spot and target. We wouldn't be able to help Nick and Christina if the cartel's thugs opened fire on us and took us out.

Dad turned off the headlights on his truck and turned into the field. Thick weeds and brush slapped at the truck as we bounced across the uneven terrain. He stopped behind another stand of trees not far from the other vehicles and we hopped out of his truck. Dad grabbed the bag of weapons from his backseat. I scurried into the trees, dropping to my knees at the base of a scrubby evergreen. Scanning the field with my scope, I spotted movement to the right of a dilapidated barn in the distance. Squinting, I stared until the image became clear.

Five men milled around. Given their relative posturing and gesticulations, they seemed to be arguing, two against three. The two were Vargas and Motley, the men I'd seen in the Waffle House. Of the three who seemed to be in accord, one of them appeared to be in charge, the other two looking to him as if for guidance. The leader wore a leather jacket with an excess of zippers and biker boots with thick chains encircling the ankles. His head was shaved, his face criss-crossed with scars.

El Cuchillo.

My heart turned a back flip in my chest and my throat swelled shut in terror. Gulping to clear my airway, I shifted the scope to take in the area around them. In front of the men, Nick, Christina, and a man who had to be Alejandro knelt side by side, blindfolds over their eyes, duct tape over their mouths, their hands tied behind them. Directly in front of each of them lay a freshly dug shallow grave.

Holy shit!
They're going to be killed!
Execution style!

"Ohmigod!" I wheezed out on a breath, beginning to hyperventilate. *Wuh-uh-wuh-uh-wuh-uh.* "Ohmigod! Ohmigod! Ohmigod!"

"What?" Dad asked, dropping the bag and kneeling down next to me. "What do you see?"

Paralyzed by my fear, I was unable to speak, unable to move, unable to think.

My father grabbed the scope from my hands, looked through it, and gasped. "Those men are gonna kill 'em! My God, they've dug graves already!"

For a moment my mind remained frozen, unable to think or react, my synapses misfiring and sparking uselessly like a frayed electrical cord. But then my mind thawed just enough for me to remember the fortune cookie.

Conquer your fears or they will conquer you.

The cookie was right.

I couldn't let my terror control me.

I had to do this.

I had to save Nick and Christina.

"Time to gun up, Dad. We're going to war."

I reached for the bag of guns, handed my father his hunting rifle and his night vision scope, and retrieved my own long-range rifle. Dad returned my scope to me and I slid it into place on my rifle, raising it to my eye.

"We can't shoot yet," I said quickly. "I don't know who's who. Some of those men might be undercover DEA."

I had no idea how many other agents were working this case with Nick and Christina. And given the limited lighting and distance, I couldn't confirm which of the two men siding with El Cuchillo might be Uvalde. We wanted to save Nick and Christina, but we couldn't risk killing another agent with friendly fire. We could only shoot if it became a hundred percent clear there was no other option and that the man we shot was a member of the cartel. At this point there was the possibility, however remote, that if any of the five men were undercover agents they would somehow be able to save Nick and Christina.

My gut twisted and writhed while I waited, hoping for things to become clear. Who were the good guys and who were the bad guys? Were they *all* bad guys? If so, we shouldn't be waiting, we should be doing something right now!

In my hyperalert state, every nerve ending tingled. The crickets seemed to be chirping at a million decibels and the musty, earthy smell of the thick undergrowth overpowered my olfactory senses. I was also aware of every breath my father drew next to me, every blink of his eyes. His presence, though, was calming rather than irksome.

Without taking my eye from my scope, I said in a hitching, quavering voice, "I'm really glad you're here, Dad."

It was true. Though I feared for his safety, I knew he was a good shot. Hell, he'd been the one to teach me how to handle a gun. He was every bit as good, if not better, than many sharpshooters. And if there was ever a time a girl needed her daddy, this was it.

"Happy to help," he said, following his words with a mirthless chuckle. "But let's keep this from your mother, okay?"

As my father and I stood there side by side with our rifles at the ready, watching through our scopes, El Cuchillo said something to the two men allied with him. In an instant, the two whipped handguns out from under their jackets and shot the other two men point-blank—Vargas in the chest, Motley in the face—the gun flashes bright in the dark night, the *bang-bang* traveling across the wide field to our ears.

The now-dead men snapped backward, arms flailing like those nylon fan-blown dancers used to get attention at car sales. They collapsed to the ground in bent, bloody heaps. I could only hope neither was a federal agent.

"Lord!" my father squeaked. "Holy Lord!"

My gut roiled and I had to fight the urge to vomit. I'd seen lots of terrible things in my job. But, until now, I'd never witnessed anyone being killed. I fought the urge to scratch out my own eyes. But I knew it would be futile. Once you've seen something that horrific, you can never *un*see it.

My lungs locked up as El Cuchillo stepped up behind Alejandro. He pulled open his jacket, revealing a sheathed knife strapped to his chest. He yanked the blade from the sheath, the metal glinting in the moonlight. His lips spread in a grin so unfeeling, so evil, so devilish, it wouldn't have surprised me to see flames shoot from his mouth.

He pressed his knife to the informant's throat. The other men made no move to stop him. Instead, one of the remaining men stepped up behind Christina, whose shoulders were shaking with sobs. The third man stepped up behind Nick. The men aimed their guns down at the back of Christina and Nick's heads.

Now I was certain.

None of these men were DEA.

I realized that shooting the men posed the risk they might reflexively pull their triggers as they fell and shoot Nick and Christina. But what choice did we have? If we didn't shoot the men, Nick and Christina would definitely die. If we did shoot the men, my boyfriend and friend stood a chance of surviving . . . *however small that chance might be.*

An odd calm and clarity settled over me, as if I were having an out-of-body experience. I knew then and there I would soon be taking a human life. I could only hope that I'd be saving one, as well.

"I've got Nick's man," I told my father, "you take Christina's." I hesitated only a split second before adding, "Shoot to kill."

My father shifted his gun slightly to the right. "Got 'im in my sight."

"Okay." I steeled myself, saying a quick, silent prayer and taking a deep breath. *"Now."*

My finger squeezed the trigger.

Blam!

My father's finger squeezed his trigger.

Blam!

The two bullets sped through the air, racing across the field and into the foreheads of two worthless wastes of human flesh. Two more men performed the arm-flailing act, the dance of death, the Macarena of *muerte,* the hokey pokey to the hereafter. They dropped to the ground not far from their earlier victims.

El Cuchillo instinctively ducked at the sound of the gunfire, putting his hand, still clutching the knife, to the ground beside him. Nick, Christina, and Alejandro reflexively dove to the dirt, inadvertently falling face-first into their would-be graves.

When he'd gathered his wits, El Cuchillo quickly scanned his surroundings, trying, unsuccessfully, to determine where the gunfire had come from. He leaped to his feet and took off running toward the vehicles, apparently intending to attempt an escape.

Operating on pure instinct now, I dropped my rifle and grabbed Nick's samurai sword from the bag. I could've taken El Cuchillo out with a single gunshot, but that would have been too good for him.

Too quick.

Too painless.

Too impersonal.

He didn't deserve better than his victims.

I pushed through the dark toward the rental truck, swinging the sword left and right to hack through the underbrush that impeded me. My father ran after me, calling for me to stop, but the thick, thorny underbrush caught on his clothing and slowed him down.

I arrived at the truck three seconds before El Cuchillo. Stopping at the driver's door, I turned to face outward, the sword clutched tightly in my hands, the blade extended in front of me, a foot crooked up against the vehicle behind me to provide leverage.

With the trees providing cover, the thug didn't see me until it was too late. He ran full speed right at me, momentum carrying him forward. His eyes went wide as he realized he wouldn't be able to stop himself in time.

If you live by the sword, you die by the sword.

His hate- and horror-filled eyes met mine as fate propelled him toward the blade. The sword penetrated his flesh with a *pop* and eviscerated his internal organs with a moist and squishy *skluck*, the force rocking me backward.

The sound of the human shish-kabob being skewered was the last thing I heard before my world went black.

chapter thirty-five

$\mathcal{A}$ Stitch in Time

El Cuchillo was lucky enough to survive, if you could call surviving an impaling only to face the death penalty lucky. The doctors had been able to sew his internal organs back together, though with all the scars he'd have on his abdomen he'd never wear a bikini again. Not that there were many opportunities to wear a bikini in a maximum-security federal prison. Or that it would be advisable to do so even if there were.

I'd needed a couple stitches, too. When I'd fainted, my head had hit the edge of the truck's bumper and been sliced open. A little embarrassing, but who wouldn't have been overwhelmed under the circumstances?

Nick, Christina, and Alejandro had been taken to the hospital, too. Though they'd put up a fierce fight when pulled from the back of the rental truck, none had any broken bones, fortunately. The doctors treated their cuts and scrapes, and kept all of us overnight for observation.

I woke at seven the next morning to the sound of the hospital room door opening. Ajay peeked his head in and whispered, "Are you decent?"

The staff had put me and Christina in a room together.

It was like a slumber party—a really awful slumber party, where the ghost stories were real and the girls blubbered and bawled all night and just wanted to go home to their mommies.

My stitches and tailbone throbbed as I sat up in bed. "We're as decent as we can be with our asses hanging out of these hospital gowns."

Ajay stepped in, carrying a white paper sack and two large coffees. He held them up. "Brought you two some breakfast. That hospital slop is tasteless."

I took the coffee and cherry Danish he handed me. "Thanks, doc. Compliments on your bedside manner."

After handing Christina her breakfast, he plopped down on the end of her bed. "Frankly, I think they should have put you two in the psych ward. Anyone who voluntarily goes up against a drug cartel must have some screws loose."

"Did someone mention screwing?" It was Nick's head peeking through the door this time. His left eye was bloodshot and bruised, his lip was swollen, and his knuckles were purple and raw, but other than that he was intact. He'd spent the night in the room next door. Drug wars were good for no one but the health care industry.

He opened the door wider when I waved him in. A nurse passing by in the hallway outside took a quick peek at Nick's exposed, firm butt, her brows quirking in approval as he stepped inside.

"Coffee?" Nick's eyes locked on my cup as he headed toward me. "You're going to share, right?"

"Share my coffee?" Teasing, I pulled the cup back out of his reach. "It's not enough that I saved your ass last night?"

"You still hung up on that?" He rolled his eyes, teasing me right back.

I handed him the cup and he took a long drink, but when he went to hand it back to me he found my hand shaking too hard to take it back from him. Setting the cup on the tray table and rolling it out of the way, he sat down on my bed and leaned in to look me in the eye.

"You did what you had to do, Tara." He reached out, putting a hand on each of my trembling shoulders.

"I know." *Damn.* Even my voice was shaking now. "Still sucks, though."

He gave me a soft smile. "Pratt and Holloway, CPAs, is sounding pretty good right now, huh?"

I had to agree. Though I knew my father and I had had no choice but to shoot the men who'd aimed their guns at Nick and Christina last night, the knowledge that we'd ended two lives was a hard truth to face. The men might have been violent criminals, but they were also someone's son, maybe a brother, perhaps even someone's father. I hated them for putting us in this position.

But losing Nick and Christina would have hurt infinitely more.

Still holding me, Nick leaned in and gave me a big kiss on the forehead, being careful not to get too close to my stitches. "It's going to be okay," he whispered against my skin. "Eventually."

A wail came from the hall, followed by Bonnie's voice shrieking, "Where is he? Where's my son? What's happened?"

Nick let go of me and bolted to the door, yanking it open. He set one foot into the hall and gestured. "I'm in here, Mom. No need to panic."

"I'll be the judge of that!" Bonnie stormed into the room carrying a large quilted bag. She grabbed Nick in a tight hug and choked back a sob before taking a step back. "Oh, my God! You've got a black eye!"

He waved a hand. "I'm fine, Mom. I've suffered worse."

"I know." She gulped back a second sob. "Trust me, I remember."

Nick gestured to the bag. "What's in there?"

"All your favorites." She glanced around for a place to set it down. "I figured you might be hungry."

Nick put a hand to his belly. "You figured right."

Nick and Ajay pushed my tray table and Christina's together to form a larger space, and Bonnie unloaded the bag. Paper plates, napkins, forks, a large thermos containing more coffee, and several foil-wrapped homemade breakfast tacos.

"Wow, Mom," Nick said. "You brought enough to feed an army."

Good thing, because after being on the front lines last night we felt like soldiers.

I'd just taken a big bite of a breakfast taco when there was a knock on the door. I looked up to see my mother and father in the doorway. Unable to speak with my mouth full of tortilla, potato, and salsa, I waved them in with my taco.

"How's everyone this morning?" Mom asked.

Like Bonnie before her, my mother carried an armful of homemade goodies. A coffee cake. Apple turnovers. Blueberry muffins. Obviously she'd been up all night baking, too worried and upset to sleep. I felt guilty to be the cause of her insomnia.

I swallowed my bite. "We're all great." I looked to Nick and Christina. "Aren't we?"

The two of them forced smiles at my mother. Dad wore a stoic face, but I knew that he, too, was in emotional turmoil. Another reason for me to feel guilty.

Christina turned to Ajay. "Go see if you can find Alejandro. He risked his life to bring down the cartel." True. If they'd discovered that one of their own had ratted them out, he would've been in for the worst kind of torture. "The least we can do is share this breakfast with him."

Ajay nodded and went in search of the informant, while

Dad rounded up a couple of extra chairs from Nick's room. When Alejandro entered the room, I introduced him to my parents and Nick introduced him to Bonnie.

Dad shook his hand and gave him a pat on the shoulder. "You've got some rather large *huevos,* son. I'll give you that."

Alejandro offered a small smile and a *"Gracias."*

The eight of us sat around, stuffing our faces and trying our best to keep the conversation light.

At seven-thirty, a nurse arrived with our covered breakfast platters. She glanced around at the remains of our veritable buffet. "I suppose you won't be needing these, then?" she asked, lifting a cover to expose a bowl of overcooked oatmeal and a fruit salad that was beginning to turn brown.

Christina and I exchanged glances. "We'll pass," she replied for both of us.

All of us patients were released at noon. We had little left to say, still processing the events of the night before and trying to come to terms with them.

Alejandro shook our hands one last time. He squeezed my hands so tightly between his I feared he'd snap my fingers in two. "I owe you my life."

I shrugged. "Just doing my job."

Christina gave me a hug then held me by the shoulders, looking me in the eye and giving me a look that said more than words ever could. That she was infinitely grateful my father and I had come along when we did. That our jobs had once again asked us to pay a very high price, but that we'd proven ourselves up to the task and sacrifice. That she understood how overwhelmed I must be feeling now. That we should go out for margaritas soon, maybe check out the new spring shoes at Neiman's. Our silent exchange complete, she turned to my dad. "Thanks again, pops."

My father gave her a nod. "Anytime."

Ajay raised his hand to give my father a high five. "Next time you're in town I'm buying you a steak."

Dad nodded again. "It's a date."

Ajay wrapped his arm around Christina as they made their way out the automatic doors of the hospital to his car.

Alejandro was released into the custody of U.S. Marshals. Given his cooperation with law enforcement, he'd be issued a new identity under the Witness Protection Program and relocated somewhere the others in the cartel would be unlikely to find him. My money was on Pocatello, Idaho.

Bonnie boo-hooed all over Nick and got him even more gooey than I had before he'd gone out on this investigation. "I'm so glad this is over!"

She wasn't the only one.

When his mother finally released him, Nick turned to me, stared into my eyes for a long moment, then grabbed me and held me so tight my ribs threatened to break. He put his lips to my ear and whispered in his sexiest voice, "Don't think I've forgotten that punishment I owe you."

I put my mouth to his ear and whispered back. "I'll be at your place the instant my parents leave."

chapter thirty-six

$\mathcal{M}$y Own Little Ass Whooping

My parents dawdled around my house all Sunday afternoon. My father replaced the burned-out light bulb on my back patio, oiled a couple of squeaky door hinges, and topped off all the fluids in my car. My mother made chicken-fried steak, a tuna casserole, and a huge pot of butter beans, sticking them in the freezer for me and Alicia to eat during the coming week. Mom washed all the dishes, did my laundry, and even vacuumed and dusted, insisting that I stay in bed and rest all the while. Hey, who was I to argue with my mother? Besides, it gave me a chance to catch up on my television shows.

I walked them out to Dad's truck early that evening, giving both of them a big hug. "Thanks for . . . everything."

My father and I exchanged a glance. That "everything" entailed far more than it should have. No man should ever have to kill for his daughter.

"You keep an eye on those stitches," my mother advised as my dad helped her into the truck. "If they get red or puffy or oozy, you call the doctor right away."

"Ew," I said, adding, "I will."

I stood in the driveway, waving as they backed out and headed down the street. When they'd rounded the corner, I turned and hightailed it down the street to Nick's.

He and Daffodil were standing on his porch waiting for me as I sprinted up. "I've been checking out the window all afternoon," he said. "I thought your parents would never leave." His lips parted in a sexy smile. "You ready for your punishment?"

I slid him a sexy smile right back. "Am I ever."

Though Nick gave me one solid pat on my naked rump as we climbed into his bed, I'd be hard-pressed to call it a spanking. In fact, his ministrations and foreplay were far more slow and gentle than usual, as if he were savoring each and every second and sensation. After last night's swift and severe brutality, neither of us was in the mood for a rushed, rambunctious bout of sex. Rather, slow and languid lovemaking better fit our mood. It also put less pressure on my still-sensitive tailbone.

Nick looked into my eyes as our bodies joined, and continued to gaze at me as he stilled himself inside me. "I missed the hell out of you, Tara."

"Right back at ya."

His voice was hoarse with emotion when he spoke again. "There were times when . . . when I didn't think we'd make it out."

I was quiet a moment, blinking back fresh tears. "I can't imagine what I would have done if you hadn't." In fact, I *refused* to imagine it. I gave him a soft, lingering kiss on the lips.

He remained motionless for several moments, as did I. The lack of movement was as sensually exhilarating as it was frustrating.

When I could take it no more, I ran my hands down Nick's hard-muscled back, resting them in the warm curve of his spine for a moment before cupping his buttocks and applying some pressure. Still he didn't move. "Um . . . what are you doing?"

He pulled his head back and looked at me, smiling softly. "I'm not doing anything."

Smart-ass. "Let me rephrase, then. Why aren't you moving?"

"I'm exercising."

"Exercising *what*?"

He chuckled. "Restraint."

I narrowed my eyes at him. "Why?"

He ducked his head into the crook of my neck and exhaled a long breath that feathered over my skin. "I just want to be close to you."

I slid my hands back up to his back and leaned my cheek against his dark hair. "That's all I want, too."

We remained interlocked and motionless for several more moments before he mumbled into my neck. "I think my restraint has gotten enough exercise, don't you?"

Now it was my turn to chuckle. "Hell, yeah."

Nick pulled his head back and gazed at me as he began to move.

"So," I said, gazing back at him. "Fifty bucks on September, huh?"

He groaned. "Don't talk about marriage. It'll spoil the mood."

"Oh! You did not just say that!" In an instant, I'd flipped him over onto his back, where he lay laughing so hard his chest heaved.

Daffodil raised her head from her bed on the floor and whimpered in concern.

"It's okay, girl," Nick assured her, reaching out to give her a pat on the head. "Daddy'll love every minute of what Tara's gonna do to him."

And he did.

chapter thirty-seven

$\mathcal{U}$h-oh, SpaghettiOs

Lu called me into her office first thing Monday morning.
"Take a seat," she said.

I plunked down in one of her wing chairs.

"You did a great job helping Nick out on the cartel case,"
she said. "The shooting was clearly justified, so there won't
be any problems there. Nevertheless, you know procedure.
Lethal use of weapons means I've got to put you on paid
administrative leave for two weeks."

I cocked my head. "You don't expect me to complain
about an extra two weeks' paid vacation, do you?"

"'Course not. I expect you to get some rest, go somewhere fun, and come back in two weeks ready to work
your butt off."

I gave her a salute. "Aye, aye, Captain."

She made a shooing motion with her hand. "Go on now.
Send me a postcard. Or maybe bring me one of those souvenir snow globes."

"Will do."

Nick took some vacation time, too, and we spent several days rolling around in his sheets—careful to avoid
my fractured coccyx—and a couple more in his bass boat

out on the area's various lakes. Daffodil loved sunning herself on the boat's deck and taking the occasional dip in the water, shaking herself all over us when she climbed back aboard. I kicked back with a brand-new copy of Rose N. Bloom's Scottish romance novel and a glass of wine while Nick fished, catching only a swim mask with a broken strap for all his trouble. He didn't mind, though. He seemed less interested in fishing for the take than in the meditational opportunities the quiet, serene activity provided.

As Lu had suggested we went somewhere fun, making a weekend trip down to Austin. I showed Nick all of the places where I used to hang out while in college and we even climbed to the top of Mount Bonnell, enjoying the view of the lake down below. I bought Lu a snow globe featuring the state capitol building and sent her a postcard with a photograph of the city's skyline.

> *Dear Lu,*
> *Following orders and having fun!*
> *Your favorite special agent,*
> *Tara*

Thanks to information provided by Alejandro, further evidence gathered by Nick and Christina during their investigation, and the leads I'd given them, the DEA identified and arrested seventeen members of the cartel in the days following the shootout/shish-kabobbing. The roundup included several major players operating from the apartment complex I'd staked out near Town East Mall. My lead had not only netted the DEA a number of arrests but, according to Christina, had shortened the investigation by weeks if not months. *Hooray for me.*

While most of the men arrested refused to talk, one of the more minor cartel members agreed to *hablar* after a plea agreement was made, guaranteeing that prosecutors would not ask for the death penalty or return him to Mexico, where he'd surely be murdered in prison. His life now secured, he spilled the *frijoles*. Per his testimony, El Cuchillo had convinced his cronies—the men in the Avenger—to double-cross the cartel by stealing drugs and money. Their plan was to frame Vargas and Motley, the two men they'd shot. When Nick, Christina, and Alejandro got in their way, they'd decided to get rid of them.

They just hadn't counted on Tara Holloway and her father showing up to save the day.

Neener-neener.

Nick resumed his position as captain of the Tax Maniacs and led the team to three successive victories, earning the MVP designation each game. Of course the MVP was required to buy beer for everyone after the game, but Nick was happy to do it. He even bought beers for the losers at the Food and Drug Administration, a majority-female team that, against the protests of their outnumbered male members, called themselves the Sausage Inspectors. We also made it to the Rangers' season opener, double-dating with Christina and Ajay.

Chase Burkhalter was charged with multiple counts of fraud, released on $500,000 bail, expelled from college, and kicked out of his frat. Poor guy. Looked like he'd miss the massive zombie-themed party prior to dead week. At least the victims would likely get some of their money back. Chase had run through a good deal of the stolen funds, but his parents had liquidated some of their retirement funds to pay restitution on his behalf, hoping the gesture would encourage the judge who heard his case to give him a lighter sentence.

Norman Peele agreed to a plea deal involving a prolonged probation and a stiff criminal penalty for his part in helping the Kuykendahls evade their taxes. Quent and

Kevin Kuykendahl were each sentenced to five years in prison. The sanctuary property was seized and turned over to a legitimate animal rescue organization that made immediate improvements. Simba was returned to Paradise Park, where he was given a much larger and better maintained habitat in which to live out the rest of his days.

My tax refund came in. Combined with my $25 in scratch-off winnings, I had enough now to buy a pair of designer sunglasses. I stopped by the Brighton store and treated myself to a new pair of shades. No more knockoffs or cheap sunglasses for me.

I spent a couple of nights with my parents back in my hometown of Nacogdoches. My father and I even stopped by the family church for some counseling with the pastor. He'd always been a pragmatic preacher, and, rather than offering us a bunch of meaningless platitudes, told us that the battle of good versus evil sometimes required those on the side of good to do some very difficult things.

He nodded to my father, then took my hand in his. "It'll take some time," he said, "but you're Tara Holloway. You'll work through this."

He was right, of course. I'd always carry this with me, but I was nothing if not resilient. Besides, the American taxpayers needed me back on the job.

When I finally returned to work, a large vase of fresh red roses greeted me from my desk. There was a card attached, addressed *To My Everything*. I glanced into Nick's office, and he smiled up at me from his desk.

"They're gorgeous!" I called.

"So are you!" Nick called back.

"Get a room!" called the agent with the office next door.

Lu stepped into my doorway, blocking my view of Nick. "No time for hanky-panky." She held up a thick file and proceeded to plop it down on my desk.

"A new case?" I asked, pulling the file toward me.

"You had no trouble taking down a drug cartel," Lu said. "Facing the mafia should be easy peasy."

The mafia?

Holy cannoli!

Don't miss the next Tara Holloway novel

Death, Taxes,

and a Chocolate Cannoli

Coming in October 2015 from St. Martin's Paperbacks

…and be sure to sniff out Diane Kelly's
K-9 mysteries

Paw Enforcement

Paw And Order

Laying Down The Paw

*Available in August 2015

From St. Martin's Paperbacks